By William Kinsolving

Mister Christian
The Diplomat's Daughter
Bred to Win
Raven
Born with the Century

Mister
Christian

A NOVEL

William Kinsolving

SIMON & SCHUSTER

New York   London   Toronto   Sydney   Tokyo   Singapore

SIMON & SCHUSTER
Rockefeller Center
1230 Avenue of the Americas
New York, NY 10020

This book is a work of fiction. Names, characters,
places, and incidents either are products of the
author's imagination or are used fictitiously.

Copyright © 1996 by The Kinsolving Company and William Kinsolving

SIMON & SCHUSTER and colophon are registered trademarks of
Simon & Schuster Inc.

Designed by Irving Perkins Associates
Manufactured in the United States of America

1 2 3 4 5 6 7 8 9 10

Library of Congress Cataloging-in-Publication Data
Mister Christian : a novel / William Kinsolving
p. cm.
1. Christian, Fletcher, 1764–1793—Fiction. 2. Sailors—Great Britain—
Fiction. 3. Bounty Mutiny, 1789—Fiction. I. Title.
PS3561.I58M57 1996
813'.54—dc20   95-33683   CIP
ISBN 0-684-81303-3

For Carol

Author's Note

In the South Pacific on 28 April 1789, a mutiny took place aboard HMS *Bounty*.

The captain of the ship, Lieutenant William Bligh, was forced overboard with eighteen other men into an open launch. Dangerously crowded, they were left in the small boat to fend for themselves upon the wide ocean.

The leader of the mutiny, Acting-Lieutenant Fletcher Christian, then sailed the *Bounty* in search of a haven, safe from the long arm of the Royal Navy.

After an heroic voyage of 3600 nautical miles, Bligh and his men reached Coupang in the Dutch East Indies.

Sixteen of those left aboard the *Bounty* eventually chose to return to Tahiti, where they subsequently were captured by the Royal Navy. Ten of them survived their return to England, where three were hanged.

Fletcher Christian finally found a mischarted island called Pitcairn where he, a group of eighteen Polynesians, and the remaining eight mutineers established a community.

These tales are true and often told, though endlessly debated. Their usual conclusions are William Bligh's triumph of survival, and Fletcher Christian's escape to Pitcairn.

What follows includes the rest of the history.

Introduction

While crossing the South Pacific in February of 1808, Captain Mayhew Folger, of the American sealer *Topaz,* spotted a rocky island that should not have been there. Checking his navigational charts, the captain concluded that the island was Pitcairn. It had been mischarted by more than two hundred miles. Having sold his cargo of gin and rum in Australia, Folger was eager to find seals in order to fill his hold with skins for his return to Boston.

With that hope, the captain set his course for the reportedly uninhabited island. But on his approach, he was surprised to see smoke rising tranquilly through the lush verdure growing above the high stone cliffs that loomed from the sea. He was even more startled when a Polynesian-style canoe approached his ship and he was hailed in fluent, if strangely accented, English by its three native paddlers.

> I went on shore and found there an Englishman by the name of Alexander Smith, the only person remaining out of the nine that escaped [in 1789] on board the ship *Bounty,* under the command of the archmutineer Christian. . . . After they had remained about four years on the island, their men servants rose upon and killed six of

them, leaving only Smith. . . . However, he and the widows of the deceased men arose and put all the servants to death which left him the only surviving man on the island with eight or nine women and several small children. . . .

The community of which Captain Folger wrote in his ship's log was populated by the descendants of the mutineers and the native women they brought with them to Pitcairn in January of 1790, eight months after the mutiny. Included in the curious group who welcomed the captain were three children of Fletcher Christian.

Because there were no seals on the island, Folger was eager to return to the *Topaz*. He stayed only a few hours, during which time he tried to find out more details about the fate of the mutineers, in particular their leader. Smith, whose legal name turned out to be John Adams, was reluctant to discuss the past; as a mutineer, the man faced hanging if ever found by a British ship. His stories were vague, contradictory, and, to his listeners, they seemed purposely misleading. Of Fletcher Christian's death and burial, he gave a garbled story, one he changed with each telling. Captain Folger recorded that Christian was shot in the back by the native men during their massacre of the mutineers. The location of his grave was not entered in the log.

For his part, Smith/Adams begged for report of the world, about which he had not heard in the nearly twenty years since the mutiny. Folger told him of the French Revolution, Napoleon's inexorable rise to power, and how the seemingly endless European war against France was spilling over the oceans of the world. After hearing of the great British victory at Trafalgar, the old mutineer rose and swung his hat over his head, calling out "Old England forever!"

Captain Folger told of his amazing discovery when the *Topaz* called at Valparaiso, Chile. An official report was forwarded to the British Admiralty, where it arrived on 14 May 1809. The news received scant attention, the war against Napoleon taking precedence with both the Royal Navy and the public. As mutinies go, the *Bounty*'s had been a minor example when compared to that aboard HMS *Hermione,* where ten officers were hacked to death, or the subsequent great Nore Mutiny of 1797, involving 50,000 seamen and 113 ships.

What happened aboard the *Bounty* had been, after all, bloodless. Those mutineers who had been captured were court-martialed; those found guilty were hanged. The hard-core band under Fletcher Christian had disappeared. The mutiny itself was memorable mainly due to the survival of the *Bounty*'s captain, Bligh, who, with eighteen of the crew, piloted the ship's dangerously overcrowded launch on an astonishing 3600-mile voyage to Timor. The Admiralty was content to neglect Captain Folger's report, and the survival of any of the *Bounty*'s mutineers was officially ignored.

Coincidentally, in that same spring of 1809, there were persistent rumors in Cumberland, where Fletcher Christian was born and raised, that he had been seen there often and made frequent visits to "an aunt." Soon after, Captain Peter Heywood, who as a young midshipman had been kept aboard the *Bounty* during the mutiny and who, in spite of his friendship with Fletcher Christian, was subsequently pardoned by the King after his court-martial, reported that he glimpsed Christian in Fore Street, Plymouth Dock. When Heywood approached, whomever he'd seen fled and disappeared.

A year and a half later, in November of 1810, King George III began to slip permanently into madness and the final Regency crisis began. The war against France was at a critical point. Napoleon had reached his zenith. Having married Marie-Louise of Austria and annexed Holland, he was also reigning as Emperor and King over Spain, Portugal, Italy, and Prussia. England and the

Duke of Wellington were the only obstacles to the Emperor's domination of Europe, and the only hope against his ambition, which was turning fatefully toward Russia.

During the British governmental crisis, when royal authority was edging its way toward the willing but profligate Prince of Wales, one of the mad King's doctors was Sir Jeremy Learned. A renowned physician specializing in brain disorders and lunacy, he shuttled between Windsor Castle and the hospital of St. Mary of Bethlehem in hopes of gaining insight to his royal patient's desperate condition. Popularly known as "Bedlam," the hospital was the second oldest in Europe for the chronically insane. It was notorious for the extreme cruelty of its treatment and care, a tradition with which Sir Jeremy, according to his journal, was familiar and which he instinctively abhorred. As his mental condition worsened into violence, the King became the object of intense political and medical bickering. Thus Sir Jeremy had less time for visits to Bedlam, and less tolerance for the appalling practices he found there.

The King's repeated bouts of mental illness had brought the attention of reformers and Parliamentarians to the antediluvian methods of care for mad people. During his own investigations into alternative treatment, not only for his royal patient but for the cause of reform, Sir Jeremy discovered a private clinic in York, run by a Quaker father and sons, who were treating their patients without the time-honored physical restraints of manacles, whipping, strait-waistcoats, or chains. Sir Jeremy had recently suggested this new "moral therapy" at Windsor to his colleagues and to Queen Charlotte, only to be roundly ridiculed by the former and silenced by the latter.

According to his journal, on 10 December 1810, in the course of a late-night Bedlam visit, the doctor visited the solitary cell of a patient whose wrists were bolted into iron manacles imbedded in the center of the stone floor. This had been done to prevent him doing harm to himself and others. The manacles prevented the man from standing, allowing him only to kneel or lie on the floor, positions which necessitated his eating directly from a bowl as well as defecating where he lay.

The doctor had observed the man a number of times. Offering no other authority than his firm command, Sir Jeremy ordered the patient released. When the resident apothecary and his staff refused because of the man's past violence, the doctor ordered them out of the cell. In the light of a lantern, he knocked the bolts free himself. Instead of making a savage response, the patient crawled painfully into a corner and, watching the doctor, rubbed his scabbed and festering wrists.

Like many patients in Bedlam, little was known of him, certainly not his name. He had lost an eye; from the tattoos on his chest and buttocks, the doctor deduced that he had been a sailor. From the scar on his back, it was clear he once had been shot. A long scar above his ribs indicated a stabbing wound. Seven months before, he had been pulled from the Thames after jumping off London Bridge. When he regained his senses, he attacked his rescuers with such raging madness he was delivered to Bedlam. After he made many frenzied attempts to kill himself and anyone who came close to him, his wrists were bolted to the floor. He had lived in such fashion, eating like a dog, sleeping in his own filth, and being hosed once each fortnight, or whenever his rages took control of him.

Standing across the cell from his patient, the doctor asked a number of simple questions, which were answered with a nod or shake of the head. The man seemed calm and lucid, so Sir Jeremy chanced a careful intimacy, explaining his urgency to learn, not of the patient's identity, which he seemed so loath to reveal, but of his madness. In exchange, he offered the man greater comforts. Approaching him, the doctor asked, "What is it that you want?" He meant the question to apply generally to the broad spectrum of his patient's needs.

The man's reply was specific: "Foolscap, a quill and inkhorn . . . not to mention a large batter pudding, if you've a mind."

The doctor automatically regarded the quill as a potential weapon. He smiled, attempting to conceal his suspicion. "No pudding, I'm afraid, but why . . . ?"

"I'll use them for naught but writing," the patient said sarcastically, his voice a rough whisper, his accent difficult to place.

"What is it you wish to write?"

"A story, that's all."

"Why suddenly now?"

The patient stared at the lantern's flickering light. "I have my hands now," he said angrily, "and perhaps even my mind as well—a thrilling combination, don't you think? You can read every word I write if you've an inclination. I'll not bother to write about the crime itself; too many others have told their versions of the same tale, so believe what you like. But now, since they've found them out there on that 'island paradise' "—he laughed, though the sound was a groan—"the story could become some pitiable romance, a shallow parable of mankind's evil. But sir, there's something more to it than that!" His voice rose against his own doubt, then he covered his eyes with one hand.

Later that night, Sir Jeremy noted the conversation in his journal, and that the man's left wrist was suppurating. With his habitual precision, the doctor listed the medications he had prescribed for Bedlam's apothecary to supply. Then he concluded:

What the patient was saying seemed humourously frantic, yes, a definite though perhaps malign sense of humour; better than reading Blake, which is the same kind of aberrant illusion. The man illustrates my theory that creative production is often a disciplined expression of one's madness and should be encouraged. The true artist obviously has an ineffable force beyond craft to create sublimity, a process unique to each artist and, needless to say, beyond anyone else's understanding, and probably beyond the artist's as well. Blake is my primary example—a contained madness energising genius—as well as Turner, Coleridge, and of course Paganini. This patient has no such genius, but he wants to write a story; certainly that is better than destruction, no matter if what he composes is blather.

When I assured him that he would have his paper, quill, and ink, he offered no thanks. Instead, he took his hand away from his eyes and stared into the dark as if confronting his damnation.

PART ONE

Escape

Pitcairn

September 1793

That day; there was no before, there was no after. I dared not think, but tried in my wisdom to concentrate only on the row of yams I was planting. The light seemed blinding; the green of the coconut palms seared my brain, and the blue sea, glasslike that day, mirrored a glare that cut through whatever it was I thought to be my soul. But I could not stop my mind. I considered in explicit detail how a seed might grow in the rich red soil of Pitcairn. Yet every time I opened the earth with my wooden spade, I saw blood there, glistening. I accepted that on that lost island there was more blood for me than there was earth to cover it, so much blood that it surely would drown me if I did not give such privilege to the sea. That day, my straight, orderly furrow of seed and blood very neatly cut my life in twain. I could no longer endure my past, and the possible future offered me nothing but madness and death.

I planned to kill myself that day. My determination was to sow a crop for my family and, once done, to rid them of what most surely would destroy any chance of their happiness. By then I could no longer bear the island to which I had brought them. If I remained I would begin to disdain my woman and our children and finally detest them as part of my prison. In my growing madness, I also believed that I would have abused them, harmed them, even destroyed them. Such degradation of mind and spirit made certain my purpose to end my life. I was five days short of twenty-nine years. When the row of yams was done, I would turn and walk to the cliff, The Edge, as we so appropriately called it. The tide was in; I would hurl myself into the sea, which by then was Heaven and Hell, and for me the only God that existed.

Then I heard people coming. I turned my back to them, thinking that my face would give away what I saw in the ground or what I intended to do. I heard them stop and I dug harder, hoping to avoid conversation. The shot rang out. I felt the ball's impact in my back and was knocked forward, falling on my face, senseless.

I lay unmoving on the ground for hours, into the night. Thinking me dead, no one touched me. Then, something ran over my neck. I tried to raise my right arm, thereby causing pain beyond anything I'd ever experienced. Whatever the thing was darted away, a spider perhaps, leaving me lying, I realised, in the dark as I tried to breathe. My nose and throat were clogged; my cheek was stuck to the rock on which I'd fallen, sealed there with dried blood. I coughed and gasped with more pain; my face felt shattered. For a time, I did not try to move again, but my mind began its utterly contradictory work. Without a thought of my former suicidal intention, I began to consider what I had to do in order to survive. Brought forth in that same instant was what had long remained stillborn in me, the decision to escape the island.

Tentatively, I moved the fingers of my right hand, then the wrist. When I tried to bend the elbow, the pain started to intensify, but it was not the stabbing hurt of shattered bone. Instead, I felt the tear of flesh and nerves, and I dared to hope that there was less damage than I'd feared. Suddenly despair gave way to anticipation, futility to expectation, surrender to determination, all whilst I lay on the ground unsure of how or whether to move.

I conjectured whoever had loaded the musket that had inflicted my wound had done so with too little gunpowder, otherwise the ball would have accomplished its purpose. That led me to the conclusion that my murderer had to be one of the natives whom we had instructed on the use of our weapons for our ease. It was they whom we sent out to hunt the descendants of the *Bounty's* pigs, which lived wild on the island. To the native hunters, the powder was magic; a little more or less made no difference to them. My white colleagues would have been more exacting in their measurement, and my right side would have been torn through.

I rolled my face off the rock where it was stuck. The intensity of my new resolve was so strong, I felt my heart begin to pump whatever blood was left into my eyes and mouth so that I not only saw but tasted my purpose. I spat the blood and squinted into the black sky, remembering with a sailor's care that there would be no moon. With excruciating toil, I rolled onto my left side. Using arm and leg as a crab would do, I began a steady crawl toward the cliff line.

Agony is best left undescribed, for in reports it often tends toward bluster. I had my agony that night; others have suffered worse. Here, at least, the caprice of memory serves us well, allowing pain to numb itself into our little monuments of scars and sore old wounds. I was surprised to bear such torment, but I remember too, in that dragging time, I saw the path, not only toward survival, but also for escape, as clearly as if guided by the stars on which I had so long depended for direction.

Earlier, I had planned to seek a place on the cliff face where I could hurl myself directly into the sea. During that first hour of inching, I indeed headed to the same precipice. Twenty feet below it was an outcropping wide enough to hold my bloody blouse for all to see. I did not know just how I'd remove it, neither did I know how I would contrive to reach the Other Side, the name we called the western part of the island, which was all steep gullies and forbidding slopes. It was difficult enough to walk there, much more to crawl. Nevertheless, that was where I had to go. I knew of springs and streams, of places to hide, of plantain and coconut trees.

I thought of my cave but rejected it as a hiding place. If my blouse was not found right away, the cave would be the first place anyone would look for me. And I doubted I had strength to climb the sheer path up and around Lookout Point, the high jutting pinnacle of rock that rose up at the northern end of our settlement where the cave was. Rainwater was collected there, as well as muskets and a brace of pistols that I'd taken up years before when the place was my fort against potential seizure.

At the cliff face, I rested for a time; then, still prone, I unbuttoned my tapa blouse with my left hand. A single Royal Navy button, saved carefully over the years, was left from my old dress tunic. I bit it off and held it in my mouth. The other fasteners were carved stubs of ironwood, more difficult to manage. I struggled with one a good quarter hour before the blouse was loose. To get it off, I had to sit, which I knew might be impossible. I was halfway there before fainting, from pain or lack of blood in the brain, I know not.

Nor do I know how long I lay there, or what awakened me. It was still dark, and this time I managed to sit upright. My teeth chattered from a cold I had never felt before in the South Pacific. The button was still in my cheek, drawing saliva, which cleared my mouth of blood. With my good arm, I peeled off the blouse. Reaching for a stone nearby, I wrapped it in the bloodied cloth, made so painstakingly by the women from the bark of the mulberry tree, then let myself fall to the ground again and crawled to the very edge. Leaning over so that the blood rushed to my head and started my nose bleeding again, I pushed the weighted blouse over and watched it fall into the dark.

Through the ever-pounding roar and hiss of surf to which we had long grown deaf, I barely heard the stone crack against the rock below me. As if the sound were a starting gun, I began my crawling race against sunrise, cold, and a sudden thirst so intense I felt it in my teeth. Sucking on the button in my mouth, I dared to hope that the blouse would be found, free of its weight, close enough to the edge to create the impression that my body had fallen farther, into the sea.

Pitcairn is a lush but forbidding rock of an island, bound up from the ocean by its high cliffs, traversed by spiky ridges, the main one, Gannet's Ridge, running the island's length from east to west. I had to cross that ridge to reach the Other Side, with my hopes of hiding and recovery. The sun was good to me, staying for some hours behind low clouds, allowing me to reach the top of the ridge as its namesake birds were awakening. I managed to slide down most of the incline, landing finally in a stream where I gently washed my face and drank my fill. Then as carefully as I could, I laid my back across the stream to let the water cleanse my wound.

My nose was broken, there was no doubt. The bullet was still in my back, but several times in my progress over Gannet's Ridge, I had involuntarily and painfully been forced to use my right arm, which made me even more certain no bones were broken. I could probably live if I wanted to, and strange it was to know I did. Once accepted, curiosity was first upon my mind— who shot me? Who was left alive? I remembered hearing several at my back before the shot was fired. Was it a native rebellion? Were all the mutineers dead? Had my woman, Isabella, known of it and this time not told me? Had she delivered yet, and would revenge include the white men's children?

I cared again, too much for what I planned to do. Threading the button onto the leather thong around my waist, I tried to think of how I could manage my escape, alone, in a canoe, one of those we'd made in native fashion, with its outrigger float, running out against the wild and never-ending surf that rolled across a thousand miles of open ocean to pound into the cove we called the Landing Place. There the *Bounty* lay, fired and sunk within a week of our arrival for fear of her discovery by other passing ships, as well as against the chance of someone having a change of heart and quitting the island, thus betraying our existence.

If any of the mutineers were still alive, they would oppose my escape for this very reason. Even though my discovery anywhere in the world would mean my own capture and death, my fellow mutineers could only fear it would mean theirs as well. For no matter if I swore upon my children's lives never to reveal this place, they could never be sure that when facing the noose, I would not bargain for my life with their discovery. My escape would have to be in spite of everything that they could do to prevent it—if any were alive. If none were, I would have to escape from those who already had tried to murder me.

Holding those pleasant prospects in mind, I dared to stand. Even if I managed to escape the island, fought through the crashing surf to open water, what did I expect? There was no scheduled pacquet! From my cave, I once had seen two ships on opposite horizons within a single month, but the ordinary time between such sightings was a season, more often half a year. And if one chanced by when I was out there, would a lookout ever spy a twig in the endless ocean? And what of storms, and food, and water?

In the same moment, I vomited. After so many years on an island, I feared the sea just as any landsman. Over the days that followed, of hiding, fever, nausea, and never-ending pain, I refused reason, consuming only water and fruit, while I convinced myself to trust the sea again.

Often only half conscious, I saw my visage reflected in a pool and could not recognize myself. A beard was growing. My face was deeply bruised from my having fallen on it, my broken nose spread flatly over my tanned but hollow cheeks. At one point, I tried to set the bone with sticks in either nostril, but my hands were far from steady, and the pain coursed through my head like chain shot. The black around my eyes and cheeks gave me the look of a rabid bat. I thought that whoever had survived on the island might well be terrified into obeisance by my mere appearance.

The wound in my back was far more serious. I could not see it or reach it. I attacked it too with sticks, hoping to prod the ball out and let infectious fluids flow. I may have been successful in the latter, but the ball stayed lodged, a little sun of burning torment between the bone and sinew. The effect on my right arm was great, leaving it dangling, nearly useless.

I spent the days sleeping, the nights searching for food and building my strength. The infection in my back came and went, worsened, then became a dull throb, thick scab, and itching. I lived on wild yams and raw taro root, with shaddock and mango. If I died, it could not be from starvation on Pitcairn. On the sixth night, I had the strength to crack open a coconut and feasted on its milk-soaked meat. By the end of the second week, I made my way to the water's edge, the Other Side being the only place on the island where the cliff line broke, providing a more gradual descent to the rocky shore. There I searched for crabs and mussels, eating them hungrily and filling what finally had become a firm stomach.

In all this time I had seen no one, and I presumed no one had seen me, awake or sleeping. It was time for me to find out who my unsuspecting allies would be, for I was sure I could not escape alone. My strength was sufficient for me to commence observing what remained of our community. I waited to approach until it was dark and then, only when there was no moon. Climbing the ridge, I crept down the other side without disturbing a pebble. Not knowing whom I might find or where they might be—it surely was possible others might be hiding and wandering at night—I made every move as if someone were close enough to see or hear me.

I spent three nights moving about from mutineers' houses to gardens to footpaths. Finally I chanced to stay into a morning, thus better to judge from my concealment who was still living, and, yes, if I had another child. The latter question was answered when I saw my woman, Isabella, stride from our house with the two boys on their way to bathe, she still belly full under her shift, still strong backed, still beautiful in spite of the grim tension shrouding her face. They passed by, not ten yards from where I hid deep in a thick hedge of hibiscus. For a moment, everything else I knew dropped from my mind, leaving a sad stump of love for them. But the hard look on Isabella's face halted my urge to call out, rush to them, and hold them. I heard a noise and looked back at the house.

Stepping out onto our porch from the front door was Ned Young, holding a musket. He called and smiled at her with an intimacy that couldn't be mistaken. She returned his smile, though sadly, before she disappeared on a turn in the path.

Pitcairn

October 1793

Ned Young was the only officer of the *Bounty* who had stayed with me from mutiny to Pitcairn. I know not why he did. I suspect he realised that, as a mulatto, he had no great future in the Royal Navy. From the West Indies, St. Kitt's as I remember, he was a nephew of Sir George Young and with such status had been well schooled. The Tahitians adored him as one of their dark-skinned own.

When he arrived on Pitcairn, Young had already chosen Teraura as his consort from the dozen women who came with us from Tahiti. The two of them lived together the entire time, but they had no children. All of us knew that he was tiring of her, and that he was a favourite of the other women. I also knew that he lusted for my woman, Mauatua, or "Mainmast" as the mutineers called her for her height, straight back, and strong stance. I believe she, too, had an inclination for Young, although I never knew if they had done the bush dance. I could not blame her if she had, for I was going mad, and she needed joy.

I'd called her "Isabella" for a distant cousin by marriage, the subject of a boyish fantasy from my past life, a life I would never see again. My island Isabella was everything a man could wish while thinking to forget his own civilisation. Her skin, the colour of dark honey, seemed always warmed by the sun. When she swam, her long black hair formed a thick veil down her back to her rounded buttocks, giving her the sleek look of a wild wet sable. Her legs were long, thin but muscled so that even when her knees touched, there was a space between her thighs that was crowned by her smooth, naked womanhood. It was the Tahitian custom to pluck out pubic hair, as some civilised women, in the past, had plucked eyebrows or shaved back their hairlines. She wrapped a piece of cloth around her narrow waist, never for modesty, which did not exist, but for comfort. Her breasts were full, and she carried them proudly. Even after child-birth, her body recovered these attributes with astonishing rapidity. She told me it was because of her desire to attract me again.

I chose to believe her, for I had come to torture myself with how close I had been to a successful life when, for a few hours, I gave in to rage and madness, and put the captain of a Royal Navy ship over the side. I had been twenty-four, already with six years of experience. Good seamen were always in demand by an island nation, and the possibility of reward and glory, particularly in a war where spoils could amount to thousands of pounds, were multitude. As war with France was a constant cloud in the British sky, I believed the timing of my career was fortunate. By my thirtieth year, I might have made post-captain.

But imprisoned on Pitcairn, I would never even sail a ship again or feel the pitch of wood against water as the wind filled the soul of her and drove me toward a future of surely something more than rotting on an island.

I thought all of this as I watched my island Isabella smile sadly at her new mate. I do not boast when I say that jealousy did not reach down my throat and grab at my heart. My first reaction was that Ned would help me off the island, the second that he would care for my family. That he was there so soon after my supposed demise was no surprise in our tight civilisation. The musket, in fact, implied his protective role. He stood for a moment, watching, listening, his lips parted, revealing his teeth, rotted from sucking sugarcane as a boy, his bare chest glistening from the humidity, the dark olive skin of his breeding made strangely golden by the years in the tropical sun.

He and I had been known as "the two gentlemen" by the mutineers, a social status that was respected by them for ten minutes. Ever after, it was the subject of ridicule and laughter to which neither Ned nor I objected, so eager were we to find a new life without such social distinctions. Before anyone, he realised I was looking back on my life and warned me of the danger. And longer than anyone he stayed my friend, even as I went mad, even as he grew increasingly eager to have my woman.

As I crept around the various "plantations" of each of the mutineers, only two of them were in evidence, Ned himself and Alexander Smith, who was staying in Ned's house and from what I could see, had been badly wounded. His neck and hand were swathed in a combination of tapa and remnants of sailcloth from the *Bounty*. When he came out onto the porch, Ned supporting him, the man's face looked oddly pale, mottled by the scars of the pox he had suffered when a child. Stumbling, he bellowed with pain as Ned held him up and then helped him back inside the house. Several of the women came and went, but I saw no Polynesian men, which seemed to confound my theory of revolt. Soon after, I saw the remains of Isaac Martin, the American, shot dead and still lying just before his house, as well as William Brown's body in his own garden, his head staved in. By the time I returned to the Other Side, I still was not sure what had happened or who was left. I was, however, certain that Ned Young knew all, and that he had much to gain by helping me off the island.

Enervated by the effort and the heat, I sprawled in a pocket of rock but was too excited to sleep. I would have left the island that moment, but I knew I had to rest, eat, build up my strength, and then climb to my cave. I fell asleep when the sun was high, only to awake at the sound of an argument not ten feet from my place of concealment.

"I say let him lie there and rot. We don't bury no savages, do we." It was McKoy, the Glasgow tar whose violent life was mapped by the scars on his face. He carried a musket.

"Then let's get him into the sea," said Quintal, as brutal a man as there was, the first to be flogged on the *Bounty,* the most hated by the Polynesian men, the abuser of his woman, Tevarua.

"Do as you like," McKoy replied. "I'm not putting a finger on him."

They were quiet for a moment, during which I didn't breathe.

"Should we go back to our houses, then?" Quintal asked.

"No!" McKoy answered, belligerent as always.

"She said all the savages are dead, and if we did Manarii, who's to fear?"

"Fear your shadow, mate," McKoy growled, "you'll live longer. Come on."

"Where to?"

"Over to the Cut, maybe to Aute Valley, wherever we can hide. We'll drowse tonight and then start counting heads."

They walked away, and I began to breathe, knowing that I would have to escape as those two slept. The three-quarter moon was high in the afternoon sky, and still sleep would not come to quench my planning and agitation. If anyone opposed me, I would have to kill, for they would not hesitate to kill me. Some-one, probably Ned or Isabella, might have doubted the death my blouse had indicated, and perhaps one of them had prepared the cave in some way to announce my arrival there. When we first had anchored at Tahiti, Ned had been one of the few on board who could swim, having grown up in the West Indies. He was soon swimming as fast and as far as the Tahitians, a talent that would serve him well before dawn.

Slumber finally came, but it was a restless doze of forgotten but terrifying dreams. When I awoke I was sweated. The moon had fallen to the western horizon and my ally the dark was near full strength. I foraged for a large meal, for I knew not when I next would dine. Then I climbed Gannet's Ridge toward my first objective, the towering rock of Lookout Point.

I knew the path to my cave by heart, having shaped its zigzag course across the face of the peak; it was a progress of stepping stones that I had used a thousand times. Nevertheless, the dark and my own wariness slowed my climb, which was fortunate, for stretched almost invisibly across the final ledge, attached to the single tree that grew there and leading to the cave, was a thin string made of fibres stripped from the leaves of pandanus palms. Stepping over it, I followed it into the cave's entrance, there to find it attached to the *Bounty*'s teakettle, placed on a rock overlooking the precipice. Had I tripped the string, the kettle would have made enough clatter as it fell five hundred feet down the cliff face to alert everyone, awake or asleep. I was sure it was Ned's work.

Inside, I found that most of my own preparation had been obliterated. The muskets and powder and shot were gone, the device I'd built for collecting rainwater had been neatly dismantled. The books from the *Bounty* were still there—Hawkesworth's *Voyages,* in which I had first read of mischarted Pitcairn's perfection for our disappearance, Parkinson's, Ellis's and Forster's books on Captain Cook's explorations, all favourites of Captain Bligh, who had underlined his occasional mention in their narratives. I went to the back of the cave and fell to my knees at a place I long ago had prepared. Clawing at stone with my good hand, I uncovered a cavity I laboriously had dug out during the two years after our arrival. There I found my brace of pistols, carefully mounted in their case, with powder and shot, as well as my midshipman's dirk, all wrapped in what was left of my rotted Royal Navy tunic.

When I hid them, my grand intention had been to wear my uniform during the last fight, should it come, and to keep the last bullet for myself, for I would never be taken, never returned to England. I did not think on the memory, but loaded the pistols. From the thong around my waist, I unstrung the single button and placed it at the neck of the tunic with a reverence I did not understand at the time, then reburied the uniform. Jamming the pistols and the dirk in the goatskin thong that held the nearly formless tapa trousers around my waist, I carefully set the kettle out of my way. Leaving the cave, I quickly descended the cliff face.

Before I reached the bottom, I heard a loud commotion, the sound of women calling to each other, urging action of some kind. Our house was nearest, for Lookout Point was on my land, and as I approached I heard what they were yelling. Isabella had started to give birth, and all the other women were arriving to help. They had lit numerous candlenut torches, so I could see from my hiding place that all the ten women were there, along with the six children, who were kept on the porch in hopes of their sleeping. Isabella made less noise than any, only calling for water and urging our elder son, Thursday October, to go to sleep, a command the three-year-old was avoiding wide-eyed, but which Charles, his younger brother, already had accepted.

Ned Young would not be there that night. As had been the case with previous births on the island, the men were excluded from the process, allowed to visit only after a suitable time to view the offspring. I started immediately for Ned's house, not allowing myself to think on what was, one way or another, a final parting, a last glimpse of a family I would never see again. They were the better for it, even the one as yet unborn. I hurried to be gone before that being came.

Ned's house was lit but quiet. I watched for a quarter of an hour before daring to approach. As I did, I heard loud snoring. Looking in at one of the windows, I saw a single candlenut torch burning next to Smith, who was making the great noise as he slept on a goatskin-covered plank bed. Across the room, Ned lay on the floor. His musket leaned against the wall within reach.

Putting the dirk in my weakened right hand, I took one of the pistols in my left and moved toward the porch. Once upon it, I did not hesitate to let a squeaking board make any sound of warning but swiftly moved inside and knelt beside Ned Young, holding the barrel of the pistol to his face just as his eyes snapped open. I put the dirk's blade to my lips to signal for his silence. Taking the advice, he did not move, his one reaction after several moments of surprise, a slow satanic smile.

"I found the kettle," I whispered. "Clever Ned."

"Is it for revenge you've come," he replied, "or is it flight?"

"I've no need of vengeance. If I did, you'd be dead by now."

"I've been expecting that for some weeks."

"Help me away, Ned. The island will be yours."

I gestured toward the door and urged him toward it. We rose together, understanding all, eyes locked, I with weapons, he with nothing but his evil and decaying smile, perceiving my plan and presuming it would fail. His grin included sympathy, as if he were some crossbred Vergil leading me toward my hopeless exit from the cliff-bound circle of our infernal paradise.

"Oh God!" It was the wounded Alexander Smith, risen up and staring at me as if at death. "So he's come back from Hell for us, he wants us there to keep him company!" He bellowed on as, painfully, he tried to stand. "Well, I'll not go! Jesus God, don't take me, Mr. Christian. I followed you as far as Pitcairn, and that should be enough. You tell the Devil to stay in Hell, he'll not have my sad soul in his collection." He managed to stand, but not for long, falling first onto his knees, then pitching unconscious to the floor.

"Let me see to him," Ned said, "then we'll go."

I nodded. Ned lifted the wounded man back onto the bunk. I saw a water bag hanging on the wall and slung it on my shoulder. There was a seed pouch lying on the floor, filled with pumpkin seeds for planting. That, too, I put in place as I held the pistol levelled at my fellow mutineer. Smith was snoring again, but this time it was more of a gasp.

Ned stood next to him and said, "To the Landing Place?"

Again I nodded. He smiled and headed for the door, then stopped there to say, without looking at me, "I'll help you go, but whatever happens to you, don't come back. I'll watch, and if I see you, you'll never reach The Edge."

"If you see me," I said, "I'll come from Hell, as Smith suggested," and I followed him into the night. He walked briskly on the path leading to The Edge, which lay above the surf-torn cove where the skeleton of the *Bounty* lay. Leading down to it was the tortuous path we called the Hill of Difficulty. As Ned and I descended single file, I remembered the curses uttered against the climb during our first days off-loading the ship of everything worthwhile, before Quintal found a cask of brandy, drank it off, and fired the *Bounty* where I'd run her on the rocks.

"Ned," said I, "Quintal and McKoy are over the Cut somewhere, planning to come back." He kept walking as he listened. "They have a musket. I heard them say they'd killed Manarii."

"Were you with them?" Ned asked.

"No. They passed a place where I was hidden."

"Then all the native men are dead."

"I heard them say so. One of the women had talked with them."

"I sent Teio to find them, to tell them it was safe for them to return. Better to have those two where I can see them."

We had reached the top of the Hill of Difficulty. Ned stopped and faced my pistol, no longer smiling. "Our brotherhood of blood is at the flood, Fletcher. Do you want to know of it?"

"I only want to go, Ned. Tell me nothing that would cause trouble, for either of us."

He seemed eager to share the tale, so I let him talk.

"The native men gave me a choice to help them or be murdered with the other mutineers. God knows they had reason. We'd taken their women, given them no share of Pitcairn, made them our slaves. I gave them a plan for their massacre, but they had little talent for it, as you now know, although wounded, and your nose broken so you look like one of them."

"What of Isabella in all this?" I asked.

"She's been silent throughout, waiting for the child to come. I showed her your blouse, but she said nothing."

We walked on until we reached the rocks on which the boats were propped above the surf. It came crashing in to swell and choke the tiny cove, then pulled back to gather force anew. Piercing the waves was a matter of exact timing, difficult in the light of day, foolhardy in the dark. And yet we clambered over the rocks past the rotted skeleton of the *Bounty's* cutter to the boat of our choice. We had to judge the timing of the waves by ear, not eye, but all of us on Pitcairn had learned well that skill from the natives. My gun and dirk once more in place in my belt, I helped Ned lift the outrigger, and, waiting for the best moment, we plunged it into the rising flood and leapt aboard, swept out into the cove as the sea recalled the wave unto itself. As we offered our pathetic effort of mad paddling, trying to control our headlong plunge into darkness and deluge, we heard the hiss and roar of water rising up before us in the cresting wall through which we had to pass. Ned was before me, paddling furiously as I used my bad arm to crutch my paddle as a rudder. All I could hope to do was keep us straight so that the force of the oncoming wave would take no notice of our passage through it.

We saw it the instant before it hit us. The boat began to rise. The outrigger lifted from the water as we commenced to roll. I heard Ned yell. Both of us lurched larboard to keep the boat level. Then the massive wall was on us, reversing its backward undertow by which we were drawn into its forward purpose. We rose up to face the force that could return us to the rocks and the oblivion we both deserved. But then we were engulfed as our canoe shot through a ring of foam and landed on the wave's broad back, and we were deafened by the crash behind us. Without pause, we went through half a dozen waves more before we dared to rest.

Bad arm or no, I paddled hard and felt my wound split open. I was in a boat at sea again, perhaps paddling to my doom, but Pitcairn was behind me. My sailor's exodus as always placed guilt and responsibility deep in the bilge of my mind. As I paddled, I did not look back; sailors seldom do, their sights set on the horizon before them. The horizon I saw was black, still unlit by any dawning rescue or solution, but I was at sea once more.

Without warning, Ned turned and swung his paddle at my head. I saw the move in time to deflect the blade with my good arm. Once failed, he did not try again, for as I drew my dirk, the pistols being wet and useless, he dove overboard to avoid a cut, which would invite the sharks. Swimming underwater to a safe distance, he surfaced and, effortlessly treading water, called out to me.

"I'd rather have you dead," he called. "Now I'll always have to wonder if you reached anywhere, and whom you've told of us along the way."

"I'll tell no one, even to the gallows, until I see an angel. Believe me."

He laughed again. "I wish you luck, Mr. Christian"—he said the name with sarcastic formality—"both good and bad. If you survive, no doubt you'll be hanged for your sins . . . which may be what you truly desire. And if you reach the world again, remember me to no one, for even as it is, this is a better place for any man of mixed blood. And I will make it better, I assure you!"

I could not see him, but could hear his arms slap against the water as he swam. "Don't tell Isabella that I lived," I yelled.

He stopped to yell back. "I'll tell no one. Why should they be tormented? I'll tell Smith you were a nightmare. Except to me and the Admiralty, you're a dead man." He swam on, and soon the distant surf muffled his strokes.

I picked up the paddle and felt the fresh ache of my shoulder. The canoe was far enough out to sea not to be carried in again to Pitcairn. Although I felt a slow trickle of blood down my back, I paddled as long as I could in hopes of being out of sight of the island when daylight came. The sun would rise before me, I hoped bright enough to turn an eye from my direction. The route of most of the ships I'd seen was due south of the island, and as I struggled with the paddle, I could not stop the tormenting thoughts of other ships, which had passed to the east and north. This torture countered that of my back, so I was able to keep paddling until the sun glared down hard enough to make me rest.

I chanced a quick dip overboard to let the saltwater at my back, then paddled on to put a distance between my blood and the canoe. As I consumed six pumpkin seeds, washed down with a bare trickle from the water bag, I scanned both sky and horizon. Not a cloud or a bird was there to see, only the last tip of Pitcairn's Lookout Point, set like a tombstone on the waterline. In every other direction I was bound only by death and my future. With nothing but a boat and respect for the sea, I was again as much of a sailor as I could ever hope to be.

The South Pacific

October 1793

The water in the goatskin bag lasted five days, the pumpkin seeds a few days longer. I tried to shoot a gull, but neither pistol fired, and as my desperation grew, I threw the useless weapons at the birds without result. The weather held, which meant the sun beat down upon me unmercifully. The only time I paddled was to stay beneath a cloud. My boat was in a current, carrying me eastward. I rigged my white tapa pants on one of the paddles to use as a pennant in case I spied a ship, but most of the day, I used the cloth to cover my head while I lay in the bottom of the canoe.

The dirk was finally lost the night I fought off some huge creature, which rose up before me with no warning, a great mass of scales and teeth, with eyes that glowed concentrically both green and yellow. It attacked first from one side, then the other. I stabbed at it repeatedly and finally struck between the luminous eyes. The blade lodged there, and as the monstrous apparition gnashed its teeth and sank away into the dark, the dirk was last to disappear.

The moment that the sea erased the traces of the episode, I questioned whether such a being truly had appeared, or if my arid brain created it. Thirst creates a host of demons as any sailor knows. From that time on, I tried to concentrate on stars at night and the horizon through the day. I held their trusted constancy before me as I floated on the deep abyss of water that could end its toleration of my boat in an instant. Soon the days and nights became confused, and I began to see strange lambent-white horizons in the blackness. And then as time and any semblance of sanity dissolved, the comets and the planets began to plummet into the sun.

On one bright night, I saw the moon reflected red upon the ocean. When I gazed into the sky, the blazing sphere was blinding white, so that I knew before I dared look down again that all the sea was blood. And like a wind that came from nowhere, groans in chorus filled the air, which I could hear even though I stopped my ears with trembling hands and bellowed loud myself to drown the noise.

When next I moved, it still was night, whether that same one or another was beyond my apprehension. I could not separate the ocean from the sky except for the horizon glistening in the distance, a circle round me made of what I thought was ice, dividing black from black. I stared at this surround and realised with growing terror that the cincture was beginning to close on me. I then heard no sound; in fact, I thought I'd gone completely deaf for I could not perceive the howls of fear that I myself was making. Coming ever closer, the ice contained my noise as suddenly the world somehow turned sideways; all my sense of balance was lost, and as I watched, the circle rose above me and my boat, becoming a circumference punctured in the universe through which everything, whole seas, whole planets, moons, and stars, could come or go.

In the center of that hole's vast emptiness, I saw a massive ship with seven masts, full rigged, its sails on fire, and yet she travelled through the void toward me as fast as any frigate, with no benefit of wind that I could feel except a breath like that exhaled in death. And with what speed she came, whether through the night or sea I could not tell, nor did it matter, for I thought the end had come and welcomed it.

In the swirling smoke, I stood with paddle raised. But as I paused, my useless weapon held aloft, I saw cutting through the fog a bowsprit, then a female figurehead, with breasts revealed, who stared at me with arch surprise. Before the ship crashed into the canoe, I saw a lookout standing on the footrope to the flying jib, his startled glance the lady's twin. He yelled as I was thrown into the sea, the sound of splintering wood the last I heard.

I know nothing of my rescue, how they found me in that fog. The first sensation I recall was brandy in my mouth, followed by intense and stabbing pain cutting through my back. I groaned and saw a pair of bloodied arms lift a bottle to my lips to pour more liquid in my mouth. A voice was angrily commanding me in some strange language. I drank until oblivion returned, which did not last as long as I'd have wished. For when I woke, or rather came again to my senses (for surely sleep was not what I'd enjoyed), the pain was still so burningly intense that I scarce dared to breathe.

I was in a ship's surgery, my rope-strung pallet suspended from the deckhead above me, allowing me to stay relatively level as the ship rolled with the contrary sea. From the size of the cabin, I gathered the ship was a small one, perhaps a barque. The other two pallets were occupied by men ill with what I thought was scurvy.

One of them took notice that I was alive and scowled his disregard but called out with words I did not know. A man came in, carrying a musket and wearing a uniform I recognised as that of a Dutch marine. He disappeared, and soon thereafter there appeared three men who were immediately identifiable as two officers and the ship's surgeon. They spoke quietly amongst themselves, then one of the officers approached and said as he pointed to himself, "*Hoa.*" It was a Polynesian word for friend. Then he gestured for the loblolly boy, the surgeon's assistant waiting behind them, to bring me the bowl he was holding. He did so and spooned some gruel into my mouth. I realised my hunger and took as much as I was offered.

"*Tama'a,*" the officer said, which meant "eat a meal."

I dared to nod. They began again to speak amongst themselves as I finished the gruel. Apparently they had concluded I was a Polynesian native, having pulled me naked from the sea, my skin scorched brown, my hips and breast with requisite tattoos. My hair was black enough, my eyes brown, my height, as was the native men's, above the average European's. I remembered how I'd looked reflected in Pitcairn's pool, my nose no longer prominent but spread flat across my face.

Abruptly, I realised I had returned to civilisation. I had to act accordingly, and think, and most of all remember much of what I long had chosen to forget. As ever, war had been on the horizon when we left England. Almost six years had passed. We had fought the Dutch before; they were rivals for the Indies' trade. It stood to reason that Holland might be at war with England.

"*Maitai?*" the officer asked, his vocabulary becoming more specifically Tahitian, "Good?"

"*Mauruuru,*" I replied, a Tahitian phrase of satisfaction and gratitude with which I sealed my identity in their eyes. The officers smiled; the surgeon came to examine me. It was only then that I realised my entire shoulder, front and back, was wrapped expertly in bandages. The surgeon reached into his pocket and proudly held between his thumb and forefinger the ball that he'd extracted. He watched me for a sign of understanding, which I gave him with a happy smile and several *mauruurus*. Then I went to sleep.

The moment I awoke, I wanted to know everything. Yet I

dared not ask a question in any language. Being an Englishman was dangerous in itself, but being an Englishman with Tahitian tattoos, plucked from anywhere in the South Pacific, could easily lead to the identity of Fletcher Christian, a name well known on any ship, I could be certain. Those in the launch with Captain Bligh no doubt had perished, but there were the sixteen men left on Tahiti after the mutiny, both loyalists and mutineers who chose to stay there rather than sail with me to an unknown fate. Once the *Bounty* was overdue and considered lost, the Admiralty would have sent another ship to find her. The searcher's first objective would be Tahiti. Once there, those of the *Bounty*'s crew who had remained loyal to the Crown—for none had much allegiance to Bligh himself—would tell the mutinous tale, and word of our crime would have spread with the wind over the oceans of the world.

Lying on that swaying pallet in the Dutch barque's surgery, I once again shuddered at the steady progress of mistakes I'd made from the moment of mutiny. Judgment, perception, equanimity, honour, all qualities of leadership I once believed were mine, all had been efficiently corroded in the three short months from mutiny to our run before the wind to the unknown. If any further process was needed to assure my character, three years and nine months of murder and madness on Pitcairn took my life to its rotten extremity. The travesty I had become was exactly what Bligh had described in his raging diatribes on board the *Bounty*. His smirking face had told me that he believed me to be no more than an overbred boy, with charm and talent enough to make my way on deck and in the drawing rooms of influence to which I had my family's access. I knew he envied that access, but he implied mine was a mere social gloss, a brittle core easily cracked by the stress of manly duties. I thus became, as he called me before the ship's company, "a coward, a thief, and a hound." But I had surpassed his opinion by becoming so much more.

And yet I chose to live, without honour, without reason. I lay there with no burning intention to rectify what I had done. There was too much. There was no way to turn and face my past, explain it, or even tell the story with the idea of gaining absolution from others. In spite of that, I was returning. I did not know exactly where the Dutchman was going, but my objective was England. I'd given up my claim or hope for home or family, though I held an unfocused wish to see my mother. I had no conceit of courage for going to her house, the place most obvious for my capture. It was my attraction to what I'd known, to return to the place on land where I'd been most alive, as well as curiosity to find out what had become of the rest of the ship's company and how my actions were regarded. But as to any purpose or worth in what was left of my new life, I saw none. If I was destined to be caught and hanged, so be it. And once again, I heard Ned Young's contemptuous observation that hanging might be the official absolution that I craved, and wondered if he were right.

Within days, eating the ship's diet, I had strength to stand, and then to walk. Within a week, I was on deck, sitting against the bowrail in the sun, letting the fresh air have its way with me, watching albatross hover in the air above the mainmast on their oceanic journey. The crew regarded me with momentary curiosity, some with sullen contempt, reminding me that I was a native to some, an Indian or nigger to others. As I watched them work, I itched to be at it with them, climbing the shrouds, up the ratlines and out in the main royal yard. The sight of full canvas was as effective a cure for me as any physic.

By then I was dressed in the rags presented to me from the ship's slop chest, that fetid trunk of overpriced, rotted goods that every purser on a voyage used to line his pocket. Having no payment to offer, I was given the poorest garments, which turned out to be alive with lice. To these I was no stranger and battled them accordingly. My hair and new-grown beard were cut short, and a sulphur salve liberally applied. The surgeon, proud of his work, took endless care with my wound, changing bandages regularly and showing the results to all the other officers, a way of reassuring them of his talents, I gathered, for he was known to consume a gill of rum with a frequency that caused concern. Nevertheless, I was soon out of the sling he had fashioned and doing the exercises he prescribed, using at first a six-pound roundshot, then graduating to the twelve.

The ship, called the *Zaandam,* was an East Indiaman carrying teak and silver. Her half a dozen small guns on deck were not for battle, but to offer a modicum of protection. From my reading of the stars as well as the position of the sun, I knew she was headed southeast toward the Horn at the tip of South America. A typical beamy Dutch-built ship with rounded bows, she was undermanned, as were all merchantmen, to save their owners' money. She belonged to the V.O.C., the Vereenigde Oost-Indische Compagnie, or United East India Company, which controlled trade in the Dutch East Indies. Merchant rivals to the British East India Company's ambition in the East, the Dutch were fine shipbuilders and admirable sailors. My respect for the captain and the officers of the *Zaandam* was immediate. I felt a nostalgic twinge for their command and privilege aboard the ship but suppressed it in order to be accepted by the crew, 'tween decks. When I was ordered to work, I went to it willingly although I had to feign an ignorance so that no one would think I knew what I was about.

I proved a fast learner, which I heard the officers and crew explain away as the natural physical adroitness of Pacific natives. For my part, I showed them on the foremast how properly to climb a coconut tree, walking up with feet and hands rather than shinnying with thighs and arms. After that, my prowess on the ratlines was never questioned and was called on with increasing frequency as we neared the Horn.

Inevitably in a merchant crew of ten dozen sailors, there was an Englishman on board, one Henry Hillendale, whom the Dutch called "Hoondy." A ferretlike man with an upturned nose, protruding teeth, tiny sunken eyes, and a mangy beard, he fixed a hate on me that came from being hated and finding someone of a lesser status to punish for his own inadequacy. Reviling me in English in front of anyone who'd listen, he used me as a butt of ridicule to which I dared not answer with anything but my happiest smile. Enjoying thus the private meaning of his public invective, Hoondy would often try to force me to show the crew how the Polynesians dance, pulling me up beside him and giving his own spastic-hipped version as an example.

"Ow, come on, you bleeding nigger, show us how it's done. You wiggle here, and wiggle that . . . Get up here, you big brown monkey, an' shew these dumb dike builders how to twirl your bird in a figure eight. Oh yes, that makes your fat-lipped women wet, don't it, mate?" In a pretense of camaraderie, I became instantly awkward, hobbled a few happy steps, then tripped over myself and collapsed. Hoondy then would kick me once or twice, referring to me as whatever filth was in his mind at that moment, for the amusement of his audience. I did my best to avoid him, but a ship, originally made from a thick forest, becomes too bare for hiding, and his need for me was great.

Fortunately he was inclined, living thus in his Dutch void, to talk out loud in English at any opportunity. A natural complainer, he ofttimes compared what he regarded as the shoddy Dutch routine to that of an English ship, on which he'd sailed, one or another, since he was twelve. "Here we are again, joggin' along Dutch fashion with sails trimmed by the Devil, and them standing on the poop as smug as a duck in a ditch. If Christ Hisself came walking on the water and told them to bring in their sheets, they'd let 'em out a foot and pass Him by like a witch. Wait till the Horn when they hold too long to their topsails and watch them blow away to make tents for the penguins."

An inveterate critic of the food and his hammocked accommodations, he took pleasure only in his plug of tobacco, which nevertheless also gave him much to grouse over. "I've chewed on this plug through the watches now, and it's dried out like an old woman's thigh. I'd rather eat my hat," which he soon did after the quid was at last consumed. He'd kept it in the lining of his hat, which, being soaked with tobacco juice, he soon was chewing.

His use of me soon gave way to cruelty, and he began to beat me with a rope or a fist on any occasion that suited him. I cowered and protected myself as best I could but knew it had to end, for I could not see him ever having enough. As we came to the Horn and the winds became as fierce as nature can provide anywhere on earth, one day I worked my way to stand next to him on the royal yards when we were furling sails. There were thousands of square feet we had to take away from the possessive gale. I knew that Hoondy had resented the Dutch for putting me with the topmen, a lofty status on board of which he was inordinately proud and loath to share with a nigger. He was always fast up the ratlines, scolding aloud his mainmast section mates for being laggards and cowards. He was usually first to scuttle out to the extremity of a yard.

That day I stayed with him and listened to his angry insults as we worked against the blow to gather sail. The deck was far below, and few eyes could watch the details of our work, the results being all that mattered. I gathered in the sail but held it rather than tying it off until he leaned over in his work toward me. Releasing the sail, I watched it pop out into the wind, tearing from Hoondy's grip and throwing him off balance with no defence against the pitching of the ship.

In a bare second he looked at me with terror, knowing what I'd done, but then the wind took him back from the yard and he screamed. My plan had been to let him fall and rid myself of his constant punishment. But in that second, I did not want to kill again, too aware of how it had become too easy for me. My hand shot out, and as he lost his footing, I grabbed his wrist. As he fell to twist in the gale, he let out a shriek that was heard by our mates, two of whom hurried to my side. I stared down at Hoondy's face and saw what he would look like as an old man.

His tiny eyes swelled from his head to look at me as a fine foam of fear was torn from his mouth by the blast. When we hauled him up, he went silent, holding frozen to the yard until they bellowed at him to do his work or we'd all be blown away. Slowly he took up his work again, too carefully to do much good at first, but soon with his usual dexterity.

I realised I'd caught him with the hand that had been weakened by the musket shot and was no worse for it. We finished on the royals and descended to the topgallants, the skysails long since furled. I let three men separate us, but no one heard his usual commentary on their faults. Once returned to deck, he did not wait to criticise those who came behind but screamed at me, "You're no nigger from the sea, but some black devil come from Hell to take us there." He ran below and stayed apart from all of us.

The ship traversed its treacherous route around the Horn. We seamen stayed below as often as possible, trusting our lives to the captain and the shipbuilders. The sea, so long our partner but now a menace that every sailor knew and cursed, would more easily destroy us on deck. As we braced ourselves as best we could 'tween decks, I often saw Hoondy watching me from some dark corner, his usual angry look quite perforated with evil-eyed query.

The reaction of the crew to his rescue was to gain me audience with the captain for an expression of Dutch gratitude, as well as appreciation from my mates, resulting in biscuit with less weevil in it, as well as an occasional solid piece of salt pork. I still was not provided with a hammock but slept on the deck, nor was I invited to sit at mess with anyone, for I was still a savage.

From that day on, however, Hoondy left me to my own pleasures rather than using me for his. He never spoke to anyone again, even to himself. And when at last we put in at Buenos Aires for supplies, he was over the side and gone the first night. I was relieved; my English was always too close in my throat. If he had heard it in an unguarded moment, he gladly would have been my undoing.

After so many weeks on the *Zaandam,* I could understand enough Dutch to follow orders and know where we were going. The ship had picked up its cargo of silver and teak in Batavia, the V.O.C.'s main port on the north coast of Java. She was headed for Curaçao in the Dutch Antilles, then on to Rotterdam. I was content to stay aboard at least until we reached the Caribbean, for I had sailed that sea on merchant ships with Bligh on two occasions before the *Bounty.*

From what I could glean with my new-found tongue, there was a war and it was a large one. But France seemed to hold the crew's conversation more than England did. We sailed into the Caribbean ten days after Christmas, passing north of Trinidad. The weather there was as always the year's best as it began. I was staying on the open deck at night, but with less and less sleep as my anticipation grew. I hardly dared believe I could return to England, but if I did I had to ask myself, where would I go? A city was the only place that I could hope to hide. If I appeared in my native Cumberland or at my mother's house on the Isle of Man, I feared I would be known, broken nose and burned skin, or no. Yet I knew my first objective would be to see my mother. Each time that I allowed myself the luxury of planning a return, the vigilant itinerary foundered on the question, who am I to be? For Fletcher Christian would not be allowed to live for long in England.

I wondered what I'd do when finally I arrived at Curaçao with nothing but the slops I wore on my back. I thought of staying in the West Indies, working hard and long enough to save some money. But how? I could not work on any ship in a capacity that would attract attention. Signing on as seaman meant ten years to save enough to buy a decent set of clothes. And even with the costume of a gentleman, where was I to go? What role to play? And once again I dared to hope I could return to my mother, my family, to those who might admit to being mine, arriving secretly, of course, with little expectation of a welcome. For sure I knew exactly what my act had meant to those who shared my name and thus the shame when society made its quick and shallow judgment.

I could not sleep for fear of what I'd dream, as well as my restlessness of purpose. Leaning on the rail, I stared down at the fine feather of a wave our bow cut through the sea. Others were asleep on deck, taking pleasure in the fair, warm breeze. Earlier that night there'd been a blow and then a rain, which washed the deck already cleared for action, I presumed, against privateers. The six small guns were in position, which appeared to me to give enough protection to repel a bathtub full of children. The close quarters of timber baulks had been put in place around the afterdeck, but with the kind of care that Hoondy would have criticised, this time with damned good reason.

I wondered if the war I'd heard about had spread so far as to that brilliant blue and sparkling sea, and if the privateers, with which we'd had our troubles when I sailed with Bligh, were still nothing more than pirates working for one government or other under a flag or letter of marque, or if with war they had become imbued with patriotic purpose. Then I thought of my own devotion in a war where, if I served my country, she'd hang me if she learned of it.

As I conjectured thus, there was the slightest change of dark, an errant shadow moving in the night ten cable's lengths away to starboard. Staring hard, I tried to see into the blackness as my old cold sweat of warning came upon my brow. At first I only saw the starlit night play tricks upon my eyes with waves and clouds. And then I saw the blot of dark again, still just a shadow but enough of one for me to recognise a ship with not a single lantern burning to reveal her phantom presence.

Instantly I ran to find the lookout in the bow. He was asleep as most were during early watches. One of those who looked on me as less than worthy of his company, he cuffed me when I woke him, then again when through his sleepy eyes he could not glimpse what I was urging him to see. He pushed me back and took his place again against the foremast. I did not await his snores but ran astern and climbed the quarterdeck, forbidden to an ordinary seaman, particularly a native. Jabbering Tahitian, I urged their quick attention starboard.

They all looked, the two helmsmen, the quartermaster, the officer of the watch, and a bosun as well as two other lookouts from amidship. None saw anything, nor did I. Whatever I had seen had disappeared, into the dark or from my mind, I knew not. The bosun threw me down, and one of the helmsmen came to aid in my punishment, but as they started on their work, the officer of the watch gave a cry and, staring hard astern, began to shout his orders, making all the others run. The bosun's call piped for all hands on deck, and as the quartermaster leapt down to fetch the captain, I looked through the spokes of the taffrail and saw a ship closing on us, no longer just a shadow but a full-rigged frigate cleared for action. Then there were two flashes from her bow-mounted guns, followed by a roar that reached us with the twelve-pound roundshot, one of which fell short, the other shattering the transom of the captain's cabin, I'm sure as rude a waking as he'd ever had.

I crawled as quickly as I could down to the main deck as the seamen boiled up from below to take their places at the guns amidship, useless as they were. Others came to grab muskets, tomahawks, and pikes, although there weren't enough to go around. Everyone was yelling, many fearing what was sure to happen, for as the unlit ship again came starboard, its slim frigate's speed overtaking our fat and beamy merchant hull, I counted in a glance a dozen twelve- and nine-pound guns, along with one-pound swivel mounts of brass, to spray a deck with grapeshot.

The captain of our ship could count as well as I, and as his men rushed back and forth to arm and aim our guns with unrehearsed endeavour, he bellowed a command that, when repeated by the bosuns, caused the men to find their cover and go as silent as their graves would surely be. Crouching near an unfilled gun port, I knelt down and saw forty yards away the frigate raising colours on her stern halyard. I was at a loss, never having seen a pennant such as that, but those around me murmured of France with anguish in their throats. Even in the darkness, I could see the frigate's guns were manned, the black tarred barrels run out through her gun ports and trained on us.

And yet we saw no flash of firing but instead heard a bellowed greeting through a speaking trumpet.

"*Bonjour!*" The voice was jocular. "*Parlez-vous français?*"

Netherlands Antilles

January 1794

My schoolboy French, unused for a decade, was only good enough to understand the barest details of the negotiation. The Dutch first mate knew the language and bellowed through his trumpet to the Frenchman, agreeing to a boarding and removal of whatever cargo was wanted in return for the safety of the ship and all aboard. In spite of having little choice, they must have known that one can never trust a privateer. That vessel's grand pennant indicated some legality; but as with all of their fraternity, they sailed with but a single motive: avarice. And for their service of disrupting shipping, they gained entitlement to whatever booty they could capture, whether of patriotic benefit or no. What's more, it did not serve their purposes to let witnesses go free, for no one ever knew if, in some far-off port, a face remembered just might bring a noose, or draw a dagger in the back.

They boarded us with grappling hooks and bloody cries, then shoved the crew, including officers, together in the bow. Thus guarded, we watched as they tore through the ship, working in the dark to haul the silver bars across the rails of the grappled ships. Then came the barrels of rum and casks of brandy, transported with considerably more care than were the ingots.

All this time we were forbidden by our guards to speak, although several of these who were themselves Dutch spoke most persuasively to our seamen, asking if any might wish to go along on the privateer, for its crew was short. Some half dozen of our worst soon volunteered and, laughing at their silent mates, were shoved across the rails. The French captain surveyed and directed the scene from his position in the shrouds. Observing that I was excluded by the other men, he leapt down on deck and asked the French-speaking officer what I was. I cowered appropriately while the explanation was offered, then the smiling Frenchman prodded me with his cutlass, urging me hastily aboard his ship.

Before their job was done, the privateers began to treat themselves to drink, and their enthusiasm for their work increased. The moment the bullion was safely stored below, the French captain shouted an order, and the Dutch crew was herded down the *Zaandam's* hatchways, the explanation given that the captain of the privateer demanded time to disappear into the dark. But as the hatchways were covered with their grates, which then were wedged with boarding axes, I saw the men aboard the privateer readying their guns. I ran toward the still-joined *Zaandam,* but those seamen who had left her tackled me and held me to the deck. The privateer cast off, and when but fifteen yards of water separated us, the French captain, even as we heard the cries of the imprisoned Dutch, shouted his order.

The broadside's report deafened me, and I was left by my Dutch captors who then rushed to the rail to see the damage done. The crew of the privateer, with cheers for their easy triumph, crossed over to the starboard side of the deck and there prepared those guns as we tacked neatly around the listing Dutchman. The cries from her belowdecks were of pain and terror. The helmsman of the privateer, with expert skill, brought her within half a chain's length of the *Zaandam*'s larboard. Then the captain's bellowed order came again. Another broadside thundered out, shattering the Dutchman's huge beams. Already listing badly, the merchantman began to founder, and flames appeared, throwing shadows through the dark. The privateer maintained her course as the crew began to shout and dance in celebration of their treacherous victory. In the *Zaandam*'s firelight, I could barely see some of her crew crawling through the holes made by the twelve-pounders.

I knew their freedom was for naught but had no time to think on it, for I was grabbed by several laughing pirates who dragged me to the helm, before their captain. After quick examination, not only of my looks, but how I smelled, he laughed and gave his men some orders. The slops I'd worn since I'd been rescued then were cut away right where I stood, and someone brought a set of clothes, fine-made striped breeches and a waistcoat made of silk, a lackey's uniform. From which ship they'd stolen such a costume wasn't worth a guess. Little of it fit, but no one seemed to care, the effect they wished having been created.

The captain disappeared below during my metamorphosis. Once it was complete, I was again escorted, this time into the galley where a silver tray was being prepared with fruits and nuts as well as what I thought was fresh-killed meat. I'd noticed several goats on board and gathered that the cook had tended his pots during the time the boarding had taken place. He exhibited great pride in how the platter looked, fussing over his design of nuts in gravy. I restrained my own temptation, for the smells and sight of such a meal made my stomach ache with hunger. Finally the platter was placed in my uncertain hands, with savage orders from the cook. I was then led by several escorts to the captain's door. One guard banged upon it with the hilt of his cutlass, then hearing his captain's order shouted from within, opened the latch and urged me forward with his blade. Taking several stooped steps, I held the platter as the cook had directed and heard the door slam shut behind me.

The sight that greeted me was one beyond any expectation. The French captain stood expectantly looking at a woman wearing a ball gown. Her face was first in shadow, then in candlelight as she turned to glimpse my arrival. Not having seen such a woman in half a dozen years, I was staggered. She stood before the transom window, her green eyes burning with scorn for the captain. Several intricate gold combs held her raven black hair in place, piled on her head. What was most astonishing to me after so many years in the tropics was the whiteness of her skin, accomplished without benefit of powder, as if she had been exposed only to moonlight. Her straight, almost pointed nose majestically separated the thin-browed, slightly tilted orbs of green, while her mouth, even though locked in rage and disgust, was full lipped and seemed as wide as her face would allow. There was a tiny mole just to the side of her left nostril. Her cheeks, flushed with anger, burnished by candlelight, rose high and straight to the prominent bones below her temples.

"Here he is," the captain said in accented English, "as I promise you." A rodent-faced, oily man, he had put on, in spite of the heat, an ornate brocade coat over the sweat-stained shirt and waistcoat worn to board the Dutchman. Still with cutlass in hand, he gestured with it for me to put the silver platter down on a table, which I saw was set for only one. There were, however, two goblets next to a bottle of wine.

"Who is this?" she asked, her low throaty voice revealing the fear to which her beauty had blinded me. And no wonder. She was dressed in all the feminine intricacies of wealth, a gown of light blue taffeta fitted tight around a tiny waist and falling over petticoats almost to the floor. I saw her shoes were soft white leather. Her bodice, cut low, revealed her breasts, held up to view by a firm corset. I could not believe in such a vision.

"He is your servant," the captain shouted at her. "You cannot dress and undress yourself; he will do it. I am bored with the struggle. And then he shall watch over our pleasures. I think you have need of a savage audience."

She looked at me with as much chagrin as dread. Still in character, I tried to indicate that I understood nothing. The captain sat down and, pouring wine into the two goblets, laid his cutlass across the table.

"Send him away," she said softly, "I can undress myself, as well you know."

"No!" the captain yelled. "Tonight I wish it different. *He* will undress you. If you resist—" He stood up suddenly and, leaping at her, he tore open her bodice with both hands, then shouted at me, "This is what you do, *sauvage. Comprenez?* Tear it off." Without caring if I understood but knowing that she did, he turned away, peacock proud, and resumed his seat at the table.

"You like some wine?" he asked her, smiling.

Holding her torn dress in place, she shook her head.

"You don't worry about the dress," he said as he began to carve his meat. "There are so many in your trunks, enough to last us many weeks. And if you do not tell me who you are by then," he shouted, "you'll be sent to feed the fishes!"

"I'll never tell you that!" she said. "You may as well feed the fishes now." She started for the transom window, but his cutlass was quickly on her throat and barred the way.

"Not now," he said. "Now back so I can watch your savage do his work." He moved her with the blade still on her neck to where I stood. He then commanded, "Show him what to do."

She looked at me and gave an apprehensive frown, then turned her back and pointed to the laces of her dress. I played confusion, then I did as I was bid as the captain began to cut and chew more meat, his cutlass laid again beside his place.

The noise of merrymaking on deck surrounded us in raucous chorus. The Dutchman's store of fine old brandy, which I'd tasted only once, was providing fuel for celebration. Hearing first a fiddle, then a squeezebox as the brigands shouted in their dance, I reached the bottom of her lacing. She then shrugged the garment off her shoulders, causing it to fall and thus reveal the strange construction of her undergarments.

The captain laughed and made a sucking noise between his lips. "These things you women wear are like a skeleton, new bones to make you into something else. Go on, go on, and let me see what's real." He then stood up and, sipping wine, he walked around to lean against the table. From his waist, he untied a heavy shammy bag that hung there on a leather thong. Putting down his goblet, he opened the bag. "What do we have for you to wear tonight?" he said, as he produced an emerald earring, then a ruby and diamond ring. She took no notice of the jewellery but stared into a candle's flame.

I knew that I was going to kill again. Somehow I'd come to think or hope that all my murdering was in the past and of another time and place; for after all, I was returning to the world of civilised behaviour. I thought that saving Hoondy proved the point, that having come round the Horn and left the savage life of blood behind, I'd somehow been transformed.

But all such delicate interpretations fall away when battered with the larger truth we call experience. For as I measured how much space there was between my hand and the Frenchman's cutlass, and if that distance might be shorter than the depth of his lust for her, I realised the greater truth, that savagery is not a matter of geography. There are no longitudes of chaos, latitudes of crime, nor is there an exact equator marking halves of right and wrong. We chart our lives ourselves, our route unsure, our destination our own creation, ever changing, nothing certain, other than the fact that we shall die. As a savage in a savage circumstance, I was going to kill again, as quickly as I could.

The captain licked his lips, put the bag of jewels down and reached toward her breast. Once done with all her laces, I had stepped aside to cringe and whimper, wide-eyed in the dark, which he enjoyed. With one hand deep within her corset as the other held his goblet, he was occupied enough for me to leap the distance to the cutlass. He had time to turn his head but not to yell. I swung and severed it.

"I want you to cry out," I said, just as he fell, before she had a chance to move or cry. "Go on—as if you're horrified to be here."

She did, and made a strange sound, certainly surprised at who from Hell I might be and that I spoke the King's good English. Stepping round the captain, his head hinged and pouring blood, I swung the transom window open. Above, no one stood beside the taffrail. Through the deckhead, I could hear the feet of those in charge, but they stood forward far enough to hinder any notice of our flight. I turned to her to find her lovely viridescent eyes upon me.

"Under such a circumstance," I whispered, "I regret to say that you must take off everything. We have a long, hard swim."

Her eyes just barely narrowed, then she stepped out of her petticoats and was at her stays. "Damn. Help me, sir," she ordered, finding knots.

With care I placed the blade upon the corset's laces. "Yell again," I said. She did. I cut, and the encumbrance fell away. Without the slightest hesitation, she began to strip away her shift. I undressed as well, a simpler process with my borrowed lackey's costume.

"You do swim?" I asked.

"As well as you, I'll wager," she replied, and made straight for the window.

"Whether you decide to jump or dive, cut yourself smootherly into the water." Unused to my own language, I had uttered a pidgin English phrase. She took no notice, but climbed into the transom window and crouched on the sill. Her body was long and thin. I was too used to female nudity to be unduly moved, but I was startled at the unfamiliar black wisps of hair between her legs. She skillfully dove into the ship's wake with barely a splash.

Quickly gathering up the jewels, I put them in the shammy bag and tied the thong around my waist. I followed out the transom window and into the ship's wake, swimming as far as possible underwater. When I surfaced, I saw the privateer's lanterns receding into the darkness. A shout of argument, then laughter floated across the water with the music, but I saw no sign that they had discovered their headlessness. I looked around for her and felt a splash on the side of my face.

"Which way?" she demanded.

As far as I could tell, the Dutch ship had been boarded as she passed the Islas Los Roques, east of the Netherlands Antilles. From that time with Bligh when I studied my charts night and day, I knew that there were many islands in the group, most uninhabited, but offering good chances of our finding fresh water. In the barest outline from the early edge of dawn, I could see two islands, one east, one north, equidistant. For no reason, I pointed to the east, and she, without comment, began to swim.

We were lucky. At the point of exhaustion—I judge after an hour and a half—we reached an easy surf that carried us upon a beach. We saw a stand of trees growing in a clump; underneath was a stream that cut through the beach's sand. Our mouths burning with salt, we staggered to the freshwater and drank our fill. Sleep took us where we lay, face-down on the sand, which was still warm from the previous day's sun.

When I woke, she was not where she'd slept. I turned to find her sitting nearby with her back to me, a pile of fruit beside her, a large palm branch held to cover her nudity. I noted that her hair, as black as any I had ever seen, hung down her back, almost like a native's. Two gold combs had survived the swim and held the hair above her ears. She'd fashioned a hat of woven palm leaves to protect her face from the sun, which had risen high by then. Turning her head, she saw I was awake and lofted a pawpaw to me.

"Good morning, sir," she said as if we were meeting on the High Street somewhere. I was instantly reminded of the formality of speech, of "sirs," "madams," and "misses" that had long since escaped my vocabulary. I doubted my ability to reestablish the habit, so I didn't try. In modesty, we spoke to each other over our shoulders.

"You haven't seen any sign of the island being inhabited, have you?" I asked idly.

"Not so far. I couldn't help but notice that your bottom is . . . well, black," she said as if making idle conversation. "Would you mind terribly telling me why?"

I laughed. "Fancy, aren't I?"

"Seriously, sir," she urged.

"It's called *tatau,* or tattoo, a custom in the South Seas." I was instantly aware of how difficult it was to tell her nothing.

"I see. And those narrow lines of arrows and designs above it, like belts around your waist, and the star on your breast?"

"Vanity, pure vanity. May I have a guava, please?"

She threw me one. "How is it done?"

"The natives make a kind of lampblack from the ash of nut-shells. Then they prick it under the skin with bones or shells that have sharp teeth cut into them."

"Painful," she observed.

"Very," I agreed.

"You're not a native, though?" she queried.

I smiled at her confusion. "No."

"But your entire bottom is—black?"

"In the South Seas, it seems appropriate."

"And are you—that way—all the way around?"

"You'll see for yourself any time now."

"Yes, I suppose I shall." The prospect was one she chose to ignore. "Where did you have this done?"

"I don't plan to tell you that," said I, "or anything else about me. When we're found, I'd ask that you say nothing about me, that you escaped on your own. No one will ever say different, me or that Frenchman."

She watched me as she finished her pawpaw. "I see," she said. "And may I not tell you anything about myself?"

"As you wish."

She smiled with interest and looked out at the sea. "That might be quite diverting." Then she fixed her green eyes back on me. "You said, 'when we're found.' Are you certain we shall be?"

I stood and tried to get a bearing, wondering if my navigational guesses were anywhere near correct. If so, it would not be long before ships passed. If not, we might be there a long time.

"Yes, I'm sure," I lied. "But we should have a signal fire and build a shelter. The rains come suddenly here in January."

When I looked down at her, she was nodding, but examining forthrightly where my tattoos ended. She then met my eyes with little awkwardness and said, "I'm sure you were relieved that the *tatau* custom didn't include the logical conclusion."

"There were other customs involving that."

"Indeed, sir? You must explain them to me sometime." With that she stood, still holding the palm branch, and faced me with the worried vulnerability of not knowing what I'd do to her. "How do you propose to start a fire?" she asked, distraction being her only defence.

"I'll make a string and show you. If you'll gather some wood . . . and don't worry that I'll cause you any distress."

Grateful for the assurance, she straightened regally.

"You seem quite used to . . . this state," she observed, gesturing obliquely.

"I am."

"Obviously I'm not, although I'm hardly an innocent . . . as you may have guessed in that French reptile's cabin."

"There was little time for guessing."

"No," she agreed. "Thank you for helping me escape from him."

"My pleasure, for sure I was getting off that ship as soon as possible myself, and now I much prefer the company to being here alone."

"For sure, and so do I," she said in imitation of my phrase. "I'll go find some wood." She smiled as she started down the beach. After half a dozen strides, she let the palm branch fall.

She spoke a very grand kind of London English, and hearing it for just that brief conversation had shaken out of my tongue the slight brogue of the Cumbrian North Country. The pidgin English that we spoke on Pitcairn was a different sound, more a stew of the seamen's accents. She'd imitated me and thereby showed that she'd heard more than I would have her know. As she walked toward a pile of driftwood down the beach, I realised how much I had to tell, waiting there behind my teeth, thus making it a danger to say anything at all.

She turned, catching me still watching her, and called, "What shall we call each other?"

"Anything you like," I said.

"A name we've never used for anyone before."

"I'll have to think on it awhile."

"Or perhaps none at all," she said quite seriously, then went back to her collecting.

There were pandanus growing near the beach, and from their fronds I fashioned cord as I'd been taught on Tahiti. With this, I made a small hand bow, then found a piece of wood relatively flat and with a knothole indentation. She brought me a straight, strong stick, and, wrapping it around with the cord of my bow, I put one end in the knothole and pressed down on the other with a shell in the palm of one hand. Then I sawed the bow, twirling the stick around in the flat wood fast enough to create a burn to set a handful of palm trunk fibres afire. In a glance, I saw her amazement. Once the fibres were alight, I threw them beneath the kindling of a fire I'd laid atop the highest hill on the island. She applauded. I nodded my acknowledgment.

We worked the rest of that day collecting wood, and palm leaves to make our fire smoke should we spy a sail. The island was small and uninhabited. While she searched for wood, I buried the shammy bag beneath a cactus plant. I was no expert of gems, but the weight of the bag redefined my possible future in more ways than I dared let myself consider, being lost and naked on an island. If she noted the absence of the bag, she made no comment. When the work became too hot, we went back to the beach to swim. By then all modesty between us was lost, and I became increasingly aware of how long I'd been without a woman. I tried to make our work distract me from such thought, but each of us caught the other looking at each other's body. I know not what she thought of mine, but hers caused me any number of awkward stumbles.

Before we lost the light, I built a hasty lean-to shelter large enough to protect us and our wood, as the trades were pushing clouds about on the horizon. Then we hurried down to search in tide pools as the sun sank through its slot into the sea. We collected crabs and conch for an evening meal, and I showed her how to use her toes to tempt the crabs to leave their hiding places. Several seized the bait before she could withdraw it, causing her to shout and kick the crabs into the air. She in turn showed me the many different kinds of shellfish native to the West Indies, calling each by name and thus revealing a familiarity that told me something more of her background. Halfway through an illustrated lecture with a washed-up shell of spiny lobster, she realised what she had revealed and said, "It's hard to hide who we have been."

"Indeed."

"But still, I'd like to try, not so much to hide as to forget." Restlessly, she stepped onto a rock and bent down to wash the shell off in the water.

"Good luck with it," I said before caution shut my mouth.

Noting well my doubt, she replied, "But surely we can overlook, forget the worst, what we've been forced to do, or had done to us?" She looked at me a moment, as if she thought I could relieve her of the burden of her question.

"I wouldn't know," I said. "I've had no luck with choosing memory."

She turned back to the shell. "I suppose that just as often, what we choose to overlook shows a certain kind of cowardice. Forgetting grows into a private, somewhat lethal lie, doesn't it?"

She smiled grimly, and held the lobster shell before her eyes to study it.

Suddenly she threw the spiny shell into the surf and said, "Sir, I wish to tell you of the privateer. You know a bit of that already, so I'll be giving little away." She paused, not wishing to admit what she thought was a weakness. Her voice took on an imperious tone of defence. "I have a need to speak of it to someone."

"That's fine, for if we never see a ship pass this way, you might as well be talking to yourself."

Reflecting the last embers of the sunset, her eyes found mine and held me with appreciation for the thought. "Yes, that's true," she said, then smiled quickly before she frowned. "I'll tell you over dinner, if I may." She then leaned down and lost her balance on the rock. I reached out to prevent her fall and, for a moment, held her arm and waist. She recovered in an instant, and I let her go, wondering if that touch had affected her as it had me.

We collected our shellfish and carried them to the hilltop, where the coals of our fire were still white and hot. The mussels and the conch we cracked open and ate raw. The crabs we baked on sticks above the fire until they turned the colour of the fast-escaping sunset. Watching as the stars escorted it away, we feasted as she, with no preamble, described what she had a need to tell.

"The privateer came on our ship at night, as she did on yours. The moment I heard the alarm shouted, I hurried to destroy any trace of my identity for fear of being held for ransom. I ordered the captain, as he was agreeing to a boarding, to burn the passenger list and swear to keep silent, which he did even as he and his crew went down in a thousand fathoms, the French scum having broken his word as I, and you, discovered was his habit. He told me he never kept a ship as a prize, for it slowed him down." She closed her eyes and passed a hand over them as if to wipe away what she had seen. Then she looked into the sky and, seeing Venus there, seemed reassured, for she resumed her narrative.

"I was travelling . . ." She hesitated, I thought to consider how best not to say too much. "I was going to . . . a new life, shall we say. Not a better or a worse, but a different one. I'd wished to leave as much of what I'd been behind. Of course I had enough dresses in my trunks to clothe ten women for a month. Perhaps the pirates will find them useful for their usual pleasures with each other, which I was forced to watch while I was aboard.

"The captain had a varied menu of appetites, a few of which I seemed to satisfy. His demands were seldom forthright, that is, I seldom knew what he was going to do to me. The only constant of our relationship was humiliation, which he exacted from me at every opportunity. Nothing he did shocked me, in spite of his many attempts to do so. By the bye, I'm twenty-six, which I rather enjoy telling you. God knows I've had a full and varied life. It's only that what he did, he did so badly, and with such a pompous cruelty to prove himself a man."

I saw her shiver, whether from her story or the evening chill, I could not tell but stood to put more wood on the fire. As I worked, she continued talking, sitting on the ground near the fire, her legs drawn up, her arms around her knees.

"When you came aboard, I'd been there four days and four nights. I'd never lost the will to live, but I had reached the point where, rather than give in to him, I was more than willing to die. That wish I knew he planned to grant if I didn't tell him who I was so he could use me yet again, for ransom. By then he'd made me do things to him, done things to me that I wouldn't force animals to do. It didn't seem to matter to me then, for I presumed my life was finished, it being only a matter of time until he tired of me.

"Then you appeared, to be a part of his amusement, as strange a savage as I'd ever seen. When you first spoke, in English, and him with his head cut off, I thought that I'd gone mad. You know the rest except that, now that I'm alive, I find I have all that to remember. When I thought I'd die, what I'd been forced to do didn't really matter. Now it does, for I cannot avoid the sense that what I did with him made all that a man and woman do for love, at least for joy, utterly repugnant, sickening to me."

A few drops of rain fell on my back, and I propped the shield I'd made of green palm leaves over the fire to preserve the coals. When I looked at her, I thought at first her tears had caught the firelight, but it was only rain on her cheeks. And as the dwindling flames covered her with colour, her eyes came up to mine. There was no doubt what she wanted.

"Please . . . quickly," she said with a forced determination and yet did not change her knee-clutched position. I knew too well her fear of time passing and making the horrible indelible. Her words released my own desire. I went to her and sat on the ground, not touching her, but close enough for her to touch me when and if she chose. She remained drawn up in a tight ball as the rain came gently, making the hot stones around the fire hiss, shining our bodies with a burning reflection. I waited until she finally turned her head to glance at me. The fear of memory was still in her eyes, along with a pleading. I held my hand out to her, and she watched it for a time before she unlocked an arm from around her knee and slowly wove her fingers through mine. I leaned against her then, and when I felt her respond, I put my arm around her shoulders. We sat there, side by side, her legs still drawn to her as were mine, to hide the insistence between them.

"I should tell you something," she whispered and sucked the raindrops collected on her lips. "I left it out before. When I realised the Frenchman intended you to watch what he and I would do, I was so appalled that I'd have killed him or myself at any second. The night before, I'd been quite sick just at the moment of his utterly selfish bliss." Then she turned her head, still rested on her knees, so she could see me. "I wondered as we swam last night about that first reaction I'd had to you. Did I know somehow that you were other than you appeared?"

We leaned against each other once again, turning to watch the fire steam, I aware of my intensifying need, yet content to let the agitation grow.

I shook my head. "I doubt it. But they say that when the fearsome times descend on us, we're capable of sensing things and having thoughts we never knew before."

She must have heard my own memory in my voice, for she squeezed my hand and reached out with her other to touch my face. Watching my mouth, she moved under my arm toward me, taking the hand she held and holding it between us. I moved to kiss her, but she held me back by my hair, grown long enough to grasp. "Could we ever know each other in a better way than this one, knowing nothing?" she asked.

"Perhaps we wouldn't want to."

She drew me to her and kissed me gently, then she said, "I'd want to know everything about you, but for you to know nothing more of me." With no warning, she moved toward me, and, off balance, I fell back on my elbows. Kneeling beside me, she looked forthrightly over my body and frowned with the apprehension her memory provided. She shuddered, then bent down to kiss me as she straddled me. But as I felt her breasts press on my chest, I felt her tears fall on my cheek and mouth, and when she pulled away, tasted their salt as they dissolved in water drops. She stood up awkwardly, her hands raised in anguish to her face, her black hair, heavy with the rain, pouring over her shoulders.

"Too soon," she said, and started to walk away.

"Perhaps," I replied.

She stared at me, oblivious to the rain, and said quietly, "What does one do to forget?"

"Nothing," I said. "We can only make more memories, to crowd the others out."

She watched me for a moment, then turned and, moving swiftly, disappeared down the path we used to reach the beach. I let her go, knowing there was little I could do to ease her mind of what she had experienced. The rain fell hard, and I stayed busy propping palm leaves high enough above the fire to protect it and not smother it. Then I lay inside the lean-to but could not sleep, thinking of her, wondering, had we met under any other circumstance, if we would have even spoken to each other.

Two days passed. I saw her on the island but let her stay to herself. I put food on a stone where she would find it; she stacked wood there for the fire. Then I heard her coming back. It was night again. The rain had stopped, and still the fire burned. Lying on my back, I didn't move for fear of causing her disquiet. I could see her standing near the fire, watching me, her body still reflecting a moon that wasn't there. Then she came and, knowing I was awake, she climbed on me again astride. Straight armed, she leaned forward, her hands pressing down on my shoulders. She shifted on my hips and moved against me. As her mouth opened, she arched her back and pushed down, drawing me deep into her. For a moment, she didn't move, but gazed into the dark. Then she said, "Please . . . let me do everything."

For a sailor long at sea, it was a simple favour to grant.

Islas Los Roques

January 1794

A ship appeared leeward during the sixth day, another on the tenth. Each time, we ran to the top of the hill and, being sure it was not the privateer returned, threw green leaves on the fire. But the smoke was not seen. I watched my island partner, looking for her disappointment. It was there the first time, but when she saw me watching her, she laughed aloud, embraced me, and then gave a parting wave to the receding sail. The second time, we did our duty to the fire, though she regarded it an irritating interruption to the search of our best tide pool.

Thus reassured about the possibility of rescue, we lived a carefree life. Our only work was the tending of the fire and carrying wood for it. Otherwise, we searched the island, found fine coves but no inhabitants or animals, and kept our watch of the horizon from our hill. I kept her in the shade as much as possible, but her skin went red in spite of my warnings. She was sore the first few nights, peeled raw by the fifth, then took on a glowing burn that deepened with each passing day. Because she wore her palm hat, however, her face remained almost as moon white as before. Once I commented on her double-hued colouring.

"I'll never be quite as fancy as you are," she countered, with a significant glance.

During the first week, I taught her much of island ways, of fishing, making tools with rocks and shells, climbing palm trees, then navigating by the stars and predicting tides. She in turn told me of the world. I learned that since the loss of the American colonies, England jealously guarded her islands in the West Indies as a vital part of her empire. Then again, so did France, which held sovereignty over a number of other islands. She told me there had been a revolution in France, the King had been executed, and war declared on most of Europe, including England. The world had changed beyond my speculations.

"When did they execute the French King?"

"A year ago, and ten days later, they went to war with England. They guillotined the Queen last October, along with anyone who remained loyal."

We had our longest talks at night when stars and crescent moon provided entertainment as we lay beneath them on our backs beside our fire. The mats of palm which she had woven for us made the sandy ground a pleasant lair.

"What is 'guillotined'?" I asked.

Apparently the question revealed a surprising ignorance, for she paused before answering to consider the disclosure.

"It's a beheading machine. A weighted slanted blade is fitted in grooves, held high between two uprights above the neck of the victim who lies below, face-down, waiting for death to fall."

"Then who leads France? Who runs their war?" I asked.

"The People," she said sarcastically, then sadly shook her head. " 'Tis a horror now. When it began, it was glorious. For a moment, the entire world looked to France to tell the future, but then the sewers of Paris overflowed. Thrown up on the streets were manipulators like Marat, Danton, Saint-Just, and Robespierre . . . Have you heard none of these names?"

As ever, I offered no response, although she guessed my ignorance.

"They kill each other now, proudly calling it the Reign of Terror, or so it was told in the thirty-day news that reached us just before I . . ."

She stopped to see if I had noticed what she'd divulged. I did but indicated nothing. To those who lived in the West Indies, news of Europe was a thirty-day sail away.

She hastily continued. "They organise the daily guillotine display at the Place de la Revolution. Thousands have been executed so." With her correct pronunciation of the French, she revealed still more of herself. "It seems in troubled times, the man most willing to invent the worst extremes will always find a wider following than one who tries for moderation."

Her observation hit its mark in me, although she did not know it. To hide my reaction, I hastened to respond.

"How do they wage a proper war while in a state of anarchy?"

"You must ask the Belgians, Dutch, and Germans that, for they have felt the French invasion firsthand. The French began by fighting for their principles, in self-defence against the Austrians. But now they're after a wider world, so much so that the Admiralty in London measures daily the steady shrinking of their moat, the English Channel."

I knew that every question asked would further date my absence, but I had to know. "And what of England? Are they fighting yet?"

"On the sea, yes. The British have blockaded France and launched an offensive here in the West Indies. Last year, the Royal Navy took Tobago, and occupied Martinique, Saint Lucia, Guadeloupe, and Port-au-Prince. Therefore, in Paris, the National Assembly is playing with the idea of freeing all French slaves and seeing how the English in their own slave colonies would cope with the uprisings that must surely follow."

She paused and smiled bitterly at something in the past, saw me watching her, then continued. "In England, the people's rag-

ing all takes place amongst themselves, where grand ideals im-
ported, though bloodless, on the wind from France have caused
a bothersome kind of havoc called 'reform.' It centres on the King
of course, the poor mad King . . . You knew that he went mad for
a time, and in the crisis, almost lost his power to the faction hovering about his son, the Prince of Wales. That was in '89."

She offered this as information rather than a question that she
knew I wouldn't answer. But I didn't know and was amazed. 1789
was the year of the mutiny as well. I grasped a thread of hope
that in a year of revolution, Royal crisis, and such violent currents
of change, my own "extreme" of mutiny might not have gained a
steadfast place in public memory. If those we left on Tahiti had
survived, it might be possible that they returned to preparations
for a war, where the need for their services was more than the
need for blame to be examined and assigned. Besides, to anyone
who cared, the villains on whom guilt should finally be heaped
had sailed away to hiding or their destruction. After nearly five
years of infernal history, who would still be dwelling on this tale?

"The last we heard," she said with ever-greater ire, "arrests are
commonplace in London for speaking out and publishing dis-
sent, or anything the government so righteously proclaims to be
'sedition.' They send drunken chandlers to the Tower for bellowing forth an insult to a Royal horse's bum. But even so, each
week another thousand join the clubs that preach in pubs and
fields the politics of revolution. They dare the Tory government
to do its worst, and call Pitt preserver of a cesspool for the privileged." Her glance to me enquired if I had the slightest jot of
what she spoke. She had her answer instantly.

"It's sure you know your politics," I said, turning talk away from
it, "and have a fair passion for the subject."

Knowing well what I was doing and accepting it, she took my
hand and kissed it, then held it to her cheek. "Our game of telling
nothing has changed. We're also trying to avoid revealing what
we've learned about each other in spite of the game." She smiled.
"I wonder what you've learned of me. Probably we should have

swum to separate islands." Rolling over to me, she put her head on my chest.

"What good would that have done," I said, "except to make the time we have here lonely?"

She lay quietly a moment, then said, "Even with no clothes, no costumes as it were, no theatre of my life with all the usual sets, façades, and furniture to give away my role, I know I must perform as I've been taught, to best accomplish an effect, or a response from you, my unknown audience of one." She smiled and rolled away to look back at the sky. "My accent, which I'm sure has cast me in your mind, or my carriage as I walk, or even how I do my toilette, naked on an island. We're not really naked, are we? Those heavy trunks we carry from performance to performance always stay with us . . . even when alone."

She sighed, bone deep, and then was silent until I heard her chuckle. Lifting herself up, she leaned on her elbow and said as if confessing a wicked crime, "I've always thought that the only way to escape ourselves, other than being all alone, is to become someone else, to start afresh, unweighted with the past. In that guise, newborn almost, one would avoid accumulating any more of those familiar burdens that a life presents. Have you ever wondered, if you were completely lost somewhere, that at the very moment, in that place, at once relieved of all your previous life, could you start to find exactly who you'd really be? Could you do that?"

I was alarmed and searched her eyes to see if her suggestion came from what I had unknowingly revealed about myself. I saw no guile, but only her own yearning for escape, from what, I could not fathom.

"No matter if you disappear," I said, "and live alone an Eskimo in Greenland, sure you'd carry a small portmanteau of the past still, unless you could go mad and thus remember nothing."

I watched agreement crease her face with sadness. "Then we're trapped in life by memory."

"Oh yes," said I ruefully. "Oh yes." I stood to feed the fire, worried that she'd somehow see my reasons for concluding that ours was such a memory-infected fate.

"Thank God for this one, then," she said softly. "I can imagine what I would have become without it." Watching as I stoked the coals, she laughed softly. "I'll tell you something else. If another ship appears, I'll keep you from your work around the fire."

"And how would you do that?"

Lying back, she propped herself upon her elbows and raised one knee above the other. Her long black hair lay over one shoulder, and her breasts and belly caught the glow of the fire. "I'd try distraction first," she said.

"You'd need nothing more," I replied and went to her.

Thus we spent our days and nights, keeping to routine, avoiding revelation. But in spite of our resolve, we found out much about each other without being told. I knew, for instance, that her home was in the West Indies, probably Jamaica, but that she'd spent much time in London, and perhaps in France, as island ladies did to learn the proper accents. Her family's wealth was obviously stupendous; besides the clothes I'd seen her wear aboard the privateer, she had "ordered" the captain of her own ship what to do, even at the moment of a boarding, and he had stayed silent unto death. Few women could command such obedience. She'd never been alone, which suggested servants ever present, and hangers-on, of whom there were and are a goodly number always hovering near a country house, a palace, or in Jamaica, a great house on a sugar plantation, cane being the only occupation to provide such wealth as she exemplified.

She did not lack experience in making love, but I detected the deep core of sadness that pervaded our encounters. Even in the very heights of intimacy, I would lose her to something, occasionally to the point of tears. Always she returned, explaining that the tears, or distance, were for joy or rapture. She knew I had no faith in her excuse, nor did I question her about it, ever conscious that she was more willing to reveal her history than I, and if begun, my own might follow.

We therefore kept our silences and, on those few occasions when I was alone and out of sight of her, I'd look upon my private choice of sadnesses, still wondering if I'd ever find a way to live with them. Having been away from Pitcairn only four short months, I looked ahead toward the family I hoped to see, rather than backward at the one I'd left behind. I felt remorse for both, but knew that one was in the past; the other, I hoped, was yet to come.

I'd go to see my mother first, on the Isle of Man, and as I thought it, I saw her sitting in the narrow parlour of the ancient row house where we'd lived in Douglas after losing our true home in Cumberland, Moorland Close, to bankruptcy. The light was always dim; the larger windows of the building faced the bleak northern sky. I saw my mother serving tea, using her great-grandmother's china, one of several prizes that survived the move from the mainland, along with varied furniture to which she would point and proclaim, "That's good, a good piece," then describe its history. She was a Fletcher, as good a name in Cumberland as Christian, one that was far older, with a claim in its ancestral line of having aided Mary, Queen of Scots, while in her flight, and Mother had brought Moorland Close as dowry to her marriage with my father.

She was alone when last I saw her, several months before I was to sail as master's mate aboard the *Bounty*. "Your father would have been so proud of you," she said, and passed my cup to me. I rose to take it as her eyes, a piercing blue, were suddenly o'erflowing as they once again examined details of my uniform. My father still remained a vital presence in her life, which image she made every effort to enhance in her children's. I let her, and always paid him homage and respect, but only for her sake. He was less than dead to me, not even someone whom I missed, for he had died before he cast a solid shadow in my life.

"Your father would have been *so proud* of you," my mother said again with emphasis, her pride shining in that darkened room, its dimness furthered by curtains washed that morning. I responded with my hopes for her.

"I'll take you back to Moorland Close," said I, the wind of fortune in my sails. "We'll sit beneath the apple trees in the quadrangle, and every Tuesday, we'll take tea in the old watchtower, just for fun." That made her laugh, the short snort of a lady containing levity. She gazed beyond me, seeing what I had described within the cold walls of that small room, and then she tilted her head with the wonder of it. Her hair, once a lustrous brown, had turned since coming to the island and crowned her face with ordered waves of grey. And then I saw the fear behind her eyes hit hard upon the vision I'd described. Her head snapped back as she assumed the rigid posture with which she faced that room and her existence.

"No more of that," she ordered with a shaky voice and passed the plate of scones she'd made for me.

How could I face her now? What could I ever do to make up for the shame I must have caused her? I knew the answer: nothing. Even so, I allowed myself to hope that if I could buy back Moorland Close for her, she might find a way to forgive me. Presiding over whatever it was I called a conscience was that picture of her, head aslant and eyes aglow, seeing for a moment what I'd promised her.

I must confess that on the island when I thought on her, I also questioned my return and considered instead that after rescue, I would pass from ship to ship, thus keeping to the silent oceans for a semblance of a life. I'd known of many men who found a way to bury who they were upon the surface of the sea. In time, I knew I'd hear about the fate of those involved with me aboard the *Bounty,* even about my family. All it would take would be the luck to find a Jack Tar from Man, then stand him to a pint of rum to make the gossip flow.

But I detected something more than reason to return. I realised how compellingly I wanted to understand what I had done. If somehow I saw it from a different viewpoint, if I watched from a distance of time and place, and comprehended beyond my shame and my admitted guilt what happened to me on that ship that day and why, I then might see a way to live on this unreasoned globe.

Thinking thus one day, I found my island companion at the fire, covering it with green leaves.

"We've been found," she said with more regret than joy, staring at the sea from the hill we'd made into our momentary home. We'd lived there for a fortnight and a half.

The schooner had sharp ends, a pair of raking masts rigged with topsails, holding a full spread of canvas. After coming about, she dropped anchor in our island's heart-shaped bay and put her quarter boat over the side. We watched dejectedly behind a stand of bougainvillea so we could not yet be seen through any of the schooner's telescopes. "The flag's a Yankee one," I offered, "carrying molasses, coffee, maybe rum. They'll get you back to Kingston."

She did not react to my suggestion of her destination. Standing naked at my side, she took my hand in both of hers. "You *must* come with me."

"No. Remember, we agreed. I'll wait until the next one comes."

"It doesn't matter who you are or what you've done—"

"No!" I said it hard and heard her take a breath. But then I squeezed her hand, and she placed mine against her breast.

"I don't believe that I can possibly go back," she argued. "I'm not who I was and don't wish to be. I can't be."

"In another fortnight's time, you won't believe this happened," I said, hoping that it wasn't true. "You haven't changed, except to know a part of you that probably you didn't know before."

"The best part, I suspect."

We kissed each other as she raised her leg and put it round my back. We had discovered the position quite by chance while on the beach, standing while we made love in order to avoid discomfort from the sand. When we were done, she'd let her feet fall to the ground, then stood back from me and curtsied, saying,

"Thank you so much, sir," as if we'd danced an eightsome reel. I then bowed, and we ran into the water, laughing. It had sounded odd to me, for I had found no cause to laugh aloud for many years.

"Please . . ." she pleaded, "someday, come back to me. Let me believe, I must believe that someday—"

I saw the quarter boat's long oars reflect the sun as they were drawn in unison. This time she did not step back to offer me a curtsy. Holding me, her tears fell on my shoulder. The quarter boat was lifted by the gentle surf, which pushed it forward on the sand.

"You must go down," I said.

She nodded, then she watched the sailors spring from the boat and haul it farther up onto the beach. "I think that I've forgotten how to be a modest lady."

"Sure it will come back to you."

"What if they attack me?"

"I'll be there."

She took my hand. "Come down with me. They won't see you. I have something I must tell you."

I hesitated but could not refuse. The plantain and palm were thick enough to hide us.

"The game is over. I must tell you who I am," she said, "so that, if you choose, you'll know where you can find me."

"Don't do that!" I ordered. "Never even think I'll look for you."

"But let me hope you might. And I could never bear to think you couldn't come because you didn't know exactly where I was. I am Daphne Lewis, 'Lady' Daphne Lewis. My father owns a sugarcane plantation in Jamaica, the largest, he insists. He always likes to say that by the century's end, he'll be the British Empire's first and only millionaire. Because of his control of seven rotten boroughs in Parliament—his share of the Sugar Trust—I have some interest in politics." She looked at me for a reaction, but I gave none.

"When the Frenchman captured me, the ship he sank was one of ten my father owns. She had been separated from a convoy in a storm. I was en route to London to be married to the Duke of Cleyland. I'm told he has a mistress who has fathered him two daughters. Our marriage, then, concerns convenience only. He gets land and income, I a match which is deemed appropriate. You see, I am a widow. His Grace's interest in me as his duchess is considered by one and all to be a glorious solution for me. I'm expected to provide him with an heir, but that is all!"

We heard the sailors yelling to each other as they started up the beach. She kissed me quickly, knowing it would be our last, and took my hand in both of hers. "Cleyland House is on Berkeley Square; Puddington is his estate in Wiltshire. One place or the other, that's where I shall be. And please, don't dare to say goodbye to me."

She pulled her hands away, turned, and ran away toward the beach. When she was sure that she was seen, she fell onto the sand as we had planned. The sailors rushed to her and, with an instant chivalry, stripped off their shirts to cover her as one of them ran back toward the quarter boat to fetch its rescue sail.

I watched as they took care of her, and noted their reaction when she told them who she was. The youngest Yankee actually performed a gallant little bow. They helped her climb into the boat and rowed her out to board the schooner. Sitting straight backed in the stern and wrapped in sailcloth, she never once looked back.

I didn't realise, or I should say I didn't let myself admit how much I missed her until I was aloft the mizzen of the Spanish brigantine that took me from the island nine days later. I was back in purser's slops, working as a topman to earn my passage to Cádiz, understanding not a word of their Castilian, only following their gestures, doing what the ship had need of. It was difficult for me to put her name and future title to the memory I had of her, the naked woman whom I taught to use her toes as bait for crabs, the lover who had clung to me whilst standing on the beach and then had curtsied thanks. High up and hanging from a yard, with northern gales tearing at my hair and at the reef points in my hands, I let myself adore her, then I told myself out loud, muttering into the fearsome wind, "Daphne Lewis, Daphne Lewis, never can I be with her again!"

Cádiz

February 1794

Cádiz was tailored to my needs. When I arrived there on the brigantine in February 1794, I found a city sodden with winter rain, frost-encrusted mud, and war. The harbour stank of rotted fish and tar, and the water was clouded by refuse and sewage. My Spanish rescuers took little time in showing me ashore with nothing other than the slops I wore, the sole remuneration for the work I'd done aloft. I didn't mind; I'd made no friends among them, my Polynesian charade keeping me apart. Besides, they were appalling sailors, so much so that it was difficult for me to manage my contempt. To leave their ship for land was even more a pleasure than was usual after an Atlantic crossing.

Yet the moment I set foot on the quay, I felt a terror with being at the place. I stood there deaf and dumb as tars and coolies passed me by, most yelling in some effort, paying me no heed except when they ran into me and shouted out a curse, which sounded strangely as it would have underwater. I could not quite look at anything; whatever I espied reflected blinding light, a mirror to the sun. My awkwardness was also due to lack of balance, not the usual adjustment to the solid earth a sailor feels when he returns from months of walking on a swaying deck, but rather that peculiar sense of nausea and faintness felt before one falls into a swoon. I stood in that state and tried to breathe, to think of what to do, for even though I knew the fates had brought me there, my mind would not let me accept the fact of my arrival.

Staggering through grimy puddles of muck tossed from boardinghouses facing the harbour, I was knocked off my feet and almost senseless by a porter's pole hung with kettles made of Indonesian tin. In the ensuing din of crashing kettles, porters' kicks and curses, I blindly crawled until I reached a wall against which I could lean and gain assurance that the land might once again convince my mind that somehow I would find my place. And to that end, I forced my thoughts toward the practical. I thought of food and clothing, money and the danger that I faced, no matter if the world to which I had returned was distracted with war.

Horrified by the slaughter of monarchy, the overthrow of feudalism, and the pillage of the church in France, the Spanish King had joined with other nations to control the spread of the Republican contagion. As such, he was a current ally of Great Britain. Within moments of my crawling to the wall beside the teeming wharves, I heard the native Spanish perforated with the varied accents of my countrymen in shouts and brawls and laughter. There were ships from every compass point aligned to left and right along the quay and many more at anchor in the bay. The blockade with which the Royal Navy bottled up the revolution allowed clutches of British officers to enjoy the seamy streets of Port Cádiz, from which they took their pleasures while their ships took on supplies. When both needs were fulfilled, they took their leave, returning to blockades northward in the Channel, or south around Gibraltar to the Mediterranean.

The sound of English was no welcome one to me, for knowing nothing of the fate of any of my former shipmates, I knew it could not be blamed upon coincidence if one of them appeared in such a port at such a time. I had to move, yet my senses continued to confound me. Still cringing to conceal my size, I made my way into the town to find a place where I might be ignored and where I could extract the pirate's jewels from their painful hiding place.

I'd ample cause to wish that as the human body long ago had taken form, a pocket had been made a part of an appendage. Lacking that, the male side of the species has but one small, inconvenient orifice that might be used for hiding. Even that is limited to part-time occupancy, where a carefully constructed pacquet might be hid if one were, as I had been, discovered naked on an island.

I had little doubt that any rescuer would soon relieve me of my treasure if they knew of it. The first thing that I did when Daphne left the island was dig up the shammy bag and pry the gems from their settings. I then soaked and stretched the shammy to a thinness sheer enough to wrap the thirty diamonds, two dozen rubies, and sixteen emeralds into a compact shape. When finally the Spaniards came to my rescue, I slipped the pacquet in my body's only secret place, where it remained until the crew's attention passed from me and I could extricate the parcel. My treasure then was placed below among the ballast at the bottom of the ship, whence I retrieved it previous to our landfall at Cádiz.

Before I found the man I dared approach to sell the smallest diamond, I began to starve and freeze, for beggars were the beneficiaries only of the kicks and anger of the passing crowds, and surely not of charity. Now back in civilisation, I foraged not for guava but behind the taverns for their rubbish. Like the alley cats with whom I fought for food, I listened, watched, and waited in the shadows.

I knew my first stone would not fetch its worth, a buyer being well aware that in my savage situation, I could hardly bargain. Finding such a man in any port town was a simple matter; planning the transaction was my challenge. I did not intend to carve out an identity by selling such a prize, and yet a buyer would most certainly be curious. Therefore, the Polynesian with the diamond had to disappear as soon as jewel and money were exchanged.

I chose the man and followed him for several days before I dared approach. He was a Turk who wore a fez, which made his daily route from home, to spice store, to brothel an easy triangle to follow. I saw too many sailors enter his store to think they went there for frankincense and myrrh. Gold or its substitute was their objective, and to obtain it, from what I could observe, they left the Turk a wide variety of objects, a shrunken head, a samovar, and an ivory pipe among them. When finally I confronted him, it was on the street before the brothel, where he, too, wished to avoid establishing a presence. I showed him the stone, which impressed him, more for its bearer than the jewel itself. Nevertheless, he offered a price in Spanish, then in the face of my apparent ignorance, in French, German, finally English, and then Russian before I snatched the stone away, refused his offer with a blend of foreign syllables, and ran away into the dark.

I met him thus for two more nights; each time he added several hundred pesetas to his multilingual offer, and finally I nodded my agreement. By then, my stomach wouldn't let my head say no in any language. He gestured for me to go with him; I refused, afraid he might have cohorts waiting to relieve me of my prize. He then said he'd return the next night with my price, and I agreed. But when he came, I met him two streets closer to his shop, and we exchanged our goods where I could easily escape him down the alleys of Cádiz if he or someone else perchance might try to follow.

Not only had I plotted my escape but my rejuvenation. Clothes came first, then food, and then a decent room with access to a bath. I took each step with care, avoiding any sense of celebration, barely speaking, doing nothing to attract attention. My disguise had no further need to claim a savage; European curiosity about exotic South Seas climes already brought too many stares in my direction. In that first bath, I shaved myself into an ordinary visage, but still retained a moustache and a neat, well-ordered beard behind which I could hide, for I had stayed clean-shaven all my life until the years on Pitcairn. I avoided the coiffure of gentlemen, leaving my hair loose and without powder. Clothing, too, was carefully considered. I chose trousers rather than breeches, wore shoes that others had worn before me; coats, hats, and greatcoats I'd buy from merchants of the streets. With my mask of broken nose and hirsute face, I made myself believe that, even though my skin would lose its burn without the South Pacific sun, I still might face the world and even my dear mother without being recognised. This conviction I carefully nurtured and soon walked cautiously into the streets of Cádiz, although never free of fear. But even with my fear, and still with sensate tricks of balance, blindness, echoing sounds, and the ever-present feeling that I did not quite inhabit the space in which I found myself, I plotted my return to England.

I dared not hurry; one mistaken step would end my life in shame before I could conceive of any other possibility. In order to avoid remaining permanently in Cádiz, I ventured forth by coach to Seville to test my wealth by selling a few more of the jewels. Ever careful, I took rooms above an ordinary tavern, found my jewellers, spoke no English, all the while apparelled in decent but undistinguished clothing. I soon realised that I possessed treasure that a career as wartime Admiral of the Blue might not accumulate. My potential buyers commented about the quality of each stone, expressing opinions that reflected on the preeminence of their original unknown owners. I sold nothing more, realising that gems were the most efficient method in which to transport wealth. Moorland Close was assured, as was a careful future. In spite of my exhilaration, I remained rigidly circumspect. Nevertheless, I succeeded in attracting interest from beyond the usual realm of gems.

I suspected nothing when I walked into my rooms the third

night of my visit and was seized in darkness without any chance to resist. When I was seated, bound, and gagged, they searched my person, discovering the pesetas from my original sale, but not the other jewels, which I'd sewed into the lining of my coat. I saw a candle being lit, behind which stood a Spaniard with a pair of hooded serpent eyes, a grandee's coiffure, a goatee and moustache sprouting from his leathery, wrinkled face, and a flat and lipless mouth from which I thought surely a forked tongue would appear.

"You are English, no?" he asked and took his place in a chair opposite me. His confidence assured me that he and his accomplices who stood behind me were no thieves, rather officials of one sort or another. When I did not indicate an inclination to respond, he sighed and stamped his boot impatiently on the floor.

"Señor," he said, as bored as if he were involved with repetitious children's games, "we do not care that Mr. Pitt has sent you to Seville with your jewels. In fact, we guaranteed the price you asked of every buyer. What we fail to understand is why you come to Spain for this exchange, and if you can explain to me the reasons, I am sure that you will avoid delay in your return." The last phrase was a threat, after which his straight lips stretched across his face in what I supposed he intended as an angelic smile.

Though bound and gagged, I almost answered it, for in that moment, whether from excitement, fear, or instinct to survive, I felt I had at last arrived upon that chair and in that room, existing on that continent. The man had many other interests than who I was, and I felt that I might as well shout out the name of Fletcher Christian, for he wouldn't give a fig. He thought I was an English spy, and I saw little reason to dissuade him. Therefore I made noises through the gag, which he removed.

"I needed pesetas quickly," I explained, not knowing what a spy should say and, therefore, staying with the truth.

"In Seville?" he asked, his doubt apparent.

"No. I came from Cádiz."

"There are pesetas there."

"The price is better here, and I chose not to be observed—an effort in which I obviously failed."

He assented with a blink of his eyelids and said, "His Majesty has every wish to be a friend to England in our common struggle with the French. However, he does not wish to be used, particularly without his knowledge, for any plan that Mr. Pitt, his gold, or any of his many agents might see fit to execute while in this realm. You understand me?"

"Your English is sublime."

The angelic smile appeared again. "Thank you," he said. "My mother came from England, which is where we wish to send you with this message. Tell Mr. Pitt that we resent not knowing what he plans to do here, and that if the practise is repeated, he will lose his agents and their jewels. You'll leave tonight, and so will I," he said, revealing his regret for such a trip.

"Tonight? To where?"

"I to Madrid, you back to Cádiz, where you'll sail for Jersey."

The word began to echo in my ears, and I was suddenly unbalanced in my chair. Jersey was an island I knew little of, only that it lay near France, just off the coast of Normandy. But it was English soil and thus was guarded by those ships and men I'd seen along the quay at Cádiz. Even with the width of the English Channel, it was too close to where I wished to be. For at that moment, discovery was not my main concern. The place was England, and I believed that I was not yet ready to confront the many conflicts and confusions of what being there would mean to me. To be on any piece of England made me once again into a mutineer and murderer.

"Please give our regards to Monsieur Tinteniac on Jersey," the Spaniard said as I was untied and we prepared to leave the room. I could not speak, my mind was whirling so. The man mistook my silence for professional composure, yet I stumbled awkwardly and dared not face him. "Tell him that his humble colleagues of our Paris Agency have much to do in France without a need to dally with his jewellery in southern Spain." Clearly he was bragging, competition in the game he played requiring such a pride.

He said nothing more but only watched as I with awkwardness climbed up, still silent, into the Spanish saddle of a proferred horse. One of his men signalled me to follow him and spurred his mount into the darkness. Two others came along behind, an escort that quickly revealed their purpose to be rid of me in Cádiz with all deliberate speed.

We rode all night, our only stops to rest the horses. I was numb with cold at first, but then the saddle managed to impress itself, inclining me to stand above it in my stirrups. I was grateful for discomfort, trying as I was to think of anything except the phantoms that would form my welcoming committee when at last I landed on English soil.

Staring through the rain, I questioned my objective. If truly a new life I wanted, why had I worked my way toward England, where each step, each smell, each sight would engulf me in my past? For though the crimes I had committed were half a world away, they were against that country, my honour, my family.

I rummaged through memory yet again for a reason to justify what I'd done. I saw Captain Bligh, heard him call me dog and cur before the crew, saw him point his finger at my face, accusing me of stealing—not money, not rations, but coconuts! For weeks before, he'd flayed me, rage succeeding rage, then afterward invited me to share his table as if nothing had occurred. Even so, the fact was that I put him overboard with eighteen men. The longboat had but half a dozen inches between the gunwale and the sea. I sent him off to die, for we were far from any civilised retreat, and those few islands possible for them to reach were occupied by murderous savages.

And yet I didn't kill him outright.

He was my captain; even with my cutlass at his throat, he held my honour in his hand. My honour, that great luxury of manly pride, went down with Captain Bligh in the storm that surely found that overloaded boat, the same southwestern blow that blasted the *Bounty* within twelve hours of the crime.

There I stopped my mind, for I had no desire to think beyond the captain to the eighteen souls whom I'd condemned along with him. They were both best and worst of our bedeviled crew, but none deserved the fate that I'd inflicted on them. Suddenly my horse shied from a lightning flash, and reared up as the thunder crackled around us. I held on and calmed the horse and knew there was no clean new life for me. I was Fletcher Christian, mutineer and murderer, still alive, who was, for no wise reason, going home.

Thus two weeks later, still saddle sore to the bone and fevered with an ague, I glimpsed the soil of England once again. An island of an island nation, Jersey's nine square leagues stood only five short leagues from Normandy, and little more than double that from Brittany, the two French coasts reaching out around the isle to form the Gulf of Saint-Malo. My ship, a small British cutter, had taken me aboard with little curiosity expressed by any of the crew. Arriving at dawn, we slipped into St. Aubin's Bay. Apparently such cargo as a silent man who made no effort to converse was not unusual, for when we tied up at the wharf of St. Helier, I was allowed to go ashore with just as much attention paid as to my embarkation in Cádiz.

But I was not allowed five private steps or even time to breathe the temperate air already weighted with the slightest scent of spring before I was surrounded by a half a dozen men. Without a word of explanation, they marched me down the cobbled quay and then around a corner to a timbered house that overlooked the bay. Inside, I was escorted roughly to a room with little furniture except a table and some chairs and searched, though nothing was taken from me. A man was working at the table, making notes on maps, two candles still lit and burned down so the wax had pooled and spread unnoticed on the surface. My arrival caused him to look up and note that the dawn had come. He watched me as he shielded the candle flames with his hand and blew them out.

"Who are you?" he said, a French accent thickening his words.

"He has pesetas," one of my escorts offered.

"A sailor," I replied, the safest truth I knew.

"Why are you here?" He rose and came around the table. My escort was still in the room. I noticed little detail, only the daggers, pistols, and cutlasses they carried.

"I had no choice. A Spaniard sent me with a message."

"To whom?"

"A Monsieur Tinteniac." I saw a glance exchanged beside me, but my interrogator revealed nothing.

"And what was this message?" he asked.

"He thought I was an English spy and told me that my presence was resented without Mr. Pitt's acquiring previous permission from the Spanish King. He said to tell Tinteniac that the Paris Agency was too busy in France to worry about the English in Spain."

He smiled slightly, but his eyes still watched me carefully. "He knows the Spanish King could change his mind at any second to join with France. And are you an English spy?"

"No. I attracted his attention when I sold some diamonds in Seville." I did not make him ask his questions, for I'd practised my recital aboard ship. "I'd recently sailed around the Cape, and in Cape Town, I'd saved my captain at a card game from a pistol shot by taking it myself. The captain had been caught at substituting cards. In gratitude, not only for my shielding him but for remaining silent on the subject of his cheating, he gave me a bauble that he'd purchased in Bombay for his wife. I chose to sell the stones in Spain—"

"Where did the bullet hit you?" he interrupted.

I hesitated, which made his eyes widen with anticipation. "Here," I said and pointed to my back.

Disappointed, he nodded to a member of my escort. A dagger cut through coat and blouse. I was roughly turned as they were further ripped to allow my questioner's inspection.

"And you of course are honour bound and won't reveal your captain's name," he suggested cynically enough for me to follow suit.

"Not for honour's sake, but for his, I have forgotten him, as well the ship on which we sailed."

After his examination of my scar, he asked, "Are you as good a sailor as you are a liar?"

"For sure much better, for I've had more practise on the sea."

He nodded thoughtfully, then said to my escort, "Take him to our suite for guests." And to me, "We'll ponder how you might be useful in return for your passage here."

The cellar of the house was stone and mortar, cold and damp. There was a wooden pallet with a rotted blanket, a chamber pot, and nothing else. I did not fear what was to happen. Incarceration in a cellar was an appropriate welcome. The place protected me from the discovery that I feared would come before I was prepared for it, as well as from the press-gangs, which were active even when I left England. I had every reason to believe that with a war, the gangs of pressmen still roamed any port to find all able-bodied souls to man His Majesty's fleet. Once seized, a man was kept a prisoner on the ships he served and might sail about the world for years without return.

Even though I had no better place to go, I was curious to find out about the world in which I found myself. What did it know of the mutiny? What of Bligh's death and the longboat, of the men I'd left behind me in Tahiti? What of this war? This "Terror"? As days passed, I asked for London newspapers; there were a dozen printed daily when I left. My gaolers gave me nothing, and the mysterious food served twice a day in a bowl became worse.

From what I'd gleaned from my encounter with the world of spies, identity was whatever one made of it. No one had asked my name, it being understood that such a question seldom would reveal the truth. One's personal past was always suspect as an unfathomable murk impossible to penetrate, and therefore of little concern. What seemed to matter was one's instant usefulness. I discovered this on the night when my gaolers led me back to the wharf. Under a dim and hazy quarter moon, I saw the small cutter on which I'd arrived, making ready to sail. There was a difference. A carronade was mounted on the foredeck. My French inquisitor met me at the rail and said without the slightest tone of warning, "Now, we'll see how fine a sailor you are. If you aren't, I'll shoot you. You'll be second at the tiller for now."

"And might there be a captain?"

"You see him before you."

"Where are we—?" I didn't finish, for he'd turned away to other business, as did my escort, who fell to the work of casting off. I hurried aft, noting the southerly breeze. The jib and topsail were already set to catch the wind, which took us out into the darkness toward the coast of France.

Gulf of Saint-Malo

April 1794

The cutter was built for speed and soon proved herself as we took the southerly wind. I shared the tiller with a taciturn old Jerseyman who knew the currents and tides from a lifetime of intimacy, as well the numerous small islands scattered about in the gulf. He steered our course, about which he informed me with instructional grunts, having no real need of my talents. The binnacle before us, we sailed due east toward the Cherbourg peninsula, which I remembered from my charts.

The ship's single mast held all her sail, her square-rigged topsail as well as fore-and-aft rigged jibs, with her mainsail stretched aft on the boom over our heads. Looking forward toward the bowsprit, I saw the shadowy movement of the crew in the hazy quarter moon as they sheeted the topsail, then moved to clear the four great guns on either side, eight-pounders to my eye, as well the larger twenty-four-pound carronade on the foredeck. There were two dozen of us, sailing in near silence. The only words I heard other than from my colleague at the tiller were,

"Grape, grape, roundshot for the carronade," given by my French gaoler, now my captain, to the gunners as they ran out their guns and lit the slow-burning matches at the end of the linstock wood.

He paid little attention to me as the breeze increased from moderate to fresh, producing long swells and a good spray across the deck. The wind was on the beam, so we were moving as much north as east, but my main helmsman seemed untroubled; the fore-and-aft sails made good use of the angle, and the square-rigged topsail was braced around to catch as much of the wind as possible.

Although performing my secondary role as lee helmsman, I nevertheless could feel in the rudder the natural urge of the ship to head up into the wind. The mate called for storm capes as wind and spray made a frigid combination which we were bound to stand and endure. As I wrapped the garment about me, I stood without support on the pitching deck, realising my cellar prison days had not relieved me of my sea legs. I sensed the exhilaration of freedom and the usual relief from facing landward matters, even knowing so little of where I might be going, only that we were cracking on with no sails reduced and a fine fan of sea spread high by the cutwater, the deck at a healthy rake of some twenty-five degrees as we plunged through the troughs of waves.

A man lay out at the very end of the bowsprit among the rigging, another clung to the masthead, standing on the topsail yard. Both were lookouts, for what I knew not, only hoping that their talent was seeing through the fog, which came on us like a wall, quickly quenching the moonlight into blackness. By then we'd seen the outline of the shore and several lights, identified by the topman in a call to the deck as Lessay. An order was shouted, and the men were up the shrouds. We turned her slightly into the wind to luff. The topsail and mainsail were furled, and the ship was brought around, leaving us to progress slowly with only jib sails set.

And then we waited. The French captain came to the tiller and stood, holding a pocket chronometer, reading it every few minutes by the storm lantern at the binnacle, then pacing along the starboard rail. The fog seemed to blanket the waves and calm the wind; the roll of the ship, now that we were off the wind, caused no jarring, and the breeze through the cutter's heavy rigging varied through several notes of pitch instead of keeping to the single tone of a steady blow. The captain paced, barking an order for silence when a seaman began to speak nearby. Again he held the chronometer in the light, then stared landward into the fog with increasing concern.

"They can't see us," the captain said to my colleague at the wheel. "Take her in closer."

"You daren't," the helmsman said. "We're as close as the draft of this hull allows."

The captain did not argue. "Mr. Gimming, a single musket shot."

I saw a number of faces turn to him with alarm, and I knew why. Any ship discovered this close to France would demand French attention. Although I'd heard the French fleet was blockaded in its ports, that did not mean that there were not smaller French vessels—brigs, snows, brigantines, even bugalets—armed to patrol coastal waters. I had no idea what degree of naval endeavours transpired over the Channel between England and France, but on water, a musket shot could be heard by anyone.

The flash of powder at the end of the muzzle for an instant lit the two jib sails. The report cracked then rolled away across the water. We listened, for what I knew not, but the crew seemed certain of purpose. Then the sound of two shots came back from aft of us, leeward, my partner pulling the tiller on the first, the topman up the mast calling down after the second, "On deck, there, I seen the blast of their gun."

The captain allowed himself to call, "Where away?"

"Three points aft the leeward beam."

We were around and gliding through the fog, again in silence, listening. Suddenly there was a scream—a woman's—then several voices yelling in French.

"*Silence!*" the captain shouted through a speaking trumpet, just as I saw an overloaded boat appear through the fog, six men rowing single banked, with a group of people bailing desperately by the tiller in the stern. We hove to as a wave swamped them. There were more shouts of alarm. Bull's-eye lanterns were turned on them. I thought I saw a trunk in the boat. The rowers boated their oars and grabbed at the lines thrown them from our quarterdeck. Just before they disappeared from my view, the sight jolted a memory of Bligh and the eighteen. A man stood up in the stern, giving impatient orders just as another swell came under and pitched him overboard.

The resulting outcry and reaction of those on board gave me to believe that the boat was overturned and all were in the water. I stayed at the wheel as more lines were thrown and orders shouted; then screams of drowning commenced, as well shouts for swimmers. Gathered at the rail, the cutter's crew looked helplessly back and forth, as would the crew of nearly any ship on the sea. So few sailors ever learned to swim.

I took off my storm cape and coat, leaving my fortune with the unknowing helmsman for safekeeping, and leapt to the starboard rail. The boatmen were clinging to the overturned hull, but the passengers were thrashing and sinking in the heavy swells. I kicked off my shoes and dove in. Hitting the cold surface was like hitting stone, taking away my breath. Someone grabbed me before I had time to surface, and I had to force my fingers into his mouth to make him gag and set me free. Pulling him to the surface, I saw a woman going under nearby and took hold of her hair. A line was landed expertly on my shoulder. I gave it to the two of them and went after the others, six in all besides the boatmen.

By then the accommodation ladder was over the side and the crewmen were on the steps, lifting folk out of the water. I heard our captain angrily urging quiet in both French and English, as I began to lose the feeling in my legs to cold. Pulling the last passenger to the ladder—the boatmen had all been taken up—I let him go first, noticing the heavy military braid on his sleeves, the epaulets of a high-ranking officer. As I was lifted from the water and up the side, I heard the wailings of loss and arguments about blame and what to do. But as I cleared the rail, barely able to stand, I shouted, "Look to the lee!" For slipping into view through the fog was a two-masted snow with its snausnout bow and try-sail, and ten ports on her starboard open with guns—twelve-pounders—run out and ready.

In those next fifteen seconds, I learned what a crew we had. Without orders, everyone moved except the boatmen and pas-sengers, who finally were silent with horror, shock, and cold. Three men were up the shrouds, tearing at the gaskets holding the topsail, four others at the taffrail halyards to raise the main-sail. All the rest save the helmsman were at the larboard guns, ex-cept the captain who stood with a gun crew behind the carronade on the foredeck.

Our luck was that the snow came at us suddenly, crossing our bow from lee to starboard. Her colours—the same as those of the privateer in the Caribbean—broke loose from the stern halyard as a French demand for our identity was shouted through a speak-ing trumpet. Her broadside could not be brought to bear, al-though one gun fired when we made no response, the roundshot skipping over the water not twenty feet to starboard. Our car-ronade, however, was set as a bow-chaser, and in the same mo-ment that the sails were reefed home, filling and moving us forward with a fine lurch, the helmsman brought the bow to bear on the snow's stern. I saw the carronade's crew madly trying to traverse the gun's carriage to clear it from blowing off the rigging on the bowsprit. I found my legs and joined them, putting my weight on the handspike until I heard "Clear!" and "Fire!" my head snapping with the concussion of the explosion, my ears deafened as I leapt out of the way of the gun's recoil. The smoke blocked our view until we sailed through it and saw the damage done: the snow's rudder was broken loose and shattered, its re-mains hanging by a single gudgeon.

The seamen had little time to cheer, but they gave one as we passed the snow's unprotected stern, giving her the insult of our four-gun broadside of grapeshot. As I reached the tiller, we jibbed hard alee with the wind in our quarter and disappeared into the fog. It would take hours to jury-rig that rudder, so pursuit was no longer a concern. But there was little relief in the fog, for the exchange of great guns would attract attention from a long way off, and anything might be bearing down on us.

The captain was already conferring with the new passengers. All spoke French. The boatmen were sullen, not having expected a voyage of any length, but nevertheless grateful to be alive and free from capture by the snow. The passengers were less reticent, both men and women giving vent to grief, fear, and anger, although the man in the uniform retained control and dignity, speaking at some length with the captain before he followed the others below to be out of the wind, which was shifting to the southeast.

"They lost everything except the ladies' jewels," the captain, my gaoler, said when he came aft. Until that moment I'd forgot about my coat, and I quickly put it on. "Their gold was in a trunk they'd brought." He shook his head at the folly, said, "Once again the sea's enriched," then issued orders to the helmsman, telling him to set a course for Weymouth. I said nothing but felt my heart begin to pound. Weymouth was in Dorset, halfway between Portsmouth and Plymouth, the main bases of the Channel Fleet. As the helmsman spun the wheel, the captain took me by the arm and led me aft to the taffrail.

"The general thanks you for saving him and his family. He has nothing to give you at the moment but this . . ." He held out a ring with a crest on it.

"I'll not have the man's jewellery when he's lost—"

"It's but a crest, he wants you to have it. It's doubtful that it will be useful to you, but should he ever return to France, it might be."

I took the ring. It fit my middle finger.

"You've earned a choice," he continued. "I'd be glad to have you stay with us. We pay well, more than any sailor ever makes. Or you are free to go ashore at Weymouth."

"I'll think on it and make my choice at Weymouth, if I may, sir."

He glanced at me with no little suspicion, my phrasing of a sudden being too much that of an officer. I turned away and changed the subject. "Who are they? What is it that you do?"

"He is Herault de Marbeuf, a general who helped liberate Toulon from the British last December, but whose name is noble and whose wife was once at court. For that, they are condemned. They have managed to escape the guillotine, which is what we do—help those who are victims of the madness in France flee the country. In their case, our people took them away a quarter hour before the arrest warrants arrived at their château, no time even to change their clothes . . ."

"They kill their generals when they're at war?"

"They kill everyone, these politicians of the Terror. He just now informed me they have arrested Danton." He laughed contemptuously. "They're devouring their own entrails . . . You're soaking wet, my friend. Find your storm cape and go below."

My teeth had begun to chatter, and I did as I was told. The hold of the cutter was already crowded with the others who'd been overboard. Their misery was apparent, except for one of the oarsmen, who'd fallen asleep. The general saw me come down the hatchway and motioned me over, introducing me to each member of his family, all of whom offered thanks in French, the two young daughters stifling their tears, the two grown sons respectfully standing, or stooping, for the hold was too low for our full height. His wife kissed my hand, the one with the ring on it, and said, passionately, something that I didn't understand.

I found a place to sit, across the hold, and wrapped the storm cape around me. Slowly the chills diminished as I watched the devastated family try to confront their unknown prospects. No, they had not lost everything. Home, wealth, country perhaps, but not each other, not who they were, not reputation. They could walk in the world, struggling as themselves, with a family and history to support them. I watched as the general discreetly took an inventory of his family's jewellery—rings, bracelets, pocket watches of gold, necklaces and earrings of diamonds and other precious stones. My recent experience informed me that their immediate future was secure, allowing them the time to find their place and begin anew, even in as difficult a place for any foreigner as England.

I turned away. I could never take advantage of the general's ring, which I slipped off my finger and put into a pocket. I had saved the family's lives, and I could only hope that I would never see any of them again.

I'd quickly decided that I'd leave the cutter at Weymouth to go to my mother. I had to see her. I knew Weymouth from my midshipman years. There were private banks there where I could exchange my pesetas for banknotes. The mail coaches would take me north to Cumberland and Whitehaven, then the pacquet across the Irish Sea to the Isle of Man. And there the return of Fletcher Christian would be known, as well the true accomplishment of my life thus far, by one who no doubt had suffered the most for it.

I'd sell enough gems to give her the money to buy back Moorland Close. If she'd allow me to do that, I'd ask nothing more of her, no forgiveness, no welcome, no endearment. It seemed to me that it was the only good thing left that Fletcher Christian could do for anyone. Whatever else I could do—whoever I was going to be—was a different matter. And even as I so neatly cleaved my life, it split the bulkheads of my memory and spilled out all the carefully contained hopes I'd so rigidly forbidden myself. Once Moorland Close was again our home, would any friend's doors be open to us? "Us"? Who would that be? My brothers, my mother and I? Would we ever be welcome in Lakeland again?

"Weymouth is off the larboard beam," the captain said. "Have you decided?"

"If you please, sir, I'll leave the ship."

He looked at me quizzically again, curious about my naval formality but not so much as to ask me more. "As you wish," he said. "I'm not surprised. There's too much—what's the word?—'purpose' in you. When yours is done, you know where to find us. We have a purpose, too."

I nodded my thanks and watched him return to the hatchway. Then I sneezed mightily, which is usual when I sneeze, startling the general's family, all of whom called, "*Santé*," in such a unison that we all laughed quietly together.

Closing my eyes, I noted that the population of my Lakeland world had dissolved, leaving me with my despair that I would ever see any of them again. *Purpose,* the captain had said of me. Beyond my mother and her home, I wondered what my purpose was, particularly when compared to his—a war to win, escape for its victims, the destruction of a government still beyond my understanding. I doubted any purpose for my very existence, dependent even for being a son on a mother who had every reason to abhor me.

And then in the dark behind my closed eyes, in the dark of the hold of that cutter moving over a black sea through the darkest part of night, I was nearly blinded by the sun shining on a white beach on which lay a naked Daphne Lewis, smiling at me.

"Witch!" I said aloud, and hurried forward to the hatchway to distract my enchanted mind with Weymouth.

PART TWO

Home

From Sir Jeremy Learned's Journal

dated 23 December 1810

After what I see at Windsor, where the mad doctors, John Willis and his tribe, insist on total control over His Majesty, cupping and blistering him, keeping him locked up, constrained, and refusing to allow him even the shortest visit with the Queen, I find Bedlam by comparison almost salubrious. It is, of course, little better than a zoo, its four keepers looking after up to three hundred inmates; men in one wing, women in another, the dangerous mixed with the placid, and only the violent locked away in chains and gyves by themselves. I suspect that Mr. Crowther, the surgeon, is close to mad himself, but he is seldom in attendance. The place is supervised by its apothecary, one John Haslam, who spends an hour a day on his rounds, except when he has business elsewhere, which I understand is often.

We have five Napoleons in Bedlam, three Jesus Christs, a pair of William Pitts (like himself, both dying drunkards), a Fletcher Christian, and a Chatterton; among the women, a varying number of Virgin Marys, a Madame de Staël who never stops talking, and one terrifying Catherine of Siena. (Of course, no one could be so terrifying as the original.) Add to these the lycanthrope who howls at the moon which only he can see, and we have a fair representation of our society.

The simple wish of some is merely for their story to be heard. Each is certain that with enough attention, the world can be convinced of the story's truth. I must confess that one of the Napoleons, the cross-eyed one, is extraordinarily persuasive.

But we—the sane—know better, we think. The rantings of the mad illustrate the symptoms of their madness, not the cause. Such is the interesting theory that my colleagues the "moral therapists" put forth, they who've been banished from Windsor for their troubles. They point out that the madman is most definitely capable of reason, perhaps his own unique reason, but nevertheless, the mind is working.

Because he—or she—is sick with some invisible bodily malfunction, a taint of the blood, too much black bile, a wandering womb, what he says is ranting, nothing more. My listening to the story, and by so doing giving it validity in the patient's fevered mind, may only deepen the conviction of his belief, instead of giving him reason to control his behaviour, or convincing him that his jabbering is not worthwhile.

Is it in the body where the initial causes lie, some tumour, some poison in the blood? This is my quandary. In His Majesty's case, I believe it is, although I am helpless to discover what. Or is it some greater reality, a truth that somehow creates the need of fantasy to reach it? For instance, in the case of the alleged Fletcher Christian, he seems to have invented a greater and more precise truth than his own, whatever that may be. He goes to extraordinary lengths to convince me (and himself, perchance?) of who he is. Any man can create himself into another, be tattooed at will, describe relations with the famous. Even so, the patient's plethora of detail is impressive. Of course my cross-eyed emperor can tell me step-by-step about the triumphs of his Italian campaign, and one of the Jesus Christs has managed the requisite scars of his Passion. I must also remember that being Fletcher Christian would result in his hang-

ing still, and death was indeed the fellow's only purpose when he arrived in Bedlam.

I'll keep reading this Fletcher Christian's story, but won't fix it further in his troubled mind with any comment. His testament may reassure him of his truth, as well as provide me with a conclusive document of his madness. It occurs to me that allowing him this exercise may be dangerous, for writing in and of itself moves thought, whether deranged or brilliant. Yet he remains placid, churning out his chapters, watching me for a reaction when I call on him. When he receives none, he ignores me and goes on writing with an intensity I dare not interrupt.

If I were not his physician, I should be tempted to discuss his history, for, as it happens, I attended the wedding of the Duke of Cleyland many years ago, to Lady Daphne Lewis. (See Journal, about November 1794, in which I noted her sad beauty.) She was the only child of the infamous Sir Frederick Lewis, therefore his heir. Before her wedding, she indeed had been captured by pirates and found naked and alone on a Caribbean island. It was a well-known adventure, which caused the Duke of Cleyland to delay the marriage (until her father urged him to the altar with a fatter fee, or so the gossips hissed), and which the London press inflated to their gross capacity. Any man then living subsequently could have made of the well-known occurrence an intriguing part of his own fantasy.

A thought: My old friend Sir John Barrow, Second Secretary at the Admiralty. Call on him to see if he knows anything germane about the Bounty.

It's 2 A.M., and I've just been summoned back to Windsor. The King does not improve. The Tories are terrified of losing his support, the ever-poised-for-power Prince of Wales perches like an overdressed vulture with the Whigs, waiting for his Regency. The King suffers, horribly and unnecessarily, I believe, in his restraining chair or strait-waistcoat. Sadly, his mad tale is totally ignored. And Napoleon, the real one, licks his lips and prepares to devour his next continent. Half the world of 1810 is marching in lockstep to Bedlam. What a merry Christmas!

Douglas, Isle of Man

April 1794

"Mother."

She didn't recognise me when she opened the back door of the house on Fort Street. As if the word had not been said, she spoke as she would to any stranger at her door in a hard spring rain.

"What is it that you want, sir?"

"Mother, it's Fletcher."

Only then was she drawn to step out, close to me in the dark, for I'd waited until night to come to the house. But immediately she stepped back.

"Shame! Shame on you for tormenting me so," she said angrily. "Are your friends watching," she demanded, squinting around the tiny garden's slat-board fence, "or are you alone?"

"We planted an acorn on my eighth birthday, outside the square tower at Moorland Close."

Her gasp silenced me, and she pulled away, stumbling on the forgotten step behind her. I reached out and caught her before she fell, but recovering her balance, she twisted away from me. In the threshold of the dark kitchen, she didn't move.

"May I come in?"

"I'll find a candle."

"No need. I know this house by heart."

At that moment, I wished I hadn't come. She said nothing, but stepped back as I went in. The wet from my cloak and duffle—I'd bought new clothes at Weymouth—was dripping on the floor, no doubt scrubbed that morning. I whipped my tricorn hat back and forth out the back door before I closed it. I heard her striking at a tinderbox without success.

"Mother, let me . . ."

Finding her hands, I took the flint and iron and struck them above the box that held the cotton rags. They smouldered quickly. "A match?"

She held the stick of wood on the rags while I blew, and when it was alight, she held it away from her and close to me. Even in the glare, I saw her eyes, though sunken further than I remembered, her lips drawn tight as backstays in a storm. The grey I remembered in her hair, held back by a patterned scarf, was now white. Even when the flame began to shake, she didn't take her hand away but stared at me, appropriately as if I'd returned from the dead.

She said at last, "Even your own mother wouldn't recognise you."

"I know some of the changes, but surely not all that you can see."

She stared at me a moment longer, then turned to the wooden table and lit the candle on it. I took a step toward my old cane-seated chair, one of six that had come with us on the Whitehaven pacquet when we left Moorland Close. I was eager to talk with her in the kitchen, for there our diminished family once had good conversation.

"Leave your cloak and bag to drip in here," she said, "we'll go to the parlour."

It was to be a more formal meeting. She took the candle, allowing me to work in the dark. I thought of leaving, writing her a letter, but of course I followed her down the short hallway. She'd lit another candle, on the mantel underneath a round gilt mirror, discoloured on its lower edge by the years of heat and smoke. It was a cold room, even in the daytime. The mirror and an old tapestry were all that adorned the walls. The ceiling was damp and flaking. I would have lit a fire, but it was April and she never wasted coal after the first of that month.

She sat in the stuffed armchair and didn't look at me. The north wind rattled the window frames and moved the lace curtains. Beside several heavy chairs with needlepoint designs was a low table, "a good piece," on which was placed a well-remembered silver tray that gleamed in the candlelight. I could see the Christian coat-of-arms, its unicorn head, the motto, *Salus Per Christum.* That crest went back a thousand years on Man. Entwined in the island's history with Vikings and Druids, the family had controlled Manx politics, with generation after generation being governed by a Christian family First Deemster, the chief judge of the island. The best land was ours, the best marriages, the family's fortunes made and spread to the Cumbrian mainland when civil war turned our story. The tray had been my grandmother's, through fourteen generations a direct descendant of King Edward the First and Eleanor of Castile. And here sat Ann Christian, near destitute, with her son the mutineer and murderer.

"Where did you come from?" she asked. "How did you get here?"

"I was rescued in the South Pacific and, after some months, found my way to Spain, then Jersey, and finally reached Douglas by mail coach and the pacquet."

She thought a moment, then slowly gazed at me. "With whom have you spoken?"

"I came here first, as soon as I could. Speaking with people or asking questions were risks I avoided."

She took a sudden breath. "Then you know nothing."

I thought she'd be the one unknowing of me. "Very little," I replied. "I read the papers as I travelled. A war with France, the Terror there, something of a revolutionary fervour in England and Mr. Pitt's fear of invasion . . ."

"I do not speak of politics," she interrupted, then hesitated.

"There was no reference to the *Bounty* . . ."

"And surely nothing about your two dead brothers!" She said this in an unrecognisable growl, her body tensely poised in the chair as if she were going to leap at me.

"Oh God . . ." I murmured, "who?"

"John . . . and Humphrey." The names broke her anger's spine, and although she didn't weep, she collapsed back into the chair. The candle on the table next to her shuddered with the impact.

"What happened?" I asked, already certain the blame was mine.

She didn't answer for a time, breathing in quick gasps. Then she said, "John, already near dead from grief, his own two children taken by disease, my only grandchildren . . ." I resolved that second to say nothing of the three on Pitcairn. "He gave up any struggle when the news of the *Bounty* engraved our family name throughout England . . ." Her eyes overflowed, and she covered them with her hands.

This affected me more than my brother's death, for he was near a stranger and deeply resented by me for those expenditures and loans that had made my mother poor.

"Tell me of the other," I asked softly, and waited for her to staunch her tears, which she did rigidly.

"Humphrey . . ."

"Yes . . ." I had loved him very much.

"He'd joined the Army, stationed on the coast of Africa, was sick with the local fevers, then died a week after news of your mutiny arrived there." She then glared at me, accusation burning in her eyes. "Why are you here?"

"If I'd known of this, I wouldn't be."

She leaned forward in her chair, gripping the arms. "How

could you have done it—forced your captain and eighteen souls into a twenty-three-foot ship's launch? How could you?" she demanded, more incredulous than blaming.

The weight of known details fell on me, making explanation awkward. "There were reasons, Mother," I said sharply, defensively. "I didn't come to excuse myself, but to explain . . ."

"Captain Bligh said that you mutinied to return to the women in Tahiti."

My legs gave way. "Bligh *survived?*" I had to sit and fell down on the couch. Even in my nightmares, this was not possible. Extremes of emotion battered through my head and heart, joy that so many respected friends might still be alive, coupled with an awakened abhorrence and sudden fear of Captain Bligh.

My mother seemed as shocked as I. Looking to heaven, she said, "Does God intend a mother to lose two sons, then tell the third of his damnation? Well then, I must tell you yours. Yes, Bligh survived. He sailed that launch through thirty-six hundred nautical miles of open sea, from the mutiny to the Dutch settlement of Coupang on Timor. Only one man was lost, killed by savages on an island where they landed for water. Six more died of fever after they arrived, due to their weakened state."

She paused for breath again, then turned to me. "I am your newspaper," she said scornfully. "Read me well. Bligh returned to England a hero, wrote a book that everybody read . . . was presented to King George at a levée . . . promoted post-captain, given a new command to sail back to Tahiti for the breadfruit and take it to the Indies, which he did with great success . . . presented with a thousand guineas by the Jamaican government, and a hundred guineas worth of plate."

The bitterness of the telling tired her, and she sat gasping in her chair. I tried to sit quietly with her, but my need to ask became an urgency.

"I won't attempt an explanation of why we mutinied. Just know that it wasn't to return to Tahiti, and that it wouldn't have happened if William Bligh had not been captain of that ship. Of those things I'm certain. The rest is still an ever-changing quandary in my mind . . . But Mother, we left sixteen men on Tahiti. Was anything heard of them?"

"The Royal Navy frigate *Pandora* was sent to find you. It found those men instead, or those that hadn't killed each other by the time the ship arrived. All were put in irons, most chained in a cage on the frigate's deck . . ."

"All? But some had opposed the mutiny . . ."

"Four drowned when the frigate sank on the Great Barrier Reef." Against all effort, she wept again before she said, "George Stewart was one . . . I see his mother each week at Douglas marketplace."

A great rock fell on my heart. He'd been my messmate, my friend, a fellow islander—from Orkney—and a loyalist who'd opposed the mutiny, kept aboard the *Bounty* only because there had been no room for him in the launch.

After a time during which we both were silent, I asked, "What happened to the rest?"

"They were returned, and all faced a court-martial. Three were hanged from a flagship's yardarm in Portsmouth Harbour."

"Who were they? Was Peter Heywood . . . ?"

She'd known the Heywood family since coming to Douglas. With a bitterness I'd never heard, my mother said, "When Bligh returned, Peter Heywood's mother, just a widow, wrote to him asking desperately after her son. His answer was nearly as cruel as the boy's death would have been to her, saying that Peter's baseness was beyond all description. I hate the man for that."

I hoped she'd hate him for my sake as well. "Did Peter hang?"

"Peter was condemned," she said. "Bligh charged that anyone who stayed aboard was part of the conspiracy . . ."

"That's a lie, which he knows. Peter was innocent. He was kept below, under guard, throughout the mutiny. What conspiracy? It was an explosion of the moment."

". . . But the King himself pardoned him."

"Pardoned him? Of mutiny?"

"And others, too. The admirals of the court-martial were served with a fine taste of the other side of Bligh's story."

"You mean there's sympathy . . . ?"

"Not for you. Be assured of that."

"I know, Mother. I'll never hope for that. But for the men, the reasons for it?"

She didn't answer but watched me, a decision to be made. Finally she gripped the arms of the chair and with effort, stood and walked to the small shelf of books, which I with my double vision of memory saw on the library shelves of Moorland Close. She pulled out the family Bible, opened it, and took out a folded cutting from a newspaper.

"This is the only article, of hundreds, that I kept," she said and handed it to me. "It tells of Peter."

I took the cutting to the candle on the mantel and unfolded the newsprint.

It was an article from the *Cumberland Pacquet* of 29 November 1791.

After the hangings a month ago, aboard HMS *Brunswick,* of the three mutineers of the *Bounty,* there has been a silence in the press and the public about the matter, as if the case were, if not resolved at least partially settled. That silence promises to be but a pause as the following letter, received by Mr. Edward Christian, brother of the accused leader of the mutiny, from a former officer on the *Bounty,* will surely attest.

For the honour of this county, we are happy to assure our readers that one of its natives, Fletcher Christian, is not that detestable and horrid monster of wickedness and depravity, which with extreme and perhaps unexampled injustice and barbarity to him and his relations, he has long been represented, but a character for whom every feeling heart must now sincerely grieve and lament.

The letter to Mr. Edward Christian is dated 5 November

1791, barely a week after the hangings in Portsmouth Harbour:

Sir, I am sorry to say I have been informed that you were inclined to judge too harshly of your truly unfortunate brother; and to think of him in such a manner as I am conscious, from the knowledge I had of his most worthy disposition and character (both public and private), he merits not in the slightest degree; therefore I think it my duty to undeceive you, and to rekindle the flame of brotherly love (or pity) now towards him, which, I fear, the false reports of slander and vile suspicion may nearly have extinguished.

Excuse my freedom, Sir:—If it would not be disagreeable to you, I will do myself the pleasure of waiting upon you; and endeavour to prove that your brother was not that vile wretch, void of all gratitude, which the world had the unkindness to think him; but, on the contrary, a most worthy character, ruined only by the misfortune (if it can be so called) of being a young man of strict honour, and adorned with every virtue; and beloved by all (except one, whose ill report is his greatest praise) who had the pleasure of his acquaintance.

I am, Sir, with esteem
Your most obedient humble servant . . .

The officer remains unidentified for the moment, and Edward Christian, a barrister of considerable reputation in Cumberland and London, says that he has already spoken with three other officers and two seamen from the *Bounty*. He assures us that all questions will be resolved, and that shame and infamy will descend on those most deserving.

My tears had begun halfway through the letter, tears not of any relief, but for the friendship and courage of Peter Heywood. As close to death as he had come, as tenuous as his reputation in the Navy would always be, he still put himself forward to defend me, in writing, in public. I also realised that my brother Edward's re-action initially had been to agree quickly with the world's worst judgment of me, no surprise for we had a history of brotherly anger. I did not speak when I handed the cutting back to my mother, content to know she had chosen it for the family Bible.

"No matter what this says," she barely whispered, "they'll hang you if you're discovered. Where can you go?" She replaced the clipping and the Bible.

"Beyond seeing you, I made no plan."

"You must hide, leave Douglas. The Navy press-gangs roam through every port, seizing anyone they find to man their ships. Here, Whitehaven, any fishing village where a seaman might be found. The Home Office has spies abroad searching for radicals and French sympathizers, even here. If they catch you, I fear they'll find out who you are . . ."

I looked for maternal concern but saw only worry of further at-tention. Even so, I said, "I'll take that fear for caring and ask noth-ing more of you than news of my two remaining brothers."

"You mustn't see them!" she said urgently. "Let no one else know that you're alive. It's such a . . . weight," and then she sat down again as if the load were too much to bear. "Charles resides in Hull, a surgeon. He barely survived news of your mutiny. He became stupefied and took to his bed, until he recovered his strength. I went to him and lived there for a time. We gave each other what-ever comfort we could. To see you I think would kill him."

"I don't believe that, Mother. Charles was a strong man, and we were very close as brothers. But I'll respect your wishes, for I agree that the fewer who know of my return, the better, whatever 'better' might come to mean. Where is Edward now?"

She didn't answer but sat staring at me, her closed mouth working nervously in silence.

"Mother . . ."

"London, at Gray's Inn. Fletcher, don't see him. You and he have such bitterness between you."

"Do you know his purpose for interviewing the men from—?"

"If you go to London," she burst forth, "they'll take you and you'll be hanged. For the love of God, please, don't put us through that."

"I've no intention of being hanged, Mother, or caught for that matter. I've means to die should either possibility present itself."

Her eyes widened in horror. "May the Lord God forgive me. Look at what I've become. Oh, Fletcher, I can't trust myself. I no longer know what I can bear, so I look at you with nothing else but fear."

Slowly I knelt beside her chair to see if she'd allow it. When she did, I took her in my arms. She did not resist, nor respond. "I have no faith in God, dear Mother, but I do believe in Hell . . . for there must be such a place for one who's caused you all I have. I'll never ask forgiveness of you; there's too much to forgive. But know that my regret is as deep as this blighted life allows, which I'd give gladly if I could relieve your pain."

"No, no," she said urgently, "do not mistake me. What I fear most is your death, for I don't know how, after losing so many, I would . . . behave. Live! Oh God, Fletcher, live. I'll gladly sacrifice any knowing of your life if I never hear of your death, for that would, I think, destroy me . . . It was better when I didn't know what had happened to you. No matter how I hated what you'd done, no matter what was said, I could think of you alive and safe, hiding on some undiscovered bit of land in some far-off sea. But now you're here, I can only imagine your being caught and . . ."

"I'll not be caught," I said before her tears began again. "There are a thousand places in the world that you can think of me alive and safe," although I couldn't think of one.

Reacting to my confidence, she broke away from my arms and stood, suddenly agitated. "My lodger's due. He mustn't see you. He's a postal officer on the Whitehaven pacquet, he stays on the nights the ship is here."

I stood, regretful of the need she had for lodgers, and reached inside my coat for the banknotes I'd bought with my pesetas in Weymouth. "Mother, perhaps with time, there'll be a way that I can be your son again. For now, I'll disappear and cause no further grief. But let me leave you this . . ." I handed the thick stack of notes to her; she took them warily. "I sold a diamond in Cádiz. There's more, enough to buy back Moorland Close. I'll send it as soon—"

She was already shaking her head. " 'A diamond in Cádiz' . . . Poor boy. Do you think I'd take a shilling from you, money such as this must be? Moorland Close? Do you really imagine that somehow we'll have our home again, take our lost and rightful place of honour in Lakeland once again? We're still in debt to relatives here and there. If I appear with enough money suddenly to buy back Moorland Close, won't someone suspect that you're alive, even a pirate on the *Bounty?* No, my son, for you are and ever will be my son, we are the mutineer's family now, and can be nothing more."

She let the money drop, and some of the notes fluttered as they fell to the floor. We stood staring at each other and both heard the lodger approaching up the front walk. She gestured urgently toward the back of the house. I stepped forward to embrace her and was gratified that she kissed me. Then I hurried to the kitchen for my hat, cloak, and bag, going out the door as the front door opened. When safe in the darkness, I turned back until I saw the candle glow returning to the kitchen. She'd had to pick up the banknotes, surely. She'd hide them in the bread crock and go about mopping up the wet evidence of my visit.

The rain blurred my eyes, and quickly I turned away, not wishing to damage memory any further with the presence of a lodger in our room.

Cumberland

April 1794

I left Douglas on the next morning's pacquet, having slept beneath the hull of an overturned fishing smack on the pebbly beach. There was no harm to it besides an aching back and the stink of red herring, which, alas, accompanied me throughout the day, having seeped into my clothes. It did prove useful, however, in avoiding that particularly prying conversation of fellow travellers.

My plan, such as it was, was to head inland as quickly as possible in order to avoid the press-gangs. Even in '87, when I'd left England on the *Bounty,* there was an impress service under the Admiralty. That was during peacetime, but we were never far from war. In Whitehaven, there had been a regulating captain who had two lieutenants under him, each leading a gang of six to ten men, depending on the availability of louts for hire. Their headquarters had been a tavern on the waterfront called the Zephyr and the Wren. Here the captured men were brought for examination, then were locked up in a gaol-like chamber called the press-room until they could be delivered to one of His Majesty's ships. Aboard they would stay, as much prisoners as seamen, until they died or the crew was paid off. The former end to it was far more common, and desertion was difficult; in most ports, the ordinary seaman was forbidden shore leave, kept on board and under guard by the detachment of Royal Marines aboard all Navy vessels, except the *Bounty,* which might have changed our history.

As the pacquet tied up at Whitehaven, I watched the crowd milling about on the pier for the telltale frayed and unkempt uniform of a press-gang's lieutenant. These were usually older officers who by choice or lack of being chosen had given up the sea for a regular life without watches or ship biscuit, and often with the steady lubrication of rum. Although they usually did their work at night, when more prime candidates for pressing were about, one did not depend on such an agenda. I was too large to overlook and just the age to beckon them.

All went well through Whitehaven. A warm sun appeared and made the still-damp cobbled streets glisten. Spring's slight heat was evident on the buds of a cherry tree and the warblers that perched there, as well in the stench of my clothing, which improved to a high fume as I traversed the familiar town toward the coaching station. It was a route I'd taken often when I was a student at St. Bees. I feared a familiar face as much as I did a pressman, for recognition had the immediate danger of hanging, where being pressed had the long-term result of years at sea as an ordinary seaman. As a former officer, I was well aware of the horrendous life lived belowdecks, but it was life and, therefore, to be preferred. Or so I supposed on that fine day.

I reached the station and paid my fare on the first coach going inland. Beyond that, I only hoped for Lakeland, for I knew it well from my youth and was certain that I could hide successfully among the crags, fells, and forests around the waters there. Abandoned mines and old quarries would serve the purpose as well. I was in luck, for a coach was scheduled to leave for Penrith within the hour. There was a stop in Cockermouth, the town where I'd grown up, but I would chance that, remaining in the coach if need be. I had little choice, as every minute in Whitehaven was a more immediate risk. Sitting in the tavern next door to the station with other passengers, I stayed in a corner, eating my breakfast of eggs, black pudding, taty scones, and coffee. No one sat near me, and the woman who served me took not a breath in my vicinity.

The post chaise pulled in and disgorged its passengers, sore and stiff as I had been two days before from the hours of jolting that made the pitch and roll of a ship seem a feathered experience. There was a change of horses, with choruses of yells and curses from the hostlers. Inside, the coachman had his dram and soon proclaimed his intention of leaving—horses, passengers, baggage, or no. I waited to be last, unconcerned with the comfort of a window seat, only with remaining inconspicuous. When the rest were in their places, and the hostler was strapping on the baggage to the boot, I stepped out into the bright sunlight, which reflected instantly off the faded gold braid that lined the hat of the lieutenant who waited there. I saw him from the corner of my eye and, keeping to my path to the post chaise, surrendered my bag to the hostler. But as I stepped onto the footboard, a hand fell on my shoulder and turned me around.

"You walk as if you've reefed a sail or two," the lieutenant said, as four of his gang gathered around him. His eyes were red and rheumy, his hair loose under his soiled officer's hat, which he wore halfway athwart.

"More than a few, I'd say. I'm a fisherman," I said in my best North Country accent.

"Oh, we can tell that, can't we, mates?" the lieutenant said as he and the others reacted to my red-herring rankness. I saw another man step to the other side of me, as the coachman climbed to his boxseat and blew his horn, announcing his departure, if not mine.

"I've a protection from the Admiralty," I said, knowing that some few fishermen had the document for the national good.

"Haw, haw," the lieutenant bleated, "been a while since I heard that old fish story. Let's see it, then."

"It's in my bag."

The coachman roared, "No more delay. We're off." And he jammed the brake staff forward.

"Then I'll be truthful," I said. "It's not convenient for me to go with you just now."

"Oh, indeed," the lieutenant said and smiled. "We'll show you convenience, mate . . ."

Before he took a step, I slammed the door closed, kicked the man beside me between the legs, and gave the haunch of the nearest horse a hard, quick smack. The startled animal leapt forward in his harness and started his three teammates. As the post chaise lurched by with the driver raging a warning to anything before him and grabbing at his reins for control, the press-gang jumped back to be out of the way, allowing me to pivot and grab hold of a boot strap holding the baggage in place. I took two bounding steps, but when I had to kick loose one of the pressmen who leapt at a leg, I lost my footing and was dragged behind as the chaise plunged over the cobbles. With that special force survival provides us, I managed to pull myself up on the baggage and perched there until normal strength returned.

I clambered over the top of the chaise to join the still-bellowing coachman, now in control of his team but not yet finished with explaining their shortcomings to them. My appearance turned his instruction to me with a vituperation of the most original smut. I agreed with everything he said, which seemed to placate him at about the same time I handed him a gold half sovereign. We then rode in silence on the boxseat, which was pleasant for me on a spring day, and surely more pleasant for the passengers below with whom I would otherwise have been confined. The airing greatly improved my herring taint and made me think that with a good boil, I would save my clothes from burning.

It was a dozen familiar miles to Cockermouth, and the ache of home began soon. The season and the weather made it worse by bringing all the world to its perfection. The bracken on the fells, which began to rise up beside us, was the colour of old rusted anchors, all that was left of last year's growth. But the first green shoots were pushing up, ready to uncoil. Among the stands of budding beech and oak that spread to the crests and down the other side, chiff-chaffs and willow warblers sang their conversations loud enough for me to hear above the thundering progress of the chaise. The flowers—celandine, speedwell, wood anemones, and even a glimpse of violet—performed their customary magic. I could see, smell, and feel them, and I swore I could hear the bees already searching through their blossoms, and taste their sweet fragrance when I opened my mouth to breathe in the sensate air of my home. Then, before I'd time to prepare, we passed below Fellbarrow and Whin Fell, the hills I saw from my bedroom window at Moorland Close. Halfway up their grassy sides was a thick scattering of Herdwick sheep with a bawling choir of leaping newborn lambs. Around them and above was a blanket of yellow gorse, while sailing with untroubled grace under the white-blue sky was a vulture, ever watchful for a stray.

I knew that if I but looked larboard—or to the left, as I was on land—I'd probably glimpse Moorland Close in the distance, at least the tower and the old battlement wall around it. I did not; the bitterness of not owning it kept my eyes forward. As my reward I saw the spire of All Saints Church in Cockermouth. I tried to prepare for the past, but there's always too much to put into place. As the chaise's wheels rumbled over the cobblestones of Main Street, fifteen years of youth came running after, caught up with us, and, as the coachman braked and pulled in his reins before the station at the Lion and Castle tavern, I thought I'd sink and drown in sudden retrospect.

If only, if only, if only was my silent chant. Of course I looked around as the passengers stepped down to stretch. There was no change of horses, so the stopover was short. From my vantage point on the boxseat, I saw the whitewashed cottages down Kirkgate by the river Derwent, their thatched roofs still glistening with dew in the sun. Next to the church was the Free Grammar School where I sweated through the hours of Latin, Greek, and trigonometry, then played hide-and-seek among the nearby gravestones.

My eye moved quickly to the grand palisaded double-fronted building over on Market Place. With its many parlours and marble mantels, it had been my brother John's office and premises when he practised law near home. He'd finally been good enough to sell it when our mother's struggle with bankruptcy began, but by then it had been too late.

Across the Derwent was the remains of Papcastle, built in the twelfth century with additions in our own. This was where my mother's ancestor, Sir Henry Fletcher, took pity on the condemned Mary, Queen of Scots, in 1568. He gave her several yards of crimson velvet for a new dress in which to be beheaded. I could glimpse any number of fine homes nearby, although most of the houses of the successful merchants and attorneys-at-law stood outside the centre.

We had known them all. I had shared my youth with the children of those families, in school, in play, at parties, and on rambles through these same spring-covered fells that surrounded us. The two rivers, the Cocker and the Derwent, crossed each other there within sight of my perch. They were the shared arteries between us, we having cavorted and talked and discovered so much of ourselves along their banks. I didn't look at faces, nor did any look at mine, for it was market day, and there was no time for idle observation. The crowd was active, with an auctioneer in full cry among the bids for sheep and cows, the greetings of friends, the bartering for goods, the excited cries of children free from their parents.

I had to leave and made the mistake of urging the coachman to my need. With a fair grapeshot of explosive verbiage, he blew me off the boxseat, insisting that I ride inside the chaise so that I might more comfortably note the speed I demanded of him.

When I took my place, he turned his abuse to his team of four, whipping them forward down Main Street and on to Keswick.

My relief was immediate, my despair corroding enough to stop my senses, so that I rode for some time through the spring, no longer aware of the season. Loss was all I felt, until I noted the knees jammed against mine and looked up to see my companions in the carriage staring at me with repugnance, their noses shrivelled in disdain. Apparently my ride in the sweet-smelling air had not accomplished all I'd hoped it would. What bothered me most, however, was the fixedness of their silent criticism, for although they would note the smell first and foremost, they might remember the face, and I was eager for no recall anywhere, much less from someone travelling with me through Lakeland. I, therefore, opened the door to request of the coachman that I be allowed to disembark, the reply to which was expected by me but much shocked those passengers I was leaving. Another gold half sovereign managed to free my bag from the boot, but not to stop the flow of the sublime saliva-spewing diatribe that continued even as the post chaise drove off.

I found myself at the northern end of Bassenthwaite. After staring at the lake's familiar beauty, I left the road for the path I knew down its eastern shore. It led through meadows that would be abloom, and woodlands alive with wrens and nuthatches, even a goldcrest if I was lucky, or some red deer. For the whole of the eight miles to Keswick, I was in the lee of Skiddaw, the majestic fell I'd climbed at least once every spring between terms at school. The weather came from the southeast that day, pushing an occasional fleecy cloud across a sky further decorated all at once with a flock of moorhen or coot, mallard, teal, or tufted duck, each flight quite certain of its different direction. Within the hour, I saw a heron fishing near the shore. He stared at me apprehensively, then reassured, went back to searching the shallow water.

With only nature's presence, I could feel a simple welcome home. It was an indulgence I allowed myself. I knew these fells and lakes and woods as well as family and friends, had as many memories of them with fewer complications. As long as I was alone, I walked without the fear of discovery, which in turn allowed my joy at being in the place to fill me with a certain exultation. I even sang, though only phrases, for my singing voice alarms animals and children.

By the time I reached the end of Bassenthwaite and was following along the bank of the continuing river Derwent, I'd decided to remain in Keswick for a time, as much to salve my mind as to plan my future. The exhilaration in my sinews made me realise what ten years spent on ships at sea had done to my talent for walking. The decks and gangways that I'd known allowed the most pathetic practise, and tiny Pitcairn barely let me stretch a leg. In Lakeland, on the contrary, walking went with breathing; if you could do one, you naturally performed the other or you must be dead. As I strode into Keswick, with the stunning panorama of Derwent Water before me and Lonscale Fell and Blencathra rising up behind the town, I felt more alive than I'd allowed myself to be, certainly since 28 April 1789, which was how I came to realise that it had been five years since the mutiny to the day.

I could not stop the sudden rush of recollection. The room I took above a tavern, even though it viewed the lake, offered no distraction from the images of the *Bounty*'s quarterdeck and of the overloaded launch. I fled from the place, which wasn't practical, for I carried the devils with me. But as I strode along the street, I viewed Latrigg, the little mountain between the town and Skiddaw. With the fervour of a convert to a new religion, I bolted for the fell's wooded slope and rushed up the well-walked path toward the grassy crest until my sailor's lungs rebelled and slowed me to a steady pace. I knew the view I'd see and trusted that it and the act of walking would be a similar expiation to what I'd felt earlier in the day. The path being relatively short and accessible to the town, I was not alone, occasionally passing others of the faithful coming and going but taking little notice of them in my zeal for nature's absolution, or some such magic.

As if a ritual sign were needed, the rain began to fall the moment my eye caught an eagle circling slowly in the updrafts that rose before Lonscale. During the following days, I became a fanatical devotee, spending little time in my room but striding off before dawn, walking around Derwent Water and up Cat Bells one day, climbing Skiddaw through Dodd Wood another, then the steep face of Blencathra, sliding on scree every other step.

In a wood, I found a hard, gnarled branch that I broke to my length and which served thenceforth as my walking stick. I kept to the paths most of the time, leaving them only when fancy or a better view drew me off, avoiding other walkers as much as possible, and greeting them perfunctorily when necessary from under a low-brimmed hat I'd bought for the purpose of shielding my face. Although alone and renewed by my familiar surroundings, I was wary still of discovery, and I examined faces quickly for any glance of recognition. Even so, with time and that sense of well-being my walks gave me, I began to consider what I was going to do and how best to do it. Somehow the strength I'd gained from Lakeland allowed an order to my ruminations, although conclusion remained as unsure as each day's weather.

I was lost in such a deep study one afternoon, when a man said something to me, suddenly appearing around a crag on the steep bank of the Whit Beck, which runs down Lonscale Fell. I hadn't been aware of him and instinctively raised my stick. A woman a little ways behind him shouted a warning, which made him recoil.

"We mean no harm, sir," said he soothingly.

The woman came quickly to her companion's side. "Only company for as little or as long as might be to all our pleasures."

I recognised them from previous walks. Younger than I, both were dressed genteelly, if somewhat threadbare beneath their cloaks. The man was quite tall and thin, his hair was cut short, and his brown coat was missing several buttons. His old top boots were down at heel, and his waistcoat, what I saw of it, was buttoned high but still showed he had no shirt.

"I've seen you before, sir," I said accusingly. "Do you follow me?"

"Not at all, sir," she said, parting her cloak and pulling down the fitted jacket she wore over her plain muslin frock. "We live nearby and walk the fells daily, as you seem to, following nothing but our inclination, which you've invaded on occasion." Under her close bonnet, she dared a demure smile, too winning and straightforward for guile.

I let my stick fall to its ordinary use. "I beg pardon. I didn't hear you approach."

"You seem dedicated to the walking way," the man said, all taciturn North Countryman, with the accent I'd known since birth.

"Just learning it again," I replied.

"How fortunate for you," she said liltingly, "as we are experts." She smiled again, an invitation and a dare. "That is, if you care for company."

I'd spent a week avoiding it and was apprehensive of any liaison. But their offer was so unaffected, and in her case so humourous, that I found my defences dissolving. Besides, they were there, walking, obviously members of my new congregation. I quickly rationalised that sooner or later, I'd have to learn to live with people, so why not practise on these two?

"I'd be honoured," I said, and coughed nervously.

"Good," she said. "Now the first thing you need do is put that one large foot, there, before the other." The glint in her eye challenged me to laugh, which I did with an ease that surprised me. They both joined me and we quickly started down the narrow path as a bare gentle rain began to fall, nothing beyond our cloaks' capacity.

Our conversation was of warnings about the path, or exhilaration about the view. We gave personality to the fells around us, speculating on what each mountain might think of the other, or of us climbing about on their backs. I realised that the couple also avoided details of their past and present lives, he with a cautious rectitude under a rather stiff exterior, she content to share her enthusiasm for what she sensed and saw. Willingly I joined in the diversion from my own moil, for every new angle on a hillside would present a view that either humbled or exalted me, all this with the pleasure of their easy conversation.

"We've seen you several times," he said.

"Yes, the first was on Latrigg," she continued. "We'd worked all day, too late to take a longer ramble."

"I walk every day," I offered brilliantly.

"We thought so," she replied. "We call you Gulliver, 'our great wanderer.' "

"You've named me already," I said, trying to suppress my alarm.

"We name everyone we see," he said, "whether we meet them or not . . ."

". . . and then create stories about them," she added, finishing his thought. "I'll tell you yours if you'd like, and you'll see how close we came."

Fortunately a rainbow stopped that idea. The rain had drifted to the east, allowing the afternoon sun an angle of access to break into its arc of colours. We stood silently as the faithful do, the ends of the rainbow on Clough Head and Blencathra, enclosing the vibrant green and violet-tinged valley along the Greta River.

We continued down the beck to the base of the mountain, then over Latrigg, talking of other rambles around Derwent Water without suggesting another meeting. When we reached a fork where the path divided, one way back to Keswick, the other along the Greta River gorge, we hesitated, unwilling to part company. There were casual speculations of chance meetings on the fells, a guessing game of where we might be on the morrow.

"Would you consider sharing our supper?" she asked without preamble or consulting her companion. "We live nearby, and although the fare will not be exhilarating, we shall be."

Every instinct of survival warned me against going, and of course I accepted the invitation. In his dour way, he seemed as pleased as she, and we walked a short way to a farm cottage and outbuildings not far from the river. They were situated just where a wind blowing down the valley between Blencathra and Lonscale Fells whipped around Latrigg. The couple led me into a small but pleasant farmhouse room and carefully began those social obligations of identity. I prepared myself with fiction.

"This isn't our home," she said with her usual exuberance. "We're vagabonds, really. The tenant family that works the farm are at a wedding in Crosthwaite, the most splendid, honest, real people . . ."

He was already at the fire, stirring its coals and adding kindling from the hamper nearby. "A dear friend from school offered us a few weeks here. Windy Brow it's called, an apt naming, don't you think? I fear the supper we offer is not a cornucopia. Potatoes and milk, from the farm . . . Very fresh," he added in apology. Comically, she held two potatoes up for my inspection.

"I must confess," I said, "my hunger seems to be for conversation more than beef or pudding."

"You'll be glutted with that by moonrise, that we guarantee," she said. "What do we really call you, Gulliver? I'm Dorothy Wordsworth, this my brother, William."

He held out his hand. Mine tightened around my walking stick. No fiction would suffice. I had to leave immediately.

They stood before me, she with the potatoes still in hand, he with a piece of kindling, looking at me with instant apprehension and fear. Apparently the shock of their names had appeared on my face.

"Have we met before?" Wordsworth asked, expecting the worst of something that he didn't yet know.

"Forgive me, I'm suddenly ill," I gasped, an obvious lie with which I hoped they'd let me go.

"No, I do not credit you, sir," Dorothy said, her fury as quick as her wit. "Do our names reward you for your search? Are you come from the Home Office, snuffling about for more evidence of my brother's radical activities? Or are you searching for scandal for your rotten earl, who refuses us our inheritance? We are guilty of nothing, sir. Wait. Are you here for blackmail about a certain child?"

"Dorothy," Wordsworth interrupted, "give the man a chance to speak. Sir, why do our names have such effect on you?"

"I cannot tell you that," I said, edging toward the door, sensing a panic that all was lost. "But do not fear me. I must leave now, and I ask nothing more of you than to forget this meeting. That would be best for—"

"So your employer won't discover we've found you out," Dorothy stated as she banged the potatoes down on the dining table and stepped toward me. "Be sure that we won't forget you, sir. Do you know what it is to be spied on, hunted? We'll alert every friend we have in Lakeland that you're about. I'm quite good at sketching and will sit me down and draw you exactly for the world to see . . ."

She stopped because I'd raised my walking stick above my head, preparing to strike her. Terrified, she staggered backward into her brother's arms. They stood there, watching me come, waiting for the blow. Wordsworth turned to protect her as I swung, yelled, and crashed the stick down on the arm of a nearby chair. It shattered. I stared at my work, then slowly looked at them, still cowering against the side of the fireplace.

There was only one chance I had with them. "I am Fletcher Christian."

If their names had shocked me, mine blasted them. They erupted from each other's arms, he ending up leaning across the center table, pushing piles of foolscap to the floor, she lurching across the room, mouth agape and arms akimbo. We all stood and stared at one another.

"I remember you from school," Wordsworth managed to say.

"Yes, barely . . . at Free Grammar School. You were five, or was it six years behind me. I passed your house the other day. I remember when your father died . . ."

"Did you know," Dorothy gasped, "your brother Edward was our attorney-at-law against Sir Jamie Lowther? He won for us in court, but—"

"Before that," Wordsworth interrupted, "he was my headmaster at Hawkshead School. Your father and ours were—" He stopped, as both of them had revealed an excitement of discovery about which they were uncertain. They looked at each other, then at me.

"Our families are as intertwined as a shroud-laid rope," I said. "I couldn't let you speculate about me with your friends. I couldn't let you draw any picture . . ."

"Of course not," Wordsworth agreed as wary forgiveness for my violence.

"But you couldn't kill us, either," Dorothy said, "so you may stay for supper."

Windy Brow

May 1794

What the meal lacked in variety, it provided in volume—endless potatoes, with butter, salt, and the freshest milk to wash it down. A sailor who'd been intimate with hardtack and grog would easily define it as a feast. I sat in the chair I'd broken, tied together with cord and every sailor's knot I knew. We talked at first of those families we all remembered in Cockermouth, successes and failures, marriages and deaths, adroitly skirting our own recent histories, which they seemed as anxious to avoid as I. Edging carefully into discussion of the war, we were led headlong into the politics of the day. In two minutes, I realised that Wordsworth was passionate, republican, and radical. It was also clear what he had to fear.

"... but this rabid righteousness of our local monarchists toward France takes their hypocrisy to despicable heights," he intoned, suddenly voluble. "The monarchy cannot exist without the aristocracy, which is no more than a fictitious superiority of titles, decorations, and garters that breeds idleness, corruption, and the tyranny that tries to teach the rest of us that we were born in a state of inferiority to our oppressors. We have one consolation, that as a nation, we may dash the cup to the ground, whenever we find the will to do it."

As if the words haunted him, he looked at Dorothy and me, then threw himself back in his chair with frustration.

"You mean, as France has done?" I asked.

"Ah, France," he sighed, despairingly. "No, of course not. Not this horrific extreme. But liberty must establish herself by violence. The people must have the right to choose their method of government. In England, we do not have that right. Here, simple reform is revolution. They sentence a man to six months in prison, another to fourteen *years* transportation, for what? For speaking one's mind. Is this freedom? No, sir, it is savagery."

"Do you express these sentiments publicly?" I asked.

He reached for his sister's hand. "Not since Miss Wordsworth has joined me . . . I wrote some things along these lines last year, when I was wandering about the country doing nothing."

Looking fondly at her brother, Dorothy explained, "He sent essays in the form of letters to a publisher—who refused them because *he* was afraid of being arrested for sedition by publishing them. It's monstrous."

"It's political treachery to make people fear to speak," Wordsworth said. "And now there's a bill in Parliament that will soon pass, overturning the law of habeas corpus. They'll be able to arrest anyone with no reason or cause, except the government's own choice of suspicion. Welcome back, Mr. Christian, to our English liberty. You are, of course, familiar with tyranny."

The implied reference to the mutiny caused me to pause. The implied sympathy for my crime made me alert. "Yes," I agreed, "but on a more personal level."

"Your mutiny took place three months before the storming of the Bastille," Dorothy said, and saw my immediate ignorance. "The revolution in France began when the people broke into the

Bastille and freed the prisoners. There are many who regard both actions as symbolic."

"I know nothing of the Bastille," I hastened to say, "but I assure you, the mutiny was no symbol, only a crime."

This surprised them. "You can't deny," Wordsworth asked carefully, "that Bligh is the ultimate example of the abuse of military and therefore governmental authority."

"The man was a very dictator," Dorothy added, "surpassing his authority with cruelty and arrogance, indulging himself with rages. What of the lost anchor on Nomuka, or Bligh's holding a pistol to his own crew?"

"And what of the coconuts?" Wordsworth added.

"How do you know such details?" I asked, amazed. "Did all this come out in the court-martial?"

They looked at each other. "We must tell him," Dorothy said.

Wordsworth nodded to her, then said to me, "No, the court-martial was an Admiralty affair. Seamen accused of mutiny who are facing the noose do not condemn their captain . . . Are you aware of your brother Edward's enquiry?"

"Enquiry? No . . ."

"How long have you been in England?" Dorothy asked directly, and for no reason that I knew, I trusted her.

"Barely a fortnight."

Wordsworth nodded, then said, "For the last year and a half, since shortly after the court-martial, Edward has conducted an enquiry into the mutiny. We've been privy to it all, not only because he's been our attorney, but because he assembled a number of our relatives and friends to serve on his panel."

"Panel?" I was totally confused. "By what authority . . . ?"

"None but his own," Dorothy stated, "as a member of a family whose name had been unjustly sullied."

Already skeptical, I asked, "Who was on this panel? What did it do?"

"It heard further testimony from your colleagues on the *Bounty*," Wordsworth said, "both officers and seamen, without the intimidating presence of admirals and the threat of the noose."

"There were an even dozen." Dorothy added, "Some had actually been in the boat with Bligh, the others had been returned from Tahiti and then acquitted or pardoned at the court-martial. All wished the truth to be told."

Knowing my companions' devotion to truth, I smiled and said, "Beware false idols. Truth is very difficult to find in any conflict, more so in this one." They did not seem to be amused. "But the panel. Who was . . . ?"

"It's quite an impressive group, one that cannot be questioned for integrity," Wordsworth said.

"I heard of it from our uncle, the Reverend William Cookson," Dorothy said with a growing excitement with the telling, "with whom I was staying at Forncett when he was asked to serve in the enquiry. He's a canon at Windsor and quite close to the King."

"I was in London at the time, being a free-floating island of uselessness," Wordsworth said deprecatingly. "But I ran into our cousin Captain John Wordsworth, who told me that your brother had assembled this group, including himself, most of whom I knew from Cockermouth or St. John's, Cambridge. Edward was a fellow there, and I'd been a most halfhearted student."

"You remember the Reverend Mr. Antrobus of Cockermouth?" Dorothy interjected. "He's now chaplain to the Bishop of London. Dr. Fisher, another canon at Windsor—they call him 'the King's fisher'—is a devoted friend of your increasingly distinguished cousin, Edward Law. Do you remember Mr. Gilpin and John Atkinson?"

"Yes, of course," I answered, "neighbours of ours . . ."

"And James Losh, a good friend of mine," Wordsworth said enthusiastically. "Do you remember him?"

"I've heard the name. But why these . . . ?"

"Five are highly respected barristers," Dorothy answered, "three are well-connected clergy, one an experienced sea captain, chosen for his experience . . ."

"All are friends, not only of your brother's but of one Wordsworth or another," her brother added.

"But if that's the case, won't their conclusions be looked on as foreordained?"

They both defended at once, Wordsworth with, "They're prepared to sign their names . . ."; Dorothy with, "Not one would think to commit perjury," then they looked at each other and laughed lightly, as if triumph were assured.

"Sign what?"

My lack of excitement deflated them. Wordsworth stated patiently, "Your brother is going to publish a transcript of the Royal Navy's court-martial, to which he plans to attach what he calls an Appendix, to include the further testimony of the dozen *Bounty* men before members of his panel, and his interpretation of—"

"When?" I demanded, now alarmed.

Dorothy looked askance. "The last I heard, sometime this month. It will turn the whole affair to your favour."

I pushed my chair back from the table and stood. "Never, I'm afraid. There is no favour for that crime. Sympathy, yes, perhaps a better understanding, but neither has kept a noose from tightening."

Wordsworth rose as well. "There were mitigating circumstances," he said as if I were a judge.

"Believe me, Mr. Wordsworth, there are none for an officer who leads a mutiny. My only chance, if I wish to survive, is slipping by between time and forgetting. This publication will bring focus to the crime again. I must prevent it."

I turned toward the door as Dorothy said, "There'll be no London coaches tonight, Mr. Christian. Unless you propose to walk, I'd suggest you take time to finish your supper."

"Why not?" I rejoined. "When will I ever have potatoes again?"

We laughed as I resumed my place, but Wordsworth remained standing. "You keep referring to it as a crime," he said.

"Can you think of a better word?"

"I've known men more guilty than you who exhaust their

minds with justification, arguing how unreasonable is established law, rather than accepting any blame."

"I did that for several years, as did some of the others with me."

"No longer?" he asked.

I shook my head. "Once the crime is committed, the mind searches for some explanation and at the same time, prepares you for the next crime." I, of course, was thinking of my own progress from the mutiny and on to Pitcairn. "Every step taken from that moment forgives the previous step. Once taken, there's no return. The mind indulges in its tricks, separating good from evil, making them equal. One creates a personal world where crimes are looked on as accomplishments, even to be admired, one's own blighted island."

"Yes, Bligh-ted is the word for you," Wordsworth said wryly, then added, "Rousseau said that a child will tear fifty toys to pieces before he will think of making one."

"A boy will do that," Dorothy said. "A girl will play happily with her first toy until it falls apart from use . . ." She broke off and regarded me fixedly. "Mr. Christian, if all that happens to a man, how does it stop?"

"It stops from exhaustion, I think, when nothing is left but what is unnatural, when stimulus comes only from some new degradation."

"But you've left your island and returned," she insisted with an admiration that I surely didn't deserve.

"That's geography, not expiation," I pointed out. "One thing the criminal learns about good and evil is that doing some evil has quick and clamourous results that stimulate a troubled mind. Doing good is usually a slow, silent process with subtle rewards. Be assured I've done nothing worthy so far, and in fact I don't know what it is that I might do, or if I even have the right to live in order to search."

We all sat silently for a time, of which I took advantage to finish my supper.

"Tell me, Mr. Christian," Wordsworth said intently, "what do you understand to be your crime, mutiny against the King, the state, the Royal Navy, or rebellion against a single unjust man?"

"The mutiny was against all those things . . . *a priori*," I said, letting fall the Latin that Bligh used often with exaggerated pedantry. "But in my own mind, I've come to separate all that from the true crime, the one that damns me beyond anything the noose can do, which was putting nineteen helpless men into a launch and sending them to their doom."

"Bligh surely wasn't helpless," Dorothy objected.

"And his doom is still before him," Wordsworth added.

I had to smile. "I've not imagined ever facing advocates like you. But you must know your criminal. There wasn't a man on that ship who tried to defend its captain. He was utterly alone. Those that went with him or remained loyal did so out of fear or respect for the law, not out of any affection or duty toward him. He was bound and surrounded with muskets and bayonets, including mine, I who was . . . in charge. Ha." I shook my head in disgust, at the same time amazed that I was telling it and wanting to continue.

"The fact that Bligh survived has no bearing on my crime. I forced him into the launch, certain he would die. I remember the moment when I knew this, when we cast them off, and he stood in the stern of the launch, still in his nightshirt. We drifted away from each other, calling back and forth, they for more supplies, the men aboard the *Bounty* for his damnation. I was silent, staring at the launch, watching Bligh until it was necessary to make some noises of command. I knew what I had done. What has happened since doesn't lessen the crime. His skill and his luck saved him, but neither alters my intent."

They watched me until Dorothy said, "He wrote a great deal about his skill, but not much about luck."

I nodded. "I've no doubt of that. Well, his skill gave him much to write about. He was a consummate navigator, and I'm sure that the severity of his discipline served him well with those in the launch. But one Pacific storm, so common there at that time of year, would have sunk him. Those that did come must have provided enough rainwater for their survival. Still, to have reached Timor is truly astonishing. I confess great curiosity about how he did it. Luck takes nothing away from him, and he was very lucky."

Wordsworth reached over and took Dorothy's hand. "This tale makes our struggles and wanderings seem paltry."

She gazed at him adoringly. "But our luck makes Bligh's look paltry, for we sailed separately so much longer than he, and now we're here, together."

They held each other's hands with such appreciative pleasure that I felt myself invisible until they both turned to include me once again.

"We talk of years, Mr. Christian," Wordsworth said, "of a voyage unlike yours, but from our souls and selves."

"Ever since our father died," Dorothy interjected, "ten years, no, longer . . ."

"We were orphans, raised by relatives, away from each other . . ."

"Dependent upon their charity, impoverished, yet with our family gentility, I as a young woman banned from working outside the house, imprisoned with domestic drudgery," Dorothy stated with a venom I'd not heard before, "all because of this snake Lowther, soon to be named the Earl of Lonsdale."

"Yes, you mentioned that." I paused. "I meant to ask what Edward . . ."

"Edward was our champion," she exuded.

"You remember," Wordsworth explained, his passion rising once again, "our father was Sir James Lowther's law-agent, administering his affairs whilst the tyrant corrupted the entire county and acquired ever more wealth from his coal mines in Whitehaven."

"I remember my mother used to say that Jamie Lowther was truly a madman, though too rich to be confined." I enjoyed the memory. "What is this 'Earl of Lonsdale'?"

"He bought the title," Dorothy said. "Baronet wasn't splendid enough for him. I heard he asked to be a duke, preferring 'Your Grace' to 'my lord.' We've solved that problem by calling him 'Sir Scum.' "

"He kept poor father running all over the county," Wordsworth continued, "and he, a widower, had no time or talent for raising children. Even before he died, we were shunted off to uncles and grandparents, and when he did die, he didn't anticipate it. At the time, he'd spent great sums of his own money in overseeing Lowther's affairs. This was our inheritance, and Lowther refused to acknowledge the debt."

"Until your brother took the case," Dorothy said triumphantly. "Facing Lowther's great team of lawyers alone, Edward beat them all at the Carlisle assizes."

"And so you have your independence," I said, again the troublemaker, "and you choose to spend it on borrowed farms, walking the fells of Lakeland."

Wordsworth nodded. "That *is* our choice, but, Mr. Christian, our case was won three years ago. Lord Lonsdale is the tyrant of the northwest of England. He owns its seats in Parliament, and manipulates all the courts between. We've received nothing. Look no further for tyranny than Jamie Lowther's castle."

The reasons for his politics were clear to me. "What will you do?" I asked.

They looked at each other with such genuine happiness that I could not believe them crazed.

"I shall become a poet, of course," he said, "something safe and practical."

"Not just a poet," Dorothy hastened to add, "a great poet, which means he'll earn even less."

Their joy led them into laughter at the absurdity. Finally they turned to me, I still seated at the table. The fire was down to coals, and the rushlight's wick had burned to half, leaving its powdery trail just before me. Outside, the wind objected loudly to the opposition of the cottage walls.

"You honour us, trusting us with your life," Wordsworth said.

"So we can share with you our rash and desperate secrets. I've wasted so much of my life, so much opportunity. Cambridge, I threw away, barely being graduated, unemployable. I went to France to live the Revolution, and finally had to flee, leaving a woman I loved . . . and a daughter. That is shame, Mr. Christian, pure shame." He stood there, devastated, until Dorothy took his hand. He looked down into her eyes, then said, "We have our freedom, not from want, not from guilt or fear, but to be together, to have a semblance of the home we never had, wherever we might be."

"And William will be able to write," Dorothy said proudly. "He's published two fine poems already . . ."

"Which gained vast praise from their three readers."

"No, no, William, at least five. We have that many relatives. So you see, Mr. Christian, in spite of all, happiness can truly be a pot of good potatoes."

"So I see," I agreed. "But for my own sake, I won't dare to think of it as possible for me."

"Why not?" she demanded.

"Your happiness is in each other. I no longer trust myself to be tangled in other people's lives."

"Too late," she said. "You're already tangled in ours."

Standing, I said, "I'll solve that immediately. Thank you for supper. It's the finest meal I've had since . . . well, much too long." As they went for my cloak and stick, I slipped a banknote under my plate.

"Will you be able to walk in the dark?" Dorothy asked.

"There'll be a moon by now, three-quarters full," said I.

"How do you know that? The shutters have been closed."

"The tides move constantly through a sailor's mind no matter where he is."

She laughed at this the way a sister would and made me wish for one.

"We have much to speak of," Wordsworth said as I wrapped my cloak about me, "much to learn from one another. Let us meet again, soon. But in the meantime, be careful. Know that England is a frightened place, haunted by these revolutions in America and France. Even before the war began, the feeling was abroad that our country was in decline. During periods of doubt, the prophets of repression are allowed their raging time. I'm no more than a vagrant trying to write poetry, but both of us are perfect for impressment, or worse. Anyone who once spoke out or questioned King and country, we are demons to be destroyed. To some, Fletcher Christian is as much a revolutionary as a criminal, but no matter. If they catch you, they'll make of you whatever these politics of fear demand."

"I'd be a sad example of a revolutionary, Mr. Wordsworth. I think they'll just hang me." I went to the door. "But on the chance they don't catch me, tell no one I exist." I shook his hand as Dorothy stepped forward.

"You *do* exist, Mr. Christian, for what purpose I'm sure you'll soon discover. Trust us. We are your friends."

I found myself too deeply moved. She saw what her statement meant to me, and there was a certain awkwardness. I went out the door without another word.

London

In choosing my coaches to London, I kept to the inland routes,
avoiding at all costs the port towns. I knew from my midshipman
days that London had more efficient press-gangs than any other
city. Seven lieutenants, professionals at their trade, each commanded a band of louts who enjoyed their work. A bounty system stimulated them, much as the prize money awarded for
captured enemy ships and cargo prodded many post-captains to
their heroism.

To my benefit, London had a million people packed in along
the Thames, and each one was my unknowing ally. Efficient as it
might be, the impress service had a great sifting to do through
such a population. I believed my chances were better there than
in Whitehaven or Hull.

Upon my arrival, I took a room at the Castle and Falcon, one of
a dozen coaching inns lining Aldersgate Street, opposite the
Church of St. Botolph. This was the principal entrance to the City
from the north, far enough from the docks and the Admiralty for

my comfort. London had always been a walking town to me, and as long as boots were strong and high enough to protect against the mud and filth, making one's way was a simple matter.

Aside from two boyhood visits and the months between my voyages with Bligh, I'd spent no time in the capital and therefore knew only parts of it with any familiarity. The City was more my place than the West End, in that when merchant ships came up the Thames, home from the West Indies, they berthed in the Docks, downriver of London Bridge. My mates and I would come upriver in wherries, and when the tide was at flood, would make the waterman shoot through the dangerous whirlpools around the bridge's ancient pillars. Then we'd step up the broad river stairs as if the world were ours.

I had changed, but the streets were the same—noisy, dirty, stinking. The tons of daily horse manure combined with the raw sewage of the entire city flowing into the Thames made breathing a doubtful enterprise. Someone just come up to town needed a week to accustom themselves to the stench. The garbage, mud, and refuse in the streets made walking an adventure, and the pounding of carriage wheels and hooves over cobblestones, the bellows of the drivers to their teams and each other, the patters and shouts of street peddlers and sidewalk costermongers, or-ange girls, packmen, and piemen, the howls of ratcatchers' packs of dogs, and the cries of street arabs everywhere offering for a penny to run an errand, hold a horse, carry a parcel, open a hackney's door—all shattered the recent silences of Lakeland like a mirror dropping.

My business took me through much of London the day of my arrival. Fortunately the sky was clear but for the black smoke of coal fires that those who could afford them burned even in May. I traversed the City to its ancient western boundary, the Inns of Court and Temple Bar. I knew my way to Gray's Inn, one of the four institutions where barristers not only had their offices but their residences and dining hall as well. My brother Edward had been called to the bar there, and I had visited his chambers on one occasion, although I could not remember the last time I'd seen him, our relationship never having been particularly noteworthy. It involved obligation more than fraternity, on his part I was sure as much as mine.

It was Easter Term for the high courts, so I could presume that Edward would be in residence. During the hours I waited and walked about outside the inn's main entrance, I found myself gaining a confidence of place among the endless traffic of the streets and walkways, the sheer current of people slowly dissolving my anxiety of discovery. Determined to keep my instincts sharp for survival, I stayed in the shadows and attracted no attention.

Then I saw Edward, hurriedly leaving the gated entrance to the inn and paying a crossing sweeper a penny to clean the street before him as he rushed to hail a hackney. His face and stomach both had swelled since I'd seen him, but he still walked rapidly, his whole body thrust forward, intent on his own vital purpose to the exclusion of anything lesser. I noticed also his elegant breeches with knee buckles, his powdered wig of Court rank, his white linen shirt and lace neckcloth. His shoes had silver buckles on them, his stockings were gleaming white silk, and his coat, breeches, and waistcoat were of the finest weave, a grand ditto suit of black upon black. Carrying his barrister's bluebag, he stamped his foot impatiently. A coach was drawing up to the kerb before him as I stepped forward and sang quietly, " '. . . and for loving his people, they shot the brave Illian Dhone,' " a heroic ancestor of ours and the subject of a popular Manx ballad.

He whirled around, his thin lips forming a silent O, his brows arching over his piercing grey eyes. Then he dismissed the hackney coach and looked around him.

"How very inconvenient," he said by way of greeting. "We can't talk here. Follow me at some distance."

I did as I was told as he made his way to Fleet Street, through Temple Bar to the Strand, which was even more crowded. I'm certain that was his purpose. The shoppers were out in full force, and although the Strand was less fashionable than Piccadilly or Bond Street, the London season was at the flood. The endless variety of shops on the Strand drew crowds of carriages from Mayfair.

Edward led me to the Hungerford Coffee House, a crowded establishment with a handsome façade of carved swags and small-paned windows. Inside it was dark, no matter the light from the street. Tobacco smoke further diminished vision, but in spite of this, the coffeehouse had files of old newspapers for its patrons to peruse. In the dim glow from oil lamps hanging from the ceiling, I watched Edward as he chose an enclosed booth in the back and placed an order. Two coffees were quickly delivered as he wrote a note and, offering a coin, asked the waiter to have it delivered. My brother didn't watch me as I approached. When I sat opposite him, he blinked as if I'd interrupted a more important thought and looked at me with a scientific interest.

"Mother was right," he observed. "You look a different person."

"She wrote you? I'm surprised."

"Why? She was terrified by your visit."

"Not when I left her."

"You don't think the money relieved her, do you?"

"Not then, but I'd hoped it would with time."

He leaned forward, abruptly the barrister before the accused. "I assure you, time is not your ally, no matter what your plans may be. Distance is the only possibility for you." Catching himself, he picked up his coffee and slid to the corner of the booth to sip it. "I can only delay my appointment by quarter of an hour. I sent a note."

"I'll consider your advice. But in the meantime, I'll soon have more money for mother, and I'm sure I can trust you to send it on to her."

At that, he smiled, his thin lips turning downward. "She thinks that you're a pirate, won't touch a penny of it . . ."

"Tell her she must."

I could see him debate whether or not to ask where the money came from and quickly reach the conclusion that I wouldn't tell him. He didn't ask. Instead, he frowned.

"You come at the wrong moment," he said.

"I regret the inconvenience, but I had to speak with you."

"I don't mean here, or with mother. I mean your existence on the face of the earth. Better that you had remained . . . a mystery."

"Because of your enquiry?"

He was too accomplished to show surprise. "Mother told you of this?" he asked casually and sipped more coffee.

"Quite the contrary," I answered. "I have the distinct impression that mother carefully avoided mentioning the subject, probably knowing I'd come here to stop it. I learned of it from another source."

Again his curiosity showed, but again he didn't give in to it. "Why would you try to stop it?" he asked instead with false surprise.

"Because the attention it will reignite could lead to my discovery," I said. "Besides which you haven't heard my side of the story."

He nodded once and then gazed off into the smoky room. "It may surprise you, but when I take a case from a solicitor—say of a man accused of murder, fraud, whatever—my purpose is not to discover his guilt or innocence but whether or not I can win his case." He leaned forward again to speak very quietly across the table. "I have no interest whatsoever in your ideas of what happened in the mutiny. From my own investigations, I know all that I need know of what occurred. You see, you are not my client here. My family's name is the client I'm defending, and I've constructed a defence that will at least divert the nation's condemnation, and it is hoped, will also remove the opprobrium from . . ." He almost said "Christian," but did not. "But let me assure you that my defence does not deny or excuse your act of mutiny. You may be certain that the sure result of your reappearance will forever be the same."

"I'm well aware of that," I said, adopting his emotionless method of debate, "but such a publication will renew official scrutiny. Anything I might try to do with my life . . ."

"What *do* you intend to try to do?"

"I don't know yet. I need to survive for a time to find out."

"May I presume you'll attempt some sort of atonement?"

He was goading me, and I had to ignore it if there was any hope of bringing him to my point, which already I doubted. "I'm sure there's none . . . I understand there was a panel."

"Yes," he said, "to validate the seamen's testimony. It's a distinguished group."

"How did you select them?"

"They selected each other, one leading to another. I spoke to one, he'd suggest the next, and that person would point to a third. So it went. There were several common interests beside friendship between us, which I was content to use. All were, I discovered, deeply and earnestly against the great evil of slavery." He chuckled with disdain. "I was careful to point out to each that Bligh had sailed ships for Duncan Campbell, one of Jamaica's great slaveholders, who was instrumental in gaining Sir Joseph Banks's interest and thus the King's support in the effort to introduce cheap food from Tahiti for the slaves in the West Indies . . . the *Bounty*'s single objective." Sighing with smugness, he concluded, "None of which appears in my Appendix, of course."

"But Edward"—my objection irritated him—"if their purpose was so transparent, what good can their conclusion be?"

He looked at me with pure contempt. "I did not select a jury. I selected reputation, a notion that you've perhaps forgotten. They have lent their reputations, which have considerable weight, to *my* conclusions, which have considerable sagacity, you may be sure. What will be offered to the public is admittedly opinion, but that common public gives immediate and slavering respect to any group of respectable gentlemen."

I was reminded again why I disliked him so. Above all else, he was a snob. "I ask you as my brother not to publish this enquiry," I requested, knowing that I'd have a better chance as a stranger. "You know the danger it will pose for me."

He smiled in his strange inverted way again. " 'As my brother,' " he quoted sarcastically. "Yes, I remember well my little brother's accusation before he went to sea, quite public it was, that John and I were responsible for our mother's loss of property and her life of penury."

"That is true, and you're aware of it," I said, no longer willing to plead. "You borrowed against Moorland Close to enhance your careers, to pay for your grand chambers of court, your place at the bar—"

"*She* borrowed, and gave it to us."

"But you knew where it would lead, and you and John did little to—"

"John's dead, you know." The accusation was clear.

"Yes, I know too well."

"And you are a mutineer. My God, were you insane? Never mind. It's done. Anything I can make of that to benefit this family and the mother about whom you seem so concerned, I will do."

It was a strange relief to see that he had some feeling left. "Can't you see that you'll only bring attention back to the family, back to mother . . ."

"And back to you."

"Yes."

He leaned across the table so quickly that the remains of his coffee spilt into the saucer. "I have worked on this affair for eighteen months. It's not a case before a court of law, but let me assure you, I will win it. And by God's blood, your fate is secondary to that purpose."

"I see that."

He nodded once, then sat back in the booth. "I'll reveal Bligh as the rabid bully he is. He's here, you know, in London, returned from the West Indies after finally delivering the precious bread-fruit. Each day he sits in the Admiralty waiting room with all the other post-captains, hoping for a ship. This publication will put him in drydock for years. The Admiralty hates public controversy. I hope he'll sue me so I can have at him in court. That would be bliss."

"And bring even more attention to—"

"In your defence, I'll say you were a gentleman, of distinguished lineage, well educated, but that there is a pressure beyond which the best-formed and principled mind must either break or recoil. You broke." He slid himself out of the booth and dropped coins on the table. Picking up his bluebag, he continued, "It would be best for you, and our family, that you remain the criminal who's disappeared, instead of afflicting us with a public hanging."

I glanced up at his face through the smoke and gloom of the place, unable to make out any other feature other than his eyes, shining with scorn. "When will it be published?" I asked.

"Within the month, if all goes well. But publishers are a notoriously slippery lot. A date to them is a *confetto* to be thrown about in their whimsy."

He smiled unpleasantly and departed the coffeehouse out a side door.

My anger was as murky as the surrounding smoke. My brother had good reason to publish his work and, like a hound at a hunt, was in full cry. Anything that tried to interrupt his run, brother or no, would be savaged until the object of his chase was bloodied and destroyed. There was too much irony that Bligh was his fox, and that I, the criminal, was to be defended like a dog trampled in the pursuit.

I ordered more black coffee and allowed myself to contemplate the possibility of William Bligh walking about the streets outside. Concluding that I could not stop the publication of my brother's work, and that I had some days, perhaps a fortnight in London before I'd have to leave, I spent the hour with the newspaper files. I turned the yellowed pages, looking for what was old news to the world, but new to me. Still sensing a bond of family,

I doubted any reciprocity. Hoping again that time might change their attitude, I took my brother's advice by resolving to give them all a distance.

Meantime, I had work to do in London. The jewels that I carried on my person were increasingly a weight. I'd resewn them several times since Weymouth, into appropriate clothes for spring, but there was never a time when I relaxed with security. It was time to sell them, give Edward the amount needed for mother to secure Moorland Close, and invest the rest to finance a future that I could not see any further than the dank boundaries of the coffeehouse. Wishing not to dwell upon that uncertainty, nor on the harrowing report of my shipmates' hanging that I found in an old *Morning Post,* I rose to go about my business.

What was needed were identities, a number of them so that those establishments I chose to favour with my trade could not compare me as a customer. This took several costumes, which I bought that day, and several different lodgings, which I acquired the next, giving a variety of names to the various innkeepers. By the time I entered the first jewellery shop, its quality chosen to match the worth I'd guessed for certain of my treasure, I'd accumulated any number of wigs, spectacles, and hats to conceal my features. At first, I was quite apprehensive, as if I'd found myself on stage not knowing any lines. I therefore said little, worried that my recently refurbished Cumberland accent would prove indelible to the hearer.

With more performance, however, I became more skilled, and with the feeling of success that large sums of money inspire—whether it has been justly earned or not—I began to broaden my characters, giving them idiosyncrasies as well as accents from English counties and colonies yet to be discovered. Any approbation for my creations was all my own, for the merchants had eyes only for what I offered them, and ears only for the amount that I demanded. At first the haggling went to them, I being awkward in the struggle. But fortunately I possessed sufficient merchandise to gain the upper hand, and I learned to be outrageous in my demands, only to be amazed by what they achieved.

I frequented a broad range of establishments, creating a new character for each of the six. They ranged from a small shop near the corner of St. Martin's Lane at Charing Cross, to the very fashionable premises of Roderick Streeter on Bond Street. The quality of my goods made me welcome in each by the second week, as I was at the two banks where I established accounts. At one, I took a bank box for the jewels, which I cut from my coat in a private room, then arranged a bill of exchange to be forwarded to Edward. At the other, I opened an account and bought my first five-percent government funds, their interest to flow automatically into the established account. Inventing a special signature for my fictional creation that allowed a bank draft for the balance to be forwarded by mail, I believed that wherever I might be in the world, so long as I could write, I'd have access to my estate.

Of course, I saved the finest stones until the last, steadily entrancing my buyers and luring them to speculate as to how many more I might produce. Appearing with no schedule that they were aware of, I nevertheless was constant, for which they all seemed grateful. Not until the final day did I have the slightest snag. I'd saved the largest stone for last, a Dutch rose-cut diamond—my knowledge had expanded with exercise, so I now knew more whereof I spoke. This I took to Bond Street in my previously established character of absentminded gentry, secretly come up to town from his estates to sell off the family heirlooms, in consequence of some unfortunate gambling debts. I wore a thin, crooked wig, tiny spectacles, a greatcoat even in spring, and grey pantaloons inside country boots that were obviously familiar with the sty. I'd made it a habit when offering my wares of pulling the stones out in a handkerchief from which they'd fall to the ornate inlaid floor, where any number of salespersons, more grandly dressed than I, were instantly on hands and knees.

The Dutch rose deserved more respect, and I gave it by allowing it to fall on a case filled with what I, in my newfound expertise, thought to be inferior goods. Mr. Streeter himself picked the stone up and respectfully placed it on a piece of blue velvet cloth, gazing at it with intense concentration that excluded his other customers, whom he abandoned to his clerks. While I waited, I talked to myself of country concerns and let the knobby walking stick I used slide from the case to the floor with a clatter. Finally Mr. Streeter, after a preamble of appreciation, offered a surprisingly low price.

"But, but, but," I stuttered, "if I'm not mistaken, you've given me a better price for lesser gems."

"Ah yes, good sir," the fellow oozed professionally, "but lesser stones are easier to sell. London is flooded with large jewels from the French who've escaped *la guillotine.* The market for magnificence is poor." He smiled, proud of his phrase.

"Oh dear," I said, all confusion. "I can't accept that, you see. The stone has come down for, well, how many generations? Perhaps I'd best go down the street with it . . ."

"As you wish, sir," he said with the assurance that I'd find the same result elsewhere. There was a commotion behind me, a certain rustling of clothing as people moved quickly, which distracted Mr. Streeter. I took advantage of it, holding him to me.

"Well, um, well, perhaps," I began, "you'd take the rose—my mother called it that—on consignment, for a better price."

"There'd be no guarantee of sale," he said, now eager to leave me.

"Yes, well, well, what might be your commission?"

"Please pardon me a moment, sir," he said as he urgently slipped around the cabinet between us to join the whispered agitation in the room. Suddenly on my guard, fearing my performance had been twigged, I didn't turn but rather looked for doors into the back for an escape.

Then I heard her voice.

"Ah, Mr. Streeter, you see I'm helpless, I can't come down Bond Street without a visit to your shop."

"Your Grace honours us."

I moved as casually as I could on legs that suddenly I couldn't trust. There was no place to go except toward a corner cabinet filled with Chinese porcelain that I examined with intense devotion, for its glass panes gave a half reflection of Daphne Lewis in a stunning frock of white silk trimmed in yellow and cinched high just under her breasts. Her gloves were also white, as was her bonnet that failed to contain all of her luxuriant black hair, which cascaded in long ringlets. The moon still lit her skin even in daytime; upon it, the jewels on her neck, ears, and wrist were only a distraction. She moved gracefully into the room, carrying a satin reticule, the swishing of her silk skirts announcing her presence, she looking here and there at objects of interest, chatting amiably with the decorous owner.

"No, as you know, I'm never exactly sure what I'm looking for," she said as she passed by my corner, thankfully without the slightest hesitation. "It's purely my instinct, I think. When I see something, I'll know. Besides, I enjoy looking . . . Tell me, what's this?"

She'd stopped at the Dutch rose.

"It's just come to us on consignment, Your Grace."

"What a splendid diamond. What is this cut?"

"A Dutch rose cut, Your Grace, a favourite used by the diamond cutters in seventeenth-century Amsterdam on very special stones."

"Indeed," she said and picked it up to look at it in the light from a window, which turned her toward me. "And might whoever consigned this have more of the same quality?"

"Perhaps, Your Grace," Streeter said with no reference toward me. "It is, as you've observed, the highest quality."

"And what is the price?" she asked, placing it back on the blue velvet.

"Forty-five hundred guineas, Your Grace?"

"Why, that's thievery," she said, laughing gaily. "But of course, who knows if it didn't come to be here by thievery, some pirate's treasure . . ."

"I assure Your Grace that—"

"Oh, of course, Mr. Streeter, I'm sure its history is as pure . . . as the Thames." She allowed him to laugh with her, then rewarded him. "I'll have it, and let me ponder the setting . . . perhaps a pendant. Well, you've ensnared me again, haven't you? How will I explain this to His Grace?"

"I'm sure the stone will defend you most brilliantly, Your Grace."

"Let us both hope so. Oh, and let me leave a note for the owner, in hopes he'll let you show me more."

Since everyone was listening, quill and ink, paper, blue sealing wax, and desk taper were produced in the instant. "That would be a great kindness, Your Grace."

She wrote quickly, folded the paper, and taking a seal from her reticule, pressed it into the hot wax provided. "I'm so very late. It's your fault, Mr. Streeter."

"And my pleasure, Your Grace."

She laughed nicely, then turned and with nods to those watching, bowing, and curtsying, she left the shop. As the whispers and excited comments of other customers rose in her wake, Streeter, preening, approached me with the note.

"The Duchess of Cleyland," he informed me as he handed it to me.

"Ten percent," I suggested as I took it and gave him my back.

"Twenty?" he countered professionally.

By then, the note was unfolded. It read:

CHARLES I

CHARING CROSS

MIDNIGHT

The meeting place she chose was as public a place as any on the planet. The intersection of traffic from Parliament Street and the Strand at Charing Cross is surely the most crowded and confused in all of civilisation, and standing in the middle of it is an equestrian statue of Charles I. I had time to study him while I waited. Raised high on a pedestal, His Majesty from his mount surveys a scene no less alarming than the view he beheld at his own beheading, with reattached imperiousness. He is surrounded by a kerb and narrow walk. The statue is guarded by four tall oil lamps which serve to illuminate both statue and the pump from which watermen supply the hackney stand at the side of the Golden Cross Inn.

I was there at midnight, despite the danger, after a day of struggle with whether I had the vaguest licence to appear or not. My conclusion was that I had no right to involve this woman in any fashion with my life, but that I was obliged to tell her so, which was an exercise in justification that would shame the Devil. I stood near the water pump as if I had some business there, my hat pulled down, watching the traffic of carriages and carts flow past and around, the cheapjacks and placard carriers on the sidewalks, weaving between the pedestrians. The prostitutes created their own current with their customers from the King's Mews and dark doorways, moving with the urgency of need and finance to the vile houses in the courts and lanes nearby.

She came from the Whitehall side, so I didn't see her until I heard, "We seem always to find ourselves on islands."

When I turned, she stood in the glow of an oil lamp, smiling proudly. Dressed rakishly as a man, or I should say, a Mayfair dandy, she propped her gold-topped walking stick of ebony over her shoulder. Her long hair was effectively encased in a tall beaver hat, her lithe body disguised in smart breeches and cutaway, a natty neckcloth at her throat.

"We shouldn't meet at all," I said quickly before any semblance of resolve was gone.

"Shouldn't, shouldn't, shouldn't," she mocked. "Then why are you here?"

"To convince you—"

"You'll fail at anything other than telling me how we shall meet henceforward."

I was lost and she knew it, but I plowed on. "Think, Duchess.

The world watches you, and we'll be discovered. The cost will be your ruin and my hanging."

"And?" she said with a maddening nonchalance as she shifted her weight from one leg to the other, looking up at me with amused patience for my struggle.

"I promised myself I'd warn you," I said, giving up completely. "But seeing you makes at least my price a bargain. I realise there's no life for me without having you for whatever moments I'm allowed."

She came toward me, but both of us looked around, allowing ourselves only to touch a hand.

"Where do you stay in town?" she asked urgently.

"My nearest residence is at Cripplegate, a very low inn."

"Take me there."

I didn't hesitate, leading her through the traffic to a hackney coach, a large dilapidated carriage with the coat of arms of the original owner still on its door. In a moment, we were headed down the Strand and in one another's arms. We had little interest in talk, and I found it strange indeed to struggle in my passion with her masculine clothing.

"I can't believe . . ." she said, then moaned and kissed me.

"How did you know?"

"My dearest, the diamond was mine."

This startled me sufficiently to pull back and ask penetratingly, "What?"

"A gift from my father on my sixteenth, from Antwerp, not Amsterdam." She smiled at my amazement. "And your disguise, though clever, wouldn't hide you from someone who knows you so well. Oh, how wonderful that you were still there," and she reached for me and pulled me down to her lips.

We passed Temple Bar, her hat toppled and let her black hair loose, and we did those tantalising things that couples do in speeding darkness and in clothing. When we reached the inn, I gave the coachman enough to keep him there until we should need him again. She had reconstructed her disguise to get us to

my room. Once inside, she removed the costume within moments. Our urgency was such that we barely reached the bed.
Soon after, she informed me during a moment of shared exalta-
tion, "Fletcher Christian, I love you."

She seemed delighted with my shocked paralysis at the name
and made of it everything that either of us could wish. Not until
we lay in each other's arms with a street lamp's glow through the
window on our bodies, allowing memory to feed, did I ask,
"How . . . ?"

She chuckled, the sound of pebbles in a wash, and kissed me.
"My husband is one of those grown-up boys enamoured of all
things military. Generals and admirals abound at our table. Within
a week of my arrival, I heard of Bligh, the *Bounty*, and . . . you,
whom Bligh described in his book in colorful detail, even unto
your tattoos," and she kissed the star on my chest.

"I so regret your knowing," I said.

"Would you have never told me?"

"Never. It stains us with what I've done and compromises you."

"You mean we must accept exactly who we are? My, my, how
terrible."

"You mock me, but it may be terrible indeed. Tell me what you
know."

"I read everything, newspapers, official records, anything I
could find about the court-martial. Do you know about that?"

"Not enough."

"I've put your name to my island memory for months. Tell me
what's happened to you since then."

I did, answering her questions as I considered this new danger
that I knew I'd never forswear. After I explained my commerce in
stolen jewellery, she said, "And now you're here. I never thought
to see you again. It's so amazing, after creating all those fantasies
one does, of coming round a corner and spying you in the street,
of following someone who barely looked like you. I did go regularly to Mr. Streeter's jewellery shop, and others too, with the demented idea that if you came to London, if you decided to sell

the jewels, if you'd dare chance the West End . . . If, if, if. I've lived with 'if' since the day I arrived."

"You paid too much for the Dutch rose."

"A shilling would've been too much, in that it was mine." She kissed me. "But I won't pay a thing. The Duke of Cleyland will, which he can well afford with all my father's money."

"Did your husband happen to note the attention you paid to the *Bounty* story?"

She sighed, then propped herself on one arm and gazed at me sadly. "Ah, my dear, I see what this can do to us." Then she looked away toward the lamplight coming through the window and, I think, noticed the rude sparse furnishings of the room for the first time. "Peter notices only one thing about me, that after nearly three months of marriage, I am still 'barren,' as he chooses to term it."

"Three months is not so long."

"Apparently his mistress fructifies within the minute. Another of her bastards is due at Michaelmas. My husband enjoys telling me that he's only trying to catch up with Prince William."

"I know nothing of Prince William's accomplishment."

"The King's second son. His Royal Highness has sired some ten illegitimates with Mrs. Jordan of the Drury Lane."

"That's much to catch up with. Your husband will be a busy man."

"Oh yes, busy, very busy. His perfunctory contributions to our process of procreation resemble the rather instant coverings in our breeding barn. Then he reminds me of my childless first marriage. I was married an entire year before the yellow fever killed my husband. And then, of course, I was with you for a number of weeks with no results . . . Perhaps the Duke is right, and I'm glad for it, because I couldn't stand to bear his child. The fraudulence of my life is bad enough without that."

I saw her distress and held her close to me. "I have a similar 'fraudulence' with life."

She kissed me and said, "Without you in my mind, I think I'd have gone mad."

"I tried to drive you from mine, but you kept bursting through it."

"Good for me!"

"On that Spanish brig that rescued me, I'd be up there in the yards furling sail, still playing the savage, with the wind tearing at my hands and hair, and I'd call out 'Daphne,' the name I'd never had a chance to utter. The Spaniards thought I called on some pagan god or goddess . . . They were right."

For a time, we were distracted from concern, which then came back to cover us like a tide.

"What shall we do?" she asked.

"Steal our time, never depending on the next second."

"You must always tell me where you are."

"I shall, of course. Unfortunately, I soon must leave London. Thanks to you, all the jewels are sold."

"Why must you go?"

"My brother promises to publish a defence of my mutiny any day now. My name will thus be brought forward in the mind's eye of acquaintances and colleagues, and for aught I know, my likeness as well. Even with a broken nose and this disreputable beard, I fear the chance recognition."

She turned to see me clearly, the shared fear in her eyes. "Where will you go?" My reaction, a wary cloud over my face, replaced her disquiet with sadness. "Oh my dearest love," she said, "can we survive all this hiding, even from each other?"

I kissed her. "Do we have a choice, other than to try? I don't. Before today I didn't think seeing you again was possible. Now the idea of not seeing you seems absurd, almost as absurd as seeing you does."

She hooted a laugh and rolled over on me. "I'm so pleased. I'll do my best to nurture the absurdity. Oh God! I haven't been a woman for so long." She kissed me, greedily. "Where will you go?" she demanded again.

"I'd thought of leaving England on a merchant ship . . ."

"I won't allow it."

". . . but from what I understand, the Royal Navy is pressing men right off the ships, at sea or in port. I'll not chance that, unless I have to."

"Have you never thought of Wiltshire, lovely Wiltshire, where a certain country house is never far away?"

"And where a certain Duke's friends and followers are forever about, who would enjoy nothing more than spying the Duchess, in mannish clothes or no, on her way to some humble cottage, occupied for her private pleasure by a mutineer and murderer."

"I haven't loved you enough. Come here."

When she was done, I said, "I'll go, I think, to Lakeland, which I know as well as I do any place. There are people there whom I might know, but when I left for sea, I was a boy and very different. Surely they'll not recognise me."

Excited, she jumped up to sit cross-legged on the bed. "Tell me a coaching inn nearby that, during the third week in August, you'll swear to visit every day to meet the post chaise from London. The season here ends on August twelfth. Parliament adjourns, and the Duke starts the next day for his grouse moor in Scotland. I've already told him that I wouldn't dream of going, and he was rather relieved. My man's clothing will take me safely to Lakeland, at least for a week, even two. How perfect! I'll bring your brother's publication. Tell me, Fletcher, are there tide pools in Lakeland?"

"No, but there are rills that make music, and tarns that change their colour under a breeze-blown cloud. Have you never been?"

"I've been to Istanbul and Paris and everywhere between, but no farther north than Hampstead."

"Oh to show you Lakeland on a fine summer's day. Daphne, come to Keswick. I'll find a cottage on Derwent Water, as beautiful a place as any on this globe. I haven't known exactly where I'd go until this moment. Now I see it clear, with you walking up the fells with me, for no other purpose than the view and each other."

"Does such a heaven exist on the earth?" she asked, talking more to herself than to me.

"Come to Keswick," I said just as doubt began to bubble, then erupt with logic through every corner of my brain. I pulled away from her, rolled over, and stood dumbly beside the bed.

"What's the matter?" I heard her say, and stopped myself from shouting, "Everything!"

"Come. Get dressed," I said. "We're playing island games. I have need of London streets to see if this is possible."

"It is!" she insisted as she leapt off the bed. "It must be," she added as my doubt spread quickly to her.

We didn't speak again until I told the hackney coachman to take us to Berkeley Square.

"We can't go there," she objected. "My servants . . ."

"We'll not stop. We'll circle round the square, and then I'll let you off at any destination you choose."

She glared at me, knowing what I was about and fearing it. We held each other silently, as if the coach were our tumbrel. I felt her tremble once, but she didn't look to me for confidence, which was fortunate. I felt myself grow cold with candor and contempt for having allowed the indulgence of such a far-fetched, dangerous whim. As we came to Mayfair, then circled and continued past Grosvenor Square, I felt my heart turn to ballast stone. I barely breathed as we reached our destination.

"Which part of the square, sir?" the coachman called through the slot from his boxseat.

"Just go slowly round and come back here," I said as I saw through Daphne's window the porticoed and pillared stone splendour at the south end of the square. Because of its great size, iron gates, courtyard ablaze with oil lamps, and three floors of high windows, some even at that hour leaking light around their draped curtains, I assumed it was Cleyland House. As we drew closer, I saw two liveried footmen of equal height standing guard at each side of the main entranceway—this just before dawn.

"Can you possibly imagine how I loathe that place?" she asked.

"Yes, I can, because we both regret what we've become," I replied. "But we dare not deny it, or pretend we're anything else."

"I *am* something else than what is not of my choosing, but inflicted by the man's world I inhabit. If you don't understand what I am, then I have no hope."

"I am here, undone because of failing my supposed role in that same man's world. But that is the world. I have a life of running, hiding, and no matter where I am, of planning an escape. I sit here holding you but I note the alleys as I pass and am ready to jump out and run at the sight of a press-gang or constable. There'll never be a time when I might not disappear without a word or warning. If I'm found, or if we're found together . . ."

She pulled back from the window as the coach passed before the gated courtyard. "No, no," I continued, "look at that façade. It's your stage setting, whether you wish it or no. You're my exact opposite, for your life is a public performance. You can't run away or hide, and any escape that you attempt will be half delusion, half pain. Although your husband seems to be careless with you, it's doubtful that his tolerance will stretch to include anything that we might be."

"You make it sound impossible," she said angrily as the carriage passed the town house and went up the other side of the square.

"It is," I said flatly, "it always has been, and it always will be. There is no island for us anymore. Never forget that. But never forget that even in our little time I've learned a love far beyond my ruined life's capacity to do it justice, even if I had you to myself. I think of your returning to him, which you must do, and I am wild with murder, which I must not do."

She didn't turn but took my hand. "We're prisoners from each other."

"In very separate cells."

She embraced me. "I shall go mad without you."

"And I'll have to find some other reason to live, a very doubtful goal. That's why I'll be at Keswick every day the second part of August, watching for the London coach. But if you come, you risk everything, not least the fact that if between now and then I'm suspected, I won't be there."

She slipped to the opposite seat in the coach and stared at me for some time. "Well," she said, "I've never seen the lakes. The trip won't be a total loss." She raised her ebony stick to knock twice on the boxseat above for the coachman to stop. Then she leaned forward and kissed me longingly. "But damn you, Fletcher Christian, be careful every second and don't rob us of our pleasure."

"If I'm not there, I will be damned."

We kissed each other again, and she opened the door of the coach. When she stepped out and closed it, I slid open the window. Before I had a chance to say a word, she was gone.

Derwent Water

June–August 1794

I left London a dozen hours later, which was fortunate, for my brother's publication came out the next day. For a fortnight, there was intense consideration of it in the press. I travelled north before the newspapers, so I saw little of the attention at the time, and the provincial papers along the way revealed no interest in the subject. Upon my arrival in Keswick, I did read several maddening articles in *The Cumberland Pacquet* that spent brief space on summary of Edward's Appendix, then lengthy paragraphs on my local history and conclusions of my good character, all of which did more to exonerate the county than anything else. By chance, I overheard in the tavern where I at first ate my meals, occasional discussion of the topic, which caused a sweat of nerves. What surprised me was the hardness of opinions, both for and against me, and the vast array of fact proclaimed on both sides, almost all of it wrong.

Such argument died out, for within the month, news arrived of the Royal Navy's victory in the first great fleet battle of the war. Twenty-five British ships-of-the-line under Lord Howe defeated a French fleet of twenty-six, capturing six of the enemy and destroying one. Such colossal triumph in a nation starved for any success made the *Bounty* matter something of an unsightly blemish.

I was delighted with the public's new perspective, and admit to the pride and envy in my bones for those who'd fought so well in what was quickly anointed "the Glorious First of June." By then I'd learned enough about the French to realise a true enemy, one that looked greedily beyond its borders to impose its will on its neighbours, and that included England. Plans for an invasion lacked only the opportunity, which the Royal Navy thwarted with its command of the seas and its blockades of the French ports. I suppose this was the first moment when I thought of going back to sea, where I belonged and might be useful.

In a careful, limited way, I went about establishing an identity. The Wordsworths had gone, so there was no one to dispute who I wished to be. A village memory, though uncaring of strangers, is long, and I was remembered by some from my previous visit in May. I built on that, creating one Christopher Harden, a London tea merchant, recently widowed and alone. He (I) had tired of the capital and was finding his peace among the fells and waters of Lakeland.

It was not an original role in the area and was accepted by the shopkeepers and tavern keepers where I took my trade, as well the landlord of the cottage that I found empty on the rise of Castlerigg Fell above Derwent Water. I'd walked around the lake once a week, an eight-mile hike with views that never were the same, changed with the minute by sun, cloud, mist, or rain. A miner's cottage, it stood on a cliff of scree overlooking Barrow Bay. Across the lake was the summit of Cat Bells, and beyond, several arms of fell, Knott Rigg, Whiteless Pike, and Wandlope. Above the cottage itself was the steep, bare rise of Falcon Crag, and just to the north the deep ravine of Cat Gill. Before I took the cottage,

I'd plotted six escapes that no one but a fool would follow. Less than two miles from Keswick, with no other dwelling in sight, the place provided privacy, protection from surprise visits, and a view of the world not to be equaled.

I spent the summer weeks improving the cottage, which had been vacant for a number of years, being less convenient to the mines beneath Cat Bells than those across the lake. The basic structure was firm, as was its thatch roof, untroubled by the mice that dwelled there. The white mortar of the walls needed paint inside and out, which I applied, as well as grey to the shutters. Beyond that was cleaning, which I did a section at a time, dispossessing at least a thousand spiders and two nests of furious thrushes. The kitchen fire was at one end, and the family fire was at the other, in the sleeping room. After I rid them of more nests, both stone chimneys drew well, although it being summer, I barely tested them. I bought two chairs to complement the old round table in the main room, and in a burst of domesticity, acquired several books to read during idle time, though there seemed to be so little.

All this was done in my driven state of anticipation. Emphatically, I infused doubt into every scene I created, but it was always overcome by imagining her first sight of the cottage, where she'd sit at meals for the view, how we'd wake, and dress, and spend a morning sitting in the sun outside the cottage, which led me to construct a rough bench that I painted a sky blue.

In spite of my efforts, she invaded everything I did, every thought I had. I wondered if she'd enjoy the perch I took from Derwent Water. When on my walks I came upon a new view, a tarn or waterfall, I felt it wasn't really seen until she saw it with me. And when news of the rest of the world came (for instance when I heard of Robespierre's death under the blade he'd used with such alacrity on others), my first reaction was how it might affect her visit. Would France's new leadership pause in war, thus keeping Parliament in session, delaying the Duke of Cleyland's departure for Scotland and Daphne's arrival in Lakeland? Thus is history put in order by a man in love.

The first half of August was slow agony, and on the nineteenth, the first day she could possibly arrive, I filled the cottage with field flowers and hurried up to Keswick two hours too soon to meet the London coach. I admitted to myself that I was demented and let myself laugh aloud when I hoped I was alone. In the village, I prowled the streets to pass the time, urging on the clocks, the sun, the universe to get about their business and move on! I spent the last half hour marching down the Penrith road, demanding of the air that I see the carriage at the first opportunity, then marching back when it was late.

Of course she wasn't on it. By the third day, I stood implanted in front of the coaching inn, not moving, holding my breath as the travellers descended, then going forward to inspect the empty coach in case she might still be within. Walking back to the cottage was an endless task, and I saw nothing on the way. By the end of the week, I waited as I'd promised, but I'd accepted the fact she wouldn't appear and made plans to give up the cottage, for I couldn't imagine staying there without her. Of course the entire fell around the place was stripped bare of flowers, for I'd put fresh blossoms about the rooms each day.

And then she was there, stepping out of the carriage and walking toward me in her man's travelling clothes, with a smile that struck me dumb. I'd prepared my speech, which I mumbled, "Ah, Mr. Crab. Welcome to Lakeland."

"Oh, Mr. Pawpaw, your devoted servant," and she reached out to shake my hand.

There were those at the coaching inn who had witnessed my week of waiting, so we remained circumspect as an hostler handed down her portmanteau. Walking through the village, we contained ourselves with nevertheless passionate descriptions of what the delay had cost us, of His Grace's dithering over buying yet more land in the West Indies, which kept him from Scotland for a week, of the condition of her bones after so many days of joggling in the often springless coaches of the Royal Mail.

And then she stopped and took a short breath of surprise. We were alone on Friar's Crag, and Derwent Water spread before us just as a bank of cloud released the sun and turned the lake to shimmers. Even in our urgency to be at each other, we were held by what we saw and stared silently about us, trying to see it all and, as had everyone before us, failing. She came into my arms, weeping, said, "I can't believe I'm finally here, and once here, I can't believe the place," and kissed me so that a week of waiting was forgotten in the time it took a dozen wrens to land in the cotton grass that lined the lake.

The walk along the shore was interrupted constantly by views that could not be denied. We passed Stable Hills, Scarfclose Bay, and through Great Wood, the path becoming peaty and soft as she told me of London matters that seemed to me of another planet. By the time we began our climb up the stony path to Falcon Crag, our laughter seemed to skip over the lake to the other side, until I suddenly began to be concerned about the cottage. It was, after all, a rough, rude place, and she was, after all, a duchess. How absurd to think that she would find pleasure in discomfort.

But once again she eased my mind. The instant she saw the cottage, she ran up the final slope before me and stood before it, gaping. She didn't wait for my arrival but went inside, so that by the time I reached the door, I could hear her wash-of-gravel chuckle as she moved about, her fingers touching surfaces of tables, windows, bed, as if she were a faerie giving them existence. She gathered up the yellow celandines I'd put in a pitcher and held them to her face, breathing in their perfume, then, having seen the vista through a window, ran again outside to see it better, finally collapsing on my blue bench, where I joined her. We sat quietly until she said, "When I die, this is what I'll see." Then she was up again and at the door, holding her flowers and pausing to say, "I think I'll change out of these travelling things."

"May I be of help?"

She surveyed the cottage. "I don't suppose we run about without our clothes, as was our custom."

"Outside, no. Inside is another matter."

For the first few days, inside won out, and only hunger finally forced us down to Barrow Bay to fish for dinner. By then she deigned to wear clothing, a simple frock of muslin, but she left her bonnet hanging on its wall peg beside the bed, allowing her hair to fall free. Our fishing was conventional, for us, with pole, hooks, and bait. Within a quiet hour, we had our fresh dinner, as we watched an engrossing progress of storm clouds slowly gathering over Borrowdale to the south. We raced the first drops back to the cottage, and I brought more wood in for the cooking fire. As I struck sparks upon the tinderbox, she put our catch into a pot. I heard nothing more until the flames were rising.

"Fletcher," she said doubtfully, staring into the pot.

"What is it?"

"I'm not sure what to do. I don't cook."

"Ha! The helpless nobility . . ."

"I'm *not* the nobility. I married it."

"Well, the first thing you do is gut the fish."

" 'Gut the fish.' You never taught me that on the island."

"It was crabs and shellfish there. You had better learn this or you'll starve in Lakeland. Here, I'll do one, then you."

I picked up the fish knife and went to work, showing off my surgical agility. "You save the guts for bait, then wash the fish, here in the bucket, then salt it." I then formally offered her the fish knife. "Have at it." She looked at the blade with disgust but made no move to take it. "The fish is dead by now. Won't feel a thing."

This did little to reassure her, but she put her fingers around the handle of the knife. Picking up the fish was nothing to her, but the incision was. She didn't look at what she was doing, only feeling it and putting whatever she pulled out into the bait box with lip-curled revulsion. Hurriedly she picked up the remaining carcass and plunged it into the bucket with such relief that I had to laugh. She rewarded me for my attention by throwing the wet fish at my head.

Even so we managed yet another splendid meal, with summer vegetables from local farms, berries from the meadows, and wine I'd laid in as part of my preparation. We lived for a week without concern and hardly a thought about anything beyond our Lakeland life, a condition so unreal that it could not last, and did not.

"We must always have this place," she said one evening as we lay in bed.

"A strange word."

" 'Always'?"

"For us. There's such a permanence to it."

This saddened her. "How often I've wished that we'd met when you were sailing in the West Indies."

"You'd have been about fourteen."

"I'd have driven you wild at fourteen."

"No doubt. I'd have deserted and you'd have saved Captain Bligh the pleasure . . ." of his mutiny, was what I started to say but didn't, unable to quip on the subject.

Sensing my discomfort, Daphne said, "Captain Bligh is a crazed tyrant who outrageously abused power on his little wooden world. I read your brother's work on my trip. It's quite damning of your captain."

"I'm certain of Edward's legal dazzle," I replied and sat up on the side of the bed. "All that seems a plague I'd hoped we'd escape here."

Her head touched my back. "We don't escape it, we crowd it out. Remember?"

Then she drew me back to bed, and within the half hour we were asleep. But not for long. I awoke sweating from a heart I could hear in my head. She was not awake to restrain me, so I left the bed, put on clothes, and crept into the other room. The coals from the cooking fire still glowed, and from them, I lit a rushlight.

The book was still in her portmanteau. I took the bound quarto out and placed it on the table by the rushlight's flame. Its attempt at official validity began with its formal title:

Minutes of the Proceedings of the Court-Martial
of those charged with mutiny
on board His Majesty's ship Bounty
with
An Appendix
by Edward Christian

Opening the book was the same as drawing a theatre curtain. There was the great cabin of the HMS *Duke* two years previous. The court was in resplendent costume, no doubt, headed as it was by Lord Hood, commander of the fleet at Spithead. Eleven post-captains joined him in the deliberations. They sat in an imposing line behind the admiral's banquet table, framed by the wide transom windows of the ship-of-the-line's stern gallery. Red-coated marines stood outside the cabin to keep order and summon witnesses and defendants from the lower decks.

They appeared one by one, those loyalists who'd gone with Bligh in the launch, giving their often conflicting views of what happened during the mutiny (for who could remember what occurred with each of forty-five men during every instant of that shattered time? I couldn't remember everything I did or said myself). Then the ten defendants testified, most of them alone. My rage and sorrow alternated as I read. They answered the court's questions and defended their actions as best they could. Hovering over the proceeding was William Bligh's dour spectre, for though he was conveniently absent on his second breadfruit voyage during the court-martial and thus was safe from cross-examination, his accusations had been submitted previously in unquestioned official reports to the Admiralty.

There was little doubt about the innocence of Norman, Byrne, Coleman, and McIntosh, for Bligh himself had written that they were detained on board the *Bounty* against their wills. Their acquittal was obvious from the first. Likewise, the guilt of Ellison, Burkitt, Millward, and Muspratt was as obvious. I knew them all to be enthusiastic mutineers, as I was.

This left James Morrison, the boatswain's mate, and Peter Heywood, my friend and fellow Manxman, acting midshipman, the only officer among them. As I read of various cross-testimony that threatened these two, I rose from the table in frustration. Going outside to breathe the predawn air, I tried to calm myself. It was the only time I left the book, and I was quickly back to it.

Peter Heywood was in the most desperate trouble, for he was accused of neutrality. An officer cannot be neutral during a mutiny. Several witnesses corroborated his claim that he was prevented from leaving the ship with Bligh by those sent below to keep him in his cabin. This was true; as I remember, I'd ordered him to be taken below under guard along with George Stewart. Heywood had come on deck when the mutiny began. I don't remember seeing him until I ordered him below. I knew he shared my attitude toward Bligh, but he was no mutineer and would never betray his duty to the King. I remember deciding in a frenzied moment not to let him or Stewart go with Bligh. I needed them both to help me sail the ship.

As I continued reading, Daphne woke, saw what I was doing, and dressed quietly. A cup of black China tea appeared at my elbow sometime after, but I didn't take time to touch it. The ashes of the burnt rushlights that I'd used were brushed from the table, and I smelled a porridge.

As it happened, Peter Heywood was found guilty of mutiny, but the court recommended him for the King's Royal pardon, which was granted. I remembered that Captain Albemarle Bertie, one of those sitting in judgment, was related to Peter Heywood by marriage. I had no doubt that the Heywood family had played a large part in that conclusion. Morrison enjoyed a similar fate, and the four obviously innocent seamen also were set free.

The four mutineers were found guilty and sentenced to hang. Muspratt's attorney-at-law, however, earned his fee. He found a legal loophole. Muspratt had wanted two of the innocent to testify for him, but the court-martial would not allow any of the accused to do so during the trial. Muspratt appealed, claiming he'd been denied his rights. After an initial delay, he was freed. But Ellison, Burkitt, and Millward did not escape the noose.

I read no more, but closed my eyes to see the scene aboard HMS *Brunswick,* which I already knew from reading the old newspapers in London. At nine o'clock, a morning gun was fired. The yellow flag was hoisted, the call to witness punishment. Delegations from all the other vessels at Spithead rowed over to the ship. Large crowds lined the shore, waiting noisily for the event. At eleven o'clock, the three men were brought on deck, accompanied by a clergyman and Morrison, who'd resolved to spend the last moments with them, an act of courage and compassion I admired deeply. Millward had a speech: ". . . take warning by our example never to desert your officers, and should they behave ill to you, remember it is not *their* cause, it is the cause of your country you are bound to support."

The Navy didn't make a hanging quick by dropping a man with a view to snapping his neck. The three stood on the cathead with sacks over their heads. The nooses were fitted, a gun fired, and the bosun piped "Haul away." In expectant silence, twenty seamen pulled on each of the ropes, running aft. The three were hoisted aloft, twitching and struggling, one to hang from the fore starboard yardarm, two from the larboard. Their strangles and gasps lasted twenty minutes; their bodies were lowered an hour later.

Ellison was sixteen at the mutiny, carried away by the excitement of it and a boy's chance to flaunt authority. How could he hang and I sit thinking on it? Millward had deserted the *Bounty* on Tahiti and on his forced return was awarded forty-eight lashes by Captain Bligh. I remembered that even with those wounds still healing, he wavered about mutiny and only at the last took up a musket. Burkitt, although an enthusiastic mutineer, yelled down Quintal's objection to our giving Bligh a compass, without which his miraculous voyage in the launch would not have been possible.

Was any of this remembered by anyone but me? No. None of it excused mutiny, which had its single punishment. Once more I assailed myself, for they had hanged because they'd followed me. I asked myself yet again what design or reason could there be for me to be alive and once again accepted that there was none. And yet my grief for those three men was such that I'd have gladly made exchange with them if it would've done some good. It wouldn't; my hanging would not have prevented theirs.

Beyond my grief, I realised that, whatever my brother's motivation for writing it, his "Appendix" was a devastating condemnation of Captain Bligh. And although exoneration was nowhere evident as his intention, he nevertheless succeeded in constructing the testimony of those shipmates who had appeared before him and his panel into a flattering portrayal of my attributes, a number of which had barely existed but had been emphasised in the telling. I had never been so certain of my brother's skill, for any ordinary reader would come away roundly condemning Bligh, which was Edward's primary purpose.

Then why was I not pleased and filled with gratitude? Because it wasn't true. It was a legal brief, as brilliantly incomplete and one sided as such documents always are, set down for a single purpose: to win the case—right or wrong, evil or good, and justice be damned.

What was missing was any word, any questioning on Bligh's behalf, which even courts of law provide, thus turning my brother's Appendix into little more than biased polemic to those of idle interest. Worse was Edward's determination to divert blame from me to any other. The most execrable example was his statement that I would never have thought of mutiny had not George Stewart, who discovered my suicidal attempt to leave the *Bounty* on a raft, distracted me from that purpose by saying, "When you go, Christian, we are ripe for anything." Thus was I supposedly convinced to lead a mutiny.

It was a lawyer's ploy to use a dead man's words. I was appalled, sickened, and all the death and blood that followed the event pulsed through my brain to blind me. Holding my head, I stood and staggered out the door. Daphne called to me in alarm, but I went on.

"Fletcher!"

I saw myself on the cliff's edge before the cottage, my balance lost. Daphne grabbed an arm and pulled me back, both of us stumbling to the ground. I could tell from the look on her face that mine was frightening her.

"My dearest, what's the matter?"

"It's all wrong! I'm the one . . ." And I knew that I'd broken again, the strange fizz flowing through my brain, affecting sight and thought, the pure pain of assault, the purer rage of revenge, all roaring without control, ready to seize on any action that might relieve the madness. I was chagrined that she was there, seeing me rave, which I confess I did. "I always did my duty as an officer ought to do . . . I would rather die ten thousand deaths than bear . . . flesh and blood cannot bear this . . ."

"Fletcher!" she shouted. Startled, I paused to watch her. "Look about you. You're here. In Lakeland. With me."

I gazed across Derwent Water to the fells beyond, and as if the lenses of a telescope cracked and distance fell away, I saw the present view and cried, "But why am I here?" My strangled voice did little to reassure her. She took my hand and led me to the blue bench. There we sat, I holding her as if I feared drowning, she leaning toward me to hearten me with her nearness. We were silent a long time, during which I realised how I must have trusted her, to reveal that part of my mind that I didn't know even existed.

"So many died," I said, trying to explain, "because of me."

"Not one in the mutiny," Daphne responded, casually I thought, as if the conversation were about the possibility of rain. "How many bloodless mutinies have there been?"

"But since then . . ." I began.

"That was not your doing," she replied. "Besides, it might have happened very differently, with still more horrible results."

"More horrible than three men hanged; six lost at sea, drowned in a cage; others murdered, by natives or each other . . . ?" This was dangerously close to revealing Pitcairn, and I silenced myself.

After a moment, she asked calmly, "How horrible do you think it would have been if you'd succeeded in leaving the *Bounty* the night before the mutiny?"

"The mutiny wouldn't have taken place."

"Oh? Your friend George Stewart warned you that if you went, the crew would be 'ready for anything.' 'Anything' surely includes mutiny, particularly after Bligh's demented behaviour over the previous three weeks, particularly with a crew so volatile with fear and hate that any spark would fire them, particularly when the second in command, rather than serving such a captain, deserts the ship with little chance of survival and the ship facing the considerable dangers of the Endeavour Strait. As you remember, Bligh with his usual charm threatened to force his officers and young gentlemen to jump overboard."

She revealed more than she had read in Edward's publication. "You've been very busy," I said.

"I told you I've read everything. There was a journal, of one of those seamen acquitted, that made its secret rounds through the Admiralty. I read that and more than even your brother did, I'd warrant you."

"Be careful," I warned her. "He had twelve actual witnesses and still got it wrong."

"His purpose was different. Wrong or right, he only wanted to defame Bligh in the eyes of the world. Did rather well, I'd say."

"And what's your purpose, then?"

"Well, I have no interest in convincing the world of anything, for the world will hang you for the crime without a thought or care of how it came to be. That we must accept, my love. The purpose here is smaller but probably more difficult: to convince you that you've a right to live. You see, I'm an interested party."

"You'll fail," I stated. "The facts can't be bent into such a pleasing shape."

"No, they can't," she responded with anticipation, "and remember that you said it. But you do accept the basic premise that officers require respect of each other in public, no matter what occurs between them in private. Without that public respect amongst themselves, officers will inevitably lose the respect of those serving under them. Do you agree?"

When I nodded, she rose from the blue bench and began to pace before me, as fine a performance as one might see in King's Bench. In spite of my deep skepticism, I watched her, entranced.

"Then you'll also agree," she continued, "that over three weeks previous to the mutiny, ever since you left Tahiti, Captain Bligh had humiliated all of his officers in front of the crew, and you, his second in command, more savagely than the rest. In other words, he'd effectively destroyed his officers' ability to command. Besides that, he called you things that no gentleman could tolerate without demanding satisfaction, 'Coward, hound, thief,' et cetera, et cetera. Men's honour is a prickly thing and sometimes as comical as an outraged porcupine. Still, it is imbedded deeply and is as much a part of a man's being as breathing. But a duel on a ship was out of the question, and England too far away to provide a delayed solution in some future meeting. On top of this, Bligh's behaviour during the coconut episode, aside from being scurrilous, bordered on the bizarre if not the lunatic. You concluded that to preserve a semblance of honour, you could not do battle with Bligh. Your duty would prevent it, so instead you would leave the ship, suicidally, at risk to your life, which would have brought considerable and appropriate shame and insult to Bligh when your absence had to be explained. And you might very well have survived. There were islands in the vicinity, perhaps with friendly natives. You spoke a little Polynesian, you had the required tattoos, water and food were available, and the women there no doubt would adore you . . ."

She paused to give me a murderous smile. I did not return it. "I was not so rational at the time," I offered.

"No, you were distraught, as any man would be. But even in that agitated state, when you were reminded by your friend George Stewart of your duty, of the greater danger to the ship, you realised that mutiny might occur if you left. And if so, to what extremes would that mutiny go? On the instant, you changed your well-laid plan to desert and resolved to stay, come hell or no."

"You mustn't do this," I entreated her.

"Mustn't? Mustn't?" she demanded, standing before me with the grace and determination of a greyhound paralysed by a scent. "Have I bent fact in any way?"

"You've constructed it to your own purpose."

"And it will stand. Unlike your brother's argument, mine involves none but you. So you must listen, for I have no other panel or jury, no public to impress. The most important fact to remember is that when George Stewart reminded you of what the crew was ready to do, you believed him. You believed at that moment, that if you left the ship, the crew might very well rebel, that the captain of the ship was in a doubtful state of mental capacity, and that if mutiny took hold of the crew, that captain, his officers, and any of the crew who opposed it—if previous mutinies are any example—most probably would be slaughtered. You see where this leads. If it were not for your demanding of each man as he joined you that he forswear allowing or causing a drop of blood to fall—

remember that, my dear?—Captain Bligh would never have reached the launch. Can you deny that there were half a dozen men, Churchill, Quintal, McKoy, to name a bloody trio, who would have pinned him to the mast with a bayonet had you not been there guarding him, listening to him rant, for three solid hours? No one, except you, protected Bligh. Remember that you and eleven men took over the ship, the other crew and officers numbering thirty-three. Not one opposed you with anything but words."

"They were not armed; we were. Daphne, the mutiny wouldn't have happened if I hadn't recruited each man to join me . . ."

"You don't know that. In all these years, you've only considered your own actions, and blamed yourself for everyone else's. Each man who joined you made his own choice. Each man who managed so little opposition did the same."

"Not the innocent, the ones who drowned in a cage coming back to England, or died of fever after surviving in the launch. They didn't choose that fate."

"Nor did you inflict it. In his haste to return to England, Bligh selfishly left the others to fend for themselves. The Royal Navy bears singular responsibility for the cage."

"Without an officer to lead them, the mutiny would never have begun, much less succeeded."

"Perhaps not that day, but what of after one, two, or three weeks more of Bligh's ravings, cutting officers' rations, viciously attacking their characters as he'd attacked yours, with you gone to an uncertain fate, and him knowing what it meant and what it would mean to others? You tell me. What would Peter Heywood, George Stewart, or the strangely invisible—at least in the mutiny—Ned Young, officers all, have done with a rebellious crew and an uncertain captain leading them into the Endeavour Strait? They had their honour as you did. And their breaking points. Once you were gone, which of them would Bligh have favoured with his ferocity, and how long would it have taken for a similar response?"

"I put Bligh and eighteen men in the launch and sent them off to die . . ."

She smiled as if watching some sort of prey walk into her trap.

"Did you give Bligh a compass?" she asked.

"I allowed one to pass to him."

"Did you personally give him your own sextant?"

"Yes."

"And in spite of vociferous objection from your fellow mutineers, you allowed the carpenter to take a number of his tools. As well, a time-keeper and the tables of latitude and longitude found their way into the launch. You also allowed five days' provisions, enough for them to reach any one of a number of nearby islands where they might forage, wait for rescue, or even construct a larger boat. If you intended them to die, my dearest, you did a frightful job."

I abruptly felt the most intense agitation and rose, intent to flee. "I can't hear more of this," I mumbled and started to walk away.

"But why?" she demanded, following me. "I've not misused the facts, have I?"

"No matter what you say, I'm not innocent of mutiny."

"I never said you were." She took my hand and stopped me. "If they catch you, you'll hang, with no defence possible. But if they don't, you'll live, and you must understand exactly what you did. The facts tell that in your moment of decision to stay aboard the *Bounty,* even in a fractured state of agitation, you took the mutiny on yourself, to control it and, in the only way open to you, to preserve a semblance of your honour, which would not allow you to avoid taking your part. Thus, you sacrificed the life you surely would have had, and by so doing saved the lives of many men, not to mention that of Captain William Bligh."

She let me go, stumbling blindly along the path down to the lake. Why I ran, I knew not at the time, but now I think it was because I feared believing her. I'd known guilty men who managed to convince themselves of innocence. In time, an arrogance and indignation took the place of fear and vigilance, and they were caught. I dared not believe her.

"There's more for you in life than that, you know," she called after me.

I didn't stop, but called back over my shoulder, "Such as?"

"Well, at least another day or two with me."

London

December 1794

In spite of what we'd agreed, she wrote once, on plain paper, folded and sealed anonymously with a business letter's red wax, addressed to my alias at my favourite tavern in Keswick.

28 October 1794

Yes, yes, yes, I know this is forbidden, but if someone does read it, he won't know who it's from, will he (or she, of course)? And of course, I shall be most careful about what I say here, which is after all, nothing more than a love letter, nothing that will set the Home Office afire with fear of invasion. I must confess I rather like the idea of unknown people knowing of us, for secrecy about such joy is very irksome. I so often wish to proclaim it, not for the sensation it would cause (you'll be relieved to hear), but because I am about to burst with it.

Because you see, my dearest, we are possible—not in the easy way of most couples on this earth, but nevertheless, we have proven that in our own restricted terms, we are possible. And even imprisoned in these extreme separate lives, we've managed to find each other and be together, quite blissfully, as I remember. Although the future can never offer any certainty (as you reminded me over and over again to my considerable irritation), I live now with equal certainty that at least we will always be trying to reach each other. I therefore wait for our agreed-upon December, although I hasten to assure you that the public's fickle attention has long since flitted to new and ever-blooming scandals and corruptions, not to mention the hardships of this endless war.

I've concluded that our greatest danger is that we'll be driven mad by not having what any man and woman who love each other might expect: time, a home, a freedom for joy. But that's the trick, not to compare us to any human couple ever known. (Can you imagine a more unlikely pair?) We are different animals, two strange fish who discovered each other so deep in the ocean that no one has observed us yet. In our luscious darkness, where no ordinary laws of nature apply, we may not find each other as often as we wish, but longing will keep us searching and alive, even when we're forced separately to the surface in our other colours and disguises.

This paper is too small, but I don't wish to burden your friend the tavern keeper at the Scarlet Spur with advancing double postage for a second page. He might refuse. In future, we'll arrange a place where both of us may write. (There's little doubt that letters sent me here are read by others, so don't consider it.) I have astounding things to tell you. Beginning 15 December, I'll greet Charles I every day at noon in hopes that you're with him and I may join you the same midnight. Please don't make me wait as long as I made you. Remember all that we discussed and admit that I was right. Remember me sitting next to you on the blue bench after supper, as well as other comforts, as I do. And don't dare forget how much I love you.

I've put this letter down from a permanent memory, for by the time I left Lakeland, I'd read it so often that it was whole only in my mind, the sheet itself in pieces from my daily unfolding of it. I publish it here as the best illustration I might offer as to why I continued to strive over the following years to live. At the time, I'd concluded no other purpose for my life, and although not suicidal, if not for her, I surely would have become uncaring of my discovery and less rigid in my caution. The chance of seeing her was the very essence of my existence, and waiting was its curse.

Remaining in Lakeland took a control that barely lasted to December. I rushed away as the first snow began to fall. The fells, which had given off every shade of colour through sunsets and sunrises, were covered in pure white, and Derwent Water was black after its summer and autumn of greens and blues. I left with every intention of returning with her, although when and how were the usual mystery.

The trip to London was complicated by the weather. A bridge washed out, necessitating a dangerous fording; a woman was taken sick, and her need of space allowed me the pleasure of riding on the box with the coachman. Fortunately, he was good enough to share the warmth of his hammercloth with me against the brutal wind. The city in winter was less reeking than in summer. The stench was subdued by cold, but the fog was worse, with the coal fires burning in every home adding to the already grey thick clouds of soot and smoke, as well as a sickly yellow tinge to every breath of air. The streets were still well supplied with refuse and garbage, so that walking held its usual hazards.

The coach arrived at a place unfamiliar to me, the George and Blue Boar in Holborn, at which there was an extraordinary traffic of coaches to and from the north. It was therefore crowded, and although this was my usual comfort, still I was unable to judge the elements of the congestion for press-gangs' lookouts or curious constables. I walked as quickly as possible through the jammed thoroughfares to an inn I knew, then hurried to Charing Cross, which I reached by noon of 15 December, the first possible moment of our agreement. I stood about the statue, watching for her carriage, knowing I might not recognise it. Staying there an hour without a sight of her, I then returned to my inn and slept. I'd know at midnight if she'd seen me. If not, I'd return the next day at noon.

When the great bells of St. Martin-in-the-Fields began to strike the hour that I'd waited for nearly four long months, I was standing in the Golden Cross Inn's carriage passage, staring out on Charles I as if he could protect me from any harm and in his munificence was bringing me my love. The shops around the square were decorated for Christmas, something that I hadn't noticed during my earlier vigil, so intent was I to spy her. On the sixth bell, I let myself consider how we might spend Christmas together, and stepped out of the cobbled passageway onto the paving of the walkways, intending to cross through the carriage traffic to the statue. But before I reached the kerb, I heard a voice say, "Begging pardon, mate, but how'd you like to see the world?"

I turned to see a man in a shabby and soiled lieutenant's uniform leering at me, as his colleagues, eight I counted, came at me from all directions. There was an ease to their efficiency, and I took no time to analyse my chances, plunging through them back up the passageway, hoping I could lose them in the Golden Cross's stable yard. But they were practised louts who brought me down within a dozen steps, and as the dozen strokes of midnight came to an end, I had a couple of them holding each appendage.

The lieutenant said, "It goes easier without the struggle," as he stabbed a rag into my mouth and they set about tying my arms behind me. In doing so, they turned me, and I faced down the passageway to Charing Cross just as Daphne, in her man's clothing, crossed the square to Charles I. She turned under the street lamp, an expectant smile on her face. I kicked two men from one leg, managed to free an arm and smash a face. Then I saw the lieutenant raise a marlinspike above my head. I turned quickly to take the memory of her already showing a glimmer of doubt, and then I saw nothing.

My feet being dragged down steps brought me back to consciousness. Blood blinded one eye, and the pain through my skull made me wonder if the marlinspike had been pounded in with a sledge. A door opened before me, and I was dragged into the middle of a crowded room filled with other press-gangs and their leaders, waiting their turn before the rheumy-eyed senior captain who sat behind a plain table and spoke in a rumbling basso whose vibrations hurt my head. Thundering at everyone, he paused only to command the clerk who scribbled next to him and to imbibe whatever was in the dark bottle on the table, which seemed to have no effect upon him whatsoever, other than contributing to the immense gutty protrusion that defied his breeches and naval coat, both of which he left open for comfort.

I was allowed the floor to wait on, and lying there attempted to regain the use of my brain, which balked at the effort. The room was dank and dim with the candlelight that only lit the senior captain's table. The noise was typical of a press-gang rendezvous, the shouted pleadings of its victims being urged to silence by the bellowed threats of their captors. I knew my fate would not change there and spared myself the effort. By the time my turn came, I was recovered enough to fear examination, and to remember who was surely still waiting for me at Charing Cross.

I was lifted to my feet as the senior captain dispensed with the gang before mine, whose victim was near hysteria.

"Stuff your mouth, you whoreson scum," the senior captain suggested to the hapless young recruit. "You'll love the Navy, and you'll be an Admiral of the Blue in a hundred years." Loud laughter came from everyone but the recruit and me. "Take him to the tender, and when you're rid of him, I'll expect three more from you rotten lot by dawn, or I'll hold your pay. Next."

I was urged forward and stood unsteadily before the table, keeping my eyes lowered, trying to contain my anger. The captain was silent too long, and when I looked up, I caught him smiling contentedly as he examined me.

"We've got a bleeding sailor here," he said as he rose and came around the table, holding his stomach contentedly with both hands. He stood before me and took a deep breath. "I can smell the old Stockholm tar on you. Am I right, Jack?"

"I can smell you, too, but it's not of the sea," I said stupidly, loud enough to cause snickers from those listening.

The insult didn't bother him; instead, he squinted an eye for closer examination. "Now what's that accent? A touch of elegance, I'd say." Then to my captors, he blasted, "You didn't dare drag in some gentleman who'll call on his friends and sink me in influence?" He walked around me, eyeing my clothes. "Good sir," he requested with snide respect, "have you papers, an Admiralty protection?"

I shook my head, but it wasn't enough.

"Shall we strip and search you, sir?" he rumbled. "I'm not eager for complications to my life."

This was what I feared; the clerk was already taking down the scene. I didn't want a record made of my tattoos. "There are no complications," I assured him. "I have nothing to show you."

Assuming I had much to hide but not caring about it, he smiled again and returned to his seat behind his desk. "Then you'll love a few weeks' cruise on our tender until the Royal Navy decides what to do with you. Take him. And if you whoreson dogs aren't back within the hour with another recruit, you'll have belaying pins up your sagging arses."

They dragged me outside to where a wagon waited, already loaded with the still-weeping recruit and one other with their escorts. It was the last chance I had, so I took it, lurching free from the hands that held me and running. The yells came fast, the shot faster, which fortunately missed. But a truncheon was thrown at my legs, tripping me up, so that four of them were on top of me in an instant, and in the next I was bound and gagged again.

I rode as cargo in the wagon, thrown onto it and left to lie face-down, with a heel on my neck and back. The ride to the river wasn't a long one, and I was dragged off the wagon, cut loose, and set marching down the steps to a launch with a pistol in my back. Sitting in the stern were two marines holding muskets with bayonets in place. They were warned, "Watch the tall one, he enjoys a chase." I took my seat, still looking for escape, but a marine let his bayonet drop and held it just opposite my heart.

They rowed us to a vessel anchored in the middle of the Thames, downriver from London Bridge, where we were greeted in silence by more marines, who escorted us below. The recruit who'd been undone was containing his grief in tearful mutterings to himself, but when we reached the bottom of the hatchway, he screamed, "Gracious God, what hell is this?"

I put a hand on his shoulder as the marines ascended and the grating was slammed shut above us and bolted over the hatch. What we saw were some forty men crammed into the hold, without enough space for all to sit or lie down. The air gave strong evidence of sweat, vomit, and waste. Two lanterns, fore and aft, did little to the darkness except make it possible to avoid trampling someone. I prodded my fellow recruit to move ahead of me, stepping over bodies toward the bowed side of the ship where I saw a space to lean.

"It's not so bad," I said to him. "It's almost full. If you're first aboard, you wait for weeks."

He looked at me, fear and horror distorting his cherub's face into a foretaste of his old age. "What happens to us now?"

"A few more days should do it," I encouraged. "Then we'll sail to one of the home anchorages, the Nore at Sheerness, perhaps Spithead at Portsmouth, and transfer onto whatever ship-of-the-line is short of crew."

"For how long?"

"As long as we're needed."

His face seemed to shrink, and out of his mouth came another shriek. "Ah, good Christ, my wife's with child!"

I grabbed him by the shoulders and shook him. "Be quiet, man. Find your courage. Women have done quite well at having children without us, and we must be as brave as they."

My convoluted logic seemed to help him but did little for me.

PART THREE

Able-bodied Seaman

From Sir Jeremy Learned's Journal

dated 28 January 1811

. . . *and it was a bitter confrontation, our insistence that the King's mania should be treated by promoting his happiness, thereby increasing his own desire to restrain himself, Dr. Willis and sons adamantly holding to their idea that a lunatic was not a sick man but "unchained animality," which can only be mastered by discipline and brutalising. Thankfully the Queen, in spite of being terrified of her husband in his condition, nevertheless has a great compassion for him and swayed the committee overseeing His Majesty's condition to allow us at least to attempt a cure, using a careful management of hope and apprehension, providing small favours, giving him a show of our confidence in him.*

We were profoundly gratified to see our theories have effect almost immediately. His Majesty's tendency to violence seemed to be equalised the moment we released him from his strait-waistcoat, I suppose because of surprise as much as anything else. (Note: The gamble was similar to the one I took last month releasing the Fletcher Christian in Bedlam from his manacles. From that endeavour, all this has flowed.) Within a day, the Queen entered his chamber for the first time in months. They embraced and wept. I understand that tomorrow, her committee will send an official letter to Parliament informing them of the King's apparent recovery, thereby throwing the Regency succession into the maelstrom of doubt once again.

Even so, a great stride has been taken toward further reform of mental care, going beyond the lax terms of the County Asylums Act of 1808. I would not be honest if I did not add that the occasion has added a small but brilliant diadem to my reputation, good for little other than a sudden florid respect at Court, and the satisfaction of watching those in charge of Bedlam react to my commands without the slightest hesitancy.

I take little credit for the accomplishment, having copied Dr. Richard Warren's course of action in 1789. Similarly a physician to the King, he too sought to match his Royal patient during his original seizures two decades ago with lunatics in Bedlam who had similar conditions of madness, with an idea of predicting the chances for His Majesty's recovery. This was of great interest to the vulpine Parliamentary Committee appointed to examine the prognostics of the Royal illness. Fortunately the King did recover completely, as I hope he will at present. My own investigations at Bedlam were something more than observation surely, and I was perhaps lucky that my experiment with the theory of "moral treatment," wielding the gentle weapon of the desire for esteem, found such a cooperative subject as the one who wishes to be Fletcher Christian. I, and the King, owe him much gratitude.

It is largely for this reason that I have responded in a singular way to my mutinous patient, with attention not usually lavished on one who has come to such a pass as he. I've done nothing about which he has knowledge, beside reading his endless and hopelessly fantastical tale. . . .

With the Royal Navy

1794–1797

I could not have known, as I gazed into the boy's overflowing eyes reflecting the lantern light in the hold that night, I was seeing my future for the next three years. That is how long he and I served together on a variety of ships on a variety of seas. And not once in that time were we allowed to put foot to land. As pressed "volunteers," we and those like us were looked on as necessary on the high seas but prisoners in port. We were kept aboard as others had their liberty, allowed only the pleasures brought to the ship on bumboats—rotten food, tainted rum, and infected whores, along with the maladies each provided. I'd previously learned my lessons about all three luxuries and respected a safe distance, such apparent righteousness earning my seaman's nickname, "Pope." It went well with the name I'd assumed for the ships' rolls, John Gulliver.

My young friend, on the other hand, indulged in any excess that came his way as antidote for his longing. Such conduct only succeeded in keeping him on the ship's surgeon's venereal list, burning out his stomach, and introducing an unknown infection to his blood—they guessed—that caused the sudden loss of hair over his entire body. His nickname thus became "Egg." A draper from Eastcheap, his bitterness at his fate turned to acid, particularly after the letter arrived announcing the birth of his son.

I of course received no letters, nor could send none. I tried on numerous occasions to beg shore leave, to no avail. Most maddening of all was when we returned to a home port after a long and wretched time on blockade or convoy escort and our ship headed for drydock, the crew being paid off. I never reached a quay. Before the ship dropped anchor, press-gangs from other ships would arrive, and those of us who'd been pressed would be turned over to yet another ship in search of its complement so it could sail on the next tide. Needless to say, our pay was overlooked and then forgotten, meagre though it was and evaporated by swollen prices that were deducted by the master for the necessary clothes and goods from his slop chest—storm cape, boots, needles, knives, tobacco. One does not accumulate his fortune rated as an able-bodied seaman in the Royal Navy.

On two occasions, I swam for shore. Once I nearly drowned, the other time I was nearly shot. Both efforts gained me a month in chains below the orlop deck, fighting with the rats for my biscuit. After that, I accepted my captivity and waited for the tiny chance that sometime I'd be set ashore. The frenzy for reaching Daphne gave way to despair, and all the conscious imaginings of what she'd done that night, what she'd thought having seen me there that day, and what had happened to her since sank into nightmare as I tried not to consider the questions when awake. I was not a popular one to sleep next to in a hammock, and suffered mine being cut down any number of times as objection to my nocturnal noise.

My main distraction, besides the complication that duty demands on any sailing ship, was teaching Egg to be a sailor. It was a challenge, for not only did he have little talent, he hated every-thing about it. It took him double the time it took others to sur-vive seasickness, and once able to stand a deck, his main motivation came from the bosun's "starting" by way of lashing with a rope's end. The angelic boy quickly became a bitter man. In spite of it, I helped him to the tops with me and taught him how to furl a sail. For even in the lowest ranks of the fo'c'sle, sta-tus eased the stress of life, and being a topman was regarded with a degree of respect by seaman and officer alike.

The other skill I shared with him was one I had much to learn about myself. The basic purpose of every Royal Navy ship, from first-rate three-decker ship-of-the-line to sixth-rate single-deck frigate, was to be a floating platform for guns. The officers were responsible for making the ship move, but the seamen were re-sponsible for fulfilling its purpose. I'd had experience with sev-eral nine-pounders on my first voyage to India, but they were popguns mounted on a rail compared to the eighteen- , twenty-four- , and thirty-two-pounders, each weighing two to three tons, each mounted on its own carriage with block and tackle attached to eyebolts on the side of the ship to haul it out for firing and to limit its recoil. A gun crew numbered between four and eight, de-pending on the great gun's size. Each man had to be precise at what he did, or all would suffer. I started as a handspike man be-cause of my size. This involved traversing the gun carriage after the gun was loaded and run out for firing. The handspike was a long straight crowbar, jammed under the carriage to move it side-ways as the gun-crew captain sighted on the target. With more experience, I became the first loader, one who sponges the bore of the gun, rams home wads and charge, then helps haul on the tackle to run the carriage up to the gun port. In describing it, the process sounds nothing more than brutish, but in truth it de-manded the finesse and timing of a team of acrobats.

Egg became my partner of sorts by loading in the wads, charge, and shot, which I rammed home and our crew captain then fired.

The boy's head was as round and smooth as the shot he loaded, his intensity such that he talked to himself in shouts of wrath throughout the process. He had no hesitation to berate those twice his age and experience if they dared shirk their effort. Gunnery practise, which happened all too seldom with live charges and ammunition (for the ship's captain had to pay for powder and shot used in practise), was the only time I saw Egg happy, or at least intent on something other than his bitterness. The rest of the time he complained, or found a way to fight, or wrote letters to his wife, over which he could be seen to allow his tears to fall. He spent more time with the rats than I did, and on two occasions suffered twelve of the cat for insubordination. None of it cured his rancour but deepened it instead, and as we moved from ship to ship, his demeanour tautened from enraged to deranged.

Our first seven months were on the *Royal Sovereign,* a ship-of-the-line stationed off Brest, a first-rate of a hundred guns and more than seven hundred men, exclusive of the officers and their servants. I'd never been on a ship that size and was lost on her for a month before I was sure of my place and duties, my back receiving the blessing of a bosun mate's starting rope in almost daily stimulation. My duties were as various as any rated able-bodied seaman's, first and endlessly as foretopman in the larboard watch and handspike to number twenty-eight gun, a twenty-four-pounder on the gun deck. I also had my place at the capstan to raise the anchors, and at the pumps during a storm when we took on water. There was work with the backstay falls when we put about; at the approach of a storm, when the topgallent masts and yards were taken down, I helped toggle the halyards. For each man rated able-bodied seaman, there were some thirty responsibilities to perform with a precision that belied the apparent confusion of a crowded deck, not the least of which was scouring it each morning with holystones. Those great blocks of Portland stone that each of thirty couples hauled back and forth between them over sand reshaped the backs of those that pulled them. Egg was my partner there as elsewhere, for no one else could tolerate him. In spite of his loss of hair, he took on plaiting mine into a sailor's queue as it grew down my back.

We left that ship when she returned to Spithead, being turned over to a frigate damned to convoy escort. This was and is a hated duty, in that chances for capturing prizes were reduced to nil. It was no secret and no shame that every ship's captain lusted for the opportunity to seize enemy ships and their cargo. A crew's lust was no less, for it was the only opportunity any of them, captain or seaman, had in their lives to make enough financial gain to raise themselves above whatever disdained station in which they found themselves.

Convoy duty becalmed that ambition, for guarding a line of merchant ships, keeping them in some order of relationship with each other, nannying them along, and protecting them from attack of privateers was a defensive duty with little opportunity for capturing anything. This meant a desultory crew and frustrated officers. All believed that they were sharing unjustly in some unknown political punishment of their captain by the higher-ups who'd drafted the assignment.

It was a dead time for me, barely remembered. We were aboard that frigate for eight months and a year, plying back and forth around the Cape to India, escorting the broad-beamed merchantmen of the East India Company that were always filled to their bulwarks with rich cargo and thus were great temptations to French privateers and the pirate ships of North Africa. For want of a diversion, we hoped for some attack, but nothing came our way. The East India Company had great influence in Parliament, and so with the Admiralty. Their convoys were so well guarded that all we saw were suspect sails on the horizon as they fled. Our officers kept the ship as taut as a backstay, but it was known to all of us that the captain began his Madeira early in the morning watch, and after the first dogwatch, he seldom was seen on the quarterdeck.

We then were turned over to an ancient eighteen-gun sloop of war attached to the North Sea Fleet on which we learned that, contrary to most Christian belief, Hell is not hot at all. It is instead a numbing, blinding Baltic winter. The ship was ordered to protect the convoys bringing oak from the Baltic ports to build and repair the Royal Navy's ships, England's supply of oak having been exhausted with two hundred warring years at sea. The winter of 1796 was a damnation one had no need for. We marked our progress not by days but by the number of fingers lost to frostbite furling sails—thirty-seven by the time we limped back to home port in March, minus a foremast, a lieutenant, and four crewmen swept overboard by the waves of iron that had crested over us. Egg had lost a thumb, I had cracked two ribs falling down the hatchway as the ship lurched against the sea.

Thus wounded and with our ship bound for refitting, both of us hoped to be put ashore, even with nothing to show for our time at sea. But useless as we were, the idea of being rid of us occurred to no one, and once again we were turned over. We could not think there was a worse duty than cruising in the Baltic, but by the whim of the Royal Navy, we found it. HMS *Sandwich,* named in honour of that spectacularly indulgent earl and built in 1759, was a rotten carcass of a once great ship-of-the-line. No longer capable of enduring the high seas, she was barely afloat at the Nore, the anchorage beyond the mouth of the Thames, off Sheerness. There she was a harbour depot ship, permanently anchored as a transfer station for men turned over from other ships, those pressed, or those taken from prisons or poorhouses, criminals, Irish revolutionaries, and quota-men, who'd paid their debts with the twenty guineas offered by the government if they agreed to go to sea.

When we arrived, we found an impossible population of sixteen hundred men aboard, all waiting for the Royal Navy to decide what to do with them. Such numbers were beyond the means of slop chest and ship's surgeon to care for. Many were near naked, more were infected with fevers that covered them with sores, scalds, and ulcers, and most were foul with lice and nits. The air 'tween decks was impossible to breathe, and hammocks—even if room could be found—were unavailable.

Egg found us space under the fo'c'sle's overhang, and we made a place for ourselves clear of the path to the hatchways. I could barely contain my fury and disgust, but he, strangely enough, went about his business with a peculiar glassy smile on his face. When I asked why, he checked our privacy and pointed aft. "See there," he said, "it's the mouth of the Thames, and my son and wife are up there no more than forty miles. I'll be there soon. By God, I'll be there soon."

I'd learned not to counter such pronunciamentos, for all he'd do was yell back at me. This time, I shared his temptation, for although there were officers and marines aboard, it didn't take us long to realise that they were as alarmed and demoralised as we that such a ship should even be allowed to float. The anchorage was filled with the movement of ships coming or going to convoy duty, or joining a blockade. They were not a unified command, although some were attached to the North Sea Fleet, presumably better prepared to sail than the *Sandwich,* for Belgium and Holland had become allies of France. The Dutch fleet, should it be allowed to sail down the Texel Channel from its anchorage to open sea, would be a formidable threat, opening the way for what everyone still feared, an invasion. A squadron under Admiral Duncan stood permanently on guard off Texel to warn of such an occasion.

But as the days lengthened into a wet though gratefully warm spring, the Dutch and indeed the war became a secondary urgency to those on the *Sandwich* still capable of considering anything beyond survival. Rumours began in April and spread through the ship as explosively as a spark in the powder magazine. I had little doubt that the rest of the fleet was similarly ignited. Egg could hardly be contained as he rushed from group to group, hearing the latest and blowing his own wrath into the smouldering speculation. I was staggered, for what the rumours told in ever-more explicit detail was that when ordered by their commander-in-chief, Admiral Lord Bridport, to put to sea, the entire Channel Fleet at Spithead had refused. The largest and most vital fleet in the defence of England, each and every ship was in a state of . . . mutiny.

The Nore

May 1797

"... and I can testify that I've known 'Pope' Gulliver almost three years . . ." It was Egg, shouting as loud as he could to the assembled thousand of the *Sandwich*'s crew. They were packed around the fo'c'sle guns, now primed and pointed aft where the officers of the ship had been confined. "Those of you knows him, han't heard much of his life, but he fairly reeks of experience, and he drips with education." He took pride in his well-rehearsed phrase.

A cheer of laughter went up as many looked at me for signs of these virtues, for to my utter horror, it was I whom Egg was describing to the mutinous crew of the *Sandwich*. An hour before, they had ignored the captain's order to clear hawse and instead had climbed into the rigging to give three cheers to the rest of the fleet as a signal of their intention. Now they were choosing "Delegates" to represent the ship in what they already presumed would be a fleetwide rebellion in imitation of what had taken place at Spithead. All this had happened with bare notice taken by me, for the previous night, I'd heard such news that any slight attention paid me might bring death, or so it seemed.

"It's true he wan't part of us that took the ship today," Egg went on, his eyes burning with fervour in his great bald skull, "but we need those to stand up for us what can speak to the King!"

Another cheer went up, this one of anger and determination. I might have laughed at the absurdity, but I was terrified that I was about to lose the anonymity that had allowed me to survive. I therefore shook my head, and said, "I'm not the one for you."

As that message was repeated to those who couldn't hear, I sensed that my lack of enthusiasm was misunderstood in many different ways. There were cries of "Why not?" and "Are you with us?" even one shout of "We'll judge if you're the one or not."

I didn't respond, hoping they'd go on to someone else. Instead, several crosscurrents of discussion kept the idea tossing about, making me the focus of more scrutiny than I'd ever had. Being singularly distracted still by what I'd heard only hours ago, which had prevented the solace of sleep, I edged toward panic. I made my way to Egg, who was standing on the capstan obliviously haranguing the large group of men about me. I reached out to pull at his leg.

"Egg, get down," I requested. "You've said enough."

"And you too little," he returned, enjoying the thrill of politics. "Come up here and tell them—"

"I'll tell them nothing. Get down," I ordered. "I'll not be a Delegate."

Although I said it to him alone, others heard it and gave a quick response of angry cries as several turned and shoved me up against the capstan. "Are you opposed?" one yelled, then another shouted, "Let him be the first to take an oath to the cause." Egg knelt down on the capstan and put his face close to mine. "What's happened to you, Gulliver? Where's your courage now?"

I looked at him and those around me, recognising all too well the blind exhilaration of overthrowing authority. "Here's my courage, Egg," I said to him, then shouted, "I'll make no oath, I'll lift no finger for this mutiny. Clap me in irons, for I oppose it, and you."

There were, of course, a hundred better ways of doing it, but I blundered on with that one, giving in to the great crush and howl about me as I was grabbed and carried to the foremast. I heard that irons were too good for me, a traitor to the cause who deserved the noose as much as any officer. But like a riptide overtaking them, there were others who were louder and more forceful, besides the fact that they were armed with muskets and cutlasses. I was torn from one group and gripped firmly by another who surrounded me and dragged me to the guns aimed aft. The loud debate continued as to my future, but those who held me simply let the talk go on until its uselessness became apparent to those without arms. Finally, the voice of one of my guards, well practised for he was a bosun's mate, rang out. "We'll not begin this exercise with blood."

Another said, "The only reason they may succeed at Spithead is that they kept their discipline and respect for the King."

There was a grudging agreement, and finally a third of my guards yelled out, "This man an't worth our attention. Egg, come and give him his wish. We'll organise ourselves into a well-run crew, or fail, mates. Delegates are coming from all the other ships. We set the example."

A proud cry of agreement followed as I was shoved to the hatchway, then met by a crestfallen Egg, who furiously led me and my escort below. I barely had a glimpse of the red flag of defiance being hoisted on the halyard where the fleet admiral's pennant had been. The cheer that came with its raising followed me down to the lower deck until I stood among the thirty-two-pound guns, had irons clapped around my wrists and ankles, then was pushed down to have my legs shackled under an iron bar attached to the deck. Egg assisted in the process, silent for once, making a point of not looking at me until the job was done.

"What a mistake I made," he commented indignantly when the others hurried back to the meeting on the main deck.

"Only that you didn't mention your idea to me first."

"I never thought you were a coward."

I didn't respond, but went about discovering what comfort, if any, was possible in my circumstance.

"We have a right to do this," he blurted. "They treat us worse than the animals."

"That may be so," I said as I lay back on the deck. "But, Egg, believe me, I have no right. Besides, it won't work."

"It's working at Spithead. The King has offered pardon to every Jack Tar, the Admiralty agreed to raise their pay, and old Lord Howe himself has let them purge their ships of cruel and barbarous officers."

"That's what we hear," I said, "and if it's true, I wonder how they did it, but also why we're doing this if it's already been done."

"We owe them our support," he said, abruptly righteous. "And we owe it to ourselves."

"Perhaps," I agreed. "Be careful, Egg. Demanding what you're owed in life can bring much more than what you want."

"I want to see my son," he shouted. "Is that too much?"

"Of course not," I said as he marched off. He was right. There wasn't a sailor in the Royal Navy who was looked on as a human being, and most found themselves regarded as considerably less.

What was happening in the Channel Fleet at Spithead and now to us at the Nore was unprecedented in the history of war. The fighting force on which the nation's very survival depended had refused their orders, put their officers ashore, and made demands for better conditions of life. It was difficult for me to believe that the Channel Fleet had succeeded, but even if they had, there was not a moment during my confinement on the *Sandwich* that I didn't see the spectral nooses hanging from the yardarms for our leaders, whoever those poor souls would be. I remembered Malvolio in *Twelfth Night*—we'd done the play at St. Bees—"and some have greatness thrust upon 'em." Two decks up from me, they were thrusting greatness, chimerical and fleet, on those they needed to lead them.

I was therefore relieved, though uncomfortable in my shackles, left alone for the moment in the dark of the lower deck, its gun ports closed against the light of day. I was fairly certain that if my companions the thirty-two-pounders were called upon during the mutiny, I'd be let loose—to clear the deck for action, if for no other reason.

Once free of that concern, my mind was once again invaded by the conversation I'd been privy to the previous night. Since it happened, it had kept me in thrall with fear and anger. As ever, Egg had been exchanging rumours with his friends during the first dogwatch at our place on deck, and I was listening warily as their speculations about the Channel Fleet infected their ambitions. The mutiny was hard upon, and the need of targets for their wrath produced a long selection, not the least of which was, "Over there. See her? HMS *Director,* just put in for a fitting, sixty-four guns, and her Captain, one William Bligh."

"What, the *Bounty* bastard?" Egg asked.

"Hisself, and there you have this bloody Royal Navy. The rotten dog should have been dismissed the service for what he did, and there he is commanding a ship-of-the-line."

I didn't look, move, or speak, but I did listen.

"What was it he did?" another asked. "I thought he rowed his launch five thousand miles, or such."

"He drove his ship to mutiny is what he did . . ."

"And all those tars sailed back for their naked savage comforts on Tahiti."

"And then got hung."

"Not all. Some got away, took women with them, remember? Fletcher Christian—"

"That's right, he's the one, got clean away, hiding on some island right now."

"There's them that says he coom back."

It was Solwig, a quota-man from Perth, given respect because he could read, and did, every book and newspaper that found its way to the ship. I hoped he didn't notice that I'd stopped breathing.

"Come back? I never heard of that . . ." someone said.

Solwig was impatient of opinion countering his own. "Oh, didn't ya? It was in all the papers near a year ago. You might ha' missed readin' it." This silenced those illiterates listening and allowed him to go on. "There was these letters published, written from Cádiz, telling how the *Bounty* sailed to South America after the mutiny, and afore they was shipwrecked, they rescued some wee Spanish general in Chile. Spain brought them all back and lured Fletcher Christian to sail for them. He also wrote the mutiny wasn't Bligh's fault but done so's to return to their women on Tahiti."

As the men both remonstrated about Bligh's guilt and laughed at Fletcher Christian's luck, I wiped the sweat from my hands and forehead.

"But then the letters were forgeries," Solwig proclaimed, enjoying his oracular reversal.

"How do you know that?" someone asked begrudgingly.

"Any seaman would know that certain details written there about the *Bounty* were wrong. Also there was a notice sent to a paper, said on great authority that the letters were forged."

"How'd they know?"

"Who was it?"

I didn't ask the questions but ached to know the answers. When I heard them, I wished I hadn't.

"Wouldn't mean a thing to you," Solwig opined, giving in to his superiority. "A poet, William Wordsworth, coom from Fletcher Christian's village in Cumberland." He was right; it meant nothing to them, but it blasted me.

"So the lucky dog is still somewhere on his island then," Egg concluded.

". . . or perchance on the moon."

"That's where we should go, take over the fleet and sail to Tahiti . . ."

They laughed and conjectured further; I hurried forward to the head, for which I had an urgent need.

With Bligh across from us, Wordsworth proclaiming his authority for my existence to the world, and the fleet blazoning mutiny, being shackled to the lower deck was the safest place for me to be. My alarm gave way to anger with Wordsworth for his revelation, which in turn dissolved in what was happening around me.

The mutiny hardened, as did my opposition to it, which I expressed only when occasionally confronted by the fervent souls who came below to challenge me. One night, a group of brave ones appeared with handkerchiefs about their faces, having no other purpose than to beat and kick me where I lay chained. With no principle in mind, I stubbornly decided not to yell or fight back, but only to protect myself as best I could. I'm convinced my silence shamed them into quitting their efforts sooner than if I'd struggled with them. The result was a bloody mouth and a cracked rib, as well as a marine guard posted over me by the ship's governing council.

Those who brought me my biscuit, salt beef, and grog, or escorted me to the head, shared the news and rumours as long as they were good. I heard that the captains and all "offensive" officers on the ships had been sent ashore, that representatives had been sent to Portsmouth to confer with those who directed the Spithead mutiny, and that each ship's Delegates had every man take an oath of support. I heard a great deal of rowing about; throughout the fleet, parades of the men in ship's barges cheered. Bands in launches attended them, playing "God Save the King" and "Britons Strike Home." I was told of similar parades through the streets of Sheerness, where long-incarcerated seamen felt the land again and tasted freedom, often at a favourite tavern, The Chequers. No doubt, Egg was among them, for I saw nothing more of him, and I hoped he'd stolen away safely to enjoy a life with his son.

Two Delegates from each ship arrived daily and met in one of the starboard bays of the *Sandwich,* with hammocks hung around it as a kind of bunting. They elected their leaders, including a "President," to enforce discipline throughout the fleet. Confinement was inflicted for disrespect of orders, flogging for drunkenness and neglect of duty. The bumboats brought rum and women from shore, and both became a fixed presence aboard most of the ships. Since few had received their pay anytime in the last six months to a year, which was the greatest cause and justification of the mutiny, the men took the art of barter to an extraordinary complexity.

I witnessed much of it from my recumbent position on the lower deck. In fact, I saw and heard more than I might wish, for when a financial transaction between a sailor and a woman was completed, there was little thought of gaining more privacy than the space provided between the great guns. The nighttime traffic was intense and varied in its expression of snores, shrieks, demands, and crying. None of it contributed to a prisoner's sleep, although one night I was offered sympathy and solace by a pursy woman seemingly intrigued with my shackles. As artfully as possible, I declined the pleasure.

In such an atmosphere, I was therefore surprised by a visitor who arrived during the middle watch, a week after the mutiny began. My marine guard greeted him with respect and retired across the deck to give the man whatever privacy he wished. He had brought his own lantern, which allowed us to examine each other before he pulled over a half-empty grapeshot box from one of the guns to sit on.

"May I join you?" He was of medium height, with black hair worn long, an aquiline nose (I'd become enviously judgmental), and dark eyes that looked about him with a quick intensity.

"If you don't mind the angels' chorus about us," I said as invitation.

He gazed around with a curious smile. "There are certain traditions that even mutiny will never change. You are Gulliver, well-travelled no doubt." He spoke in a good Scottish burr with an educated polish to it, at least he knew of Dean Swift.

"I am, and like my namesake, find myself tied down and helpless."

He was amused and said, "I'm Richard Parker," and then as if
embarrassed, "The Delegates elected me their President."

"A dangerous occupation in a mutiny."

"Agreed," he said, and waved it off. "I saw you that first day
when you refused, when you opposed the cause. They might
have hanged you. Did you consider that when you spoke out?"

"That, as well as knowing that I'd surely hang if I were a Delegate."

"You were very brave."

"Only practical, and now uncomfortable."

"Enough to change your mind?"

"No. The consequences are still the same."

"What if they weren't the same?" All pleasantry was gone, his
intense excitement taking its place. "What if I told you that the
Channel Fleet has sailed from Spithead, their mutiny settled with
not a single hanging, all being pardoned directly by the King,
with their pay raised and the dismissal of fifty-nine officers, including an admiral and four captains, now on shore?"

"I'd have to think you'd lost your purpose here," I said and saw
his mouth tighten with hearing what he already knew. "But it
wouldn't change my mind."

He paused, watching me. "I want you with us."

"Why? I'm a first loader and topman who's against you."

"I care naught for your gunning, Gulliver. And I don't care what
you're hiding. You can't hide your brain, which is what I want.
Every Jack Tar on this floating prison has his secret, some part of
his life 'gang aft a-gley,' I as bad as any, for I was a midshipman
once with a future, who spoke back to a lieutenant and was dis-
rated, ended up on land, a teacher trying to stuff learning into the
empty skulls of sulking dullards. I'm come from debtor's prison,
taking my quota to pay off the debts that were my only real accomplishments, and on the journey here, jumped overboard to
save the world the trouble of me. Don't think I'll be judging you,

for what I need is your counsel. This corrupt Navy provides us with example of every human woe. We are careful to describe our conflict as being with the Admiralty, not the King. We can change this Royal Navy into a humane and democratic institution for us all. Thirty-eight ships are with us here. Soon more will join us from the North Sea Squadron at Yarmouth. Come help us, Gulliver. It does no one any good to have you wasted here."

It was a good speech, spoken with honest passion, but it infuriated me. " 'Humane and democratic'? The Royal Navy? You mean the crew will vote from the comfort of their private cabins on which battles their ship shall join? Rubbish! As long as there are wars, the military will always be pure inhuman dictatorship, inflicting order any way that serves it best, demanding blind obedience with no concern for 'humane' comforts."

"I speak of food and being paid," he said intently. "I speak of lunatic cruelty by officers who are 'inflicted' on their men and who destroy the efficiency of any ship."

I paused, not wishing to continue with a debate I knew was hopeless, or with a defence of that authority which I had overthrown in my own endeavour. "Lying here, I'm certain of just one thing: your excitement. Being 'President' of such an undertaking is heady stuff, a great flattering to have so many men entrust their lives to you. Suddenly you're in control of a shattered career, as well the fate of all who follow you. But don't mislead yourself. The King and the Admiralty have a war to fight. If the Channel Fleet succeeded in their demands, it's because of its primary importance and the totality of surprise in its action. This is a secondary fleet, not unified by purpose or command, and this mutiny is no surprise. His Majesty and their Lordships won't give in to you."

"Are you so faithful to the King?"

"That indulgence I'm denied. But I know this navy. You hope it might be changed. You forget that from our little island here, this navy rules the seas and is the only reason France hasn't overrun us. That is the power you're up against, not its failings, and that is why you'll lose."

He sat for a moment, then rose and pushed the grapeshot box back to the precise place from which he'd taken it. When he picked up the lantern, he said, "What we demand will make the Royal Navy better. The Lords of the Admiralty will recognise this, and that's why we'll win. My invitation to you stands, and whether accepted or not, I hope I may visit again."

"In my current position, it would be difficult to refuse."

He smiled, then walked away, speaking to my marine on his way to the hatchway stairs. As a result, the marine took off my wrist irons, which made sleeping easier. I recognised too much of myself in the man, the frustration and education, the seduction of leadership. Of course he led a fleet, I'd had a single vessel; he had all of England as his witness, I the privacy of an unknown sea. Therefore all of his temptations multiplied. Nevertheless our impulses were the same, and I pitied him.

It was another week before he came again, a week in which I heard the first utterings of doubt in the cause from the men. Two militia regiments appeared suddenly in Sheerness. More infantry and artillery took positions at Gravesend and Tilbury, and local furnaces were kept fired to provide red-hot roundshot against what was thought to be an invasion by the men of the fleet. The Lords of the Admiralty actually arrived at Sheerness, which gave a momentary lift to the fleet's sense of importance. It soon became clear that their Lordships would not deign even to meet with Parker and the Delegates but had come only to receive the total submission of the men, for which they would receive the Royal pardon as had those at Spithead, and be expected to return to duty.

It was during this visit that five ships showed the first signs of wavering, the red flag of defiance being hauled down from their mainmast heads, replaced for a time by the white Admiralty flag, then the red went aloft, then the white, a clear indication of the struggle on board, no doubt witnessed by their Lordships from their vantage point above Sheerness harbour. When they abruptly returned to London, their orders were to cut off supplies of food and water to the fleet. The militia was put on guard to keep the men from reaching land. Abruptly my imprisonment was shared by all.

Parker came to see me three days after food and water rations aboard were cut to bare necessity. By then the lower decks' atmosphere had altered, the bumboats having taken their passengers to shore for lack of paying customers. In the light of his lantern, I saw the price of infamy carved into Parker's face, the excitement of our first meeting now sunk into the dull black recesses of his eyes. He found an empty half cask to sit on and pulled it over to where I lay. Throwing himself down, he stared at the deck as if I weren't there.

"They've taken up the channel buoys and lights," he whispered.

There had been much recent talk of sailing the fleet from the Nore and finding some other future than what increasingly seemed certain. This was desperate madness and most knew it. Now that possibility was gone. Without the channel markers, even ships with experienced pilots would founder on the sands surrounding the anchorage.

"I'm sure you expected that," I said.

"I suppose we did," he said and sighed. "What galls me most is that they ignored us. God! Ignored us as if we were beneath their consideration."

"It is a trick of power."

He nodded. "They do it well. How can I bring them to negotiate with us?"

"Offer to surrender."

He looked at me, then shook his head and laughed. "I came down here, I'm not sure why, to speak with you, but I might as well be in the Admiralty Board Room argle-bargling with Lord Spencer himself."

"He wouldn't let you in. But you're welcome here."

"My thanks for that. It's one of the few places left. I now divide my time between those who think I've failed them and those who want me to order the outrageous. The latest is to sail up the Thames and bombard London."

"Unless they've changed since I've been down here, the men would never do it."

"I know, but those of us chosen to lead are forced ahead by those who are the loudest behind us. They command the pack, even to oblivion."

"Oblivion is your ally. Behind their posturing, they know that they can't win. It's now a question of how long it will take to starve us to our knees . . . besides, of course, the danger we create wallowing here."

"Danger? This fleet?" He laughed. "To whom?"

"To England," I shot back, impatient with him again. "Every minute that the men's pride and anger keep this fleet hostage, the chances improve that the Dutch and French fleets will pluck up their courage and break loose through our weakened blockades. The Channel Fleet could not withstand them both. The French have transport ships waiting at Calais, their army could land at Dover in hours. You invite invasion."

"You mean we should give up and be hanged by the England that ignores us?"

"No, but for the tens of thousands to be killed in an invasion, and the homes and villages occupied, destroyed and fought over for the next decade. God, man, you're not ignored. Every able-bodied seaman on a ship today is at jeopardy because this fleet is idle. The King, the Admiralty, the Parliament know that, but they can do nothing more to reward mutiny. So they have to wait . . . for you."

He chuckled contemptuously. "Would that I had such power to decide. I do the Delegates' bidding. When I counsel compromise, their favourite extremes go further than before. And you'd have us climb the yardarms now, an easy thing for you to recommend, safe in your chains."

I sat up and grabbed his arm, drawing him close to me so I could whisper, "If you'll surrender, I'll climb the yardarm with you. I'm Fletcher Christian of the *Bounty.* They'd love to have me, too. I might distract from some you'd wish to save. Use me as you will."

His jaw dropped open in surprise as I let him go. Lying on my back again, I accepted my impulsiveness and did not regret it.

"That was very rash," he said.

"True," I agreed.

"I believe you're the only man I've spoken with in the last few days who is willing to put his life forward for what he believes. Everyone else is thinking of how to escape his punishment."

"I'm not eager for mine, either."

"But you care that much for England?"

"Yes, although I've come to think there is a time for anyone in hiding when he is almost compelled to stand and yell, 'Here I am.' This seemed a proper occasion."

"I'm much impressed. You knew we put Bligh off the *Director,* didn't you?"

"I'd heard he was about."

"Yes. He's waiting for us on shore." As if this reminded him of duties to be done, he rose and shoved the half cask back to its place. Standing above me with his lantern, he said, "It's very odd. I've thought of you often since all this began, both as your former self about whom I've read, as well as who you are here. To one who's been plagued by doubt with every step I took, both of you seemed so certain. Once decided, you stayed your course come Hell and damnation. I tried to emulate that trait, without your success, I fear."

"It's easier to do with a single ship and a single life. As to my 'success,' I only had to deal with an argument. You have a cause, much more difficult, much more involved."

He nodded without conviction, then turned and walked to the hatchway. The steady progress toward the mutiny's collapse was assured in my mind from that moment, for there was an irre-

sistible alternative: the King's pardon, a second chance to return
to duty by hauling down the red flag and raising the proper
colours.

Parker struggled on, sending a petition directly to the King,
who returned it with an ultimatum and a proclamation that all
would be considered rebels if they did not return the ships to
duty. In light of that, the ships began to shift allegiance. Hoping
to divert them, Parker sent the fleet his orders to prepare to sail,
pilots, markers, or no, and fired the signal gun. Not a single ship
unfurled a sail, until two ships made a run to return to duty.
Parker himself ordered that they be fired on and worked the guns
himself of those who followed his orders. But few did, and soon
other ships slipped cable and drifted to safety on the tide, either
steering for the harbour at Sheerness or to join with other ships at
Portsmouth.

By then, those on the *Sandwich* were hungry and thirsty, and
sure of failure. Parker was the object of contempt. I sent word for
him to come if he were inclined and had no response until the
morning watch of 12 June, when he arrived with keys to take my
chains and shackles off. He did so silently, and I saw madness in
his eyes. His hair was stringy with sweat and dirt, and when he
spoke his voice was rasped and worn from shouting his un-
obeyed orders.

"They'll break up this crew into other ships, send you all
quickly to sea. You can lose yourself again, for you deserve no
more punishment." He helped me stand, which was always difficult after the shackles on my legs, and whispered hurriedly in
deference to the groups of sailors watching him, "You stood
strong against this mutiny. If England knew how much you had
affected me . . ." He hesitated because one of the groups of men
approached, intent on conversation with him. "I'm giving the ship
back to the officers," he whispered, then turned to the seamen.

I moved away as best I could and, for the first time in a month,
climbed the hatchway steps without my chains. The pain of
blood returning to familiar recesses in my feet was unpleasant

but welcome. So was the sun in which I stood by the rail during the hour it took for the transfer of command to take place, the marines to enforce order, the officers not sent ashore to take their places on the quarterdeck, and for Richard Parker to be seized by a lieutenant and, unresisting, to be confined in a cabin below under guard, mainly for his own safety.

I never saw him again. A week later, during his trial ashore, I was turned over with the first forty men to a new ship, HMS *Ardent.* Four days later, Richard Parker was hanged from a yardarm on the *Sandwich,* which was soon after broken up as being uninhabitable.

The North Sea

October 1797

"We shall have the honour to engage the Dutch flagship. Keep to your guns, and glory will be ours. The Admiral flies close action, and that's what we'll give from the *Ardent,* damned to the Devil if we don't."

The captain had his cheer, but not from me. The Dutch fleet had the advantage of the lee shore and had formed their battle line close to their coast, where their beamy, shallow-draft ships could better chance the shoals on which our first-raters might well ground. There was no time for classic strategy; the *Ardent* had been one of three ships on station off the Dutch coast when the enemy fleet appeared at the mouth of the Texel Channel. A fast lugger was dispatched with the news, which brought the entire North Sea Fleet screaming up from Yarmouth. After months of waiting, all those involved with mutiny at the Nore were eager for the chance to prove themselves to King and country before official minds might change to wreak a punishment not covered by the King's own pardon.

"Let the men know where we are," the captain bellowed.

Expanses of sea having few names, a point of land was used. "Camperdown, five leagues east-southeast."

Upon his sighting of the enemy, our Admiral Duncan had barely taken time to blink before he threw tradition to the shifting wind. Instead of forming a line of battle and sailing up to the enemy's line to fire broadsides tooth by jowl, he divided his fleet into a pair of packs, and ordered each to attack a single point. This caused havoc to the enemy's stately procession before it eased closer to the shore. He led us toward them on his flagship, *Venerable,* caring more for speed and time than any neat formation, for if truth were told, our fleet was a rushed confusion.

I was crouched beside my great gun, a twenty-four-pounder on the *Ardent's* upper deck. It was double-shotted and run out, already primed by our gun captain, who held the gun lock's lanyard, ready to fire. Headed as we were bow-first directly for them, we couldn't see the enemy through our larboard gun port. We didn't know which side would face them first, or if we broke through the line, if both sides would be firing, every one of the ship's sixty-four guns blasting away in every direction. In our thrice-weekly practises, there was a careful order to the guns, an almost dignified rhythm to the exercise. I wondered just how long such precision might last in actual combat, and if the Dutch gunners were conjecturing about the same future.

On the other side of the gun, Egg was talking to himself as usual, heaping curses on the Dutch and urging himself to heroic extremes. He'd arrived on the *Ardent* quite by chance, having been taken again by a press-gang after two months with his family. I'd spoken for him, and he was sent to the tops with me as well as to the gun, providing me the luxury of friendship, odd though it was. We never mentioned the Nore. Each of us forgave the other with silence, glad for the familiarity of our companionship. His bitterness against the Royal Navy and his fate remained a constant soliloquy recited at the start of every watch. For now my glabrous friend had even better reason. He who hadn't even an eyelash wore a talisman on a wire around his neck, a metal locket crammed full of yellow curls from his son's head. During each dogwatch, his curses to the world flowed freely as he lovingly opened the container and touched the tiny coil of hair.

"Wind from the larboard, northeast by east," the quartermaster called to indicate the slight change. There was little change in our going, for we heard the first firing from the Dutch flagship, the *Vrijheid,* answered in moments by Duncan's *Venerable* before us, which we accepted as overture for our own action.

The first lieutenant ordered silence. Even Egg had stopped his curses, and we all crouched, waiting for the forward guns to announce our entry into battle. It was my first fleet action, and I was suddenly startled by the thought that within minutes, seconds, ten thousand men on forty ships would fight a battle and a few hours later, a thousand would likely be dead and two thousand more wounded. I wondered at what level of command such numbers were considered, if Admiral Duncan included the figures in his strategy. Victory was the number of enemy ships sunk or taken as prizes. The number of men lost was a secondary consideration. I briefly turned to see captain and officers on the quarterdeck, each with his glass trained on the enemy. On deck, the other gun crews were waiting as I was, crouched by a gun, afraid of death or, if wounded, afraid of life, but even so, hoping for it and fighting down the fear with blind defiance and instant hate for the unknown enemy.

I remember distinctly that I heard Dutch shouts through the close firing before us. Then before I was deafened by it a split second later, their broadside of roundshot flew over or crashed against our larboard side, sending sharp splinters through most of us. The screams of pain began. We couldn't fire in unison, coming at them at a right angle. We had to pass the stern or bow and pour our shot into her as each gun came to bear.

Then in my memory the world slowed, although sound remained at pitch. I saw a roundshot coming over the foc's'le, but seemingly as slowly as a tennis ball, passing over us, striking the captain and tearing half his chest away, then floating half eclipsed with red over the taffrail. I felt the first of *Ardent's* guns explode, a bow-chaser carronade, and barely sensed the strange choir of my shipmates' cheer as we were released from our silent, motionless sweat. And even then, with seconds between the firing of our larboard guns as each passed by the stern of the *Vrijheid,* I felt as if I had time to observe the scene at leisure, although I was jamming the handspike under the gun carriage to move it the few inches needed to make a second shot into the enemy stern possible.

I looked up and saw the mainmast's royal yard begin to fall. It crashed into the top, split and fell in two pieces toward the deck, my bellow of warning lost in the firing, three powder boys crushed beneath. When the marines pulled them out from under and found them dead, they hurried the bodies between our gun and the next and dropped them over the side, all this a slow dance in my memory, just before my gun captain yelled and pulled his lanyard.

Deaf from all the rest, I barely heard the explosion of our gun but watched it rise up and lurch backward hard against its breech rope. In the smoke that instantly enveloped us, I was at work with worm, sponge, and rammer as Egg loaded cartridge, ball, and wad, the gun captain yelling as he pricked open the cartridge of powder through the touch hole, poured more powder down from his horn and set the gun lock. Not bothering to aim, the *Vrijheid's* transom windows being close enough for us to spit in with the wind, he barely looked to see if I was clear before he pulled the lanyard. Again the two-ton great gun lurched back on its carriage, but as I lifted the worm I saw a Dutch gun fire from the stern as we passed her. The iron ball came toward us, crashed into our neighbouring gun and split it, tearing three members of its crew to pieces, then ricocheted across to Egg's head, one sphere meeting another, the softer of the two exploding on the impact, the metal locket on its wire flying off the stump of neck and landing on the deck amidship.

I stared at it as if nothing else around me mattered, even as I rammed the gun, another man taking on Egg's loading duties, my friend's body pouring blood into the scupper. Behind me, unseen until too late, the shattered gun's carriage had broken loose from its tackle. Enough of its crew were dead or maimed so that the carriage began to slide on the deck, now slick with their blood. My gun captain yelled a warning, but it was a usual communication and I paid it little heed until I saw the carriage coming, tried to leap out of the way, but slipped and fell, my left ankle caught between a truck wheel and my own gun's bracket. I felt the crunch of bone before I fell, the loose carriage carried back by the roll of the ship. My crewmates dragged me out of its path, then left me lying on the deck, our captain bellowing impatiently for their return.

My wound was relatively minor compared to many others. In spite of pain, I stayed silent. There was no blood from my ankle, although its colour changed to purple before my eyes. We were within ten feet of the Dutchman, firing point-blank into its waist, having come up on her starboard. We were badly outgunned, not that I could see anything in the smoke, only the damage done and the bodies littering the deck. As two marines picked me up and carried me to the hatchway, I saw a powder boy holding a cartridge as it caught fire, instantly setting his face and hair ablaze. He, too, was silent, staggering to those who couldn't help him, holding out his arms for help until a bullet mercifully cut him down.

Going down two decks to the orlop was an agony, but in the surgeon's cockpit, it was exceeded by the horror around me. The surgeon and his loblolly boys were all smeared bloody head to foot, busy at their table, sawing through a leg bone. The screams of their patients, those who hadn't the luck to faint or die, pierced even my deafness. The marines who carried me found no room to lay me down, so stacked me on top of several others to wait my turn and hurried back above. My supporters groaned as I did when another was soon after deposited on me, then another, and another. Below the waterline, the air was fetid before the battle started and reeked now of wounds and every bodily excrescence. Breathing was more difficult as each body dropped on the groaning, leaking heap in which I lay, bellowing mindlessly at the horror.

How long I was there is unknown to me. The next experience of life I had was lying on an unfamiliar lower deck, my mouth filled with the taste of copper coins. My thirst was greater than the pain in my left ankle, which I was surprised to discover was still there, amputation being the treatment of choice for broken bones. The leg was, however, a strange shade of greenish purple between the dressing and the knee. Within minutes of opening my eyes, I learned from those lying nearby that the battle had been a triumph, eleven enemy ships captured or destroyed, our own *Ardent* regarded with respect for weakening the *Vriejheid* sufficiently so that she could be dismasted and finished off by HMS *Director,* under Captain William Bligh.

I might have laughed except for the splinter wounds healing on my face. I had little time for irony, for bothersome information brought the future fast into focus. We were aboard another ship, transferred from the *Ardent* to speed us to Sheerness and medical care in hospital. On pure instinct for survival, I prepared to avoid that institution, for there records would be kept. Although I'd occasionally worked over the past years without a shirt and thus revealed my tattoo to those few who took no notice, I was still wary of official scrutiny. Enough time had passed perhaps for my body's artwork not to jar immediate recognition, but I had no doubt that somewhere in the government I was still a subject of some interest. Having my description in a surgical report might make a match in some clerk's mind, making him a hero and me a prisoner.

Walking was my first concern, with money an instant second. I sat up on the deck, lost consciousness as blood drained from my brain, then after a time, struggled up to hands and knees. A crutch was a necessity, and from that position I perused the deck for shards of wood to serve my purpose. The ankle throbbed as painfully as I thought possible at the time, an extreme I was to learn was easily surpassed. Once in Sheerness, I could write my bank for funds, the postage paid by the receiver. Until they came, I had no choice but to live outside and starve, which I was certain I could do for several days, except for the unknown of what my wound would cause me. But I'd survive, I was sure of that, for when the funds arrived, I'd eat, bathe, and take the first coach to London and Daphne. With that thought before me, I forced myself to stand, the pain ending any elaboration of my fantasy.

By the time we docked at Sheerness, I had my crutch and was practised in hobbling. The ship's surgeon nevertheless silently defined the Royal Navy's hope for my recovery by giving me, still John Gulliver, an Admiralty protection instead of a sick ticket, thus implying that the damage had a permanence that no hospital could cure. This fit my purpose, and I only hoped he was the usual navy doctor who, overwhelmed by numbers, was forced to make prognoses with statistics.

His attitude was shared by those marines who helped us toward a wagon on the quay that was to take us to hospital. I told them that my friends were near; and if I were to die, I wished to be with them. They let me go, and I hobbled along to the nearest tavern I could find. Expecting to be something less than welcome, dressed as I was in the foul and ragged sailor's striped trousers, blouse, and jacket that I'd worn into battle, instead, upon my entrance I created an awed silence and then a sensation as a hero, wounded yet returning from the great victory at Camperdown.

The tavern was crowded with those celebrating the battle. I was instantly fed bread, cheese, oysters, then mutton, roasted potatoes, and carrots boiled beyond life, all washed down with a dark brown ale that did wonders for my foot. During this, I accomplished two things, one writing a letter to my bank, which the good tavern keeper took himself to the post office—no doubt noting to whom it was addressed and reaching his own, and for me advantageous, conclusions. My other success was answering questions about the battle, about which I knew nothing, having seen little before I was wounded and less from the surgeon's cockpit. So I made up whatever was needed in order to satisfy, kept eating and drinking until with a suddenness that surprised us all, I fainted dead away, falling face-first into my third helping of roly-poly pudding.

I awoke in a strange bed in a strange nightshirt, surrounded by some half-dozen women who immediately upon seeing my consciousness righteously seized me up to bathe me. I protested my modesty, and they left me with a basin and a pitcher, promising breakfast, although it was almost time for dinner. I hoped that I'd again be given that dark brown ale, for my foot was aflame, the leg's colours changed in hue toward yellow and green.

Thus was I cared for until a letter of credit arrived three days later. I never discovered who had changed me into the nightshirt and thus had seen my tattoos. Nothing was ever said. My landlord provided me with clothing, and in my honour he assembled a kind of naval-looking mufti. Nothing fit me, but I could at least look respectable in the London coach. I paid him well for all my pleasures under his roof, which included the lovely young wench sent in one night who found me in such pain, she fled in the confusion of her inadequacy to distract.

For in truth, the ankle was worse, and I knew I had to find relief as soon as possible. I was already depending on Daphne to know whom I should see, what physician could be trusted. Therefore in the coach, I gave in to imagining our meeting, our time together, recovering in Lakeland, at our cottage or another if it were already let, holding her, hearing her, seeing her. There had not been a day or a night in almost three years when I hadn't tortured myself with variations of the same dreams. I gave her credit for my having retained enough sanity to have survived, enough determination to wait for the chance to find the land again, and her. The chance was here, and no rotting foot was going to keep me from her.

The coach ride was very long, very hard. I thankfully was unconscious through some of it, the pain burning up my nerves to the spine, there to find convenient route directly to my brain. In London, I had to be lifted from my seat and, even with my crutch, found it difficult to walk. The fog was thick and yellow, making it as difficult to breathe. My fellow passengers, who'd been informed by my tavern friends in Sheerness, in turn informed anyone who'd listen that I was a hero at Camperdown. A hackney coach was summoned for me, and I was helped into it, giving one address, and then another when we were at a safe distance.

By the time I stepped down at Berkeley Square, I could barely see for the pain. As best I could, I found my way to the alley behind Cleyland House, anticipation battling with caution as I reached the carriage yard. On one side was a stable for eight horses, all in residence. On the other was an assortment of carriages in line, a covered barouche, a landau, a curricle, the largest drawn out into the yard, gleamingly new, with six ornate coronets placed on its corners and on each side of the box. An artisan was painting the door with the Cleyland coat of arms—I noted a caboshed boar's head—watched over by a head groom in grand purple livery piped in gold. Around them, footmen, farriers, and stable boys hurried about their duties—no place for a privy conversation.

"Begging pardon," I began, then gave in to coughing, the heavy fog clogging my throat.

The head groom, used to beggars of all denominations, drew himself up, nostrils flaring, dewlaps aquiver. "What is it?" he demanded.

"I'm collecting for the wounded of Camperdown," I said, amazed I'd invented so well. "Perhaps the master of the house . . ."

"Camperdown?" the head groom intoned, loud enough to get the attention of the yard. My sailor's plait and faux naval costume made their impression. He and others approached the iron gate on which I was by then leaning.

"Victory takes a bloody toll," I added for effect.

The head groom took out a coin and reached through the gate to offer it. "His Grace, the Duke of Cleyland, is in the country, most probably dogcarting with his son." This made his colleagues laugh but almost killed me. "Here's half a crown. Come tell us of the battle."

I tried to breathe and saw the fear on one boy's face as he looked at mine. "Then perhaps Her Grace might have a . . ."

"She's in the Indies, her father dying. What ship were you on?"

A horse whinnied and kicked at its stall door, turning all their heads. When they looked back, I was on my way. "I'll come another time," I said, unsure if they heard me, unsure of my next step, but not because of my ankle.

His son. And hers, of course. I was dizzied by the thought and had to lean against the first lamp post that I reached out of sight of the carriage yard. That was where fury overtook me, and I bellowed incoherently that she had been forced by social circumstance to do what she so deeply loathed. But worst of all, she wasn't there. I bellowed louder, passersby regarding me as drunk, sympathetic to me because of the wound, the visible one.

It took a little time and the return of pain to calm me down enough to consider what I had to do. A doctor was the obvious objective, but I knew of none, and I daren't go to a hospital for fear that they might force me to stay. I knew that pain was dulling my usual caution; nevertheless, I had ever-fewer choices. I hailed the first hackney coach that passed and trusted myself to the driver.

"Can you take me to a doctor?"

From his look, he'd quickly concluded my need of one. "What kind, physician, surgeon, or apothecary?"

A surgeon was the obvious choice, for they dealt in wounds and broken bones, anything that broke the skin. But they usually worked in hospitals. Apothecaries were always suspect, self-educated and often quacks, prescribing potions of their own invention for their own profit.

"A physician," I ordered, depending on the scholarship required of them, as well their private practise unencumbered by the necessity of hospital care. "The best," I added as I fell into the carriage seat.

"I knows one on Great Ormond Street; took an earl there once."

I nodded gratefully and said, "Hurry."

He did, and in spite of the terrible carriage traffic that I didn't remember, we were there in a quarter of an hour. I was kept waiting in a salon by an officious gorgon of a woman who demanded five guineas and who'd seen enough of pain to make no more of mine than an intrusion on her day. The great man himself let me know instantly how inconvenient was my interruption of his orderly routine. He was dressed in black with the requisite physician's three-tailed periwig, and his irritation quickly turned to suspicion as he examined my foot, propped on a satin hassock filled with down.

"This is quite serious, Mr. Gulliver. How did it happen?"

I thought that I should have used a different name but had no other than that on the Admiralty protection, my only identification, which I thought he'd ask to see. "A carriage went over it," I offered.

"I see," he said, reacting skeptically to the lie. "As a physician, I deal only with internal disorders, but I'll be glad to consult a surgeon and have you placed in hospital."

"I'd hoped you could prescribe some physic."

"This is a wound, sir. Drugs will not cure it. I'll prescribe laudanum for the pain, something against blood poisoning," he wrote disinterestedly as he spoke. "You should not be walking about. Gangrene is a distinct possibility."

He handed me the paper, and I struggled to pull on sock and boot. "I've wasted your time, which I regret, sir."

"You should be in hospital, Mr. Gulliver," he preached as he handed me my crutch, obviously relieved I was not to be his responsibility.

"Thank you, but no hospital, sir," I said and met his arched look of suspicion once again before I hobbled out of his sanctum.

Great Ormond Street is close to the Sick Children's Hospital, so I only needed to walk a few blocks before discovering an apothecary's shop. When I went in, I was struck by the sinister light of the place, refracted as it was through large jars of preserved body parts and tumours in the windows. The proprietor, on the other hand, was pink cheeked, wore his own hair, pure white even without powder, and gave me the impression of an angel, which I needed.

He took the physician's paper with a seraphic smile, scoffed, and looked at me. "What's your trouble, sir?"

"My ankle was crushed."

Without being asked, he sat me down on a bench and gingerly removed my sock and boot. Upon viewing the thing, he tut-tutted and sucked between his teeth. Then he smiled again and said, "I'd say you have two days. Did this grand physician tell you that?"

"No," I said. "Two days for what?"

"Two days before they'll have to cut it off or it'll kill you."

I apparently reacted, for he looked alarmed, but then there was that disconcerting smile again. "Want to try and save it? What the careful doctor prescribed would keep you drugged and happy until you had a stump or a coffin."

"What do you . . . ?"

"The names in my concoction will mean nothing to you. I'll give you laudanum now, and then you go to your rooms and take a little bolus I'll make up for you. Don't make any plans for the next week. You won't be able to move."

"Why not?"

"The only thing I'll promise you is that you won't be dead."

I nodded. He smiled. I had no rooms. "You need a room?" he asked. I nodded. He smiled. I wasn't eager to continue this exchange, but he seemed to accept my dependence, and that blissful beam of his reassured me that I'd already arrived in some earthly anteroom of heaven. When he handed me a glass of water and dropped fourteen amber drops into it, I smiled back at him and sealed our pact. Within minutes the pain had been dissolved in the tincture of opium, and within the hour I was in a room in Covent Garden, owned by the apothecary's "sister," or so he said, who seemed, in the lovely haze through which I viewed the world, as angelic as he. She poured me a glass of cider from a bottle, and he proferred the bolus, which seemed an enormous orb, more appropriate to pass through a culvert than my mere throat. Gagging with it, I eventually washed it down but not before the bitterness of the thing took a layer off my gums, or so it felt.

The moment that the pill was down, my kindred saviours looked at each other, all smiles gone, and went out the door without so much as a glance at me. As I heard the bolts close—and it was to be the last sound that I heard except my own screaming—I was flooded with the apprehension that they'd let me die, steal my money, and sell the body to the resurrection men, those specialists at robbing graves and finding unclaimed bodies for the city's medical schools. Then a lightning bolt went up my spine and fried my brains as I screamed strangely in falsetto. I fell, unconscious and presumably dead before I hit the floor.

I awoke only once during the week that I was there, a period of time discovered only after my recovery. My leg was numb, and I had a terrible thirst, but I couldn't move a muscle of my own, including those that controlled my voice. A man was moving me in great haste as a woman took my place on the bed and both of them stripped naked to consummate their financial arrangement. I was propped against a wall nearby, more concerned with the apparent loss of bones throughout my body than with the couple's amazingly gymnastic struggles and animal bawling. When they were done, I was repositioned on the bed and awarded a rather wet and searching kiss for my troubles, I presume by her.

My next waking came with a sal volatile under my nose that caused me a severe gasping.

"No harm, no harm," my celestial guardian assured me, his white hair a halo round his face. "A little ammonium carbonate to clear away the cobwebs." He smiled so intently that I could feel a heat. "Your time's up here, and your foot won't kill you. But you'll need to soak and drain it for a time, and rest, and not dare take a step on it. Otherwise all this will be for nothing."

I was weak and famished, but the body worked, my skeleton obviously replaced. What's more, the money that I had was still in its pocket. I was impressed and paid him well. My landlady agreed to let me keep the room until I could find another, and I went out with the apothecary to find food. It was a cold evening with every suggestion of winter in the fog-choked air. Walking with the crutch was difficult and became painful as blood rushed into the damage, now newly dressed and wrapped in a muffler rather than a sock and boot.

I knew I had to have help, a place to stay where I could have the steady care my ankle would need. With Daphne away, there was only one other in London who I would dare approach, and the idea of doing so was utterly repugnant. Nevertheless, within a week, by which time I'd gained the strength to do so, I waited upon my brother Edward outside the gates of Gray's Inn.

It chose to rain that day, and he chose not to appear until late that night, descending from a hackney coach, dressed resplendently in silver-buckled shoes and breeches, silk brocaded coat trimmed with gold, and lace ruffles bursting forth from every opening. Most astonishing was the absence of his barrister's wig, for it was a family joke that ever since he'd gained the privilege of the lowliest peruke for the Utter Bar, he hadn't ever doffed it, even in his bath. He paid the coachman and stood with his own thin hair pomatumed and tied behind under a large tricorn.

As he turned to the gate, I called to him. "Edward."

He stopped, gazed first at the guard at the gate to make sure he was paying no attention, then approached and urged me further into the darkness.

"If ever you come here again . . . What's happened to you?"

By then I was wet through and shivering violently. "I was wounded at Camperdown."

"Camperdown?!" His fury was evident, although contained for silence's sake. "You were at Camperdown? On a Royal Navy ship? Good God, how absurd. That battle ruined us. Ruined us!"

"How ruined?"

"Damn you, we had sullied Bligh, turned the world and even the Admiralty to our view, that your mutiny was as much Bligh's doing as yours. Do you know how hard I worked to bring that about, the friends, the favours . . . ? Then the great victory of Camperdown, and Bligh receives a gold medal for his heroism! Blast you! I'll never mention Bligh again."

"The victory was no fault of mine," I said, barely able to speak through chattering teeth. "I have more money for Mother, and I need a place to stay."

"Mother doesn't want your money, and you should go to hospital."

"I can't. You and Bligh made my tattoos famous . . . Can't you use your lawyer's gift to convince Mother to—"

"She doesn't wish to hear of you. The idea of your money sickens her."

"But did you secure Moorland Close for her?" He gazed away into the dark, which was my answer. "Then where's the money?"

He turned on me and stepped forward as if to strike. "You dare imply . . . ? Ha. What would you do, take me to Chancery Court? The money, every penny, is in a box at the Bank of England on Threadneedle Street."

"For her sake, Edward, convince her."

"She has her own mind about this. What are we to do with it? She's frightened by it. I can't even convince her to sign a will for fear the money will be discovered and point to you."

I shifted nervously on my crutch, resisting what I had to ask. "May I stay with you awhile?"

"Here? At Gray's Inn? You must be mad."

"I remember your grand chambers. There's room enough . . ."

"Understand one thing, Brother," he spat out, the relationship a curse. "You are dead to our mother and to me. Your memory is shame and embarrassment, it threatened my career until I turned it on its head. Two of our brothers gave up and died because of you. I will not. If I ever see you again I'll call the constable myself. You are a criminal, sir, and an evil one at that."

He stood before me, filled with hate and wrath, but from under his hat a lump of pomatum slid down onto his forehead from the damp. I had to smile, teeth chattering as they were.

"You are mad," he said, stalked over to the gate and disappeared.

A fever came that night, and I was in bed for another week. My landlady sent me soup on occasion, but food became less of an interest as time went by and uselessness became my everyday state of mind. I held to Daphne's return as something to anticipate, but that was a complete unknown, for she might with motherhood have changed toward her husband and toward me. I spent too many black hours at night considering that prospect. Combined with the acid concoction of life that being a cripple creates, I had little sleep. In a stupor of futility, I took to leaving my room and walking—or dragging myself along with the crutch—through Covent Garden to distract myself from my own smells, despair, and loneliness.

There was never a lack of diversion there, with costermongers, drays, the fruit and vegetable merchants, prostitutes, and theatre-goers all edging through each other with cries, laughter, threats, and occasional conflict. Still wearing my sailor's plait, I was often offered a coin for my wound without my asking, each repetition of charity solidifying my role as an invalid. My anger soon gave way to melancholy that seemed to infect my soul, which I didn't believe I had. It was my consciousness that was infected; and in those dark, exhausted, shambling hours, I saw nothing to do with myself, moving through the yellow fog from one sworl of lamplight to another as if purpose might be found in following such a route.

"Gulliver . . ."

The voice seemed an echo, and I thought that I'd imagined it. I hobbled on through the crowded street, not knowing which one, or even what day it was. But then I felt a hand on my arm, and again, "Gulliver."

I turned and looked down into the excited, delighted face of Dorothy Wordsworth.

"It *is* you. I told William so." Upon her examination, the excitement quickly drained away. "Tell me what's wrong with you."

"I was wounded at Camperdown," I said, so glad to see someone I knew, but even more so, someone who knew me. "Miss Wordsworth, what of you?"

"That's terrible. You look very ill." She looked back over her shoulder. "William's with our friends, back there, no need to worry. He saw you and sent me, we've been to the theatre. How can we see you? Why, you're a hero, aren't you?" Then she reached out to touch my arm again. "Are you all right?"

"Yes, yes. What are you doing in London?"

"Oh, so much has changed. William was given an annuity, *to be a poet*. He's written a play; your story inspired him. Covent Garden is considering it, and he's here writing alterations. We'll know in a few days. Where are you staying?"

I didn't answer, but smiled and then began to cough. She stood by awkwardly as the crowd continued past us. "Forgive me," I said, "I've forgotten how to talk to anyone. How was the theatre?"

She was impatient with the non sequitur; I might have asked her if she'd like some cheese. "Brilliant. Mrs. Siddons, *The Merchant of Venice*. You're not well, my dear Gulliver, you must let us help you. We have a house now, Alfoxden, near Holford in Somerset, two miles from the sea. The air—"

"But you're in London . . ."

She glanced back toward William. "In spite of our giddy hopes, I haven't the faintest expectation that the play will be done. We also fear the impressment gangs. William could too easily be seized. We'll be back at the house by the first of the year. Can you travel? Do you have money?"

"Yes, don't worry . . ."

"You must come. This fog, this city will kill you. Say you will. Give me your word."

"You know that promises are beyond me."

"You must."

"I'll try."

"Not good enough, but it's a start. We'll teach you how to walk again, and to talk, too. Oh, we've talkers there." She rose up on tiptoe to speak into my ear. "Remember, Fletcher: Alfoxden, Holford, Somerset . . . and your friends, the Wordsworths." Then she hurried away as I stood petrified to the spot by the sheer pleasure of having someone use my name.

Alfoxden

January 1798

The post chaise dropped me at the coaching stop in Nether Stowey. I was more dead than alive, kept from pain as well as true consciousness on the trip from London by a holy brown bottle of laudanum supplied by my cherubic apothecary. As if I needed further reason to leave town, he had informed me that enquiries had been made about my whereabouts. The original prescription that I'd given him and which he'd filled had for unknown reasons led representatives of the Home Office to him. I supposed the physician I'd approached had reported his suspicions.

I didn't care. My decision to leave London had already been made in the certainty of death and the desire to be amongst friends for that occasion, at least amongst those who knew me. The foot had become something of an unwanted and separate being from the rest of me, barely fitting in my boot, the heel split open to accommodate the foot's swelling. Again the ankle had changed its colour, this time including in the spectrum a mortal black.

Once alighted in the village, some three miles from Holford and Alfoxden, I had no alternative but to walk. A local fellow I asked for directions, upon hearing of my destination, regarded me with openmouthed suspicion and silently pointed me my way. It didn't seem far, made even less by the large sip from my brown bottle, which also had an effect on the weight of my crutch and duffle. In some odd slant of time, I found myself at the foot of the snow-spotted Quantock Hills where, nestled in a glen, a small mansion was surrounded by a wood, bare in winter. A fallow garden stood to the south, and a courtyard relieved the overbearing gabled façade with a grass plot surrounded by gravel walkways. I made my way with an increasing breathlessness until I stood gasping on the gravel as a heavy sleet began to fall. Suddenly a five-year-old boy ran around the corner of the building toward the front door. He saw me, his mouth opening with fear, then he bolted inside. Standing there suddenly filled me with doubt about my coming. The boy brought home the spectre of Daphne's son, although he couldn't be so old. I saw the heavy oak front door burst open, and out rushed the boy, Dorothy, Wordsworth, and another man with wide burning grey eyes and black loose-flowing hair, a thick nose, and full lips, at which point I managed to collapse.

"Quickly," Dorothy urged.

"What made him fall?" the stranger inquired, his baritone a stentorian projection.

"The man is ill," Wordsworth said as they reached me, "wounded at Camperdown."

Again I recognised his northern burr, hearing all this through an unfamiliar reddish haze. I even thought I heard the sea, which was impossible.

"Thank God he's come," Dorothy added. "We saw him in London."

"I doubt that God had much to do with it," the man said as he picked up the brown bottle that had fallen from my pocket.

"Rather give the Devil credit for making London his own and so intolerable to everyone else."

"Hurry, he'll freeze out here," Dorothy insisted.

"Come, Coleridge, take his feet," Wordsworth urged as he lifted me.

"One seems fearfully twisted," the man said, avoiding my wound and grasping my calf instead.

"Carefully, Samuel," Dorothy ordered as she reached out to take my hand, walking beside me and carrying the crutch. "Gently," she commanded, the last I heard of them.

I awoke with a jab of pain so intense that I sat upright, eyes wide, to see the three of them watching over an aged wrinkled crone who held the gleaming knife that protruded from my foot. From it, a purple liquid interspersed with yellow gushed forth into a basin on the floor. As if the sight rather than the pain were intolerable, I closed my eyes and fell back on the bed in which I lay, there to find oblivion again.

Whether the nightmares came before or after visions of seeing but not feeling Dorothy bathing my foot in a basin, I know not. Nor do I know if my screaming in the dreams reached reality. I was grabbed and thrown onto a pile of bodies as others fell on top of me, abruptly in the cockpit of the *Ardent* once again. My mind's creative horror gave me Egg on top of me, his separated head beside me on the deck, cursing me and the Royal Navy. I wept for him and saw his gold-ringleted son nearby, watching us, crying out for his father. I wept again, at least in the phantasm, which never seemed to end, the stacking going on, the bodies howling, Egg, his son, and I a wailing trio in counterpoint.

I don't know when I opened my eyes or why. No doubt hunger, the brightness of morning sun in the dark-beamed room, the sound of Dorothy's humming all contributed. Then I felt my foot, and it was bearable, also constricted. I managed to lift my head to look at this wonder, and found it bound, boxed tightly between pieces of wood wrapped in bandages.

"Wiggle your toes," Dorothy instructed without preamble. I did. They moved with only slight discomfort. "How splendid," she said. "How do you feel?"

It was my voice that didn't seem to work. "Hungry," I croaked.

She smiled triumphantly. "I'll bring you my bean and bacon soup. It's guaranteed to stop nightmares."

"What have you heard? I so regret . . ."

"No guilt allowed, sir. First you eat, then you talk . . . and soon you walk."

They all arrived with the soup, even the boy, who stared at me with enormous blue eyes too big for his sandy crinkle-haired head. Introductions were made and conversation galloped head-long around the room as I ate and ate, and then ate, Dorothy ladling the ambrosia from a tureen on the bedside table when-ever my bowl was empty.

"This is Basil Montague," Dorothy said of the boy as he shyly buried his head in her skirts, "the son of a widowed Cambridge schoolmate of William's. The boy's living with us as our ward for a time, until his father is settled, and we're teaching him—"

"By osmosis," my other bearer from the courtyard interrupted, moving opposite her across the bed as if it were to be their play-ing field. "The child is put out in the park to run, and by rushing along between grass and stars, the secrets of the universe are his."

"Oh, and you'd have him sitting in the cellar reading Greek," Dorothy remonstrated.

"This is Samuel Taylor Coleridge," Wordsworth offered in his deep guttural intonation. He took the chair near the fire, which was burning nicely to heat the room. "We're here in Somerset be-cause of him."

"It's all his fault." Dorothy nodded happily.

"You see what I must bear, Mr. Gulliver," Coleridge said melo-dramatically as he drifted over to the window where the sun-beams surrounded him with an aura of motes. "All this I endure, as well the contumely of my neighbours, all for the supreme pleasure of being in the dangerous company of this very great poet and his . . . overwhelming sister."

"Dangerous?" I asked, attempting to join the conversation. I was to learn there was never a need.

Dorothy filled my bowl again. "When we first arrived to live here last summer, the local folk regarded us as, well . . ."

"Immigrants, gipsies, or worse—French spies," Coleridge burst forth, anticipating the telling of his own version. Dorothy let him have at it. "There'd actually been an invasion of sorts near here at Fishkill a few months earlier. Some French troops landed, only to become lost and then mauled by the local militia, called up and thrilled to defend the nation." He moved across the room, pointing accusingly at his friends. "Suddenly, here was this strange couple who said they were brother and sister—who'd ever believe that?—with this devilish child, they only 'looking after' the wee boy, washing their laundry on the Sabbath, walking about the hills at all hours, day and night, but making maps of the pathways that led to the coast—obvious landing places for the French. The ferment of gossip frothed, and some local patriot informed the Home Office about this dangerous band of zealots . . ."

"What happened with the Home Office?" I asked, the question perhaps too close to a demand. If they were still being observed, Alfoxden was no place for me. Dorothy and William understood my tone right away and watched me with concern as Coleridge continued his story.

"They sent an agent down from London to investigate us," Coleridge said proudly. "He—the fellow's name was Walsh— Walsh took to following us about . . ."

"Is he still here?" I demanded with no hesitancy.

"No," Coleridge continued, oblivious to the tone of my interruption. "Unknown to us, Walsh was sensitive about his large, crapulous nose. He heard Wordsworth and me speaking of Spinosa, which he heard as 'Spy-nosie,' and assumed we ridiculed him. He left on the next post, quite in his cups by then, his nose thus fueled and glowing."

"Did it really glow?" young Basil queried. "I hadn't heard that before."

"The story grows with each telling, Basil," Dorothy gibed.

So the days passed, with one or all of the family—and they did seem a family to me—keeping me company at meals, Coleridge joining us almost daily. They'd wander in and speak of their work, Coleridge kindly supplying me with laudanum when my foot became bothersome. I gratefully allowed the distraction from the emptiness of my life to the fullness of theirs.

One night, Coleridge had stayed home. Because I had the Wordsworths alone, I took advantage of the situation in order to clarify an old anger.

"When I saw you in London, Dorothy, you mentioned a play . . ."

Wordsworth made a quick sound of derision. "The state of the theatre in Britain is so depraved that writing for it is an utter waste of time." His vehemence was so unlike him that I hesitated to go on. But I had my own purpose.

"Dorothy said my story had inspired you . . ."

He glanced at me, understanding my concern. "My dear friend, you inspire us all. Coleridge, still innocent of who you are, is quite taken with Fletcher Christian's adventure. In my play, I have a man corrupted by his guilt, which I assure you is my invention. His crime was to force the captain of his ship onto a barren island and leave him there to perish."

"Too close, Wordsworth." My fury made me rise from my bed. "Damnation, man, would you publicise me so?" I took two hopping steps before Dorothy rose to oppose my progress.

"No one at the theatre recognised the reference," she said steadily, "and only a few friends heard the play when William read it last year. But even if anyone did connect the stories, the *Bounty*'s mutiny is a well-known history in all of England, one that even a poet might have heard about and used for his own purpose."

"But several years ago, this poet," I said, my anger leading me to accusation, "also wrote to the newspapers about some forged letters from Cádiz, implying an intimate knowledge of Fletcher Christian's whereabouts. Doesn't it occur to you that one fine day a connection might be made?"

Surprised by my vehemence, Dorothy looked to her brother, who had not moved from his chair. "The play will never be produced," he said, "and I give my word that I'll not publish it until it can do no harm to either of us, for it is an imperfect thing." This was a difficult admission for him. "The letter I wrote willingly, at the urging of a cousin who was on your brother's panel. His supporters were not eager to have Bligh forgiven by a forger."

"Did you indicate to your cousin or Edward that you'd seen me?"

"No," he said with certainty. "No one has heard of that from either one of us. We regard your confidence as a trust until death."

Such was his probity that I felt chagrined and limped back to my bed. Dorothy accompanied me, and as I lay down, she drew the covers over me, saying, "Dear Fletcher, William doesn't even use your name. Occasionally I allow myself that pleasure, but only when alone with you. His letter to the paper caused but little notice . . ."

"A newspaper's life is half a day long before it wraps the garbage," Wordsworth stated.

"It becomes a record," I countered. "And if your name is known, now or in the future . . ." I stopped, seeing Dorothy turn to her brother again.

He rose and stood with his back to the fire, his head held high, without the slightest qualm. "There was a letter," he said, "from a friend of yours, Captain Peter Heywood."

Again I reacted with a lurch to stand, which Dorothy opposed successfully. Wordsworth gazed at the fire's shadows on the wall as he spoke.

"He wrote to ask if my apparent certainty about the Cádiz forgeries had come from any personal knowledge, which he begged to share. I replied that any knowledge that I had was far surpassed by his own, having lived through the experience he had, and that my conclusions were based only on a careful reading of the recorded history of the case and the limited access I had to the Christian family. I heard nothing more from him."

"Do you have his letter?"

"We burnt it immediately," Dorothy said.

I slumped down in my bed, my anger and anxiety infused with remorse that my past had touched the Wordsworths, and that my presence on the earth, if discovered, would obviously cause a friend like Heywood, who'd gone on with his life and career, unwanted attention to his past involvement with me.

"Fletcher," Dorothy said with deep concern, and I felt her hand on my cheek. "What is your worry?"

"Where might I start?" I said and tried to laugh.

"You're safe here, as is your secret," she assured me. Wordsworth watched from the fire, his look one of steadfast concurrence.

"Perhaps safe from without," I managed, "not from within."

Dorothy took my hand in hers, and I held to it as I would to a lifeline.

After they left, I sat up, and knowing that I risked Dorothy's wrath, unbound my foot. Strangely determined, I took away the wood that braced it and stood. In spite of their assurances and obvious affection, I had to leave them. By the time they'd finished their work downstairs, I'd circumnavigated the room a score of times and was ready for the world.

The next night, I managed to go downstairs to eat. There was something of a celebration in the dining room. Clean clothes, a bath, and my hair newly plaited—Dorothy was unfamiliar with the sailor's way but it sufficed—made me feel as if I were whole again. The ankle, still tender, caused a painful limp, but my eagerness to leave was palliative enough.

I was met with a cheer from the assembled family, which included Mrs. Coleridge, a pretty though somewhat sullen woman, with a one-year-old son named Hartley in her arms. Basil rushed around me and tugged me to my place with all the excitement of a party. Even the servant girl who'd brought my meals upstairs welcomed me with a happy smile.

"I think an ode to Lazarus is in order," Coleridge pronounced.

"There's nothing that proximity to nature cannot heal," Wordsworth intoned but with a modicum of joy.

"Not to mention bean-and-bacon soup," Dorothy amended as she slipped into her place before the tureen.

A bottle of wine had been opened for the occasion, and my glass was filled. I raised it solemnly and gained my quiet. "I wish to say that most important to my healing was knowing that brother, sister, friend, and even Basil cared, so deeply, their hearts stirred, their very souls touched . . . by my foot." Dorothy and Coleridge guffawed, Wordsworth smiled dryly, and young Basil shot looks amongst us, deciding if he might laugh. I continued somberly. "For some unearthly reason—the atmosphere about the place I suppose—a poem actually burst forth from my fevered brain. Now I, imitating my two friends' example of daily, nightly, even hourly proclamation of their work, must humbly do the same. I call it 'Ruminations on a Rotten Foot.'

> "Has any foot received the holy care
> That my extreme appendage had to bear?
> The washings, soakings, rubbings—all like prayer,
> With Coleridge's tincture, blessed and rare."

A knowing agreement rumbled from all.

> "It made me wonder if my wound had been
> To nose sublime, my knee, or hairy chin,

Would your idolatry be such a sin
That poetry and nature would drown in?

"No foot of mine shall lead you so astray.
It's now a thing to walk on one fine day,
My only hope that on our merry way
You'll deign to hear the few words that I say."

I then turned to Dorothy, and she smiled her anticipation.

"Miss Wordsworth, you who made my foot like new,
Next year I'll have it stuffed and sent to you."

My presumption was forgiven by the poets, and Basil loudly enjoyed the idea of my foot being stuffed.

"Another five drops of laudanum and he'll be the poet laureate," Coleridge opined.

I'd not seen Wordsworth laugh so heartily. "You've given us a sonnet, sir."

"I've given you doggerel and burned out my brain," I responded. "How do you two churn all those pages? I had to work very hard."

"You had a fine fever, Gulliver," Dorothy said, proud of her healing work. "That's no nightmare verse." She often had waked me from my horrors, then made me tell them her when she gave me a tea of herbs. It was then we'd ended the formality of names with each other.

Mrs. Coleridge, the child sleeping in her lap, said, "Don't waste the foot on walking with them." She was smiling, but her voice was edged. "You'll find yourself in Penzance with an empty stomach and your ears full of chat."

"Oh, Sara," Dorothy said happily, "their talk is the fuel for their exercise. I hardly need to feed them when they're walking."

"Well, Dorothy," Mrs. Coleridge retorted, "you're hardly a stranger to that diet."

We all laughed, a little more than we would to make her comfortable, including Dorothy at herself. Mrs. Coleridge seemed pleased to be appreciated, but she was envious of Dorothy's ease and equality and busied herself with the restless child, who threatened to wake.

For much of the evening that followed, Coleridge was tenacious about learning to sail the seas while still on dry land, having chosen me as his pilot. As usual, his questions came between extended blows of philosophy and poetry, leading to disjointed enquiries about the parts of ships and navigation. His interrogation continued as we walked the Quantock Hills later that night, after Mrs. Coleridge and the children were asleep. We were a lively quartet of mixed purpose, mine being to strengthen a foot, theirs to find the path of the muse.

Dorothy and I were paired by the poets' discourse and by my infirmity, which slowed me on a steep ascent. Her pleasure in her role of nurse was only surpassed by that of her patient, for her company was an effervescent joy. After hours of copying her brother's impossible scribbling into a legible form, she dove into the moonlit walk, her startlingly receptive eye darting about, feeding on the smallest details of the countryside.

"Remember," she said, "you mustn't try to keep up with those two gazelles. They are propelled by energies that we know not."

"They walk almost as fast as they talk," I said, enjoying the clear, bright night as we approached the summit of Longstone Hill to view the Bristol Channel. The still air held its edge of winter, but it was a thin one.

"William keeps up to listen, Coleridge keeps up to adore, I rush along to see what they do. A most splendid friend is Coleridge. You must speak with him sometime about his sea poem. He's struggling mightily with it."

"I will before I go."

She stopped, I thought to rest. "And when is that to be?"

"I suppose when you release me," I tossed off jocularly and saw a look pass fleetingly over her face that I was too obtuse to comprehend. Embarrassed, she turned and started off again. I followed, oblivious to little else than the splendid moonlit views, the creaking of the ancient trees around us, and my ability to move upward with little pain, dependent only on a twisted walking stick that Coleridge had supplied me.

As it happened, I left Alfoxden the next afternoon. Dorothy and I went to market day at Nether Stowey while Wordsworth was on an educational ramble with Basil. It was late morning, and I was still recovering from the excesses of the previous night, a struggle Dorothy was enjoying. As she was picking up a local cheese, she suddenly froze and gasped.

"What is it?"

"Spy-Nosie," she said and stared across the market square. Behind a wagon of turnips, I saw a prematurely balding man of perhaps forty with an incipient dewlap, a florid complexion and, yes, an extraordinary gnarled nose. But the eyes told all as they locked on me, rapacious eyes that sucked in detail, and burned with suspicion and determination. He saw that he'd been recognised and turned away, edging quickly round the corner of the apothecary shop with two local fellows who on occasion chopped wood for the Wordsworths at Alfoxden. They knew, as did the Home Office, that I was called Gulliver.

Dorothy and I returned immediately to the house, she trying to convince me that if I left so quickly, I'd give rise to more suspicion than if I stayed. It was a weak argument, and she gave it up for silence until we stood alone in the main hall, I changing into my boots and travelling coat.

"I'll walk over the hills to Porlock, catch the mail from there. He didn't follow us, and I'll be gone before he has the chance. Burn my other clothes, I'll travel light. If he comes to question you, tell him you'd met me in London, wanted to do your share for the war wounded, and offered me a place to recover."

"Can't you wait until William returns? He and Samuel will—"

"No telling where they are or when they'll come. I must ask you to give them all my thanks, for I don't have words enough to say."

"I'll try to find some for you . . . But which ones will you say to me?"

As she stood there so suddenly exposed, in the instant I saw how much I'd overlooked in our friendship. I took my hand away from the door and said, "Anything I'd say to you in gratitude would be too little. Surrounded by these word wizards, you'd not enjoy any blathering from me."

"I'd have you say a simple thing, that you'll stay, or at least come back."

"I told you once that promises were beyond me."

"But they're not beyond me." She walked slowly but purposefully to me. "I promise I'll think of you on every walk we take." Reaching up, she held my face in her hands and gently kissed me. I held her for a moment before she backed away, looking rapidly about her. "I shock myself," she said, then gazed at me with her warmest, though trembling, smile. "May you soon forget your nightmares, Fletcher Christian, and believe in yourself as deeply as your friends do." Then through the smile a tear coursed down, which she ignored.

"Dorothy, as you know better than anyone, my nightmares are of things I've done that make a doubtful gamble for any faith you'd have in me. Believe in your brother and his love of woods and hills. He was fortunate that his youthful folly never went so far that he couldn't write it all away. Lucky man. I fear at times his sacred Nature has rightfully expelled me . . ."

"Go!" she commanded. "Don't dare give in to that despair. I'll see you again before I die."

"Ah, Dorothy, I never deserved to know you, and I'm blessed that I did."

I took her hand, held it, then taking Coleridge's twisted walking stick, I went out the front door. With only slight discomfort in my foot, I hiked up into the once-happy Quantock Hills.

PART FOUR

Fugitive

From Sir Jeremy Learned's Journal

dated 10 February 1811

But I am beholden to this Fletcher Christian as my laboratory rat if nothing else. Therefore I took it upon myself to find out if there had been someone at the Home Office named Walsh. Indeed there was; he was still there. My patient once again had done his research. Not wishing to involve officialdom, which is always bothersome, I decided instead to write both William Wordsworth and Samuel Taylor Coleridge.

Asking only of "Gulliver," I took care to have both letters sealed and franked from Windsor Castle to give them more of an impressive air than a mere physician could command. I did not do this as a convert; the man who calls himself Fletcher Christian is a lunatic with a severe though quite ordinary mania of one who prefers to be someone else, famous or infamous, depending on the elements of character required. I wrote the two poets on the chance of discovering when the man's delusion had been made manifest, if he'd actually appeared to others as Fletcher Christian—and thus Gulliver—early on, in 1794 at Windy Brow, or in 1798 at Alfoxden.

My own belief is that he'd lived an educated but somehow injurious life that at some point drove him to madness and the person whom he'd become. However, I doubted that his created Fletcher Christian had actually appeared in the real world. I was proven wrong.

An answer from Wordsworth's sister, Dorothy, arrived quickly, a very brisk reply denying any knowledge of such a person named Gulliver, and wondering if my careful reference to Windy Brow revealed me to be from the Home Office rather than a doctor at Windsor. She reminded me that her uncle, Cookson, was a canon at Windsor Chapel, and should I have further need of information about her or her brother, I might consider approaching their uncle to save my good time. She would by the same post alert him of my interest in them and hope for my satisfaction. I could well imagine that alerting and hastened to Canon Cookson to assure him of only an idle curiosity about someone who had used his well-known nephew's name.

Then Coleridge's letter came. Although he was in London and the Wordsworths in Lakeland, Coleridge's message arrived ten days after Miss Wordsworth's. It was, however, longer, with three pages of military analysis as to why Wellington's bare grip on the edge of Portugal was England's greatest hope against Buonaparte, two pages about his unending faith in the Trinity, one page—Note: the writing changed dramatically into a large looping scrawl—about the Wordsworths living on their own Olympian height in Lakeland and therefore having but little time to consider the past or the nature (which he put in quotes) of friendship, and at last a final sentence in answer to my enquiry, which I record here, as I discarded the rest:

There was a Gulliver the last year we lived in Somerset, a sailor as I remember, whose mind I culled for sea nuggets that I wished to make gleam in my poem of the Ancient Mariner, and who should be introduced backwards into the bowels of hell if he is claiming, as others have (see above), to have had a busy hand in that poem's creation. I am, sir, your most obliging, etc. . . .

This petulant defence seemed as odd as it was unnecessary, and the implication that Wordsworth was already guilty of such claims led me to make enquiries. I had read the second edition of the poets' splendid collaboration, Lyrical Ballads, *and had been impressed by Wordsworth's majestic poetry of the natural world and his preface describing a new genre of poetry. But "The Rhyme of the Ancient Mariner" was surely by another unique and giant talent, just as surely Coleridge. Wordsworth's petty, even cruel comments in the book's introduction to that poem showed him to be less than a friend.*

First through gossip, then through medical colleagues, I learned that over a decade, Coleridge had become severely addicted to laudanum as well as to drink, in combination or separately. His marriage a shambles and his finances worse, he had left his wife and three children in Keswick, where he had been in residence (and in proximity to the Wordsworths a dozen miles away in Grasmere), to come to London, hoping for work as a journalist and for a cure. At present, he writes passionately of current events for The Courier *and consults various physicians—one an acquaintance of mine—about his addiction. There seems to be a frigid* crise *between the two poets, but of its reasons, I know nothing.*

Therefore, according to Coleridge, Gulliver did appear, as early as 1798. Perhaps he'd met Coleridge in Nether Stowey and expanded the story to include Alfoxden without ever meeting the Wordsworths.

Then there is this afternoon's conversation with Sir John Barrow of the Admiralty. I find I hesitate to put this down, for those rumours that conversation allows as interesting amusements tend to permanence when written on the page. But these facts are harmless here. I'm dealing with a madman, and facts, of course, only lend irony at best.

I'd intended to call on Sir John before this, but time had not allowed. I saw him at Brooks's and when I mentioned the subject of my enquiries, he revealed a look of amazement before his military mask hardened into its usual stern visage. After listening a few moments, he invited me to walk with him to the Admiralty, as his obligations as Second Secretary there were pressing. Once abroad, amongst the milkmaids and their cows in St. James's Park, I realised within a few words that his true intention was privacy.

We have been friends for many years, useful to one another in exchange of pertinent news of Court and military matters during the war. Trust is well established between us. As we walked along, he told me that the Admiralty had learned a year and a half ago that the final resting place of the Bounty *was a mischarted island in the South Pacific called Pitcairn. Only one mutineer was still alive, the rest dead by various means, including Fletcher Christian. The news had aroused little reaction at the Admiralty, which had numerous uses for its frigates other than sending them to capture a single, old, and from what the reports said, enfeebled mutineer on the other side of the globe.*

Then Barrow stopped me. He made certain that we were away from anyone's hearing and recited an insistent preamble of secrecy. Only then did he tell me that on recent visits to his childhood home at Ulverston in the Lancashire part of Lakeland, he had heard "rumours," a term he emphasised, that Fletcher Christian had been residing in the area under the protection of his cousin, John Christian Curwen, M.P., the distinguished and respected member from Carlisle, whose wife, Isabella Curwen, was the heiress to the Workington mining fortune. Mr. Curwen apparently had taken his wife's name at the time of the mutiny.

I reasoned with Barrow that such a romantic rumour was easily imagined, that indeed my patient had included a genuine nemesis from the Home Office named Walsh, and that Lakeland being a well-known refuge for fugitives of every degree, the supposed unjust infamy heaped upon a local son added to the ro-

mance. He agreed with me, but then added, again with a call for secrecy (which thereby marks this part of my Journal for the fire, alas), that a young friend of his by the name of Peter Heywood, formerly a midshipman on the Bounty *and now a captain in the Royal Navy, had actually seen Fletcher Christian a little more than a year ago along Fore Street, Plymouth Dock. Heywood had called and run after the man, but he escaped. So certain was Heywood that it had been Christian (they had been the closest of friends on the* Bounty*) that the captain was driven by duty to report his sighting, he hoped discreetly, to one who was official but who might be sympathetic. Because of family connections, he chose Sir John.*

Barrow chose to regard Heywood's story as delusionary, and thus relieved the captain of his responsibility to duty. As we continued our walk through St. James's, I idly told him more of my patient's story, even those details involving the Duke and Duchess of Cleyland. He expressed an interest in my patient and, should I regard it as helpful, a desire to read his manuscript. In his tone but unspoken was speculation that Fletcher Christian might be alive in England. I assured him that my patient was a madman and told him of our Napoleons as well as our St. Catherine, who in the last fortnight had managed to carry her imitation to its logical conclusion by starving herself to death.

I left Sir John at the Admiralty and took a hackney coach to Bedlam, not out of any sudden urgency based on what I'd learned, but to check once more on my Royal patient's surrogate, for I am due at Windsor tomorrow. Upon entering the cell, I was surprised to see the Fletcher Christian hunched up against a wall rather than where was usual, at the table I'd procured for him, as well as a stool, for his writing. Also, there was no stack of foolscap filled from edge to edge for me to read. This attempt at capturing our conversation is from memory and therefore not exact.

"How goes the writing?" I asked.

"I'm done . . . No purpose to going on."

"The telling has served a healthy purpose . . ."

"There's too much pain in the rest of it."

I decided to go around the subject. "I spoke of your manuscript to Sir John Barrow, Second Secretary at the Admiralty. He would be interested to read it, when it's done."

"For the pleasure of hanging me, no doubt. Well, he can do that now. There's enough there already for that."

"No, not for that, but for an expert reading, one far better than mine to judge the truth . . ."

He looked up at me then as if he pitied me. "You try and try to motivate my next breath."

"No matter who you are, I want to know what happened." I'd hoped for the humour of irony, but as so often happens, I was met with despair.

"You know what happened to Daphne. They made Bligh the governor of New South Wales in Australia. Blast me if I haven't lived this madness once. Another time is torture."

"Yes, another time, perhaps the hundredth time, and another hundred to come, and every time is torture, is it not?" I asked this angrily, as an accusation, which instantly secured his attention. His story was my weapon. "Coleridge's Ancient Mariner compulsively retells the events of his crime, trying to reconcile himself to what happened, an attempt in which he is surely fated to fail. You torture yourself in the same way by reliving a life that you insist has been fouled by a mutiny. But in the telling of your tale, you blindly overlook the good of it. You write that you offered your life to convince Parker to end the mutiny at the Nore; perhaps you saved England an invasion. What you suffered and accomplished at Camperdown makes any other man a hero, honoured by his countrymen. Who can tell the effect you had on Coleridge's poem? And what you describe with Daphne Lewis is an envy to us all. Why do you obliterate your glory, man?"

I'd said all this in the heated style of debate, and when I saw him rise and step toward me, I thought it was in anger and feared the worst.

"You believe me, Doctor! You cannot deny it."

"Nonsense. I do deny it," I hastened to interject, realising instantly the serious error I'd made by joining in his fantasy. "I don't believe you are Fletcher Christian. You've created a history in your mind for your own need, whatever it is, your intelligence allowing you to complete the portrait to an amazing degree, even testing it on others. If you must do all that, you must, but you must also be fair and consider the positive aspects of it."

He stood a moment, said nothing more, then with an irritating, even confident smile, he went over to his table, sat on the stool, and without regard of me began to write again. I knew from past experience that there'd be no further conversation, so I left.

After further consideration, I'm not concerned about feeding his delusion with my little peroration on his "glory." (Gracious, what a choice of word.) Rather, I believe I practised the best kind of "moral treatment," playing upon his need for esteem, which can be given simply by seeming to accept a small degree of his colossally imagined story.

What if the cure for madness is simply to believe the mad? It couldn't be worse than believing many of the sane, those charlatans whom we trust with our souls and fortunes, those heroes who lead us through this catastrophe of war. Whom would I trust to tell me of the world's sad truth, the poor King and this Fletcher Christian, or Buonaparte and Wellington?

London

May 1798

Daphne was back in London. The week-old newspaper, a copy of the *Morning Chronicle,* had slipped under the seat pillow of the mail coach I took as I was traversing Wales. There was a column devoted to the activities of the nobility, earls or above. The Duchess of Cleyland had returned from the West Indies after burying her father. Within an hour of reading the news, I was on a post chaise to Bristol, there to connect with the Flying Coach for London, accomplishing the ninety miles in the brief space of seventeen hours, with stops for dinner, tea, and supper. We would arrive at the Old White Horse Cellar, Piccadilly, near midnight, and I supposed I'd have to try to sleep until the next morning before calling at Cleyland House.

Wales had been a perfect place for me to disappear, and the spring had been sublime. I spent much of it on the road as one of the great band of itinerant peddlers, beggars, tinkers, the discharged and wounded from the war. After the convivial companionship I'd left behind at Alfoxden, the loneliness at first was like a stone on my heart. My mood was further affected by not having laudanum, which made me realise how much I'd been habituated to it and the weight it had on my mind. Avoiding conversation with those I met walking, I ached for Coleridge's swirling exegeses, for Wordsworth's chanted observations of the earth's soul, and most of all for Dorothy's effervescent wit and joy and lightning perception. The two elms in the garden where I observed their walking's thirst quenched with flip, the herd of deer in Alfoxden's park that raised their heads in unison when one appeared, gazed a moment, then bounded off when Basil ran ahead to try to greet them, Dorothy bullying me to build my strength with a basin of broth; indeed, I was homesick for a family, my poetical chimera. It was a short-lived luxury, realised only after the spending of that short time with them, so quickly gone. Dorothy's kiss, of course, forced the consideration of a possibility, one I quickly quashed in spite of deep affection, my being a danger to them and still loving another, who was at present an even more improbable prospect.

I considered all this as the Flyer, advertised as "hung on steel springs," nevertheless managed to jar our back teeth loose. I still travelled with the instincts of a fugitive, watching all my fellow passengers' eyes for undue curiosity. I didn't know how much of a look the agent Walsh had stolen of me that market day, but I had no doubt he'd returned to Nether Stowey afterward, because the name of Gulliver was growing familiar at the Home Office. The suspicious physician presumably had originally brought the name to their attention based on my strange refusal of a hospital. Then Walsh. In time of war, any suspicion caused alarm, and any repetition of a name aroused the spectre of a plot or a conspiracy.

I'd left Gulliver and my sailor's plait in Wales. As the coach jolted along the turnpike through Knights Bridge past St. George's Hospital, the coach guard's trumpet blared our arrival. I christened myself anew in time to be John Harris when I alighted at Piccadilly.

The usual crowd was gathered in the coachyard, street arabs eager for errands or a chance at a pocket, beggars, a typical gang of thieves waiting to make off with unwatched luggage, smashers from inns selling their establishments and offering to change passengers' good money for counterfeit. I even spied a pair of louts who reeked of the press-gang. With a certain flair and the security of my Admiralty protection, which I still carried, I let them see my limp, exaggerated for their sake, for my foot was healed as well as new. I still used Coleridge's twisted stick, but more as a remembrance and a weapon than for support. Slipping into the dark lanes as quickly as I dared, for I had no luggage, I made my way to a low lodging house nearby. It had a reputation for thievery, but having little to be stolen, I meant to pass the interminable hours there until I could go to Daphne.

She might not be in residence. Upon return from her voyage, she could have chosen the country, with her son. The thought of him still muddled me, and as I climbed the inn's stairs to my room, I tried again to figure how much a woman changes when her focus centres on a being she created, how much shared parenthood might perforate the wall that previous circumstance had built between the Duke and Duchess, husband and wife, but now mother and father. I knew I wouldn't sleep and didn't bother to undress but lay on my bed, imagining her family, fighting despair, and preparing for rejection.

Fortunately distraction came, although not a kind of my choosing. Having conjured the adoring family in a dogcart, laughing as they circled their castle's park, I was busy torturing myself with their happiness when I heard a carriage pull up outside, with a restless horse, stamping and blowing. The streets were ever crowded, even at three in the morning, so this was not surprising. But in my restlessness, I rose idly to look out the window, and there through a thin fog, in the lamplight, stood Walsh, surrounded by half a dozen men, all watching another hobbling about with a stick, gesticulating its twisted shape, in obvious imitation, I concluded in that second, of me.

I didn't hesitate and left my room, as well as Coleridge's betraying walking stick, and bounded to the stairway. Halfway down, I saw three of Walsh's crew being admitted at the front door by the irritated owner. Up was my only escape although a route unknown to me. I climbed to the top floor of public rooms and chose a door. Knocking loud enough to wake a dead man, I heard at last the furious blustering of an occupant stumbling toward the door, which he opened.

"You pig scum, who's this that—"

"Those of us who dwell here understand my need, which is your window."

"My window? You whoreson bleeding . . ." Sudden understanding snapped open both his eyes, and he became my conspirator. "In a dustup, are we? Help yourself," he said, indicating an already open sash. I sprang across his room without the slightest gratitude expressed and began my exit. Unfortunately I was still on the same side of the building as the street in which Walsh still stood in the lamplight. But, for my luck, the window gave me access to a drainpipe leading up a gabled window to the roof. With as much grace as my recent indolence allowed, I moved quickly hand over hand on the drainpipe, up the slanted roof. Then my luck turned fickle, and I stepped on a loose slate, sending it sliding noisily on its way to the roof's edge, then falling to the street, where it shattered within five yards of Walsh's feet.

His whistle blew. Yells of the chase went back and forth around the inn as I reached the roof's peak. Balancing on it as if it were a yard, I hurried through the fog, thicker at that altitude, toward the next roof, to which I leapt, and then the next. I had no plan and barely could sense direction, but the yells from below followed me with unnerving accuracy. I slipped and fell, holding to a ridge of tile, looking back and seeing two pursuers on the roofs, moving carefully through the fog. "We see him," one bellowed, which motivated me to scramble up and onward, wondering what I'd do when the block of buildings ended.

My faithless luck returned, for there before me was a massive construction with webs of wooden scaffolding reaching up so high it was lost in the fog. Another bellow from my hunters sent me climbing whilst refusing the consideration that "up" had limitations too, as any treed badger knew. Again my topman's skill served me well, and although the scaffolding was not as friendly as good ratlines, I had little trouble making my way. "He went up," I heard one say doubtfully, and then the other state with bravado if not courage, "And so shall we." I reached the top and found some old friends there, the blocks and tackle used to haul up heavy building blocks, hanging on a center stanchion. Tied firmly to the stanchion were the ropes that anchored it below, quite like a ship's mast held by shrouds and backstays. I couldn't see to where the ropes led but had no choice. I put the hook of a running block on the stanchion's base rope, took a firm hold on the tackle, and swung my legs up to control my descent. As I started to slide, I heard a shaky cry, "God's blood, the ground's gone!"

"Don't look down!" another voice suggested.

"I won't, and won't go up, either."

I passed between them then, gathering speed, close enough to blow a kiss if I hadn't been so occupied.

"There he goes!" "He's coming down!" they bellowed with relief as I fell past, suddenly finding my path blocked by a building beam. I hadn't time or strength to stop, so had to swing myself to one side. My back was grazed, but I plummeted on, the occasional beam avoided as before.

Breaking through the fog, I saw my rope was tied off to a huge stone block that would have made a jelly of me had I kept my speed. As I tightened my legs to brake the fall, thus scorching through my trousers, I saw Walsh running toward me. Hearing my approach, he aimed and fired a pistol. Happily, he missed, and when I reached the block of stone, I was able to push off and fly just far enough to fall on top of him. We struggled and punched. In spite of rope-burned thighs, the advantage was mine. Even in my urgency, I admit I was transfixed when I found my eyes in proximity to his nose.

"Who are you, man?" he growled, taking in each detail of my face.

"No one worth this trouble," I managed as I pinned him down.

"I do not give up, sir. I'll know you one day soon."

"But not tonight, sirrah," I demurred, then hit him hard across the jaw and left him lying for his colleagues to find. I ran through lanes and alleys until it brought unnecessary attention, then tried to melt into the cobblestones under the ever-thickening fog.

I managed an hour of sleep, lying low against a wall. When the city began to wake, I was already arrived at Covent Garden, there struck of a sudden with sartorial concerns. I bought some clothes, better than I'd worn since I'd come ashore from Camperdown, went to a rooming house for a bath, and struggled to arrange my chopped hair in some pleasing order. Still barely in control of my eagerness, I visited a coffeehouse and busied myself with morning papers filled with reports of the French fleet's escape from Toulon during a gale that blew Rear Admiral Lord Nelson's blockade squadron almost to Sardinia. My breakfast added to distraction, along with enough Turkish coffee to infect my nerves with cymbal crashes. I read vivid descriptions of the French fleet, three to four hundred transports and warships, carrying forty thousand troops with artillery and cavalry, all commanded by "the people's general, Napoleon Buonaparte." The unanswered question was, where were they going? Malta? Gibraltar? Ireland? or finally England? Whether from coffee, news, or personal anxiety, I could no longer sit still, and rushed out onto the street, to walk until I couldn't wait any longer.

I reached Berkeley Square at nine, carrying the note I'd written and sealed at the coffeehouse. Still chary of anyone's front door, I hurried to the Cleyland House carriage yard. Unlike on my previous visit, the place was frantic with activity. The covered barouche I'd seen being painted with the coat of arms was in the last stages of having its matched black team of four harnessed. The head groom, again in resplendent livery, berated everyone. Two liveried footmen and the coachman were already at their places on the carriage. One horse kicked impatiently at the splinter bar, worrying the grooms as they wrestled with the final buckling of harness.

The gate was already open, and the head groom shouted at me with imperial disdain, "Out of the way, there, for Her Grace's equipage."

I leapt aside, jolted by his implication that she was there. The carriage moved quickly past me and down a passageway to the square. I quickly approached the head groom, sure of no recognition from my visit a half year previous.

"Please see that Her Grace has this in the next five minutes," I said as I gave him my note and a fiver, a considerable sum for such a favour, but I had no edge of time for hesitancy.

The head groom was suspicious but, thankfully, greedy. "She's on her way . . ."

"Best hurry," I advised, then added, "If you're successful, I'll have another five-pound note for you."

He left me with as much dignity as his eagerness allowed. I stood in the spot as if the sheers had dropped me onto a keelson, wondering if I'd written enough—or too much if intercepted. "Charles I, one hour, urgent," was all I'd said. I suddenly thought it could be read as wishing for an hour to spend, rather than meeting in an hour. As I began to sweat with this, my costly postman reappeared, his hand outstretched. She'd be there! I paid my obligation and ran to find a hackney coach.

The hour passed, a grain of sand at a time, I trampling a moat around the statue, ever watchful for Walsh's men, ever terrified I'd missed her. Then suddenly from the Strand, the Cleyland carriage appeared in the fog, forcing its way through the axle-to-axle traffic, moving over to pass next to Charles I. When it came by, it didn't stop, but the door was thrown open. I ran to it and leapt in, landing in a heap on the floor at Daphne's feet.

I looked up as she pulled the cord and slammed the door shut. Then she turned her staggering green eyes on me. She was dressed as a duchess robes herself for town, in a visiting frock of diaphanous white silk, very thin, worn over only light stays, cinched up high under the breasts and cut low to reveal them. Over the dress was a sleeveless pelisse reaching to the knee. Her bonnet was an elaborate confusion of black-and-white dotted bows, and under it, her hair was still in long ringlets that cascaded to her shoulders. Her lips were red, and wet, and unsmiling.

"You're late," she said. "You were expected, what was it, four years ago?"

"Do we have privacy here?" I asked as I lifted myself to the seat opposite. I noted the window curtains, which had been drawn, as well as the gold sconces and flowered chintz upholstery of the carriage. There were pillows everywhere.

"Complete, except for entrances and exits."

"I was press-ganged that night, then turned over from ship to ship six times without touching shore. I was at the Nore at the time of the mutiny, then Camperdown." Her eyes widened with imagining the details. I went on. "I didn't know who might read your mail. When I was put ashore because of my wound, I came instantly to Cleyland House. You were in the Indies . . ."

"My father died," she said impatiently. "Wound?"

"My ankle stood in the way of a twenty-four-pound great gun and came out the worse for it. Better now."

She watched me without a trace of care, or none that I could see. I believed I'd lost her, that curiosity had brought her to the meeting. Then she said, "I've ached for you each day since then," and came across the carriage into my unready arms.

I didn't know a kiss could suck so much of past and pain away, but as relief convinced me once again that she was mine, I kissed and touched her for the future times that I'd have need of such remembrance. We'd as soon have avoided words, but questions sprang from both of us, and answers found their urgent path between our kisses.

"How long do we have?" she asked. "Your note almost killed me with surprise."

"I must leave England as quickly as possible. The Home Office is searching for me. But tell me—"

"Do they know who you are?"

"No, but they can read tattoos as well as you if given the chance. Are you . . . ?"

"Couldn't we hide in Lakeland?"

The idea stabbed into my purpose and twisted there, infecting me with ruinous temptation. "They discovered me in Somerset, and waited for me in London. They're too excited now, no place is safe."

"You mean you came to say good-bye to me again?"

"As I remember, that's not allowed. I came so you'd know I'm still alive, determined to come back to you, if that's your wish."

"My wish? It's one of the two reasons I breathe. The other is your son. I'd have brought him, but he's in the country with His Grace, the Duke."

My mouth went dry as the scuttlebutt in the doldrums. "What are you saying?"

She lay back across the seat against the pillows and removed her bonnet, enjoying her surprise. Her smile was enough for life. "I can count nine months as well as any, Fletcher. Soon after I left you in Lakeland, I knew that I was pregnant, before the Duke returned to London. The date of his last dutiful effort could be stretched to fit my predicament. From the moment I told him, we became the best of distant friends. He has his heir, and we've lived separate lives ever since, he with several mistresses." She reached to take my hand. "Your son, named James, for your greater assurance has your eyes and mouth exactly, as well as the courtesy title of the Earl of Bowfield."

I sat, a sack of bones and blood, bewitched. "James . . ." I repeated.

"Are you pleased?"

"Pleased? You hurl this bolt of lightning that splits me into one half exploding joy, the other charred grief that I can't know him, or be known to him."

"You can. You will," she stated positively, then laughed as she presented her next surprise. "He'll adore our Lakeland cottage, which I bought through agents who—you must trust me—cannot be traced."

Again the place appeared to me, this time with a son running about. I took her in my arms and let my gratitude complicate our kisses. She responded to my hands on her as I dared glimpse the prospect she described, but the absurdity of such a hope occurred to us at the same time. We hesitated in our embrace, holding each other, but looking off at different voids.

"What are your plans?" she asked stoically.

"To find a ship, perhaps a merchantman, to float me away to anywhere, it doesn't matter."

She sat up straight. "It does to me. I'll have it a short voyage, thank you very much." With that, she pulled a cord, which made a knock above.

A panel to the coachman slid open. "Yes, Your Grace?"

"Take us round to Blackfriars Bridge, then to the Upper Wet Dock, the dockmaster's hut. There's no urgency."

She lay back again on the pillows and reached to undo her stays. "A great many merchant captains ate well at my father's table since I was a child. We'll wander down and see who's in port, find you some proper gear. In the meantime, let me welcome you to my travelling boudoir. We have a little time, too little as always . . ."

It took us several hours to cross over Blackfriars and through Southwark. Not a minute was wasted. We managed somehow to know each other again as if we'd spent our lives together, or so we believed by the time we arrived at the dock, where a hundred merchant ships were berthed for loading and unloading, protected from the wind by the surrounding double rows of trees. Our first stop was a provisions shop where I purchased used clothing and supplies suitable to the merchant officer that once I'd been. In the crowd of heavy drays and wagons, the Cleyland carriage was noted. Daphne recognised three American ships among the first ten we passed that had carried rum for her father. The dockmaster, aware of the carriage outside his hut, was all courtesy when I made request of him for introductions, and he asked me if I had an Admiralty protection. All the American captains insisted on the document for fear of the Royal Navy's tendency to steal their crew right off their ships. I showed him mine, but made certain that the name he used for me was John Harris, a name change being a common request by sailors for any number of reasons.

When she heard the name of the captain to whom I was directed by the dockmaster, Daphne laughed aloud. "I remember him well, and he'll remember me. I informed him at dinner one day that it was rude to scrape his spoon across the bowl while eating his soup. Quite the proper little snob I was at ten . . . But you'll like Mr. Cronley. He's a tip-top man." She took a calling card from her reticule and reached into a small cabinet inlaid on the wall of the carriage. Inside was an inkhorn and a quill, which she used to scribble a note. I took it with me up the gangplank to pay my addresses to Captain Cronley of the three-masted barque *Salem Glory,* loaded with hemp and cotton for the Levant.

A craggy, pipe-smoking American, the captain's first reaction when he let his sharp blue eyes fall on the card I handed him was to chuckle. "Oh ho, she was quite the young lady, she was. Told me how to eat. So you sailed for that old goat-stomach Sir Richard Lewis? He's dead, you know."

"I'd heard he died."

"Think you'll enjoy an American ship, Harris?"

"Aye, sir. I'd be happy to be aboard."

"And I to have you with your protection. The rotten Royal Navy's stolen half my crew, pressed my last second mate right off the ship in the chops of the Channel. We sail with the tide to Constantinople, the sunny Med after this foul fog of London. Bring your gear aboard afore that, sign on the Articles, and find a place below. You're invited to my table for supper."

"Thank you, sir. I'll be there."

I hurried back to the dock and found Daphne's carriage parked at a discreet distance. I knocked and opened the door to find her quickly wiping tears away. "What are you doing here so quickly?" she accused. As I sat next to her and closed the door, she added, "And how can you be here and leaving me so quickly?"

"I'll be back."

"When?" she demanded. "Constantinople is a bit farther than Dorking."

She let me hold her then, and allowed me to avoid answering her question. Instead, I reminded her, "You wrote me once that our greatest danger was going mad from not having what other couples have . . . that because of who we'd become by the time we met . . ."

"Those two strange fish . . ."

"Yes. We'll never have all we want. We're damned to that and can't expect anything better."

"A terrible word, 'never' . . ."

"But what we have is more than most. Surely it's more intense for being so little. So longed for, it becomes the light in the rest of our dark and hidden lives. It's left to us to find the ways to overcome the world and be together. This my second life began with you, and whether with you or without you, I honestly believe I breathe with you." She laughed and smiled at me, delighted. "I even imagine that when my heart beats, it does so just to keep up with yours. They say it's madness to live like this for love, but now you've given me a son. Great bounding balls of fire, Daphne, a son! Not in name, not even in presence, but in *being,* already I'm listening for his heartbeat to keep yours company."

"If you don't come back soon, I'll come looking for you, I promise you that."

"No need. You already haunt me every minute of my life. I'll come back to you, as fast as I'm able."

Suddenly she sat up. "You must write to me. What madness! We forgot to arrange . . ."

"Do you have a friend that . . . ?"

"A duchess has a thousand friends," she said caustically, "not one of whom I'd ever trust with you. Tell me your birthday. I've never known it."

"The twenty-fifth of September."

"The twenty-fifth day of the ninth month. Write to . . . Mrs. Derwent Fish, as good a name as any, care of the London General Post Office, box 259. I'll write there as well, unless you tell me of a place as safe. If someone else has the box, I'll buy it from them."

"The pleasures of privilege."

"They're damn few, and you're most of them. Now go, my dearest. Since birth I've known the tides and yours is soon. Besides, I won't stand another moment of this leaving. Come back to me, Fletcher, as soon as you can. I want you to meet our son."

It was something beyond will and survival that moved me out of that carriage and, carrying my new duffle of stuff, back to the barque. After waiting so long to see her, I couldn't quite believe I was leaving her after what was little more than a day visit. That angry battle took over my mind, and I remember nothing of stowing my gear in my cabin and finding my place on the quarterdeck as the ship was prepared to sail. Apparently I met my fellow officers and observed the quality of the crew going through their routine of casting off, and finally I stepped down to the waist to supervise the setting of the mainsails.

It was there that memory serves again, for over the bulwark, I caught a glimpse of white, and as I shouted orders to the top or to the men hauling on the sheets, I edged my way to the rail. She was standing on the quay, watching the ship, but as we made way out into the basin, she strolled to the end of our dock and stood there as long as I could see her as the ship passed into the Thames. She never waved, nor did I. She watched until we disappeared beyond the windbreak trees, at which point I went blind again to anything aboard and flailed about on deck like some demented bat, I'm sure. Somehow I managed my duties and enjoyed the captain's table, where I learned firsthand of my fellow officers' blunt-spoken camaraderie, in which I was quickly included with that peculiarly hospitable American enthusiasm. I was to be the officer of the middle watch, from midnight to four, which allowed me after supper to begin the only letter I was ever to write on that voyage.

It went well, and was, as merchant shipping often is, tediously uneventful, except for two occasions. The first was on our return from Constantinople, when the convoy we had joined for our protection was blown in all directions by a gale. After a night as black as the Earl of Hell's riding boots, the young midshipman sent aloft at first light roused us all by informing us, his voice cracking up and down with fear, that we were within ten cable lengths of a fleet, a dozen unflagged ships-of-the-line, with two accompanying frigates already on their way to investigate us. As he raised the Stars and Stripes, Captain Cronley began a great broadside of grapeshot curses at them. If French, they'd take us as a prize; if British, they'd impress the crew. When we were in range of their guns, they broke their colours, and in spite of my own trepidation, I was glad to see it was the British ensign. As one of the frigates bore away to return to the fleet, the other hove to.

"*Salem Glory,* ahoy," came the captain's call through a speaking trumpet, but before he could introduce himself, Cronley bellowed back, "We'll have no boarding, sir. I'm short of crew myself, and can afford no—"

"No boarding intended, Captain. Our intention was to ask you to dinner to celebrate our victory. We found the French in the mouth of the Nile, and Lord Nelson allowed our fleet to cut out ten of their ships-of-the-line and two frigates. Their flagship exploded! Buonaparte is left ashore to trot back to France on foot!"

It sounded as if the frigate's captain had begun his celebration long ago. My own reaction to the news was instant joy and envy of those who'd been there. I resolved then and there that any future ship for me would be the Royal Navy, the risk be damned. I'd passed through many without discovery, and I'd do it once again.

"My thanks, but no dinner," Cronley bellowed, keeping his neutrality intact. "We'll send our compliments across with a case of fine Madeira saved for such occasion, asking in return for you to take our mail."

"Gladly done, sir, and gladly received."

The morning watch was not mine, and I hurried below to collect the four-and-twenty pages I'd written to Mrs. Derwent Fish, box 259. A fleet moved slowly, but its fastest frigates were sent ahead with messages, reports, and bags of mail. My letter would lose itself in the postal system and gain no attention except from the one to whom it was addressed. Daphne would hear a good deal more than anyone could wish about Constantinople's bazaars and the myths of the Aegean, but there were twenty-four pages of reassurance that I was coming back.

I watched our launch as it plied its way through the easy sea to the frigate's larboard. Beyond, the massive ships-of-the-line, their prizes in tow, made an imposing progress across the horizon. With a glass, I could make out Lord Nelson's long, slender, blue pennant streaming from the head of his flagship's mainmast. I do not believe in premonition, but I had the distinct impression as I examined the damage to his ship that I'd sail with him one day. Would that it had been sooner rather than later.

For the second interruption in our tedious routine was one that broke us altogether. A fortnight after sighting Nelson's fleet, we were north of Algiers, edging our way toward Gibraltar, still looking for our convoy and its protection. Our progress was slow, for in summer the westerlies prevail between Sicily and the Barbary Coast, blowing against our progress. The surprise was a northern mistral that came on us as suddenly as an eclipse. It was during my watch, and I found myself, with Cronley, tied to the mizzen as we were forced to run before a gale wind with mountainous following seas. The helmsmen fought to keep the ship true, but before I could tear myself loose, they lost control, the ship broached to and swung around into the trough. The following sea crashed over, and within minutes we were dismasted, the thick oak cracking with a sound like gunshot and crashing overboard with whatever canvas was left.

Whatever luck we had kept us from capsizing, and the captain and I rode out the storm, not daring to unloose the ropes that held us to the stump of mast still left standing. The storm passed as quickly as it had commenced, and as we released ourselves, Cronley tried to figure what to do. A sailor coming up the hatchway from below looked by chance to starboard and called, "A sail!" Both Cronley and I had kept our glasses with us through the storm, and both were trained on the visitor.

Exhausted beyond despair, Cronley said, "And so the buzzards come. Your opinion, Mr. Harris."

"There are two," I said, adjusting all ideas of the future. "A pair of Barbary corsairs, I'd say, xebecs to be precise, fourteen to sixteen guns apiece."

Cronley was silent a moment, then collapsed his glass and said, "We'll hope the Dey of Algiers is collecting hostages for ransom and not slaves for trade."

Algiers

January 1801

For more than two years, one day was a copy of any other for me and the hundred and fifty sailors I lived with in our Algerine dungeon. There's no need to describe the degrees of ghastliness of that time for it was all of a piece. The only variety was when someone went mad and was dragged out by a platoon of the Dey's Janissaries, there to be offered the solace of the bastinado, and beaten on the soles of his feet until he couldn't walk. Of course a certain number expired from torture, dysentery, or malnutrition, but death was such an ordinary event, we kept no record beyond the names. During the summer of 1799 there was a drought, and therefore water for hostages was dropped from the list of bare essentials. That was when our captain, Cronley, died. What we were given to eat—a grey gruel that we dared not smell, examine, or question—was just sufficient to keep us alive, which was all that was expected of us.

Hostages were what we were, scrofulous and increasingly hirsute, for as Europe blasted away at itself with a major war, there was our nasty little undeclared malevolence to the south. The piratical Barbary States—Algiers, Morocco, Tripoli, and Tunis—felt free to seize any ship of a country that didn't pay tribute for allowing its merchant shipping to pass. Because the European powers had navies large enough to escort their merchantmen as well as fight a war, the deys and pashas who ruled the pirate states under obeisance to the Sultan of Turkey directed their best efforts against the ships of America, a distant country, and since its Revolutionary War, one with no navy.

Our little company of desolation had been collected from a number of ships over the years. We were being priced at fifty thousand dollars for our freedom, above and beyond the monies President Adams and the American Congress had already paid in tribute for safe passage. The issue was further complicated, as we learned later, by Thomas Jefferson's election to the American presidency in 1800. One of his major campaign pledges had been "Millions for defence, not one cent for tribute," a catchy phrase that resulted in the construction of three new frigates in New Bedford and allowed us to rot in Algiers.

Having been an officer on the *Salem Glory,* I was regarded as a temporary American by both my captors and my mates; and although there were the occasional diplomats who visited, their noses twisted at the stench, eyes averted from our eyes, I was not eager to claim my citizenship. Nor was I surprised when a man from the British legation appeared, asking if "one John Harris" was present. I'd no doubt that Walsh would sooner or later visit the Upper Wet Dock, and would find what ship had taken me. The news of *Salem Glory's* capture had obviously reached the Home Office. The diplomat's request had no response from me, nor from any of my mates. I dared to hope that Daphne, too, had heard the news.

I made some Yankee friends who never asked a man about his past, discovered who the best and most reliable might be, and as an antidote to madness, I occupied my mind with planning an escape. With death, disease, and changing guards, I waited for a year before I shared my plan with anyone. It took that long for desperation to make it seem any more than folly.

Escape was, of course, impossible. The dungeon was a large cave carved out of solid rock, with iron bars dividing it unequally in two. We existed in the smaller part of it, with air and light supplied from grates out of reach above, which led to the fortifications on the ramparts overlooking the harbour. There was a row of buckets for our wastes lined up against the bars. Each morning, the few men inclined toward ignoble truckling with the guards were given the privilege of carrying the buckets out through the single gate in the bars and up the stone stairs to enjoy the sunshine and undefiled air for as long as it took them to empty their burden into a sewer.

The larger part of the dungeon was the Janissaries' domain, with tables and chairs for them to pass their time on duty, instruments of torture—a rack, a brazier with branding irons, an iron-spiked boot, nothing particularly original—for them to do their work on us when needed. We had reached a level of survival that allowed us to welcome the heat of the brazier when someone was to be punished with a brand, particularly during the violent storms that swept across the North African coast between November and March.

My plan was simple, to rush the gate when it was opened for the buckets. I volunteered to be the first. We were to overpower our guards, one hundred fifty of us against the two dozen on duty at a time, and seal the entrance at the top of the steps. The surviving hostages would hold the guards hostage and thus be in a position to negotiate freedom. To that end, we studied our keepers to find their individual weaknesses and idiosyncrasies, of which there were many.

The Janissaries were a privileged class in Algerine society, several thousand specially trained fighting men who controlled every aspect of its government and rule. As such, they were allowed to practise a very lax observance of Islamic law. We saw unending amounts of alcohol, opium, and tobacco consumed.

Their senior council elected the Dey, but it was an ominous sort of politics. If the Dey was casual in his control of any element under his authority, there were always those who would quickly take advantage of his weakness and kill him. For this reason, he occasionally appeared in the dungeon, usually to take part in the more brutal tortures in order to enhance his reputation.

We had organised ourselves as captives do in order to survive, by friendship as well as skill. At first, my plan was entrusted to only a few, and those few included others only when necessary. Our guards forbade conversation by any more than three, so communication was limited, even at night when oil torches lit the cavity in which we tried to sleep. Nevertheless, by the winter of 1801, we knew our guards like brothers and were determined to try for our release. Only then was the news spread, carefully through trios in apparently idle chat. Each man was given his duty and his position at the gate to follow those of us who would be first. The Janissaries carried scimitars, daggers, and pikes, as well as having muskets at hand in racks at the foot of the steps. There was no doubt that many of us would die.

Each day for a week, as the gates were opened for the dozen bucket men to make their ascent, the rest of us rehearsed by moving easily to our most advantageous positions for a charge. We depended on the full buckets to be used to blind and bash, our only weapons until we could seize those of our captors. As the bucket men went out, ten groups of a dozen would follow, one upon the other in a controlled attack in order to avoid a crush at the gate. Each group had an objective—the muskets, the stairs to bar the entrance at the top, the guards themselves, the collecting of their weapons. I must confess a certain pride in the intricate detail, impossible as the enterprise might seem. Of course one man's hesitance at the gate would end it all. But of one thing I was sure: in all the men was a crazed courage, which by the night before our venture was so palpable we had to work hard to hide it from the guards.

As we watched the moonlight slowly pass over the grates

above us, a new watch of guards came down at midnight. They seemed unduly jovial. Dungeon watch was hardly a choice assignment. Suddenly, they fired the brazier. We were alarmed, for none of them had brought their usual indulgences. Torture often lasted through the morning hours if the prisoner did, and our plans would be affected. We waited as the coals grew red, wondering as always which of us would be the victim. When the officer in charge pushed the end of his scimitar in among the flames, I shuddered as no doubt my mates did.

A short time later, familiar cries demanding obeisance sounded from above, and down the steps rushed a fully armed brigade of Janissaries, who formed a line and aimed their muskets into our part of the dungeon. We backed away from the bars as the Dey himself appeared above in his customary resplendent white robe and turban, carrying a long white whisk. Followed by his retinue and personal guard, he descended the steps with requisite dignity. Without looking toward us, he issued an order, which the dungeon watch hastened to fulfill. The gate was thrown open, they rushed through them, grabbed me, dragged me out, and threw me down at the Dey's feet.

Someone beside the Dey spoke. "Word has come to the Dey that you have planned an escape."

"Who told you such a thing?" I enquired.

"Secrets do not keep in a dungeon," he said, and I chanced to look up in time to see the translator take the Dey's whisk as he in turn reached for the scimitar in the brazier. I was jerked to my knees and my head snapped into a convenient position and held there by someone grabbing at my hair. The Dey raised the scimitar high above his head. He executed several impressive passes with it around my head, the red-hot tip tracing a path in the dim light. With a shout of triumph, he then expertly jammed the tip into my right eye.

As I lurched, my handlers yanked me back and let me fall, bellowing, on my back. The Dey stood above me, the scimitar hissing with gore, and held it over my heart. With a bored expression, he waited for my cries to subside, then began to speak. The translator addressed those watching in the dungeon.

"The United States Government has, after all, agreed to pay your ransom. A ship arrives in a fortnight to take you home." There was an audible gasp from my fellow hostages and then yells of joy, which I might have joined under different circumstances. "If you try to escape again," the translator shouted to gain their attention, "this fool will lose his other eye, and your ransom will be doubled."

The Dey lofted the scimitar back to its owner and, his duty done, strode to the steps. I was dragged back to the gate and thrown in without ceremony. There I received whatever solicitude my mates could offer. Many stripped off their rags to make a bed for me, others offered half their gruel until our rescue came. Other than that, I was left to deal with the pain that kept me unconscious much of the time, raving some of it, and clamping my teeth into a block of wood supplied by my captors, not from any compassion but to keep me quiet.

I hardly remember our release. I was carried to the quay and aboard the American brig sent to fetch us. Fortunately a surgeon was aboard, prepared by the American authorities for the worst, and with me he found it. Before the ship set sail, I was on my back in the sick bay with enough opium in me to believe I had a third eye in the center of my brow and would not miss the one I could feel was being carved away. And then I was afloat as well, and stayed in that condition for whatever time it took for the pain to dull and a crust to form. The major problem soon became my bowels, which had the awesome adjustment to make from Algerine gruel to the solid food that now came my way. Salt junk, greasy cabbage, and potatoes coated in something brown took a careful introduction into my systems, which for a time rejected these culinary overtures with a wide variety of rebellion.

I managed to reach the deck to see Gibraltar as we sailed by. My mates made more of my appearance there than was called for, and I was presented with an eye shield sewn up by the sailmaker to such a fit it might have been a tailor's work. My loss hardly affected me once balance was again mastered, the problem being more with sea legs lost in the dungeon than with an eye. Within a week I had some strength and took my turn with duties on deck as we passed into the Atlantic with no intention of calling at any place in England. I understood the Americans' hesitance to risk Royal Navy boarding and impressment. The month-long crossing to Boston, our destination, was a painful delay, as was the equal time for my return, presuming I could find a ship.

By that time, I should have been aware that my fate was never to be a predictable one, even for a month or two. This point was made to me at the end of a morning watch. I was aroused at first light from my hanging cot in the surgeon's sick bay by a single shot from a nearby ship. By the time I reached the main deck, I found all at the starboard rail watching a British frigate two chain lengths away, its launch approaching us carrying officers and marines through a brisk sea. Within minutes, the officers were aboard, selecting both crew and those rescued from Algiers for duty in the Royal Navy. The marines had taken their positions to prevent any resistance. The American captain kept to his starboard side of the quarterdeck, but let the British know his thinking.

"God strike me down, sir, if you haven't chosen enough. These men have been two years in prison."

"One or two more of them, if it please you, sir," the rather smug lieutenant answered as he continued his inspection, which was ineluctably coming round to me.

The American lost his temper, "You slack-arsed double-poxed hound, remember me when next we meet on equal terms."

"Your servant, sir," the lieutenant replied and saw me. "You! Over to the rail."

"I've a protection," I said, the paper having been kept by the Dey with all the rest of our identities during our incarceration, and returned at our release. I handed the lieutenant my faded paper.

"Mr. Gibson," he shouted to his bosun, "is there a Gulliver on the ship's roll?"

"Harris. I changed my name . . ." I hastened to explain.

"No, sir!" the bosun called.

The lieutenant smiled unpleasantly. "Win it at cards? Stole it, perhaps? Maybe even murdered for it? You'll love the Baltic Fleet, Jack." As he stuffed my useless paper into his tunic, he raised the bayonet he carried to within an inch of my good eye and ordered, "Over to the rail!"

The Baltic Fleet. My only thought of it was that it must sail even farther north than the North Sea Fleet, which had been the coldest hell I'd ever known. Much worse was the hard fact that my two months of Atlantic crossings had expanded to indeterminate years before I could expect to reach England. My bitterness made me useless to anyone, and I received a good deal of stimulus from the bosun's starter rope, both on the frigate and then on HMS *Elephant,* to which I was unceremoniously turned over when we reached Falmouth. I only remember the wind that day, which blew a frigid greeting from the north.

There was no rest, nor opportunity to write to Daphne, for the fleet was set to sail, to where I knew not, nor cared. I spent a week sleepwalking through my watches, bearing the bosun's starter and learning how to freeze. My bitterness gave way to a lugubrious melancholy that gained me neither sympathy nor friends. After an abysmally slow and storm-wracked crossing of the North Sea, punctuated by gunnery practise each day, which provided a momentary source of heat from the gun barrels, the fleet for reasons unexplained to me anchored off the Danish coast.

This absurdity seemed to pierce my somnolence. England had not fought the Danes or any Scandinavian for a thousand years. Our enemy was France. What were nineteen ships-of-the-line, of which our seventy-four-gun, squatty HMS *Elephant* was one, doing hovering about Denmark? Once curiosity began rattling around my brain and tongue, I learned enough to realise it wasn't absurd at all. It was blithering politics.

It seems that the mad Tsar of Russia, Paul, had taken offence at England's occupation of Malta, he being the Grand Master of the Order of St. John's Knights of Malta. He had convinced several other deranged kings—of Sweden, Norway, and Denmark—to join him in a treaty called the Armed Neutrality of the North. This piece of paper effectively cut off British access to the essential stores supplied by the Baltic countries: tar, flax, hemp, and most vital, timber, of which there was little left in England. A shortage of these would do more damage to the fleet than any battle.

So there we were, our rigging white with frost from the snowstorms that blew over us one after another, sitting and waiting for our commander-in-chief, Admiral Sir Hyde Parker, to decide what he was going to do. For the truth was that London was in a periodic uproar. Pitt had resigned as Prime Minister, hopelessly obligated to drink. In the confusion of transition, no one either at the Admiralty or in Parliament had concluded if we were to attack, or who—Russia, Sweden, or Denmark—or to blockade them all. We had the choice, for the Baltic itself was icebound and kept their fleets apart, at least until the spring. The choice, and the strategy for it, was left to the distracted, hesitant Parker.

At sixty-five, Admiral Parker had just been married to a plump and pleasing nineteen-year-old, referred to 'tween decks as "Lady Batter Pudding." He had resisted sailing from Yarmouth for this reason, only doing so after considerable goading from his second in command, Vice Admiral Lord Horatio Nelson, the hero of the Nile, whose squadron I'd glimpsed as they returned from that battle. As I dippled my ear into the weir of gossip ever swirling on a ship, I learned that Nelson, too, had similar attractions on the land, having capped his triumph at the Nile with an unhidden and much-condemned affair with a diplomat's wife. The difference was that Parker preferred to dally before battle, Nelson after, and the latter was not inclined to be dithering about the Baltic on blockade. For one thing, a blockade would allow time for the ice to melt, and the combined fleets of the Baltic states was a force of a hundred and twenty ships-of-the-line.

After a week of floating boredom, suddenly the signal flags were hoisted throughout the fleet, and launches fought their way across the turgid sea with messages. Within the hour, all hands were called aboard the *Elephant.* We stood in our divisions under low grey clouds and a bitter north wind as the bosun piped us to attention and the officers on the quarterdeck uncovered. A captain's barge was at our starboard, and the word passed quickly that Nelson was coming aboard. The first man up the side, he put his foot ceremoniously on deck. The marines snapped to and rigidly presented arms. The ship was pitching so, this was an accomplishment.

The man was surprisingly short, his uniform that of a vice admiral, but with a large star and an array of accompanying medals casually revealed under his cloak. One sleeve was empty and pinned up, and he wore an eye shield under his cocked hat, which he wore athwart. After acknowledging the quarterdeck, and with a sweeping glance over the ship, he strode toward the captain's cabin, a retinue of officers and servants following up the ladder, carrying his trunks and papers. In passing, he happened to see my eye shield and, with a gesture of his remaining arm, noted our similarity.

By dinnertime, the rumours had produced what turned out to be the truth. Nelson had removed his flag from HMS *St. George* and come aboard the *Elephant,* because he needed a ship with a shallower draft. Having convinced Admiral Parker that Copenhagen should be attacked immediately, Nelson planned to lead a squadron of a dozen ships into the city's harbour to do it.

The isle of Zealand, on which Copenhagen lies, is separated from Sweden by The Sound to the east, and from the rest of Denmark by an appropriately named body of water called the Great Belt. Across from Copenhagen itself was another small island which formed a channel that ran directly in front of the city and through its harbour. Running down the length of the channel's

centre was a treacherous shoal called the Middle Ground. On either side of it were the two navigable channels, the Kings Channel, near the city, and the Outer Deep farther away and just out
of range of Copenhagen's guns.

Within a hectic hour, we took the wind, which had blown for
months from the north, and made our way down the Outer Deep
to a point south of the Middle Ground. The squadron anchored,
watching doubtfully for the wind to reverse itself. What Nelson
needed for success was that unlikely change, a breeze from the
south, unheard of at that time of year, moving us back up the
Kings Channel and directly into Copenhagen's harbour. Four
miles to the north, Parker stayed with the main fleet, ready to attack the powerful batteries of the Trekroner Fortress, which
guarded that approach.

As we waited, we reconnoitered the Danish line of defence. In
the Kings Channel between shore and the Middle Ground was a
line, a mile and a half of eighteen floating batteries, numerous
hulks, and eight men-of-war. Behind them were the shore batteries of the city. Most difficult of all was the lack of marker buoys,
which the Danes had wisely removed.

Against all that was our presumptuous dozen, waiting through
the last days of a freezing European winter for a magical south
wind to blow us in. But my easy skepticism did not take into account the force of nature named Nelson. On April Fools' Day, as
if the cosmos took a bemused interest in such absurdity as ours,
indeed the wind began to shift. We were astounded. There was
talk belowdecks that Nelson wanted to fight so much that this
time he'd offered God his arse, buttock by buttock, for a friendly
breeze. We prepared for the Battle of Copenhagen the next
morning if the wind came true.

My duties that night were simple; being on first watch, I helped
the powder monkey stack the bags of gunpowder where we
wanted them and filed the roundshot smooth for a truer passage.
I then took a sanding stone to the deck around our gun so that
blood could not cause us to slip. There were eight of us to the

gun, one of seventy-four on three decks, ours a twenty-four-pounder. My gun captain, named Chester, was an old tar from Blackpool. He wore thick black muttonchops on the sides of his bald, pockmarked head, spoke in grunts, and prided himself in not having learned to swim during his eighteen years before the mast. During our gun drills on the North Sea, I'd found the man knew what he was about, for he had us firing a round every hundred seconds despite the foul weather. When pressed, or showing off for the quarter gunner who supervised us and our three neighbouring guns, Chester would have us sheer off another ten seconds. I was again the first loader, leaning out through the gun port to ram home first the powder, then after it was loaded, packing in the roundshot, chain shot, or coals—whatever ammunition was ordered. I had to be quick, for Chester in his diligence to pull the lanyard line and trip the flintlock would as soon have a new rammer than delay his firing.

I sanded hard, remembering well the gun carriage lurching over the slick deck at Camperdown and mashing my leg on a bracket. Before battle some ships painted their decks to match blood so that it wouldn't show, a waste I thought, for the colours of carnage make a wider rainbow than red. Of course I wondered if some of the morrow's blood would be mine. I knew it would make little difference, except to one who made me care to live, to see her once again, and to see for once my son. My melancholy gathered into a wave.

Except for losing her, death itself meant nothing. I was aboard that ship-of-the-line as much gambler as sailor, knowing the even chances that death could come with the first broadside or could linger for months over a broken body. No one dared mention the odds on surviving the battle, but to most seamen who lived to furl another mainsail, their booty was a life of hard and unrelenting tedium, with whatever brief relief one could discover on that foreign planet, land. Such was the truth for a Nelson or for any Jack Tar, a sad truth indeed, with life's chief glory being the successful destruction of an enemy, and the rest of it passing so perplexedly.

A half hour into the watch, I heard the oars of our squadron's barges dipping into the frigid waters, propelling the twelve captains through the black freezing night toward the *Elephant.* Nelson had invited them to supper in order to convince them of his strategy and to rouse them to his own level of enthusiasm for the battle to come. From what I had heard of him, I had little doubt he could do it. The man was addicted to history's glory, but unlike most flag admirals and generals, he would send no other to capture it for him. He lusted for battle, and I wondered what happens to such men if fortune gives them their lives in peacetime. In their prayers, I presumed that both Buonaparte and Nelson thanked God for each other every night.

The bosun stood not twenty feet from where I worked on the upper deck, piping each captain aboard as he climbed up the side and stepped through the break in the hammock netting already rigged about the gangway. I watched an officer of the *Elephant* greet each one and cross the rolling quarterdeck toward Nelson's dining cabin, their eyes shining in the dark, their sure sea stride revealing their anticipation. Several of the captains were younger than I, and the great "if" of my life came roaring through my mind again. Had I not done what I had done twelve years ago, might I be one of those proud men, in command of my own seventy-four, sailing into battle with Nelson? Then, as if the tortured thought needed an emphasis from hell, I heard the pipe again at the gangway.

And there stood Captain William Bligh.

Because of my sullenness since I'd joined the fleet, I'd missed much talk and hadn't heard a mention of his name. If he'd looked down, he would have seen me. I had no doubt that in spite of eye shield, seaman's plait, and a ridge of whiskers round my chin, he'd recognise me. And I must admit that in that moment, in spite of all my recent understanding about my life, I wanted him to see me, to understand that I'd survived, to leap at me and thus allow my hands to have acquaintance with his throat. I braced myself for this, but he only straightened his cocked hat, looking nowhere except toward his objective, Nelson's cabin door, to which a welcoming lieutenant led him.

As he disappeared inside, I was on my feet. I couldn't accept his passing by so closely without a recognition, as if somehow I didn't exist and, after all, was negligible to his experience. Still holding my sanding stone, I started toward the captain's cabin, gaining speed and intention with every step. The vainglory of my entering there and, before all those assembled, shouting out what he had done while punishing him with my stone weapon was full before me. Any number of lieutenants were as well, one of whom announced my advent to his colleagues, as well to the marines on guard. All sprang to action, bringing bayonets and cutlasses to bear. In my blind intention, I ran hard enough upon one of the first to bring blood and startle its owner.

"Here, where in all bloody hell are you going?" he bellowed and kicked me to the deck.

Another asked, "Who is he?"

"Topman, larboard watch, gun number five," the lieutenant who oversaw my labours reported. "Bosun, take him below. He's probably drunk, saved up his grog for some courage the night before battle . . ."

The marines grabbed hold of me and dragged me to the hatchway, my rough progress pitied by none, for I'd made no friends during my great sulk across the North Sea. Already I condemned myself to that damnation reserved for fools. As they threw me up against a great gun and the bosun's mate emphasised his lesson for the night with his starter's rope across my back, I flailed away with my own punishment, searching for better words of contempt for what I'd thought to do. They finally left me there, the bosun's mate offering the advice, "You sober up by dawn or we'll do you a ducking to help you come around." I sank down to the deck and crumpled there, ashamed and enraged that I would so quickly threaten the life that I'd so recently resolved to live by performing such a puerile stunt. I cursed the instinct for the public display of so-called honour, which I seemed to carry still, that need for recognition as a gentleman, that craving for revenge on Bligh.

"Fool," I said aloud. "Fool!" and before I could swear to Daphne that I'd not die for him, but live for her, I heard agreement from the shadows around me.

"Oh yes, I grant you that, a bloody slack-arsed fool, no doubt."

"Who gets hisself softened up for roundshot with the bosun's starter."

"Tonight he's a fool, tomorrow a corpse. Just put a bung in his mouth so he'll be quiet and float."

I joined the nervous laughter, crept up the hatchway as quickly as I could to my own gun, and went back to sanding. When the captains left three hours later, they had my back and my envy, uncomplicated by the passions from the past. I thought I heard Bligh's excited, piping voice anticipating the battle to come, and let him go with no hopes for his mishap or glory, leaving either to his own endeavours.

Within minutes, the *Elephant*'s launch set out to sound the Kings Channel as close to the Danish line as possible. I was still working when it returned. Using a pole rather than a lead and line, for the sake of silence, they'd managed to circle the nearest Danish ship without discovery. As Nelson dictated his orders of battle for each captain and had them dispatched to the ships in the squadron, my watch ended. I went below to my fourteen-inch-wide hammock suite and slept, cold as always, but with a sense of peace no man had any right to have the night before such a battle as Copenhagen was to be.

The drum woke us, and a stiff southern breeze greeted us on deck. Our first order was to haul the sheet anchor, the largest on board, as well as any other spares up and over the side, ready to drop and place the ship in a precise position. Nelson's strategy was to sail in line up the Kings Channel, the first ship anchoring and engaging the first Danish ship-of-the-line, the next ship passing the first to engage the second, pouring fire into the line of hulks and floating batteries as it progressed. The third would pass the first two, until in like manner the entire squadron was strung out and anchored south to north with nothing else to do but blast away at the enemy.

We had our breakfast—an oatmeal thicker than usual that formed a ball in the stomach that would last the day long—after which all hands were called, and we prepared to sail. At 9:45, my mainsails set, I was at my gun and saw the first three ships of the squadron weigh anchor. Our capstan started clicking soon after, bringing our anchors in, and we took the wind in line. My gun was the first, just below the quarterdeck. Nelson gave his orders to the captain, paced and joked with some of the officers, prepared his messages to the squadron with his signal officer at the sternpost halyard, and dictated his every order and observation to two clerks for the ship's log. His anticipation was as if he were headed to a day of cricket.

But joy did not last long, for a ship before us in the channel, the *Agamemnon,* ran aground. Nelson sent signal flags running up and down to change the order of attack. At 10:20 the broadsides began from the first ships in. There was a spur of shoal from the Middle Ground unknown to us, and two more British ships grounded on it. This left nine of us to take Copenhagen, and as the *Elephant* passed round our mates, we raked the floating batteries and anything else Danish that we could see. By the time we anchored, the smoke from a thousand cannon was weaving its thick blanket to smother the entire harbour, leaving our targets to memory. After the first broadsides, it was "Fire as you will," and every hundred seconds we blindly obeyed. I bellowed at the powder monkey to bring more cartridges, barely heard between the shrieks of pain and shouts to the marines to clear away the wounded and the dead. A shot hit the mainmast, and splinters from it cut our handspike man to bits. As he fell, I grabbed the implement, my duties done with loading, and with Chester's mad commands echoing in my already deaf ears, I inched the truck to his liking, then jumped back to avoid the great gun's lurch and went back to my original duties. For much of an hour I filled two roles, mates from our twin starboard gun filling in for others who'd fallen. By then the gun barrel was so hot that we daren't touch it for fear of frying flesh, making the loading of it a chancy business.

I was working the worm to clean the barrel when a roundshot hit the neighbouring gun to ours, exploding it and throwing metal through the lot of us. Because I was behind our barrel, I escaped the worst of it. Chester's punctured body lay sizzling on the cascabel where he'd been thrown. I lifted him off and called a marine. Together, we dropped him overboard, I tearing off his powder horn as he fell. The gun was loaded; another man had taken up the handspike. I went to the lanyard, looked out over the muzzle ring through the port for something that might be a target, saw the flame of a gun, pulled out the quoin at the breach for a degree of altitude, and fired, leaping out of the way.

Then I shouted, "Now, for Chester, one, two . . ." and I began to count our hundred seconds. The second loader was still alive to worm, his twin from starboard took his place as he took mine, and our little human machinery fell into place, the gun loaded and run out at fifty-two, me pricking the cartridge at fifty-eight, priming the vent from Chester's horn at sixty-five, setting the flint-lock at seventy-six, shouting for a traverse through the eighties and firing at ninety-four!

We gave a cheer we hoped that Chester heard, and as I started counting once again, the numbers were drowned out from above.

"Give me a crew of one-eyed men," Nelson was shouting to anyone who'd listen, "and I could make a ship-of-the-line fly! Fire on!" he urged us. "Fire on! They cannot hide from the likes of us. A one-eyed man can see through the smoke of hell!"

We continued our century shots into the afternoon, pausing only to cool the gun and to take water ourselves. The remains of our neighbour twenty-four was removed, and its twin from star-board took its place. It was apparent to us all that opposing fire was dwindling, not to any level of relief, but in effectiveness. What became clear in those moments when the breeze made a window in the smoke was that the Danish ships and floating batteries were badly mauled, but when they ordinarily would have struck their colours, they were resupplied with men from shore. We saw their dead and wounded accumulating on their decks and battery platforms. Our squadron had no resupply, and at the rate of fire pouring back and forth between us, the battle could continue for a week, if we could send the Danish roundshot back that crashed into us and rolled about the deck.

It was in early afternoon that I heard by chance the signal officer shout across the quarterdeck to Nelson that Admiral Parker's flagship, four miles to the north, had flown Signal 39. When Nelson ignored him, the lieutenant, named Langford, repeated the news.

"Mr. Langford," Nelson reproached him, "I told you to look out on the Danish commodore and let me know when he surrendered. Keep your eye fixed on him."

"Should I pass the signal to the rest of the fleet?" the hapless lieutenant asked, for that is what he should have done. A signal from the commander-in-chief was not to be ignored.

"No. Acknowledge it," was Nelson's brief reply. Then, "And keep our signal for close action flying."

I started another hundred count but was distracted by what I heard then from the quarterdeck. "Do you know what's shown on board the Commander-in-Chief?" Nelson asked furiously. "Number 39!"

The only man standing near enough to respond was the Lieutenant Colonel of Marines, who knew nothing of signals and asked, "What's it mean, my lord?"

"To leave off action," Nelson bawled and repeated, "*To leave off action!* Now, damn me if I do." He took a glass from an officer and put it to his patched eye. "You know, I have only one eye. I have a right to be blind sometimes. I really do not see the signal."

I laughed aloud through "ninety-six," and fired, looking as I leaped away at Nelson, who smiled at me, proud of his gall and willing to share his pleasure.

The action continued for another hour, the Danes defeated, their ships disabled but still fighting and firing, refusing to surrender. Finally Nelson sent a message under a flag of truce offering "to spare Denmark when no longer resisting, but if the firing is continued . . . to set fire all the floating batteries we have taken, without having the power of saving the brave Danes who have defended them."

Soon after, for the first time in five hours, the Danish guns were silent and so were ours. The squadron gave itself a cheer that none could hear, being still deaf from the battle. I sat down on the deck and noticed that my arms were burned raw and the rest of me had splinters. Before I had a chance to commiserate with myself, my hand was grabbed and I was pulled up to standing by Nelson, who thundered, "Come, my one-eyed shipmate, let me shake your hand." Then shouting to the crew, he said, "To the quarterdeck comes the honour, but at the gun the better man! All of you fought nobly as your country depended on your doing . . . I'll offer my appreciation to a seaman and an officer," he suddenly suggested, his excitement causing him to hop a small step before me, his lost arm's stump flapping. "Signal Officer, have my second, Admiral Graves, come aboard, and Captain Bligh of the *Glatton,* at their earliest. Bligh supported us magnificently, and this man . . . your name, sir?"

I forgot whatever it was, but before he had a chance to question further he was called urgently to the quarterdeck. I waited only a moment before heading for the hatchway. I was bleeding well enough from splinter wounds to justify my leaving the cleanup of the carnage in order to visit the surgeon's sick bay. I passed through the still-cheering men 'tween decks, who were celebrating that they were still alive, and went forward to the forehatch. Climbing to the foc's'le, I made my way to the bowsprit and, as if I had some business with the rigging of the fore staysail, I worked my way out on the foot ropes. I glanced back once to see if anyone took notice, then jumped.

The shock of cold water nearly stopped my heart, but the sting of brine on my open wounds was worse. I started to swim, aware that I would not gain notice in a harbour already occupied by dead bodies and wounded struggling to reach wreckage in order to stay afloat long enough for rescue. From the ship, I barely heard the bosun calling, "Pass the word, number five larboard gun captain, Lord Nelson's compliments . . ."

I hauled two flailing men—whether Englishman or Dane I knew not—to the planks from a floating battery. Resting there, I chanced to see the captain's barge put off from the *Glatton,* rowing smartly, double banked, for the *Elephant.* I turned away and swam for shore, where I hoped to join the crowd of wanderers that such a battle creates and lose myself until I could find a friendly fishing boat to carry me back to England.

I learned much later that four thousand men had died. Also, an entire week before our miraculous south wind blew us up the Kings Channel, the Russian Court, not wishing a blockade or conflict with the Royal Navy, had caused the mad Tsar Paul to be strangled to death. The news reached Denmark only as Lord Nelson was dining with the Danish Court, arranging an armistice. The Battle of Copenhagen had been unnecessary.

I also learned that Bligh was honoured with doing the favour of delivering for Nelson an elaborate set of Copenhagen porcelain to Lady Emma Hamilton, his mistress, in London.

Derwent Water

July 1801

After a month of hand-to-mouth living, wandering westward across Denmark, I reached the port of Esbjerg and managed to find a fishing boat bound to do its work across the North Sea, then calling at Newcastle. The impress service had a large quota to fill there, but my master was good enough to let me ashore at Tynemouth, with the perfume of red herring sunk in my pores. My wages were some decent slops to wear and enough money for an outside seat on the mail inland to Carlisle. There I found a corresponding bank to mine in London, and within a week, I could afford new clothes, a decent bed, an acid bath, and finally a doctor to examine my lost eye's cavity for anything the naval surgeons might have missed.

I of course wrote instantly to Daphne, or "Mrs. Fish," explaining the broad details of my absence, and telling her in a veiled manner of my plan to go to our cottage on Derwent Water in hopes that she might join me at the earliest. I would wait for a reply sent to "Patrick Jones"—my latest alias—in care of the proprietor of the Scarlet Spur in Keswick. If I had no reply within three weeks, I would leave immediately for London. I had no idea if she was there, or how often she passed by to look in our postal box. After years of emptiness, I doubt it offered her the temptation to attend on it each day, or even once a month.

I took the mail coach to Penrith and changed to a chaise bound for Keswick. Coming into the Greta Valley again was a dream from which I wished to wake, for I knew Daphne wasn't yet in it. This gave rise to a great bleat of reasons why she wouldn't or couldn't come, and I lurched across those pounding thoughts as the chaise approached the outskirts of the town. Once there, I gave in to the nostalgia of having been happy walking in those streets. At the Scarlet Spur, I forced memory of me from the proprietor, whom I remembered to the last broken vein in his ruddy cheeks. Giving him the money to pay for any mail that might arrive, I ate an early supper so that I might have the sunset for my walk to the cottage.

I started out and met the first full view of Derwent Water as if it were my oldest friend in life. Taking the well-remembered path along the lake's east shore, I was welcomed by meadow pipits and yellow wagtails filling the limpid air with their cries to the sun that sank into a mist behind Cat Bells. At that time of year, however, the light remained for hours giving a richness to colours that burnt the eyes. Whole fells of yellow furze, the green reeds crowding the shore spiked here and there with yellow iris, endless fields of buttercups, all these and more kept stopping me to take them in. The path itself was of leaves and sphagnum moss, with speedwell, daisies, purple clover, and white campion growing in a wild border, then cat's ear and meadow pea finding their places beneath the alternating oak, ash, birch, and pine. Breathing was like drinking crystal liquid of an unknown kind, and walking in that never-ending sunset as it played its variations through the spectrum was a music imagined though never heard.

I carried a small sea bag and felt the weight of war diminishing with every step. Not so the memories, but in that extravagant panorama, there was little room for them.

I reached Barrow Bay and hesitated, anticipating the empty cottage and doubting I would wait so long as three weeks. The thought darkened the evening, and I climbed the stony path up Castlerigg Fell, blind to the much-remembered view across the lake, which I had dreamed on endlessly in the dungeon and between too many decks. Hearing the rooks and black-headed gulls calling overhead, I didn't look up at the violet clouds for fear of greater longing.

I heard a cry. She was sitting on the blue bench. "I'm going mad!" she gasped.

I stopped breathing. She rose. I bellowed and ran headlong to her. "You can't be here!"

"No, *you're* the one who can't . . ." and just before I took her in my arms, she put up a hand in warning. "Wait!"

Behind her, leaping from the front door of the cottage, dark eyes wide with curiosity at the disturbance, was a six-year-old boy, my son. His hair was as black as rook's feathers, and I could see myself in his face, even though I no longer resembled myself a whit. We stood staring at each other, my throat gripped closed, my lost eye under its shield tricking me with tears.

Daphne was busy, too. "James . . . Look who just arrived. An old friend of mine, I've known him since, ah, before you were born."

Without taking his eyes from me, he asked, "Is he a pirate?"

"Yes," I assured him, "yes, I am."

"I've never met a pirate before. What are you called?"

Daphne and I exchanged a desperate look before she took my name from what she saw. "This is Mr. Blackbeard. My son, James Denby, Earl of Bowfield."

More impressed with my presumed occupation than his own title, he stepped forward at first to show a leg, then thought better of it and offered to shake my hand. As he took it, he asked, "Will you show me how to throw a dagger?"

"Absolutely," I answered, and hastened to add, "And how long might we have here for lessons?"

He turned to Daphne as did I. She was still taking me in, and I realised I was not as I would have wished her to see me, dirty for one, eye shield and chopped hair, having cut my plait again to avoid the press-gangs' notice. As well, the namesake beard. Nevertheless, she smiled at me as lovingly as she dared and told me, "My husband has profited so greatly in the war that he's sailed to India, I think to buy it. We'll have our time here . . . but strange and careful roles to play."

"I'll do mine better than Kemble could," I promised.

"What's a role?" James asked.

"It's pretend," Daphne said adroitly, "like the Christmas plays at the castle."

"Oh. Well, Mother, I will *not* play baby Jesus anymore. I'm too big."

I laughed, too loud with joy, it booming across the entire lake and no doubt echoing over there. James was startled, but quickly was infected with my pleasure. "What are you going to play? You should be King Herod."

"I've played too many parts in recent years," I said, entertaining Daphne. "Here in Lakeland, we should be almost ourselves."

"Yes! Oh, yes, with no one watching us," the boy said.

"No audience at all," Daphne agreed. "We've been here barely a week and haven't spoken to anyone except ourselves."

"It's been quite splendid!" James chimed in. "No stockings, no periwigs . . . How did you find us, Mr. Blackbeard? My mother said that no one knew this place except the two of us."

I gazed at Daphne with such intense love that the boy could barely miss it, saying, "She's a good friend to me. I made her swear she wouldn't tell devil or angel where I'd buried my treasure. You see, James, we'd not be safe if anybody knew."

"Your treasure's here?" he asked, mouth agape, eyes darting to the fells.

"It is, my boy," I answered, the last phrase tearing through my throat before I could stop it. I gazed at Daphne. "My treasure's here." I had to hold her. There was no more waiting. "Could you fetch a dry traveller a dipper of water? I'd be most grateful."

I saw his questions tantalise his mouth, but he held them in and dutifully ran inside. She was in my arms, and all was silence and aching and years falling away. She managed to gasp, "He'll go to sleep at eight," before she stepped back and assumed a pose so guiltily demure that I was forced to laugh again. James returned with the ladle from our water jar, carrying it with comical intensity. I drank from the ladle, watching him, still wondrous of a son. He, too, watched me, his curiosity abruptly searching beyond my treasure, for there was a wariness beside the trust in me that he accepted from his mother.

"Are you hungry for supper?" Daphne asked to break my revery. "We have some kippered herring and bread, a little wine. We weren't expecting guests. Tomorrow is market day."

"No herring, thanks," I quickly objected. "But bread and wine and you—who said that?—is a feast to a starving man." We almost took hands but turned to the cottage virtuously separate, only to be met by James's inquisitive question, "Where will you sleep?" I saw for the first time the fine edge of castle sophistication.

"Where I've slept for more summers than you can imagine," Mr. Blackbeard replied with appropriate drama, leaning down so the boy had to look me in the eye. "Under the stars with a fine wind for a blanket, but always with my shield off. When I sleep, the bad eye sees if danger's coming as far as fifty leagues away."

He seemed satisfied with the answer, even amazed, and he led us into the cottage. Inside, I had the sailor's awkwardness with home, the years of yearning for it perversely turning on the instant of return into a sad but vital longing for the sea and its freedom. I was delighted with the instinct, for it meant that I was home more surely than a deed of land, or wedding licence, or baptismal certificate could legitimise. This was my home and family, without my name, without my aid, without my life, but with my love that threatened to burst me that night and through-out the weeks of deceptive joy that followed.

The boy as predicted was asleep by eight, filled with promises of daggers and cutlasses, treasure and booty. Fortunately for Daphne and me, he, like his father (or so I was told), snored. It was a gentle alarm for us who fell upon each other with an ea-gerness complicated only by the strange need of being silent and, because she no longer slept with her husband, taking neces-sary precautions. Only once in the rushlight did she react to my scars of splinter wounds from Copenhagen, and then she forgot them, too.

It was a golden summer, the sun providing that colour to clouds, mists, and fells as surprises in the day. So much happened in that short, happy time, talk amongst the three of us falling over each other as the currents in a cascading stream. Within hours, I'd told Daphne of the Dey's handiwork with the scimitar, of Copen-hagen, Bligh and Nelson. I taught James the art of fishing as prac-tised in Lakeland, and soon we were catching our dinner whenever we wished. He was a serious young boy, matured by responsibilities beyond his years, watchful of all around him, and curious about every shift of light, flight of bug, and edge of crag. Light, bug, and crag conspired one day as we walked, causing him to fall and slide down a slope of scree. No damage was done, but by the time I reached him, there was blood from his nose and cuts on his face. I tried to pick him up, but he shook me off, preferring to stand on his own.

"Thank you, I'm fine," he said as drops of blood fell on his trousers. He pulled out his handkerchief and went to work.

"He's fine!" I called to his mother, who watched anxiously from the path above us. Then I reached out to offer him a hand as we climbed. He refused it, started on his own, but the scree gave way and he began to slide down again, struggling to climb faster than he was falling.

"Stop climbing," I ordered. "Fall down."

At first he didn't, but finally he fell and lay there until the scree stopped moving under him. Again I climbed down to him, and finding a solid foothold, I again offered my hand.

"I don't need your help," he said, flat on his back, afraid to move, but determined to do whatever he was going to do alone. I figured this faulty independence had something to do with his castle training and that it had to be changed.

"Did you hear of Nelson winning the battle of Copenhagen?"

The non sequitur surprised him. "Yes, of course," he answered impatiently as some more scree slid away under his legs.

"He wasn't there alone," I said.

"I know that," James answered, aware of the point but not wanting to admit it. "His Grace the Duke knows him."

"Does he know that there were five hundred men on Nelson's ship, and he depended on each one to do five or six different duties, otherwise the ship would run aground and all would be lost? Of course they depended on him, too. But if Lord Nelson slipped and fell on a bloody deck and the nearest man offered him a hand, don't you think he'd take it? It's give and take, James, even when you're in command."

Slowly he decided and finally reached over for my hand. It was fortunate as several hundredweight of scree came loose under him and plummeted down the fell. James was silent as we climbed back up to the path where his mother waited. Just before we reached her, he tugged on my hand and when I turned, he said, "Thank you, Mr. Blackbeard," then hurried past me to Daphne, assuring her that he was as good as new.

Later, as we returned with fresh bread and eggs to the cottage, the boy ran on ahead—carefully—leaving Daphne and me the luxury of walking arm in arm.

"That was wonderful for him to have you there," she said. "If it had happened with the Duke, six footmen would have been sent to do the job."

"And all of them would be at the bottom. Few fathers are given

such an heroic opportunity in the eyes of their child. I only wish
that he could know me."

"I do too."

"Do you think this pirate performance is working?"

"Very well. You must remember his context. With the Duke,
James is used to a wide variety of strangers suddenly appearing
in proximity. As long as he doesn't find you in my bed in the
morning, all will be well."

"He sleeps like a stone, and I rise with the sun."

"How nice for us, isn't it? After losing three years and an eye,
we deserve this. I rather fancy the eye shield . . . What is it?"

I'd stopped to look at her, something that I couldn't seem to do
enough. "You've trapped me into living, haven't you?"

"And I'll never let you out."

We were too close to the cottage and restrained ourselves, but
sat together on the blue bench, an intimacy that we allowed ourselves and seemed to pass our son's discernment.

"I keep forgetting to tell you. I heard of Peter Heywood,"
Daphne said as the light on the fells across Derwent Water
shaded suddenly from pink to violet as a cloud crossed the setting sun.

"Where is he?" I asked eagerly.

"He made post-captain three years ago and currently commands a frigate in the East Indies Fleet."

"The East Indies? I'll never see him, and perhaps it's just as
well. Post-captain! Good for him. I'm amazed, after his being sentenced to hang at his court-martial."

"His family gave him unending support . . ."

"Ah, yes, his family . . ."

My bitterness and feeling of loss were too obvious. She chose
to change the subject, rather dramatically. "There's something
else. Soon after you left the last time, I was questioned by a man
named Walsh from the Home Office."

"Why haven't you told me?" Alarm, forgotten in the weeks I'd
been in Lakeland, spread through me, an instant poison.

Her face suddenly set in an attitude of imperiousness, and she became the duchess I'd seen on previous occasions. "There's little I hold back from you, Fletcher, and much that I'm capable of managing. Walsh was a simple matter. He came to Cleyland House, was very insinuating, and asked who you were. I told him, a friend of my father's to whom a favour was owed. He became a little too insistent on details, so I gave him a few harmless ones and dismissed him."

"Was that the end of it?"

"No, over the next several weeks, I became aware that I was being followed. Sometimes their struggles to be unobserved were truly ludicrous. I told His Grace of the episode, that is, exactly what I'd told Walsh, that I'd troubled to help a friend of my father's to employment. The Home Secretary is the Duke of Portland. He's known my husband since they were boys. Dukes have a way of protecting each other's privileges, no matter if law or politics are involved. I was told that Walsh was flayed alive for his presumption, and ordered to drop his investigation. He's not thrust his elephantine nose in my business since." Then she smiled, her eyes sparkling. "Have you ever seen such a proboscis?"

I smiled but wasn't relieved, which she saw. "This is why I didn't mention it," she added. "Now you'll worry."

"Yes," I agreed.

She put her hand in mine. "I'm sorry," she said.

"So am I."

"We've been here four weeks," she responded. "If they had followed me, wouldn't they have appeared before now?"

"Of course," I said, trying to relieve us both. "And every day that passes is a greater assurance."

"I'll believe it if you will," she offered, knowing I wouldn't.

"We'll try," I responded with hollow determination, and kissed her.

We both tried, but a wariness crept into every walk we took, every visit to the lake, every climb up the fell. I watched the faces of everyone we came upon, at the same time, trying to hide my own. As the first leaves began to turn and James collected each new colour, I again walked over my escape routes from the cottage.

One day the wind shifted north, and autumn shrilly announced itself, giving its chilling warning of winter. The mists thickened, and the wind blew them across the lake in boiling deceptions. The boy and I climbed above Bracken Riggs and watched the mists above us join with those below. A shepherd's cairn marker gave us relief from the wind as we sat against it, waiting for a view to clear, at least enough of one for our descent.

"Have you visited your treasure yet?" James asked. "Is it all there?"

"Aye, it's all there for you to see when you're ten, I promise you." Somehow I'd convinced him that such age was necessary to view such riches.

"I must tell you something," James said.

"I'm glad to hear."

He spoke very seriously, beyond his years. "You should know that you're the best friend my mother has."

I could barely utter, "I'm glad of it."

"She's a duchess, you know."

"Yes."

"There aren't usually any pirates for us to talk to."

"Surely not . . . But you can talk to each other, can't you?"

"Yes, when there's time. Being a duchess is busy work."

"How do you feel about becoming a duke one day?"

He paused, and I chanced to look at him, seeing his child's face cloud with vehemence. "It will *not* be the same as it is with His Grace."

"How will it be different?" I asked as innocently as I dared, pettily grateful that he didn't refer to the man as his father.

He didn't answer right away. "I hope . . ." he started, then hesitated, I thought from shyness. "I hope . . . I'd like to know people, as I know you. I could never talk to His Grace this way."

"Have you tried?"

He thought a moment. "I don't think he wants to." Putting his head against my shoulder as he had when I read to him at night or drew pictures of my pirate travels, he said, "I wish you'd come back with us when we leave here. My mother, I'm sure, can arrange for you to do something in the household."

"Pirates do badly in any house," I explained, so moved that I could barely breathe. "We need the wind of the open seas . . ."

"Yes," he agreed sadly, "and I suppose the London constables might wonder what you are."

"Without doubt."

"But when will we see you again?"

"You mean after today? Perhaps at breakfast tomorrow . . . but no matter when we leave each other, James, I'll fight my sea battles, and if I'm still able, I'll find my way back to you."

"I'd be very grateful," he said almost formally, then reached over and gave me a hug that tore up my heart, leaving a void of yearning for the time I'd lost with him that ever remains. A week later, while Daphne and I lay in bed with the moonlight streaming over us as we delicately struggled to discuss the future, it was settled for us.

"If you stayed here," she reasoned, "you'd be as safe as if you were on the moon. As you say, the locals respect the tradition of any man having a right to hide from the world, and I'd know where you were, which I'd very much enjoy for a change. My life is my own, largely, and I'd come as often as I could, not always with James, but often . . . often."

"And on the rare occasion, I might visit Charles I," I said. As she smiled her further temptation, I sat up in bed, not knowing what I'd heard, only that our fragile plans were already shattered.

"Oh no," she whispered, as I moved quickly to the back window. A hundred yards away, a figure sank behind the rocks beside our path. There was another above us on the crag, squatting there like a vulture. Then I heard a horse whinny, too close for an idle traveller in the middle of the night.

"They're here," Daphne said, as I began to dress. I nodded, and she said, "Our postal box, I beg of you, it's safe for us . . ." Then she sprang out of bed and, naked, ran to an alcove by the fireplace. "I brought a pistol, my father taught me how to shoot . . ."

"For the boy's sake, don't murder someone," I said, pulling on a boot. "My only chance is flight. What will you tell them?"

She drew herself up into a commanding pose and said, "That I have a lover and it would be indiscreet to reveal who he is. No one dares ask a duchess more."

I went to her, and we clung to each other as long as we dared. "Wherever I go, I'll already be trying to come back to you."

"It will take time now," she said, ahead of me in realising what this escape would mean.

I kissed her. "Time stops now," I said and went to the door, then stepped over to the truckle bed and leaned down to kiss James. "Tell him often that the pirate loves him."

Through the beams of moonlight, she hurried into my arms again, her white skin burning into my eye's and hands' memory. Then we heard a high-pitched whistle sound, alerting me like any bosun's call to action. I'd heard the whistle before, when I escaped over the roofs of London. I pulled open the door, to see the muzzle of a pistol leveled at my skull. Holding it, admirably steady in the moonlight, was Walsh.

"Come out slowly with your arms held high, sir."

"There is a child asleep," I offered as I obeyed him.

"Yes, and a woman, if I'm not mistaken." He backed away as I closed on him, his pistol still well aimed.

"Leave them alone," I bartered. "Your business is with me." Several men appeared around the cottage but kept a respectful distance.

"I, bother the Duchess of Cleyland and her son? I wouldn't think of it," he said triumphantly. "Although now that we have you, I'm sure we'll finally gain a bit of her respect, which we bloody well deserve."

"Mr. Walsh, what's your great interest in me?"

"You keep turning up, don't you? You know all these interesting people, don't you? And then you run, and change your name, and disappear. Why would you be doing that during a war? Perhaps aiding the enemy? Perhaps a nice nest of your poets and lords and ladies sympathetic to those sophisticated, fancy French? I'm a more ordinary Englishman, sir, but England has no place for traitors, sir. So I plan to find out about you even if I have to skin your grand hide to do it." His moonlit smile indicated a certain anticipated pleasure.

"Sir, I fear for your life," I said, measuring the distance from us to the edge of the crag before the cottage.

"You fear for me? Why, pray?" He was amused.

"The woman inside has a pistol . . ." His eyes slid toward the door, allowing me the moment I needed to leap at him, batting his pistol aside as it fired, then to grab his neck in the crook of my arm and leap for the edge of the crag. We landed on the scree, I on my back, he facedown and bellowing. As we slid along, the scree a loose current under us, I guided myself using my arm as an oar, and as we separated, I saw that Walsh's nose held him steadily as the keel of a ship would do, sailing downward through the loose rock. No shots were fired from above for fear of hitting him.

When I gained my footing, I turned back to see Walsh lift a bloody face to the moon and howl his rage. Two men were following, trying to climb down. I started to run, the moonlight illuminating my path, familiar to me but not to them. Splashing through a beck and leaping a gill, I ran up a fell covered with whin and bilberry shrub.

What made me hesitate were two men on horseback coming from my left. I turned in time to see two more riders behind me, climbing through the shrub in great leaping strides, the riders shouting at each other that they had me. They did, so I reversed myself and ran down toward the nearest horse, waving my arms and roaring like some demented animal. The poor horse faltered, and as its rider tried to reclaim command, it reared, allowing me to grab the man and tear him from his saddle.

I was no horseman, but desperation made me one. I found a stirrup and leaped on, the poor animal under me knowing he had a howling devil on his back. He responded with an appropriate burst of speed that shot me past the other rider, who was whirling on his mount, trying to use a cutlass on me, then a pistol, which went off as I made my departure upward to the crest of Falcon Crag, along the fell to Barrow Beck, guiding my mount first above the scree, and finally hearing one of my pursuers start to slide. Turning, I glimpsed man and horse somersaulting each other down the fellside and urged my sudden friend to greater speed.

By now as wild as if he'd never been tamed, the beast near flew until we reached the beck, at that familiar point a rushing cataract of white water that caught the moonlight and made it dance. I slid off the horse to his relief, turned him, and smacked his haunch, sending him in a frenzy, galloping back the way we'd come. I then plunged into the beck and was instantly swept away downstream.

I did my best to keep my head above the surface, and to avoid the rocks that interrupted my graceful and ever-faster passage down. I knew what was ahead and chanced to glimpse two horsemen doing their best through the bracken on the bank to keep up with me. They did well until they, and I, came to the cliff that ended their chase and turned the beck into a waterfall of two hundred feet. I went over in a moonlit spray the same colour as Daphne's skin, and was lost in it.

1801–1805

As it happened, my escape was not to anything that could be called freedom. It began four years of an exile as wretched as any prison.

Going over the falls cost me a cracked rib or two; from the pain, I was never sure. Even so, I was able to hide from Walsh and his men in the wood, actually seeing him at a distance, considerably perturbed. Within hours, I was above them on Bleaberry Fell, heading north toward Glasgow.

It was a good hike, but Daphne and James had made me fit for it. The ribs gave great discomfort for a time, but not as much as I would have had jolting about, sitting bodkin in a coach. The weather held for the most part, and I found a heavy greatcoat in Carlisle. The war had put many on the footpaths, every one of them in a worse state than I. Almost every day, I shared my food with someone who was desperately hungry. From them I learned that some strange process of peace between England and France had suddenly begun. I wagered anyone who'd listen that it would be a short farce to be played only until the Corsican villain made his entrance again.

For me, the benefit of peace was the relieving of the press-gangs of their quotas, thus allowing me a slightly less difficult progress through the ports. I was still chary, thinking that Walsh had men everywhere. But the idea of going north instead of south to London was a sound one, and I found a ship in Greenock carrying corn to the West Indies. The trades were true, and in six weeks I was in Kingston, Jamaica.

I worried about Daphne every hour of every day. Not for a second did I underestimate her ability to grind Walsh into a pulp of blathering burgoo. Even so, he would make report of his efforts, and her name would surely be included. In spite of what she'd told me of her husband's broad mind on the freedom of her life (so that he might guiltlessly enjoy the freedom of his), I feared that because James had been with us, His Grace might take great umbrage. I was unsure of this, the nobility's code of ethics being a thing of wonder, so quickly changing for convenience. I only hoped that she'd paid no price for what she'd given me, which was my life.

For there I was again, at least alive, fulfilling part of my apparent destiny by running and hiding. There are those who might look upon such activity as less than dignified and surely dishonourable. A plague on such comfortable judgment. I chose to live so that I might love Daphne and James. Cat-and-mouse was a price for that luxury. I wished that I had met her as a man rather than as the miscreant half-rotted away with humiliation whom she first saw. But because I knew that she, knowing all, could honour me with an affection so reliable even while so dangerous in its giving, I dared to think she'd see me whole again before we were done. I found myself unbound by the usual expectations of manhood in this age, the rituals of birth and education, even of honour and the Royal Navy. Instead, I was defined—at least to myself—by my dance with death, not only the sentence on my head, but the chase and the battles, as if I said, "I know well my deserving, so let it come if it must. But I'll do all I can to stay alive, for there is purpose here"—to love Daphne and find myself somehow worthy of our son.

For those four years, I was a sailor again, aboard every type of foul ship that sailed among those islands, except for two longer voyages around the Horn, carrying rum to Australia. Each time I attempted to find a ship bound for England, an exercise I dared at least once a six months, I came so close to either discovery or impressment that such attempts became foolhardy. The war with France began again, and Napoleon crowned himself Emperor. For a time I was involved in smuggling British weapons to the Haitian slave armies who were fighting the French occupation.

How I do not know, but early in 1805, my involvement in this latter enterprise brought me to the attention of Government House in Kingston. With the ineluctable thoroughness of the diplomatic drones there, my description, apparently in enough detail to gain attention, eventually reached London and an all-too-appropriate desk at the Home Office. After so long a time of anonymity, I was hardly prepared to see James Walsh stalking along the quay at Kingston harbour. He did not see me, and I managed to cross the island that night. I found a boat in Ocho Rios bound for Tortola.

I moved from island to island, ever wary of Walsh, who proved exquisitely adroit in following me. Everywhere, I searched for a ship to take me clear of him, even if it meant sailing around the Horn again. There were two hurricanes, one to Walsh's advantage, one to mine. In such manner I reached Grenada, and my last hope of finding passage away from my pursuer. By then, the warring fleets of the world had arrived in the Caribbean, hoping to do damage to each other. I collected information about them as my own desperation to disappear somehow on any one of them grew. But the port of Grenada stayed empty for a week, and finally Walsh caught up with me. I saw him coming before he saw me and was forced to crash through my rented room's window, fortunately falling safely to the alley below. Rushing to the port to escape somehow, I looked out upon the astounding vision of a dozen ships-of-the-line coming in, each flying a British ensign.

I was further staggered to see Lord Nelson's pennant flying. In an instant I was away, rowing in a boat lent me for my last gold guinea. I pulled across the harbour to HMS *Victory*, and before they could shoot me, yelled greeting to Lord Nelson from a one-eyed gunner of his acquaintance at Copenhagen. Thankfully he remembered me, heard my news that the combined French and Spanish fleet had fled back across the Atlantic; and as he sent signals aloft for the squadron to form to sail, he asked me aboard.

Walsh by then was closing fast from shore, bellowing mightily for his right to me. I offered Lord Nelson an utterly outrageous explanation; even so, he was good enough to order his marines to give Walsh a warning fusillade, close enough to cause his hired boatmen to turn and pull for shore. I had no doubt that he'd be on the quay to meet me wherever I arrived, but that was something I'd consider at the time. For within the hour, I was working the tops and setting studding sails to hold every inch of the trades in order to catch the French. Lord Nelson honoured me by making me gun captain of a twelve-pounder on the quarterdeck, the area reserved for the commander's pacing. I learned that night that all the rushing back and forth by the fleets had to do with Buonaparte's renewed plan to invade England. He had his Grand Army, nearly two hundred thousand troops, massing near Boulogne, and two thousand flat-bottomed boats ready to float them across the Channel to the Kent downs. If the French and Spanish fleet was able to unite with their colleagues held by our blockades in their Atlantic ports, their combined power might be enough to allow Buonaparte and his Grand Army the two days they needed to cross the Channel.

I was as eager as Lord Nelson to have done with them. As we sailed from Grenada, he detached a frigate from the squadron to speed his plans to the Admiralty (before I had a chance to write to Daphne, alas). Nelson had not put a foot from the ship for two years and more while waiting on blockade in the Mediterranean to meet the French. He had almost as strong a desire as I to return to England. The talk 'tween decks of the scandal of him and his mistress, Emma Hamilton, was endless. No doubt His Lordship pictured another annihilation of the enemy, a triumphant return with captured ships galore, thus providing prize money for all in the fleet, and then a very eager passage to the aforementioned lady. I wished him success in all, for I hoped to imitate his progress and rush to Daphne.

But the sea is a sailor's purgatory. We run with the wind or float becalmed, chasing some nautical ambition, watching for some slight change of elements that might have meaning. But what it really is, is waiting. We fill the time with intricate routine to run the ship and keep from idleness, give in to the excitement of chasing an unseen enemy who may have sailed in another direction, or surrender to the stultifying tedium of blockade duty or port without leave. Speculation is our daily porridge, and no one dares to call another's wildest guess amiss.

So was it for the eight hundred and fifty souls aboard HMS *Victory* during those long summer months and going into autumn. We fairly flew across the Atlantic on the trades in pursuit of the enemy's fleet, but once across, Lord Nelson had no knowledge of their exact destination and had to guess what it might be. Alas, he guessed wrong, sailing directly east for the Strait of Gibraltar, while the enemy had turned northeast for the Bay of Biscay. Nelson stepped ashore at Gibraltar galled to know he'd missed them after such a waiting as his years on blockade. What was worse we learned after we refitted and started north to join the Channel Fleet to defend against invasion. A Royal Navy squadron had intercepted the enemy fleet in the fog off Cape Finisterre. There had been a battle, inconclusive and even unnamed, but it had allowed the enemy fleet to escape to Vigo on Spain's northern coast. With the enemy's ships dispersed or blockaded in various ports, the feared invasion was thereby foiled, at least for the moment. And in that moment, Nelson was granted leave.

For the five minutes of ecstatic anticipation after learning that our destination was Portsmouth, I was something of a wild man 'tween decks, clapping shoulders, yodeling my joy for everyone to hear. Lord Nelson had been ordered home, a well-deserved leave that I presumed we'd share. I was brought suddenly back to silent grief when it was forcefully pointed out by the bosun that the crew would not be sharing His Lordship's pleasure but would do such work upon the ship as was necessary after a two-year cruise to make her fit for a return to sea. For surely Nelson would not be kept idle on land by the Admiralty while the French and Spanish fleets still floated.

We anchored at Spithead on 18 August, and from the main top-sail yard I watched His Lordship's barge pull briskly for shore, my envy of his happiness an acid in my veins. I offered bribes, feigned illness, and considered a swim—none of which accomplished anything except to make everyone above me suspicious and watchful of my every move. Aboard I stayed for four weeks, of course anticipating Walsh, who for reasons I couldn't know, never appeared. I was oblivious to the rumours of our next objective, or the news carried to the ship in the bumboats with their pleasures of the port. Nelson refused to allow women on ship when under sail, but while in port, tradition held sway. Each watch did its work, then came below to enjoy the harlots who took up residence 'tween decks. Some seamen had their families come aboard for visits, which few of them could tolerate for very long. What lying down was done took place between the twenty-four-pounders, and there's little doubt that many sons of guns were conceived that summer month, whether desired or not. With lack of breeze and August heat, the stench of rum and melting tar combined with body sweats and rancid breath to make a noxious gas to breathe.

For these and other reasons, I chose to sleep on deck where, when inclined to self-laceration, I could hang on the rail to see the lights of Portsmouth and wonder how far away Daphne might be. The letters I'd written aboard, then sent her from Gibraltar, had probably arrived. I wanted her to come, then didn't. She might have been in Lakeland with James. It was summer, the London season was over, and I'd found her there in August four years ago. If so, she wouldn't have visited our postal box. Even with all those safe thoughts, I let myself imagine her in white, sitting aboard each launch or jollyboat that approached us, and felt the crushing disappointment each time she wasn't there. I wrote more letters, to be sent only when we set sail again, and wondered if they'd make her as crazed as he who wrote them that we had been so close.

As is usual in port, we prepared the *Victory* for a three-year cruise with supplies of every kind—shot and powder, barrels of biscuit, beef, and beer—and as each was stowed below I saw the sustenance for another day, week or month of my life spent waiting to return. Nelson himself had been two years away. No one counted missing as a wound. In three years my son would be thirteen, a young man who probably had forgotten me.

Thanks to the Admiralty, I was not allowed to torture myself in such a way for long. The news 'tween decks began to harden into unity. The enemy fleets had managed to consolidate while sailing south, away from the Channel, to Cádiz. There they threatened to run for the Mediterranean, or return en masse for an invasion. England could not afford to allow them the choice. Nelson was recalled on 13 September, and we sailed three days later, my accumulated letters in the last mail pouch to shore. We learned within the hour that Nelson had been given command of the fleet. For the first time in his career, he could go about his work without the need of convincing an admiral above him of his strategy. This made for an even happier mood, for there had always been a pride of place with being on his flagship. I shared the pride, but not the happiness, for by then, I'd begun to grow distrustful of glory and its eager pursuit. The thought was a muddle at the time, but what was to follow clarified it.

There was no question in any mind that we were sailing toward a battle, if only the enemy would oblige us. We also knew

that *Victory* would be in the van of the attack. The familiar conflict between anticipation, terror, and resolve began its moil in all
of us, and there wasn't one who didn't cover the struggle with
some degree of imitation of our leader. He and Captain Hardy,
who commanded the ship, put themselves on view during every
watch. Alone or together, they paced their territory on the starboard quarterdeck, often in deep discussion with each other, as
often bandying with the other officers, or even with the crew.
During gunnery practise, Nelson revealed an ongoing repertoire
of one-eyed badinage to me.

"We should start a breed of British cyclops," he suggested one
day. "A single eye forces concentration, I'm convinced. The second eye allows too much distraction. One eye for duty, the other
wanders to all kinds of wretched fribbling. Hardy, what if we
gathered all the one-eyed men in the Royal Navy and manned a
first-rate with them?"

"Never be allowed, my Lord," Captain Hardy opined in his bluff
way.

"Why not, pray you?" Nelson objected. "The Cyclops Squadron,
cruising about, staring down the enemy . . ."

"Too expensive," Hardy responded. "All those eye shields . . ."

I then fired my gun and proved His Lordship's point, hitting exactly the target of casks set afloat for us.

"Take note of that, Hardy," Lord Nelson said. "The roundshot
follows a one-eyed gaze as if it were a magnetic path."

The story made its way through the watches, and by the time
we joined the fleet waiting off Cádiz, I'd gained a strange
celebrity, not only as an able-bodied seaman who'd been noticed
by Lord Nelson, but as one who shared a magical one-eyed
power with him. A sudden ritual was born of touching my eye
shield for luck, a custom I was quick to discourage but to no
avail. Negotiating hard, I convinced my superstitious mates to
wait until we saw the battle looming.

And wait we did, after a welcome by the fleet that in its enthusiasm for Nelson's arrival in command at times surpassed naval

decorum. The first two nights, His Lordship had his captains aboard for supper, to explain his strategy of attack, should the French and Spanish fleets make sail to leave Cádiz. 'Tween decks heard nothing of that, for we would sail into battle however we were told. There was no guarantee we'd face the enemy at all, for they could stay in Cádiz harbour until the Atlantic dried.

Our fleet stayed over the horizon from them, Nelson setting up a telegraph of frigates, seven of them spread horizon to horizon, east to west over twenty leagues. The enemy saw only a single ship, obviously observing them. Even so, they had to know a British fleet awaited them, and as October crept through its wearying days, the irritating tensions of blockade doubts began to do their work. They even touched on Nelson, who after all, the doubters chided, had never commanded a battle in open sea. The Nile and Copenhagen, on which his reputation was based, were fought against ships at anchor, in areas of water nicely limited and largely protected from the fickleness of wind and sea. I didn't advertise my experience on the subject and watched the bosun break up the occasional fights that such a lively argument inevitably launched. They were few, for devotion to the "Little Admiral" was as thick and strong as paste.

And then it came, Signal 370. I heard the lookout call it down to the signal lieutenant on the poop, the morning of the nineteenth. "Enemy ships are coming out of port." Lord Nelson, who was on the quarterdeck to hear the report, took five seconds to check the wind, and ordered "General chase southeast," and I was up the mainmast shrouds for the tops before the bosun's call was piped. From there the view of our twenty-seven ships-of-the-line changing course and filling sail was a sight that tore a cheer from every throat aloft. Excitement and relief was what we felt, I skeptical even then that such a thrilling sight would be enough to overcome my doubts. We made our way to put ourselves between Cádiz and the Strait of Gibraltar, everyone devoted to the simple, happy scheme of giving Lord Nelson his battle.

It didn't come for two days, and we were aloft on every watch to shorten or make sail due to the capricious coastal winds. The frigate telegraph kept the fleet informed of the enemy's position, and we remained unseen by them until the dawn of the second day of chase. Being on the morning watch, I was already on the main topgallant yard at the lookout's call. I saw their ships stretched out to the east of us, all thirty-three with ensigns flying. They were headed south, about four leagues away, and beyond them at some ten leagues were the white cliffs of Cape Trafalgar. HMS *Achilles,* closest to them, gave us all a laugh when she signalled, "Have discovered a strange fleet."

That was the last of laughter, for at seven bells the entire enemy fleet began to wear to a northerly course, heading back in the direction of Cádiz. The wind had fallen light, so speed was not a word to use throughout the day. Even so, their crews displayed an astonishing awkwardness, taking two and a half hours to re-form their line of battle. I witnessed the exercise from the tops as we were setting studding sails on auxiliary booms attached to the yards, to catch as much of the bare southern breeze as we could.

Nelson thought the enemy would run for the port, and, having formed our fleet into two columns, was determined not to let them get away. "Prepare for battle" had been flown since the first sight of them, and on the ships across our fleet, the decks were cleared for action, with all furniture and bulkheads stowed below, the powder monkeys distributing the blue, black, and red cartridges of powder, coded for their range, the carpenters preparing their shotboards of wood and lead to plug the roundshot holes that might appear below the waterline, the bosun reeving extra sheets to the sails and shrouds to the masts. Above them, we in the tops wrapped chains around the yards' braces to prevent the yards falling to the deck if the braces were shot away. A thousand preparations were made, and then a thousand more.

When at last I returned to my gun, I ordered more shot than what the garlands held, hearing Nelson say, "I shan't be satisfied with only twelve ships today as I took at the Nile. I'm inclined toward twenty." At six bells we were piped to dinner, and the superstitious gathered at my place to touch the magic eye shield. I ate untasted salt pork and drank a deeply savoured half-pint of wine. While we ate, Nelson sent a signal up of his own creation, saying that "England expects that every man will do his duty." It took the whole meal to send it, requiring eight hoists of three flags and four hoists of seven. It was read to us below, and my shipmates gave a lusty cheer. I was silent, considering what England might expect of me.

Then it was to our places, to watch and, still in our purgatory, to wait as the ever-gentler breeze moved us toward the enemy line slower than a man could walk. Our fleet was divided in parallel columns, and it was clear that Nelson planned to break through the enemy line on that breath of air, then bear up to leeward, the chosen enemy ship being trapped between the source of motion, a gentle breeze, which could only serve to push them into our fleet's broadsides. It's what Duncan did by chance and necessity at Camperdown, but with a North Sea wind to crack him on. I was fairly certain that the strategy had attracted Lord Nelson for its sheer bravado and its ability to confound an enemy still expectant of ships coming opposite in a line to bombard each other, tooth by jowl, with roundshot.

Three hours it took us to reach the point of risk, when the bow of the *Victory,* which led the windward column, and that of the *Royal Sovereign,* which led the leeward, sailed at right angles straight into the mouth of the enemy fleet's broadsides. We knew that from that moment to when we'd perforate their line, we'd be unable to return fire and would have to bear whatever they could send our way. My crew's guns on larboard and starboard were both double-shotted, one roundshot, one of grape. The quarterdeck was open to the enemy's tops, where already we could see their sharpshooters gathered with their muskets. The bare breath of breeze moved us so slowly that my number two muttered that he'd go overboard to swim and give the ship a push.

The marine band of fifes, drums, and trumpets was playing still on the poop, although few heard its rendition of "Britons Strike Home," our attention locked on the enemy. The gun crews were naked to the waist, barefooted on the sanded deck, trousers rolled, with kerchiefs round their ears to offer them a scant protection from the firing. My shirt remained on, a habit never broken for fear of the ever-shrinking chance that my tattooed star would be noted by one who might remember Bligh's description of me. The officers who spoke with Nelson were also concerned with stars, the decorations that he wore on his uniform for all the world and the enemy to see. He put their objections aside with, "I won them in battle, I'll wear them in battle. This is no time to be shifting coats."

There was a moment of silence, as if the gods of war took breath for all that was to follow. I chanced to stand and took a breath myself. To a sailor, a single ship under full sail is a sight to fire the soul. In that moment, there were so many ships around us that the limits of the world were defined with them. To starboard was our other column, closer than ourselves to the concave crescent doubled enemy line that made a forest of varnished masts, each with billowing sail that spread across our eastern horizon, while aft was our own long column. All appeared motionless, the French ships in black and white, the Spanish red, white, and black, and our own painted fresh at Nelson's order in buff and black, all crowned with billows of white sail, all held in the moment as if an offering to the timelessness of battle and man's fate—as long as there were men—to fight them. For me, magnificence was diminished by the fact that there would ever be "The Greater Battle," even greater than one as grand as this, for men would make it so. There would always be the Nelsons and the Buonapartes, with ever-greater weapons and ever-driven ambitions, who nevertheless have the witch-like powers to inspire and to lead men into this ever-ravenous maw of glory and death.

A single French gun fired, testing for the *Royal Sovereign*'s range. Another shot and then the first broadside, which was short of her, sending roundshot skipping like ducks and drakes across the water. Then there was another silence, and I happened to glance around to see Lord Nelson, who was straining to see over the rail.

"See!" he cried, "See how that noble fellow Collingwood carries his ship into action! How I envy him!" This from a man whose own ship was minutes away from receiving its own broadside blessing. I stared at him, thinking that such a compulsive appetite was near demented. Knowing full well that of such stuff were heroes made, I turned away so that my belittling reaction to him would have no further effect on me. For I, like every other of the hundreds of men aboard, the thousands in our fleet, would need such rapture to survive, if I or they should be so lucky.

We reached the point of welcome and were greeted by broadsides from those French ships nearest us. The *Victory* took what few roundshot found her as a target, sighed and shuddered, then went on. Our lieutenant on the quarterdeck ordered us to stay down and calm, for our guns would not come to bear for a short eternity. I marked the time it took the Frenchman to reload, and then the ragged order of their next attempt at us. The months and years blockaded in port had taken their toll on their gunnery, and from their wearing, I'd say their sailing as well.

We were close enough to see which ships we were approaching to break between, the *Bucentaure* from which the commanding admiral's flag had appeared with their first shot, and in front of it, the massive *Santissima Trinidad,* she of the four decks and a hundred and thirty guns, the largest ship on the seas and a Spanish indulgence if ever there were one. I waited for the familiar obsession of the hunter, to be at them, to show what we could do with our weapon, to conquer and triumph. It didn't come. Even so, I was an animal of war, with every muscle tensed to wrestle from my gun a faster second shot.

They found us hard after that, for we floated toward them for half an hour before we had our chance. There was a long swell moving with us, and if I'd had the wit to think on it, I'd have known something of the time we had before us. A ball tore through our main topgallant sail, and we heard the Frenchman cheer. The broadsides followed, one roundshot cutting Nelson's clerk in two, another—double-headed—killing eight marines still on the poop. A shot hit the deck just before Hardy and Nelson, bounced and flew between them, sending splinters into Hardy's shoe. Smiling happily, Nelson said, "This is too warm work, Hardy, to last for long," and then continued pacing, making some remark about the courage of the men under fire. I suddenly felt disgust toward the man for his enjoyment and his need.

We stood on implacably, the intended space between the two French ships closing so that the decision was made to pass instead through the gap at the French flagship's stern. The *Victory* continued to shudder under constant broadsides but did not break. There were dead and wounded all about the upper decks before we'd ever fired. The studding sails were shot away, and then the mizzen topmast fell, making us lose wind, stretching our wait a little longer. A roundshot smashed out four spokes of the ship's wheel and cut the tiller ropes, so that Hardy had to send forty seamen below to manhandle the tiller.

By then the French knew Nelson's strategy and did what little they could to counter it. Then the gap behind the flagship closed completely, the ship abaft, *Redoubtable*, almost touching her bowsprit to the *Bucentaure*'s stern.

I heard Captain Hardy say, "My lord, it seems to go through, we'll have to board one or the other."

"I can't help it," Lord Nelson replied, I thought somewhat petulantly. "It doesn't signify which we run on board of. Go on board where you please. Take your choice."

Hardy didn't hesitate. He shouted to the master below, ordering the helm to larboard, and as the musket fire came down like hail, we swung toward *Redoubtable.* The breeze barely moved us, but the swell lifted us along until finally our purgatory ended.

The *Victory*'s larboard sixty-four-pound carronade on the fo'c'sle shot through the flagship's ornate and unprotected stern, directly into the French admiral's cabin. As each gun of the larboard broadside came to bear, the shot was copied, sending grape and roundshot the length of her, some of us indulging in two rapid rounds as we slowly passed. By the time my gun did its work, the French flagship was heeling. Looking down on her upper deck revealed only dead men and dismounted guns.

Then there was a jolt. We'd crashed into *Redoubtable*'s larboard bow, the force of impact pushing the enemy ship to face eastward with us, our yardarms locked to hers. The gun crews rushed across the decks to man the starboard guns. On the quarterdeck, we passed among the officers, captain, and admiral, the latter two still pacing. We started firing, the smoke from our previous work on the French flagship now covering us and making aim a happenstance. There were six crews for the dozen twelve-pounders on both sides of the quarterdeck. Each took pride in their work and no notice of the musket fire from *Redoubtable*'s tops. I lost a man, my neighbour gun captain lost two, but the marines, having torn off their red jackets in the heat to reveal their checkered shirts, put the dead overboard and took their places. Our lieutenant took the order from the master for gunners to shoot down, passed it on to us by signs for none could hear, and I jammed the bed and quoin to tilt the gun, sending our shot downward through the *Redoubtable*'s decks.

Silently I counted our ninety-second routine, and seldom did we go beyond it. The *Redoubtable* had bound the *Victory* to her with grappling hooks, but then they shut their gun ports to prevent us from boarding through them. The smoke was thick as pitch and blackened all of us. I barely noticed the ships of our column as they followed us through the break in the enemy's line to begin their own attack. Then as I pulled my lanyard to the flintlock and turned against the firing, I saw Lord Nelson fall to his hand and knees, Hardy, watching elsewhere, continuing his stride unawares.

I leapt over to aid him, but before I could, he'd fallen flat on the deck.

Captain Hardy was there, and Nelson choked out, "They've done for me at last, Hardy."

"I hope not, my lord," Hardy replied, kneeling beside him.

"Yes," Lord Nelson stated conclusively. "My backbone is shot through."

"Take him below," Hardy ordered. I and another seaman, with a marine, lifted Nelson as gingerly as possible and headed for the gangway. As we left the quarterdeck, I heard the order for all gun crews to go below, the musket fire becoming too intense. My arm was under Nelson's shoulder, and there was blood on my hand.

"Cover my face," he ordered, reaching for his handkerchief. "It wouldn't be wise for the men to see me thus."

The marine spread the handkerchief over his face and medals, and we began our descent through four decks to the orlop. Once 'tween decks, I saw that the *Redoubtable*'s larboard was so close that our guns could not be run out. When they were fired and lurched back, our gunners threw buckets of water through our gun ports to prevent fire from spreading to us.

No attention was paid to our procession. Nelson was a light load for the three of us and bore his carrying silently. The smoke was thick between the low deckheads; the roar and fire of the great guns continued as they were lumbered forward, then came crashing back against their tackle, their half-bent blackened crews bellowing, moving about in the lower decks' darkness that was split by the dulled sunbeams coming in through the ports. There were shrieks of pain that even our deafened ears could hear, and the acrid stench of powder and sulphur made us gag. Nelson coughed but that was all, except the bleeding that I felt. Down and ever down we went in the maddening delirium of senses, lifting what all others would regard as precious cargo, if they'd known, down scramble nets and hatchways, to the cockpit where, when we entered, the powder smoke was absent but the temper of death took its place.

We laid Lord Nelson down among those groaning or crying for relief, shattered bones and torn bodies crowding every space.

The marine went to inform the surgeon. The lanterns through the murky air below the waterline cast a greenish tinge on flesh that would be white with shock and death in sunlight. Removing Nelson's handkerchief, I saw he was alive at least, and he saw me; at the same time, anyone capable of it noticed that there was a lull in the firing from the decks above, an eerie silence that seemed to spread to even those who screamed. Then through the quiet and four decks of oak, we heard, faintly, a trumpet sounding something no Englishman would play.

Nelson coughed again with the effort of speaking, then managed the urgent, strangled words, "They're boarding us. Waste no time here, my one-eyed friend, I'm a dead man. Keep the ensign flying. Oh, God, should I die and lose!"

I backed away as the chaplain, who'd followed us down, took my place supporting him. The surgeon came quickly and began his examination as Nelson told of his wounds. The thirty-two-pounders on the deck above us began their thunder yet again, and with every shot the concussion from the firing impacted my already ragged brain. I hurried up the hatchway, not out of any eagerness to be about my duty, but because I'd begun to feel a great suspicion toward the man.

Keep the ensign flying. As soon as he said it, I was transported back to Moorland Close and the great holiday game of capture-the-flag we played there. Perhaps my perspective was skewed by it. I'd also done too much since and seen too much carnage in battle to be moved by Nelson's suffering. Even so, it seemed clear to me that lying there at the bottom of his ship, back broken and him dying with the hundreds in pain around him, that even as he breathed his last, his one good eye was fixed beyond the outcome of the battle on fame, history, and posterity. To gain his proper place, he needed to "Keep the ensign flying," keep this ultimate game of ships blasting away at each other, to have his twenty prizes and his victory, in order to become enshrined in memory.

Yet as I climbed the forward hatchway, my step quickened and the urgency of reaching the deck to fight the battle became a force within me that my doubts could not diminish. It was not because of Nelson, or whatever England might expect, or even the slightest desire for glory. Nelson had his own incentives, less troubled than mine, and surely he had more talent and gall to carry them out. I accepted his command as I reached the fo'c'sle, my motive something simpler than fame or veneration. Running to the first cutlass I saw lying on the deck, I realised that I was there only to confront death again, to continue my little habit of survival or to find my oblivion. But for the first time, I sensed the folly of it.

I bellowed against the thought like a deranged Mameluke as I attacked five Frenchmen who came across on our anchor. Joined instantly by marines sent from below to protect the deck, we beat them back, two of them falling into the sea. Then through the smoke I saw another ship appear on the other side of the Frenchman, gliding uncontrolled against her starboard. It was one of ours, *Téméraire,* and she started firing, as we had done, downward through *Redoubtable*'s decks.

At the same time, we heard a great crash at the waist of the *Victory.* I turned to see the Frenchman's main yard cut loose from its slings and fallen to act as a bridge for a larger boarding party. We rushed astern, met more marines and officers ready to oppose the boarding. I leapt for the yard and stood balanced there, slashing at any Frenchman who dared approach. I managed to stop three before one appeared with a pike that I was crazed enough to think I could divert with a cutlass. The pike found my left side above the ribs. I didn't feel a thing, my balance lost and I falling to the deck.

We cut away at the French boarding party, which was itself distracted by the arrival of the other English ship. The smoke grew too thick to breathe, or to see, and whether because of it or the wound, I stopped seeing anything and remembered even less beyond the gush of blood I discovered falling down my side and leg onto the deck.

Thankfully I remained unknowing while someone stitched me up. I somehow noted the rare sight of the surgeon cutting off the dead Lord Nelson's hair, the loblolly boy holding a bullseye lantern above them. I don't know when the explosion of guns was replaced by the roar of the wind, but the great storm that the long swells foretold before the battle came on with a shattering force.

I was moved from one place to another and lashed down for safety. Another vision that found its way to my memory was several men lifting Lord Nelson's body into a barrel marked Brandy. A good deal of it sloshed over the brim before the top was pounded on, due to the pitching of the deck in the raging gale. It continued for a week, I learned later, when my senses and appetite returned and I rejoined my watch, or what was left of it. The storm was one of the equinoctial conflagrations that plagued the Atlantic at that time of year. It caused greater havoc, death, and destruction than the battle did, which had been a great victory for us, so I was told. Except for Lord Nelson's death. I've seldom seen such grief in men, such love and admiration told through naked tears that no one bothered to control.

Nineteen was the number of French and Spanish ships who had struck their colours to us. After the battle, one exploded in a fire, eleven were cut loose and burned or parted their cables in the storm. They were lost with those wounded aboard going down with their ships, as horrible a death as there was, surely worse than Nelson's, who, once the storm had passed, rode out our limping voyage to Gibraltar in his barrel, lashed to the mainmast under guard through every watch by a single marine who had fought hard in the battle and was given the honour.

Nelson had my respect for dying well and brave, but not the adoration that my shipmates in their ardour seemed to demand. To me our solid ships, not one of which was lost in battle or storm, were the heroes that allowed some of us to survive the strategy that would make Nelson immortal. The Royal Navy would claim the victory, but everyone who felt that wind and saw the waves crashing over us knew full well that the storm did the greater damage to the enemy.

We arrived in Gibraltar and refitted for the voyage back to England. There was an attempt to have a faster ship take Nelson back, but the *Victory*'s crew rose up as one to prevent it. The brandy in his cask was changed to wine, and on 2 November, we started "home," as everyone referred to the destination. The cottage in Lakeland was as close as I could come to filling that ideal, and I let myself wallow in that ephemeral anticipation through the five hard and stormy weeks it took us to reach Spithead.

By then we'd guessed from messages sped to us at sea something of what was in store for us, but even so, there was no way to prepare for what followed.

London

January 1806

What were ten thousand bloody soldiers doing in a funeral procession for an admiral?! They, with every other official and group who could crowd in line, stretched the pageant from Whitehall to the steps of St. Paul's Cathedral. I arrived angry for the occasion, as were many of my mates from *Victory,* for since our arrival at the mouth of the Thames, we'd beheld the great frenzy of mourning in which the nation had indulged for weeks.

To me, funerals are for the living. Too often such rites are a performance with requisite displays of emotion, punctilio, and costume that would make the dead writhe if they were so unfortunate as to witness their own progress to the grave. For Nelson, every excess had been called for, and every idle officer, lord, and squire with a little gilt on his coat wished to take a part. On a cold but grand bright day for a parade, all of them spread out for a mile and a half before the carriage carrying the coffin, along with those ten thousand soldiers!

It had not been a pleasant month. We arrived at Spithead exhausted, then sailed to Sheerness, where they sent Nelson's coffin for him. It had been carved from the wood of *L'Orient*, one of those French ships blown up at the Nile, and Lord Nelson had always been rather proud of it, the stories of his plans for it told around the scuttlebutt for as long as I had sailed with him. He was on familiar terms with death, and certainly it came as no stranger. Why the nation seemed so distraught made no sense to me, except for envy and the guilt that they had not been there with us. Even so, they knew his vanity, his inclination to dare the worst, already to the loss of eye and arm, and they had heard full well the temptation he offered at Trafalgar by making himself a target with his medals. He had been determined to be this age's hero and had used his talents well to gain that glory. But many other men had died giving it to him, and where were they in that procession? Their bodies had been thrown overboard, often in pieces, their families, friends, and fellow villagers left to mourn with prayers and private sorrows.

It was because of them that I marched in that parade. The previous weeks aboard the *Victory* we'd spent keeping the curious worshippers off her. They came out in boats to surround the ship in Sheerness harbour, hoping to see the spot where Nelson fell, his blood on the deck, if possible, ghouls of fame eager to sup on the simplest remains of the dead. When refused those intimacies, they would have settled for a splinter of the ship herself, shaved off with their pocketknives, had we not kept a watch about her in the launch at all hours. Some of us who'd been wounded were begged for a glimpse of our scars by those dignitaries allowed on board, and when we refused, they blessed us for our sacrifices even so. By the time we left the ship to come up river to Whitehall Stairs, a good many of us were sick of the martyrdom being draped on the man and anything he'd touched, ignoring, of course, by righteous exception the two he loved best: his mistress and daughter by her, who were conveniently and brutally overlooked.

Those of us who fought and would have died at his command

respected the man, as much for his foibles as for his style, skill, and steadfastness. He'd allowed me the privilege of a slight familiarity, and he had as much trust, gratitude, and affection as any officer could ever have of me. But I hated the saint they were making of him. Those wounded of the crew of *Victory* who were able to walk the distance were no doubt considered tokens of the common men who'd fought their last. We took that honour with more determination than pride, and resolved to have our own way with the ceremony. Stretching Nelson's shot-blasted ensign among forty-eight of us behind the carriage that carried his coffin, we processed along with the wave of silence that greeted his remains from the crowds packed in about the streets, the only sounds being the removal of hats and the severely stifled sobs.

The walk seemed long, for I was searching the crowds for certain faces, Daphne, James, and Walsh, although I doubted that my family would be standing in the street, and doubted even more that Walsh would try to take me from this circus, so many teary eyes upon us regarding us as gods. I'd written Daphne almost every day and urged her not to come, to wait until the funeral was done, after which the world's attention would dissolve in other matters, and I would find a way to leave the ship. What bothered me the most was that I'd not received an answer, which then goaded all the devils of doubt that four and a half years of absence had nurtured in me. She might have been at the castle in Puddington for the holidays and not had access to the postal box. Or she might have heard nothing from me for all that time and given up on my existence, or directed her affections elsewhere, or any of a thousand variations on the theme that played their discord through my battle-scrambled brain. As I marched to the solemn drum behind one who would no doubt be lifted high in the firmament as war's quintessence, I knew that before I'd ever fire another gun, they'd have to shoot me.

We reached St. Paul's, most of us aching from the long walk on solid ground. Inside, every seat was filled, the organ playing dirge and triumph, us marching in a lockstep with the ensign spread behind the coffin, now carried by twelve men high on their shoulders, a canopy held by six admirals above it. Behind us came another thirty admirals and a hundred captains. We were gratified that the army stayed outside.

The service lasted four hours, with choirs and trumpets, prayers and banners waved. As we waited, I could see any number of my mates bearing up, their recent wounds rebelling against the strain of such attention. The stitching in my side began to smart and cause a sweat even in that frigid church. But every seaman's eye I met was focused with determination to do our work, and finally we followed the coffin down into the crypt.

After the interminable prayers and chants, the First Lord of the Admiralty, old Lord Barham, approached us for the ensign, which we were to fold and he to place on the coffin. But as His Lordship watched, somewhat perplexed, I gathered, we made a good tear in the flag, taking off a segment of it. As some folded what was left, each of the rest tore off a small piece and put it in his tunic. We had kept it flying, and no one would keep us from a share of the memento. My piece was meant for James, but was taken with a different attitude than those my mates would have. Several of those in authority from the Herald's Office were quite put out, but Lord Barham fried them with a glance, and nothing more was done. At long last, the coffin descended to its proper place, the choirs began the recessional hymn, and we joined the endless column going back down the centre aisle.

Then I saw her, from the chancel steps. In a pew reserved for the peerage that I would pass, Daphne was on the aisle, dressed in black bombazine, with an elaborate bonnet of the same material. A dark sable-trimmed cloak was over her shoulders, an odd covering for a woman in a church, even in the January cold. She watched me, smiled, but something was wrong. Her eyes were sunken and red rimmed, and her face, more lovely than I could have ever remembered, glistened a sickly white. As I approached, she coughed and lifted what I saw was an already blood-stained handkerchief to her mouth. Too many eyes were on the *Victory's* crew for me to speak to her. Next to her was a man, also dressed in black with weepers attached, he shedding copious tears for Nelson. I didn't doubt it was her husband. Even so, I moved to pass as close as possible to her.

"James is at sea . . ." she said faintly, and then her eyes rolled upward and she began to collapse. I caught one arm and His Grace caught the other. Together we let her down on the pew.

"I told her she mustn't come," he uttered peevishly, "but she insisted . . ."

A lady in the seat behind pulled out a smelling bottle, asking, "What's wrong?" as the recessional continued to pass without me.

"Consumption, I'm afraid," His Grace informed us, and I felt my heart wither. He then looked to his peers and requested, "Perhaps someone would be kind enough to have my carriage brought to the north porch."

A man went up the aisle as I remained on my knee, still holding her arm.

"We'd be honoured to have Lord Nelson's shipmate give us aid," the Duke said to me. I looked to see his gaze of adulation that never fixed on a single point but moved restlessly to take in any diversion. His was not an unattractive face, with fierce eyes, prominent straight nose, and a square chin. I did not respond, except to help him lift her up, and together we carried her through those still recessing, then down a side aisle toward the north transept. Her head rolled listlessly, and I put my arm around her waist to offer her my shoulder. I cared nothing for her husband or the crowd of onlookers, most of whom, in the English manner when involved with grand ceremony, overlooked any unpleasant imperfection.

The carriage, the same one I'd enjoyed some years before, came up with a great clatter of its horses. The footmen threw open the door and offered assistance.

"I'm deeply grateful," His Grace said to me as we lifted Daphne into the familiar interior and laid her across the seat. "Perhaps you'd care to call," he suggested as we covered her with the cloak. "I worshipped Lord Nelson, would adore to hear the details of the great victory, the tragic death . . ."

"I'll come immediately," I said, determined to be with her. "I knew Her Grace, in the West Indies years ago."

"Come with us now!" he offered, all excitement with capturing a Trafalgar prize. "It must give the Duchess such a joy."

I was in the coach before he could think better of it. Sitting next to him across from Daphne, I felt the jolt as the carriage turned and headed back to Mayfair. I wanted desperately to hold her but kept my place.

"Now tell me," His Grace requested eagerly, "where were you when Lord Nelson was struck down?"

"At my gun on the quarterdeck. How long has Her Grace been ill?"

"Nearly a year, poor dear. We've done everything, but there's really nothing to do against this scourge. The papers say it's killing thousands every month." He seemed honestly regretful, I can't deny that of him, but why was he not devastated? Instead, he queried, "Did you see who made the shot, where it came from? And were you boarded by then? The papers have been hopeless . . ."

She coughed again, a drop of blood falling on her chin. Her eyes opened and she saw me. Joy spread her face into a familiar smile of wicked anticipation, and she reached for my hand.

As I took hers, His Grace said, "Your old friend," startling her with his presence.

I hastened to set the scene. "His Grace kindly invited me to accompany you. I told him of our old friendship in the Caribbean."

"Ah, yes," she conspired, "that old friendship. I'm so glad to see you again. Are you able to stay with us awhile? I've so much I'd like to tell you."

"Yes, of course," I responded too quickly, so said, "but would I not intrude . . . ?"

"On the contrary," His Grace hastened to offer, "we'd be delighted." Then he leaned over to whisper, "Do it, man. I'll arrange everything with the Admiralty." He was used to being obeyed and knew his power. I graciously consented to do his bidding.

Little more was said during our progress to the West End. Daphne held my hand but kept her eyes closed against the discomfort she felt with each jolt of the coach. I had to be content with her hand, and never took my eyes from her, thinking of anything but that she was dying. His Grace rode easily along, watching the world go by outside his window. I detested him for his detachment.

A chair was waiting in the forecourt of Cleyland House, and four footmen carried Daphne in and up one side of the double staircase from the hall. At the top, she was met by doctors in their periwigs, at which point she turned to find me on the stairs opposite. Relaxing, she smiled, then she was gone into a room off the upstairs hallway. His Grace followed, leaving behind several followers who had materialised from various alcoves and corridors upon his arrival. They and I waited outside the door in an awkward silence, they beholding me with considerable disdain, my uniform that of a common seaman, not an officer. On those occasions when I nearly lost control and approached the door, their curled lips and uplifted brows caused me enough irritation to behave and hold to my advantage.

At last the door opened and His Grace came out followed by the doctors.

"How long?" he demanded of them after a footman closed the door.

"Days. Weeks," a very grand man said, obviously a physician. "A month at most."

Anger let me not believe him. "I wish her to be comfortable," His Grace directed, "some physic for the pain." Then he came to me and taking me by my arm, moved us away from the others. "She asked for you, and if you know of other friends, she seems to crave the past."

"I know of no one, Your Grace."

"This comes at a particularly difficult time," he stated, halting at a private distance. "The wretched economy of the country threatens us at every turn, trade ruined, exports impossible, my mills in the Midlands . . ." As if embarrassed to be concerned with such matters, he turned his quite piercing blue eyes on me and looked directly at me for the first time. "You know, several years ago, some fool from the Home Office reported to me about the Duchess's adventures in the Lake Country, involving a fellow with an eye shield."

He waited, watching for a response. I was practised enough to give none, resulting in an admiring smile as he continued. "I chose to ignore the man. Daphne's life has been her own, you see . . . I urge you to stay."

Admitting nothing, not even the gratitude I wished to offer him, I replied, "I'll gladly stay as long as I might be useful."

"Good! Good. You'll have a room nearby," he said, ushering me to her door. "I'll arrange clothing. Use the house as you will . . . We must call you something."

"John York," I picked without a thought.

"Good," he replied and turned to those perched and waiting. "Come," he said and led them to the stairs.

I went in, not yet able to appreciate the cluttered luxury of tapestry, portraits, wainscotting, and rich furniture that I'd already passed. Daphne's room was dark, with curtains drawn over the windows. A fire burned opposite her canopied bed, beside which stood two women servants.

"Leave us," Daphne said, and they willingly obeyed. She was in a white peignoir, propped up on a mass of tapestry pillows. Having done some magic, she didn't look ill at all, in fact was radiantly beautiful, her black hair gathered up in ringlets.

When the door closed, I stepped quickly to the bed and knelt beside her. She ran her hand through my hair and smiled. "The roles are reversed, my darling," she said. "Now it's you who keep me alive."

"If we left tonight, took you out of London to clean air . . ."

"It would kill me within the hour." She cut me off firmly, as if she'd had enough of hope. "Fletcher, dearest Fletcher, let's do something much more daring. Come sit next to me on my bed."

Still agitated, I did as I was told. "If I'd known, I'd have come. Damn my life for keeping me away."

"Nonsense. I couldn't have told you until I heard you were on the *Victory*. By then I was too sick to come to you, and it was too late to send the news." She took my hand and kissed it. "We're blessed that you're here. Could you ever imagine that the Duke would invite you here himself? . . . Of course you're saving him the great inconvenience of offering husbandly care. I'm sure he's deeply grateful."

"He's a fool. How could the man live with you and not . . ."

She leaned up suddenly and kissed me. I held her in my arms as she didn't have the strength to stay. From exhaustion, she let her head fall on my shoulder. "I found the letter that you wrote mid-ocean and sent from Gibraltar with all those from Portsmouth on the same day the news of Nelson's death and the great victory reached London. It was like a fire at Christmas with all the presents burned. I didn't know for three weeks if you'd survived. I lay abed, reading your letters over and over, and . . . died of longing." This made her laugh, the water through gravel sound I remembered, which now broke into coughing. Reaching for a handkerchief, she fell back on the pillows, trying to control the spasms that wracked her. Gradually they subsided, but not before the handkerchief was deeply stained. "Then I read in the *Gazetteer* and knew you were at least alive."

"I wrote you daily from the time we—"

"I'm sure you did, but I was unable to go to the postal box. Nelson's funeral was the first time I thought I might see you. No one could refuse my patriotism, so I was allowed to attend. And hasn't it worked out nicely . . . My dear, I'm easily exhausted, and you'll have to put up with a number of disgusting necessities, my handkerchiefs, my glorified cuspidor . . ."

"Daphne, we must do something, find other physicians . . ."

"I've found them all, believe me." Her eyes demanded me to

accept the obvious. Then they softened. "What we must do, as always, is not waste our time."

My uselessness was too obvious to me. "May I hold you?"

"Do not squeeze."

I leaned over and slipped my arms around her back between the pillows. With effort, she raised her arms and held my head in her hands.

"This will be hard for you," she said. Then she kissed me. "But then we'll be together . . . and that would make me believe in Heaven."

"Don't do it. Believing only makes dying easier. Heaven is here on earth, and so is Hell, where I'll be if I lose you."

"I promise to haunt you."

"You must. You're the only one who knows my name."

"Your son . . ."

"Have you told him who I am?"

"No . . ." She leaned back, and I laid her down on her pillows.

"He must never know. Has he been summoned?"

She closed her eyes, smiling to gain my attention. "Ever since he met a certain pirate, James has been enamoured of the sea. Last summer, His Grace arranged for him to be a midshipman aboard the *Ajax*. He's very happy there, and I have no wish for him to see me now."

"The *Ajax?* She followed us through the French line . . ."

"His captain wrote to say he fought bravely, at eleven, a natural seaman. Something he inherited, surely. He's in the Mediterranean somewhere . . . My darling Fletcher, I'm exhausted. Please, please stay."

In an instant, she was asleep. Her pale skin had always been a lustrous wonder, but now it shone with the heat of her sickness.

"Where would I go, my love?" I asked, and saw a bare smile as if the absurd question gave comfort to her dreaming.

I stayed with her from then on, leaving only to change into the clothes provided me, or to wash, occasionally to walk outside, sleeping on a chaise longue moved to the foot of her bed at her command so that when she waked, she'd see me there. His Grace came in once a day, faithfully if briskly, asking of her comfort and my needs. The staff was told I was a special doctor given the privileges of Cleyland House, the doctors told nothing other than discretion was demanded. Our meals were delivered and enjoyed together, and hours were spent telling each other of the years we'd been apart. I read the letters I'd written her and filled in the blanks of time. I gave her the piece of Nelson's ensign for James. She gave me all the letters she had written to me and had been unable to send. They told me much of my son, his badgering of His Grace to join the Royal Navy. Daphne and I shared much laughter, our joy in each other denying her illness and the world hovering about us. The door to her room became inviolate, never opened without a knock and a spoken request to enter. Privacy was ours. Quickly I displaced the women who had cared for her, providing sponge baths, at which I became proudly skilled, concentrating on my work to avoid acknowledging the obvious progress of her illness.

In the middle of a night, when I rose to stir the fire's coals and replenish them, I turned to see her watching me.

"Could you bear to come and lie with me?"

"That's a pleasure that takes no bearing."

"I'm not certain of my capabilities, but watching you at the coals has fired my mind."

"Fire has always been our friend," I said and slipped under the covers in my island costume.

"Gracious. I feel a little shy." Then she laughed, and, miracle, the coughing that we both expected didn't come. We laughed again and waited as if for gunshots, but in the happy silence that then followed, all we heard were our own gentle sighs, and later gave ourselves the luxury of sleeping there together.

So began a week of unexpected—at least by me—improvement. Some of her former strength returned. She was able to leave her bed and sit at a table for her meals. She slept more comfortably and longer. At times, she ordered me out to walk about the town so she could dictate letters to her friends who had called. One morning, I had put the coffee on the table by the window overlooking Berkeley Square and cracked the curtains to allow a shaft of grey snow-filtered light onto my morning paper. There I sat in as domestic a scene as one might have, camping out as I was in the Duchess of Cleyland's bedroom.

"Oh, I could live for this," I heard and went over to the bed to kiss her good morning, but she was standing before I reached her and gave me my kiss.

"We aren't supposed to do that, the doctors say," she warned me as she crossed to the fire.

"They might as well suggest I lay an egg."

She stared at the flames, her warning prodding our reality too painfully.

"Now that you're here," she said, "I think of all our possibilities."

She took several steps toward me, but began to waver. I stepped quickly to hold her, and her head fell to my shoulder as she embraced me. "They say that this disease allows a short and brilliant respite toward the end, unbearable as any pain, for it holds life up as mockery . . ." She began to cry, then pushed herself away and stood unsteadily, her fists clenched, staring angrily at our breakfast table.

"Daphne, tell me about these possibilities. Each one. We'll make a feast of them."

"I'll trade you mine for yours . . . I have enough to last your lifetime." She began to falter again.

"Begin," I ordered. "Start right now. Tell me the best of them."

She slowly looked up at the streak of light through the curtains and saw that snow was falling. "It would have to be the cottage. I sold it after that vile Walsh discovered us, but we'd buy it back." She reached out a hand for me as she continued. "It would be spring, next spring. We'd fill the rooms with wildflowers, and James would come on leave. The three of us would fish again . . ."

So began the end. The respite she described passed in days,

but we continued stretching time with our happy schemes. As her need of pain-relieving physic grew, it was left increasingly to me to have a dream for her waking, to which she'd add the special detail that would make it live for me. She also offered me example of how to die, and gave me my instructions.

I was sitting next to her bed one day, thinking her asleep, when suddenly she said, "The moment before I die, I want you to close your eyes, no, your eye, forgive me"—she smiled at our old joke—"and leave me, leave the room immediately, and take my life with you. They'll take care of what's left of me, which has nothing to do with us. Promise me."

I did. Another time she asked, "Are you still angry?"

"I'm used to fighting enemies and keep looking about the room for them. Lacking that, I've no one to rage against but God, and alas, I'm no believer. So yes, I am."

She reached for my hand. Hers was very cold. "Try not to be. I was, but somehow it's been replaced with gratitude for what I've had, particularly for what we've had. Think how impossible it was that we should ever meet. And here we are. That is so satisfying. I'm no believer, either, and won't go rushing to the church for last-minute reassurances about eternity. Eternity! What a waste of time. I'd rather think on the days we had . . ."

We didn't reach February. I was retelling one of our favourite creations, which I'd invented and she'd embellished, about a small yacht we'd have.

"We'll take her out from Whitehaven, sailing north to call at Isley, Mull, then the Isle of Skye and Dunvegan, to my mind, as viewed from the sea, the finest castle in Scotland. James will take the tiller, I'll be his topman . . ."

"I'll read the maps, no . . . charts, sorry. And we'll call her *Lakeland*."

"Of course, yes, I'd forgotten that."

"You mustn't forget that . . . And who's to do the cooking?"

"You, the fish, at which you excel. I, the porridge, biscuit, and of course, the grog—"

"Fletcher!" She sat up in bed, reaching desperately. I was there to grasp her in time to feel the life leave her. I disobeyed her wish and kissed her, which brought her back enough for her hand to rise toward my cheek.

"Never dare to say good-bye to me," she said, and then her hand fell.

It was then that I shut my eye, still holding her. Slowly I laid her down, and unseeing, closed her eyes, then sat a time, holding her hands. Through the lid of my eye, I could see dull shadows cast from the candle near her bed. I reached over and blindly put it out with my hand. I stood, and without looking back, opened my eye and walked from the room.

Conclusion

From Sir Jeremy Learned's Journal

dated 17 March 1811

*The two reversals in themselves, King and patient, taken sepa-
rately, would not have taken such a toll on me. Of that I'm certain.
But together, they make me question any theory of the mind's ill-
nesses. Perhaps I should consider a return to a simpler practise,
prescribing physic to dowagers with gout or some such utility.*

*I do not come to this conclusion from any social despair due to
my "release" from Windsor. My sanity is less affected than my
pride in the profession. Besides, the hooded consolations and hissing sympathies expressed by those at Court made my presence
there a painful dance. I am well rid of the Royal obligation, although I retain a gnawing compassion for the King, ironic I suppose, for it is he who so publicly proved me wrong by retreating
into madness to a degree beyond any expectation. Thank God that
the Fletcher Christian débâcle was a more private matter, although even its small circle of secrecy keeps my mind churning
during these hours in the middle of the night when sleep eludes
me. With any luck, I won't have need of seeing any of them again,*

except Barrow at the club. But he has proven himself the soul of discretion time and time again. I have no worry there.

Then why can't I sleep? Why do I retire at my customary hour— without my Windsor duties, now more customary than ever—to sleep as if dead for an hour or two and then find my eyes wide with resurrection?

After an hour spent staring into the dark, I think I see, if I can only write it down before I lose it to this nighttime whirling of my mind. I wake because of fear. Because I was so wrong after a dedicated lifetime of practise, suppressing all familial or personal distractions, after a career that lifted me to prominence and respect, I fear that I'm undeserving of either, that my attainments were a momentary chimera. Instead of curing kings of madness and lifting lunatics out of the pit of despair, I am at the last fated for quite an ordinary life. Yes. That's it. That is the reality that terrifies me.

Now, with this truth finally before me, I wonder at this scribbling. It was not my purpose here to record the life of an ordinary man, a scrivener to the times, a medical demi-diarist. It occurs to me that of a sudden, these pages are hardly worth the effort to continue with them, or to cull and destroy those parts others might find objectionable. For who will care? To justify the years of filling these endless quires of paper demands at least a memorable life, if not a spectacular one. And, yes, to gall my wound thoroughly, one like Fletcher Christian's. I laugh to remember that upon our parting, I urged him to finish his story, with aching envy I now realise.

I pray that this steady shattering of confidence will end, but as I examine each piece's intricacy, doubt breaks away another part of me. . . .

Bedlam

June 1811

This is written at my doctor's suggestion, one whom I betrayed by being something other than he thought I was. I could not change that consequence but regret greatly the effect it had on him. Taken from the Thames as I had been taken, he however did not survive his leap from London Bridge.

Contrary to the good doctor's prescription, writing of Daphne's death left me severely saddened. I felt as if I had lived it again, and the effect on me was similar to the first time. I gave up speech and eating, sinking through the days as if they were a long, dark maelstrom. Bedlam's attending apothecary remedied this by taking away my manuscript, table, and stool, thus enraging me, which was a cure of sorts, I suppose. This resulted in any number of treatments with the cold water hose. Still I didn't eat, not avoiding my food but using it to throw at the apothecary with anything else I could find. I was not far from the reward of the floor shackles again. Dr. Learned's visits had become fitful, his presence demanded elsewhere. One night when he appeared at my cell door, he found me cowering naked in a corner, having just enjoyed an evening's hosing.

"What's happened here?" he said, agitated. "I received an urgent message from Sir John Barrow to attend you immediately. Did you see him?"

I was not inclined to conversation, even after he took off his cloak and wrapped me in it. I was grateful, but still I wouldn't talk.

What changed this condition was nothing that the doctor said or did, but an astounding appearance. The door of my cell was thrown open by the apothecary, who was carrying my manuscript. James Walsh barrelled in after him, bursting with triumph.

"So there you are at last, and with your rightful name—Fletcher Christian."

I believed I was having some sort of demonic vision inspired by my hunger. He'd aged since I'd seen him last, wispy grey hair and rheumy eyes, but his nose was still a carbuncled monument, and his tobacco-stained teeth, which I'd never noted, were widely revealed for our pleasure.

My doctor rose and confronted him. "I'm Sir Jeremy Learned. This man is a patient under my care. Who are you?"

"Ah, Dr. Learned, yes. I'm Walsh of the Home Office." The doctor couldn't contain a quick look to me. "I'm sure you've heard of me," Walsh went on. "And we hear much of you, that things are not as you might wish at Windsor."

The doctor avoided a reaction by turning to the apothecary. "Give me that manuscript."

The apothecary, as close to a weasel as any man can be, whined back, "Why is he so privileged? He licks your cheeks, but he throws his shit at me!"

It was true, as he was a most deserving target.

"Besides, the manuscript's been spoken for," the vermin stated proudly, indicating Walsh.

"The Home Office has no authority in Bedlam," the doctor stated, magnificently, I thought. "If you don't give me that manuscript immediately, you may consider your position here to be at an end."

Caught between two opposing forces, the apothecary remembered how his profits came to him and handed the foolscap to the doctor. Then, as low to the ground as possible, he slithered out of the cell. The doctor then regarded Walsh, who quickly turned to me.

"I followed you in Nelson's funeral cortege, from Whitehall to St. Paul's," Walsh fairly crowed. "Out of respect, I waited to arrest you until after the ceremony. But you never came out. No kindness is ever rewarded, is it? Where've you been for the last five years?"

Having not recovered from writing of Daphne, I wished no further prodding into that time. I tell it here to complete the chronicle. In truth, I barely remember those five years, mostly spent wandering the roads. Whenever my source of income had occurred to me, I took money from the bank and travelled about, feeding not only myself but anyone in need, often seamen wandering inland with their families to avoid being pressed. Eventually, I returned to Lakeland. I went once to see our cottage and found it occupied by a raucous family of six whom I left with a bare greeting. I tried to see my mother, writing a request to her so that she'd feel free to refuse, which she did, although with gratitude for my continued existence. In the rejection, she included my brother Charles, who was living with her in Douglas, his surgical practise in Hull having been damaged by controversy and his nerves now in a parlous state. I had no wish to see Edward. Whatever had happened to the money for Moorland Close, I only knew that it had not been spent for that. I'd given it, a considerable sum, but at the time, I hadn't the inclination to fight that battle further.

Oddly enough, I spent almost a year under the generous eye of my cousin, John Christian. He had added Curwen to his name to honour his wife, the namesake of my island woman, Isabella. John and Isabella had attained everything that youthful promise

and wealth had predicted for them. She said that she remembered meeting me years and years ago, and I chose to believe
her. They welcomed me as a cousin wronged by fate and circumstance.

But then my cousin told me news gained from sources he had
in London, that the mutineers' community on Pitcairn had been
discovered and reported to the Admiralty. There seemed to be no
public or official reaction, but even so, more devils than I care to
describe descended on me. In a familiar panic, I hastened to the
conclusion that I must quit my cousins' hospitality for their sake
and quickly left Lakeland. Half of my mind was consumed with
the bizarre idea of going back to Pitcairn, the other with the possibility of being pressed aboard a Royal Navy ship to contribute
yet again to the unending war. Both would have been disastrous
for whoever might have been with me. It was their good fortune
that, as I was walking along Fore Street in Plymouth Dock, where
I hoped to find a ship, I felt myself observed. When I turned, of
all people in the world, I saw my oldest friend, Captain Peter
Heywood, staring at me as if I were a spectre of doom. He was
right. His finding me would once again connect him to my crime,
a fate he'd overcome with courage and distinction. I ran.

I managed to escape him, but any confidence in my ability to
have an unrecognised future was obliterated. Hoping that even
such a man as I could be lost in London, I came, only to go mad
with fear of discovery from either press-gang, Home Office, or a
former colleague. I became deranged, never leaving my room,
never approaching the door, finally crawling on hands and knees
to pass before the window, shouting at shadows on the ceiling. I
didn't eat, of course, and what waste I created was collected in a
single chamber pot, which soon was filled and overflowed.

Such noise and filth could not go unnoticed. The landlord finally came with a constable, no match for one as crazed as I, and
I fled, convinced by then that to die was appropriate. It didn't occur to me that all I had to do to achieve that purpose was tell
them who I was. Thus pursued, I found my way to London

Bridge, and after I recovered from my leap, I was brought screaming to Bedlam.

"Tell him nothing," Sir Jeremy instructed me. I willingly obeyed.

"He doesn't have to, Sir Jeremy," Walsh gloated. "You said quite enough to Sir John Barrow at the Admiralty, didn't you? All about this patient here, this mutineer, and him being chased about the world by that old fool, James Walsh. But Sir John Barrow, being an extraordinarily efficient man, wrote himself a memorandum, as is his habit—in great detail, by the way—all very private and confidential, of course. But unbeknownst to him, a friendly colleague of mine who works there took occasion to examine the document, saw my name, and sent me a fair copy. I've just spent the morning with Sir John, who wasn't very hospitable at all, you may believe me"—here he gave a great phlegmy chortle—"but no matter. I have my man, don't I?"

"You have a madman, Mr. Walsh," Sir Jeremy asserted, "a fact to which I'll testify and daresay I'll convince any court . . ."

"Are you so sure, sir?" Walsh rumbled viciously. "Your opinions on that subject might not be worthy of serious respect any longer, wouldn't you agree? In fact, I'll probably have you called to prove our point." He laughed again at his fine humour. It seemed to devastate Sir Jeremy, who flinched at Walsh's glee.

"Walsh, you're right," I said, my first words and exactly those that Walsh had come to hear. His face stretched alarmingly with his smile as I continued. "I thank you, Sir Jeremy, but being anyone else than Fletcher Christian, I have no life beyond Bedlam. This is less than life. Let me go with him. You wished to know the end of the story. I might serve it best by being hanged at last."

"You are *not* Fletcher Christian," the doctor stated, on an edge of agitation.

I turned to Walsh, my unexpecting ally. "You'll have to prove your case, Mr. Walsh, beyond any doubt."

My suggestion could not have pleased a person more. He

turned from us and gazed heavenward, his face alight with beatitude. "Here, the reward for persistence; here, my life touches its sublimity." He scurried to the door of my cell and opened it. "Who in all the world might offer the perfect proof of your identity, one that would . . . 'convince any court'?" He hurried into the corridor outside.

I glanced at the doctor, who seemed more distraught than I, his lips pressed tight against his teeth.

Then Walsh returned triumphant, for he was escorting William Bligh. I, being beyond shock or fear, had an inclination to laugh, which I suppressed. Both watched me for a reaction, Walsh the vulture, Bligh the god, in formal uniform, his captain's cocked hat under his arm. He stood rigidly at attention, the corners of his mouth pulled down severely as I remembered from the past, his eyes wide and sunk back in his skull when exercised. Except for a certain balding and the greying in what hair was left, he hadn't seemed to age at all.

"Sir Jeremy," Walsh said, "may I introduce Captain—I beg his pardon—Governor Bligh, recently returned from New South Wales, fortunately at home today in Lambeth, where I hastened directly from seeing Sir John Barrow. I think we may assume that any court might accept his identification of this mutineer." If he hadn't been so obsequious toward Bligh, I believe the man would have started to dance a jig.

"I'll speak with him alone, if you please," Bligh ordered in his usual brisk fashion, causing echoes in my brain.

"I think not, Captain—I beg your pardon—Governor Bligh," Sir Jeremy said. "This man is ill, and I'm his doctor."

"Nonsense," Bligh responded. "There's fire in his eye, and contempt about the lip. Leave us."

"This is a hospital, sir," the doctor stated forcefully, "not a quarterdeck . . ."

"Sir Jeremy, let us be alone," I said. "If anyone could disprove who I say I am, it's he."

The doctor hesitated, in a state of considerable anguish. Then he took me by the arm and led me to the farthest corner of the cell to whisper urgently, "You should know that Bligh is returned from New South Wales under considerable suspicion. He was forced from his office by a mutiny there . . ."

"A mutiny?!" I doubt that anything could have startled me but this.

"A mutiny," the doctor repeated. "Some have come to London willing to testify that it was justified. The court-martial begins next month. He is regarded by all as extremely vulnerable."

"Thank you," I said, wondering if he'd told me because he finally believed me. He gave no indication, turning and walking out the cell door. Walsh hastened to follow, closing the door behind him. I stayed at the edge of the cell as Bligh occupied its centre.

"I thank God that I've lived to see you hang, sir," he stated crisply. "I assure you that I shall be aboard at Portsmouth to observe it."

"You're certain that I'm Fletcher Christian?"

"Certain enough to bet my life that you've tattoos to bear me out."

"They shall."

"You seem most willing to be my vindication," he said, as curious as he was proud of himself.

"My willingness has little to do with you."

"You're not concerned with dying?"

"No more than with living. I began to lose concern for both one day in the South Pacific, some twenty years ago."

"Then you admit your crime?" he demanded, suddenly intense.

"Oh, God, Captain, I did so long ago, and will again at my court-martial. Have you waited so long for this old confession of mine?" Obviously he had. Triumph narrowed his eyes. At the same time I realised that curiosity offered a strong distraction from rage. I asked, "But tell me something—and you'll never need reveal it to anyone else—have you ever admitted, just to yourself, your part in it?"

"*My* part?" He scoffed. "You *are* mad, sir."

"Yes, surely so, but madness recognises madness. I remember too well your actions on the *Bounty*. Do you, I wonder? Do we dare speak of that time now that we meet in Bedlam? But what better place for our reunion?" Then I did laugh, which allowed him to regard me with repugnance and pity. "I was near mad even then, when you, the day before my crime, accused all your officers of the theft of your *coconuts*. Do you remember that demented episode? And when I volunteered that I'd taken one to slake my thirst during my watch, you called me a thief, a liar, bellowing that half your pile was gone. You were raving, Captain. Unfortunately I was all too susceptible to the contagion."

"Ah, so in your poor mind, the fault of mutiny is mine."

"Not at all. I embrace the blame." I then stepped toward him in order to better observe him. "Have you ever admitted to yourself that when we were in Tahiti, you, too, were distracted from your duty?"

"You *dare* talk to me of duty in Tahiti, when you and your grand friend Heywood partook in that rutting season you oversaw on shore . . ."

"You hated that friendship, didn't you, so much that you accused him unjustly of planning the mutiny with me. Do you realise that you almost hanged an innocent man?"

"He was found guilty by a court-martial! But he didn't hang, did he? Why? Because he was a gentleman, you may be sure of that. Do not speak to me of duty, sir, I who had no family to rescue me if I made such treasonous errors."

"But your duty then was to care for the ship. Yet even though you were aboard, our second set of sails were allowed to rot, as were two of the ship's boats. We found that out on the day of the mutiny. They were eaten through with worms. Such irresponsibility itself would result in a court-martial. I didn't notice that those facts were part of your report to the Admiralty."

"When I reported to the Admiralty, their interest was in more important things," he said. "The ship was missing with a band of mutineers, after all."

"And I'll hang for that. But you should know by now from where we came, Captain Bligh, from your ship, created in the three weeks after we left Tahiti, when you'd lost your set of sails, and were surrounded by officers who had joined the seamen in their common pleasures, while you with God-fearing virtue stayed chaste aboard, dutiful to your marriage vows, doubtless a vexing abstinence. During that time, you had the usual group of malcontents, deserters, and grumblers in the crew. But when we sailed away, the lashing of your tongue revealed the harnessed demons of your mind, and with them, you cut some of us into mutineers."

"You made your own monster, Mr. Christian, cut from your own whole cloth."

"Yes, the cloth was mine but you were my tailor, and for what reason? The sails would have been forgiven, for Tahiti was uncommon humid. Worms in the ship's boats were not a unique occurrence in the Royal Navy. Your solitary rectitude would no doubt have been applauded. But the imagined flaws of duty and your loss of control of the crew while we were in Tahiti—all that drove you beyond your usual edge of rage. Over the next three weeks, you cursed, insulted, and berated everyone unmercifully, under the guise of reasserting discipline."

"Discipline was needed." He was gazing into the corners of the cell, distracted, defensive. "It had become dangerously lax under your command of the shore party on Tahiti."

"You crossed over into madness," I said calmly. "Remember sending us ashore on Nomuka for water and wood, forbidding us to use our weapons against the natives, even when they attacked us? You sent us to die in order to prove your authority, then called us—me in particular—cowards when we hastened to return. You knew how serious such a charge was, particularly when overheard by others. You knew if we'd been on shore I would have challenged you, as any 'gentleman' would have to do, wouldn't he? But not on board a Royal Navy ship against my captain. Still the abuse increased, to raving over your coconuts. You said you'd make it so bad for us we'd choose to jump overboard before we reached the Strait. Do you recall that?"

"Is this what you plan to tell the admirals at your court-martial, that you led a mutiny over coconuts?" he asked disdainfully, but I detected a concern. He then gave in to anger. "You held me at the mainmast for three hours the next day with a sword at my throat . . ."

"Truthfully," I said, "did you not see yourself in me that day? If not, you were blind at the mirror. I was created mutineer in your mad image."

"My image? You took nothing from me, sir. You were of the great family Christian on the Isle of Man, twenty-three generations a gentleman. I only shaped you into a half-decent navigator. What you made of yourself was your own doing."

"You resented those twenty-three generations, even when we were friends."

" 'Friends'?" he sneered, and stepped toward the door. "When, pray, was that? As I remember, I was ever your commanding officer, that one who finally promoted you over more senior men to be my number two. Do you remember that, sir?"

"I do. You did it because I was your friend, and once on the *Bounty* it soon became apparent that you'd need at least one. We were friends, Captain Bligh. We'd eaten, caroused, laughed together over many years. You enjoyed, I think, my admiration."

"Tush. I was long familiar with the lonely role of ship's captain, the *a priori* hostility of any ship's officers and crew toward him who has ultimate authority over their unfortunate lives. You were chosen for what I thought was a talent to command. I didn't realise, to my considerable regret, that you had so little sense of honour and duty." He sniffed and glanced away as if poised on a poop deck, examining the sheets of a mainsail.

"What little honour I have I've bled for," I replied. "My duty is my own, not defined from above by an authority that, after all, is so often the veneer behind which we hide, as you are doing now."

"I do not stand here hiding, sir."

"You do, behind your rank and brilliant uniform, your bristling 'sirs' and your dependence on military respect for your commands. But after all is done, Bligh, we are two men who knew each other once, and well."

He shifted his cocked hat from under one arm to the other. "I'll not have you use my proper name."

I snapped a salute. "Beg pardon, *sir*. But that's who we are, two madmen standing here in Bedlam, all too familiar with each other and our mutiny . . . although your costume is certainly the better one for the occasion."

"And I'll not have you expound to me about that mutiny, do you mark me, Mr. Christian?"

"We were two madmen then, too, staring at each other over a widening sea. For me, it began the long voyage to this consummation where you find me. For you, it gave advantage; that brilliant edge of madness allowed your success through thirty-six hundred miles in an open launch."

He gasped as if stabbed, took several steps toward me and slapped me hard across the face. He was shocked enough to tremble, I, to smile.

"I've never hit a man in my life," he uttered, staring at me.

"Perhaps you've never heard the truth so clearly."

"That open-boat voyage was an accomplishment," he bellowed, "that will live forever in naval history."

"Yes," I agreed, "and for the opportunity, you owe me thanks."

"I OWE YOU NOTHING!" he shouted.

The cell door swung open. I bent to pick up his hat, which had fallen to the floor. We were both distracted by a young man standing at the entrance in a Royal Navy lieutenant's uniform, who immediately stepped in and saluted his superior.

Bligh acknowledged the young lieutenant with the irritation of being interrupted. I gave him his hat, which he accepted with no gratitude. Then Dr. Learned came in with a most seraphic smile on his face, still carrying my foolscap. He was followed by Walsh and a distinguished gentleman with white hair and an erect military bearing, but in a plain black civilian coat and knee breeches.

"Captain Bligh," Sir Jeremy queried, "are you acquainted with Sir John Barrow, of the Admiralty?" He couldn't help a gleeful glance at me. Even I knew who Sir John Barrow was, as did anyone in the Royal Navy, in Parliament, or at Court for that matter.

"Exceedingly well acquainted," Bligh replied coldly.

There was an intense silence as the six of us stood, eyes wide with confrontation. For the first time since I'd been there, the cell seemed crowded.

"Your servant, Captain Bligh," Barrow said, taking command as no civilian I had ever seen could do, although he spoke so quietly, all were forced to listen. "I was explaining to Mr. Walsh just now that because I'd been privy to some of this story before today and had done some research of my own, that after his most unpleasant visit to me this morning, I immediately paid a call on the Duke of Cleyland. May I introduce you to him now?"

I remember that my heart stopped beating. The young lieutenant stepped forward respectfully toward Bligh, his senior officer whom he had already saluted.

Barrow went on. "His Grace returned from the Mediterranean Fleet two months ago to settle his father's affairs and assume his title." He then drifted back to stand beside the doctor, and to watch.

Bligh did not react, still working to regain composure and to understand the new circumstance. Walsh could not leash himself a second longer. "With respect, Your Grace," he rumbled volcanically, "nothing changes the fact that this is Fletcher Christian, the mutineer, and Governor Bligh has identified him as such."

"No, no, no, Mr. Walsh," said the young lieutenant, the Duke of Cleyland, blast me, my son James. He strolled easily across the cell to have a closer look at me. "You have it all wrong. You see, I know this man." He gave me a confident smile and turned back to the others. I could barely stand. "This is Mr. Blackbeard, a dear friend of my mother's in the West Indies. I met him many years ago, and in fact, he was with my mother just before she died. I have any number of witnesses to that, you may be assured."

"He has had many names, Your Grace, and—"

James fixed Walsh with a look that stopped him breathing. "Mr. Walsh, I'm sure you know many details of this matter, but let me urge you to consider other circumstances. For instance . . ."—he took a small gold box out of a pocket and opened it—"you already know of this, Mr. Walsh." He picked out a small piece of blue material and held it up for all to see. "A piece of Lord Nelson's ensign at Trafalgar. Mr. Blackbeard gave it to my mother on her deathbed."

"His name on the *Victory*'s roll was different," Walsh interjected.

"No matter there, sir," James said, an edge of impatience in his voice. I felt a great swelling of pride, and saw him as an Admiral of the Red. He continued as he paced back to me. "My mother included this memento in a letter she wrote to me just before her death, to be opened only when I assumed my title. Her letter told me everything about him." He stood before me and, with a look, accepted me and all there was to know. I was so obviously moved that he quickly turned back to Walsh to take attention from me.

"I'm grateful to you, Mr. Walsh," he said. "Since I read her letter some weeks ago, I've been searching for this man, and you have made our meeting possible." I saw Walsh sniff the change of wind and start preening to accept the noble gratitude. James continued, "But then the question of your use of an informer in the Admiralty spoils everything, doesn't it? It will almost certainly be construed as a criminal conspiracy, if not a treasonous one in the military courts, a sad conclusion to such a distinguished career as yours."

Walsh gasped, then stepped back.

"I plan to present this remnant of the immortal memory to His

Royal Highness, the Prince Regent," my son continued, "when I explain this situation to him, as I'm sure I'll be called upon to do, should it become public." He allowed the emphasis to fall on Walsh, then turned to Bligh. "His Royal Highness's new duties are overwhelming, but even so, I'm certain that he'd be most sympathetic to Lord Nelson's shipmate at Trafalgar."

Bligh looked at me, unbelieving, but obviously concerned.

"With great respect, Governor Bligh," James said as he approached him, "for your memorable and incredible accomplishments at sea . . ." He let the compliment hang in the cell's silence, but Bligh wasn't taken in at all. He stood as if expecting a broadside, and it came. "I understand," James continued, "that you'll soon be involved in a decisive court-martial involving the mutiny under your governorship in Australia. It occurs that it might be difficult if there were *two* such courts-martial for the newspapers and the public to dwell on, both cases involving your personal behaviour."

Again Bligh glanced at me, then looked back for more. James gave it to him. "Coming here today, Sir John told me that you applied for your admiral's flag last month, but that it is being held back, pending the inquiry into this *latest* mutiny." James was as cold and hard as the stones of my cell. "I also understand that you have six daughters to see into society. How difficult it all might be—win or lose—should these courts-martial portray you . . . destructively, as no doubt they may."

"You would stoop so low," Bligh cried out, "as to attack my daughters, sir?!"

"Don't be misled by your well-known emotion here, Governor Bligh," James responded cogently. "Be assured that I will never have anything to do with you or your daughters. It is they who must live with you. Should this particular matter ever be revealed, it is the press and the public who will have their way with them. One might defend oneself effectively in a single mutiny, but two, examined in trials at the same time, might have the effect of convincing both boards of admirals—and the world—of a certain pattern of behaviour. You do remember your court-martial in 1805, that found you guilty of tyrannical and oppressive behaviour, I believe it was described as, aboard HMS *Warrior*." He glanced at Sir John Barrow, who nodded. "And were you not also involved as a ship's captain in the mutiny at the Nore?"

Bligh didn't move, barely breathed, then said, "You talk of conspiracy, Your Grace." Then he stepped forward and bellowed in James's face. "Well, here is one between you high-born—"

"You forget yourself, sir," James interrupted forcefully, "and who you are."

Bligh was silenced by reasoning, and struggled to control himself. His eyes moved from James to Sir John Barrow, then to the door, and finally rested on me. He didn't bother with hate, for he was already forgetting what had been said, as was his old habit.

"Lieutenant," he began, portentously looking about the cell, "be assured that my conscience is clear in all these matters. I've witnessed the power of privilege throughout my life, never having had that luxury myself. My accomplishments are my very own. I am content to leave this matter in the hands of God, whose justice knows no such corrupting and biased influence as is in evidence here." Then he focused on me. "Your punishment shall be damnation, Fletcher Christian, an appropriate future for you."

"Believe in it if it gives you comfort," I managed.

He stood for a moment, as if considering whether or not his duty demanded some violence of speech or action. Then with his brow raised, he walked from the cell.

This left Walsh alone to look between his retreating witness and his threatened future. Obsequiousness was his chosen attack, and of the four of us who remained, he unwisely chose the one of highest rank. "Your Grace, surely this matter doesn't warrant your or Sir John Barrow's wrath. I was, after all, only doing my duty . . ."

"Ah, yes, duty," James responded. "A great principle, and a

greater excuse. Sir John, I believe you wished to deal with Mr. Walsh."

"Mr. Walsh," Barrow said in his quiet, calm voice, approaching Walsh as a spider to a fly, "how far has this current matter progressed at the Home Office?"

"Well, not far at all. Your memorandum came directly to my desk, and I did my own investigations. I'd planned to make report when all was in full bloom." A dim hope of his great glory still shone in his eyes.

"I hope so for your sake," Barrow replied, his doubt obvious. "For we will depend on you to collect every reference in your files concerning this man, and your investigations of him over the years, and deliver them in person to me within two days. And should there ever be the slightest question raised about him, from the Home Office or anywhere else, I will see to your arrest. I suggest you use your undisputed skills and the resources open to you to protect . . . Mr. Blackbeard . . . from the slightest curiosity."

"And if I oblige," Walsh eagerly negotiated, "may I depend on . . . ?"

"Depend on only one thing, Mr. Walsh," Barrow stated. "You have used the Admiralty. Now the Admiralty will use you. You may go."

Walsh stood a moment, his mouth poised to speak, then he thought better of it and hurried from the cell. The doctor hastened to Barrow and solemnly shook his hand.

Barrow said, "We'll speak no more of this," and the doctor nodded. The Second Secretary to the Admiralty then turned to me. It was a look well known to every captain who approached him for a ship, every admiral and lord who tried to bully him. The look saw to the core of any man and reached judgment in the instant without the slightest revelation of his determination. He so judged me, and I can only hope there was something good in it. Without another word, but with a respectful leg made to James, he left.

James came instantly to me and took my hand. "I just passed my lieutenant's examination!"

"So I see, and that your tailor was the first to know." We laughed as I shook his hand, and then suddenly embraced. He was as tall as I, and strong made. "Congratulations," I managed to utter before my throat locked.

I saw the doctor over his shoulder, abruptly looking as devastated as any captain striking his colours. He stood, seemingly blasted, holding my stack of foolscap to his chest as if it were a shield.

"Sir Jeremy," James said, "it is my intention that 'Mr. Blackbeard' accept my hospitality and protection. If you agree, he'll go with me presently to Cleyland House."

The doctor seemed distracted, as if he hadn't heard, but then nodded.

"Come," James said to me.

It was not as simple as one might think, for I'd been in that cell for many months, and the corridor outside, not to mention the world, seemed terrifying. Even so, my determination took me toward the door, and I realised that all I had to wear was the doctor's cloak. He read my concern as I approached him. "Wear it," he said. "Have no worry."

James saw the situation and said, "I'll have it returned within the hour."

Sir Jeremy waved away concern and suddenly thrust the stack of foolscap at me. "You must finish this."

I took the manuscript and tried to find some words of gratitude. "I believe you saved my life, and perhaps, even my mind . . ."

He shook his head. "No, no, God, no. If I'd had my way, you'd have been madder still. Finish the story, I beg you . . . Go. Go."

I regret that because of my own anxiety, I could not understand his struggle, and am not sure I do even now.

"Come," James said, and I gathered the cloak about me and

walked slowly into the corridor. As I passed their cells, my fellow inmates recognised one of their own and sent me to my future with shrieks of resentment against their own.

It has not been an easy passage. For several months, I found the streets impossible to endure, remaining inside Cleyland House, which had its own haunted memories to avoid. James finally convinced me to travel with him to Wiltshire, where I found a certain stability to the world, and my place in it. With ingrained naval habit, I established a daily routine that I adhered to with the rigour of a demented proselyte. It included riding with my son each morning through the castle's forests, then putting down the rest of this story to honour Sir Jeremy's wish. Now done, these pages will be placed in James's green leather folder and locked behind the secret panel in the library for his future reading, should he wish to do so.

A fortnight ago, he departed for Portsmouth on his way to rejoin his ship on blockade in the Mediterranean. I found the parting unbearable, unfamiliar as I am with even having a son, much less watching him go away. There is no way of knowing when I'll see him again. The Royal Navy is disinclined to grant leave. Napoleon now eyeing Moscow instead of the downs of Kent, I needn't worry of battle for James. Dying of boredom is a greater threat on blockade. Of course, his frigate's duties take him in harm's way on a regular basis, which gives my nights their gloss of dread. The caprice of working my way onto his ship as topman and gunner I allow full play during those hours when missing him becomes too sharp.

Riding through the woods is not the same alone, and now that these pages are done, my routine is more void than content. My restlessness has affected my temper to the degree that I do my best to avoid those here who serve me so well, and so kindly. But I must leave. Extended castle living is noble rot. There's more purpose in Bedlam.

And what is mine, now that I begin my life again? I suppose

nothing less than discovering the destiny of a man who has survived his forty-six years, with the memory of a great love, a son, and no fear of death being his only accomplishments worthy of note. The mutiny is a deep and permanent scar but no longer living history to me. The world may choose to make of me what it will, but I will find my own definition. I leave this place as any seaman leaves his land life behind, going where wind, war, and fate's wheel may lead, certain of nothing but curiosity and my determination for more existence. The times serve me well, offering extremes of every description. I anticipate. I therefore am alive.

A Chronology

23 December 1787	HMS *Bounty* sails from Spithead on an expedition to bring breadfruit plants from Tahiti to the West Indies.
23 March 1788	Heavy gales keep the ship from rounding Cape Horn. After three weeks of trying, it turns for the Cape of Good Hope.
26 October 1788	*Bounty* anchors in Matavai Bay, Tahiti.
4 April 1789	*Bounty* sails from Tahiti, the ship's hold filled with breadfruit plants.
28 April 1789	Mutiny. Bligh is put over the side in the launch with eighteen others; the *Bounty* sails for Tubuaï.
14 June 1789	Bligh and the launch arrive at Coupang, on Timor, 3600 nautical miles from site of the mutiny.
14 July 1789	The Bastille is taken by the people of Paris. The French Revolution begins.
23 September 1789	After sailing for five months between Tubuaï and Tahiti, the *Bounty* leaves sixteen crewmen

who choose to remain on Tahiti, then sails for an unknown destination.

15 January 1790 *Bounty* drops anchor at Pitcairn. A week later, the ship is fired and sunk.

14 March 1790 Bligh arrives in England to write his book about the mutiny and his voyage in the ship's launch.

7 November 1790 HMS *Pandora,* a twenty-four-gun frigate, is sent to capture the mutineers.

23 March 1791 The frigate arrives in Tahiti and takes the fourteen from the *Bounty* (two had been killed) prisoner, placing most in a cage on deck, chained to the bars.

3 August 1791 Bligh, newly promoted to post-captain, sails from Spithead on his second breadfruit expedition.

28 August 1791 The *Pandora* hits the Great Barrier Reef and sinks, taking four of those from the *Bounty,* still chained, and thirty-one of the crew to their deaths. The survivors head for Coupang.

19 June 1792 The ten *Bounty* survivors of the *Pandora* arrive at Spithead, all still prisoners and facing court-martial as mutineers.

12 September 1792 The court-martial of the *Bounty* mutineers. Three are hanged six weeks later.

5 November 1792 Midshipman Peter Heywood writes to Edward Christian that Fletcher was not as portrayed by the court-martial.

15 December 1792 Baptism of Anne-Caroline Wordsworth at Orléans, her father William having returned to England for lack of funds and without marrying her mother.

February 1793 England and France declare war on each other.

7 August 1793 Captain Bligh arrives back in England after his successful second breadfruit expedition.

20 September 1793 Massacre Day on Pitcairn Island. Fletcher Christian is among those said to have been murdered in the native rebellion. The single mutineer still alive when Pitcairn is finally found (1808),

	Alexander Smith (John Adams), tells vague and conflicting stories of Fletcher's death to each new party that arrives. A grave is never discovered.
Throughout 1793	Edward Christian's panel, including cousins and acquaintances of the Wordsworth family, hears evidence from twelve members of the *Bounty's* crew.
May 1794	Publication of Edward Christian's *Minutes of the* Bounty *Court-Martial and Appendix.*
9 January 1795	Death of Raisley Calvert, brother of William Wordsworth's schoolmate, who leaves a legacy of £900 for the poet to pursue his literary aims. The Calvert family owns the farm Windy Brow, outside of Keswick.
January 1796	Bligh given command of HMS *Director,* sixty-four-gun ship-of-the-line.
7 November 1796	The newspaper *The Weekly Entertainer* includes a letter from William Wordsworth in response to the publication of a series of letters purported to be written by Fletcher Christian from Cádiz. Wordsworth writes: ". . . I think it proper to inform you, that I have the best authority for saying that this publication is spurious."
19 May 1797	Bligh put ashore by the crew of *Director* during the fleetwide mutiny at the Nore.
August 1797	James Walsh, agent for the Home Office, reports on suspected spies in Nether Stowey, Somerset.
11 October 1797	Battle of Camperdown against the Dutch fleet in the North Sea.
December 1797	Wordsworth's play, *The Borderers,* is considered, then rejected by Covent Garden. (The pertinent scene, describing a captain overthrown by his crew and abandoned on an island, is Act IV, scene 2.)
1795–1798	In Coleridge's notebook that covers this period is an entry: "Adventures of Christian the Mutineer." (The underlining is Coleridge's; the notebook is in the British Museum.)

23 March 1798	Coleridge completes "The Rime of the Ancyent Marinere" and reads it to the Wordsworths at Alfoxden.
1 August 1798	The Battle of the Nile, Lord Nelson's first fleet triumph.
12 December 1799	Buonaparte names himself First Consul of France in a bloodless coup against the Directory.
25 December 1800	Ned Young, after having three children with Fletcher's woman, Mauatua, as well as four by another, succumbs to asthma, the first man to die of natural causes on Pitcairn.
28(?) January 1801	The secret birth of Horatia Nelson, daughter of Lord Nelson and Lady Emma Hamilton, surrounded by scandal that threatens his career.
2 April 1801	Battle of Copenhagen.
1 October 1801	Ratification of peace between France and England, proclaimed officially the next March as the Peace of Amiens.
24 May 1802	The Wordsworths' claim of more than £10,000 is at last assured by the death of James Lowther, Earl of Lonsdale, his heir being sympathetic to the debt.
18 May 1804	Buonaparte is proclaimed Napoleon I, Emperor of France, and so crowns himself the following December.
January 1805	French troops mass around Boulogne, the new emperor preparing once again for the invasion of England.
25 February 1805	Bligh faces court-martial and reprimand for abusive behavior while in command of HMS *Warrior.*
30 March 1805	The French fleet escapes from its port of Toulon in a gale. Lord Nelson begins the long chase, eventually to the West Indies.
13 June 1805	Learning of the enemy fleet's quitting the Caribbean, Lord Nelson's squadron follows back across the Atlantic.

24 August 1805	Napoleon suddenly changes his mind and leads his Grand Army away from the coast in order to attack central Europe.
21 October 1805	Battle of Trafalgar and the death of Lord Nelson.
9 January 1806	Burial of Lord Nelson at St. Paul's Cathedral.
February 1806	Bligh sails for Australia, newly appointed as Governor of New South Wales.
26 January 1808	Bligh arrested at Government House in a mutiny against his government.
1808–1809	Rumors in Lakeland tell of Fletcher Christian being in the area, under the protection of his cousin John Christian Curwen. The rumors are subsequently reported by Sir John Barrow.
14 May 1809	News of the discovery of the mutineers' colony on Pitcairn reaches the Admiralty.
March to June 1809	Captain Peter Heywood is ashore to assume a new command of a frigate. He reported later that he had seen Fletcher Christian in Fore Street, Plymouth Dock.
25 October 1810	Governor Bligh returns to England, "victim" of yet another mutiny and determined to gain vindication.
November 1810	King George III's madness begins again after the death of his favorite daughter, Princess Amelia.
December 1810	Bligh puts in for his admiral's flag.
20 December 1810	The Regency Bill, shifting royal power to the Prince of Wales, is introduced in Parliament.
8 January 1811	The first court-martial brought by Governor Bligh concerning the mutiny in New South Wales ends, to his consternation, with an acquittal of the accused.
29 January 1811	The Queen's Commission reports on the king's momentary improvement.
5 February 1811	The Regency Act is passed. The king's decline continues unremittingly.
5 June 1811	The second court-martial brought by Bligh. This time the accused is found guilty of mutiny but is only cashiered, not hanged.

31 July 1811	Bligh is gazetted as Rear Admiral of the Blue but is never given command of a ship again.
11 April 1814	Buonaparte, defeated by Allies, abdicates at Fontainebleu and is then sent to Elba.
March 1815	Buonaparte leaves Elba and raises new armies.
22 June 1815	After his defeat at Waterloo, Buonaparte signs his second abdication and subsequently is exiled to St. Helena.
7 December 1817	Vice Admiral Bligh dies, aged sixty-four.
29 January 1820	Death of George III.
30 March 1820	Death of Ann Christian, Fletcher's mother, at ninety. She leaves no will.
14 November 1822	Death of Charles Christian, Fletcher's brother. He leaves no will.
1823	Edward, by now the Chief Justice of the Isle of Ely, dies, also leaving no will.
1831	Sir John Barrow, Second Secretary to the Admiralty, anonymously publishes his book *The Mutiny of the* Bounty, which includes the story of Captain Heywood's sighting of Fletcher in Plymouth Dock.

Acknowledgments

This novel is not an attempt to settle the long-raging debate of whether or not Fletcher Christian survived Pitcairn and returned to England. That consideration is the work of many scholars and historians, whose diligent investigations and often conflicting opinions have given me such pleasure while writing *Mister Christian*. Their achievements have allowed me my presumption. I have used the preceding historical data only to stimulate and limit conjecture. As to the fiction, I stand by what Thackeray allows, that "novelists have the privilege of knowing everything."

From a long bibliography, there are four sources that deserve special mention, for I referred to them almost daily: *Fragile Paradise,* by Glynn Christian, a direct descendant of Fletcher; Sven Wahlroos' *Companion and Encyclopedia to the* Bounty *Adventure;* Sir Walter Besant's *London in the Eighteenth Century;* and *Nelson's Navy,* by Brian Lavery.

At a time when I was trying to learn to sail ships-of-the-line (on land) and was foundering badly, I happened across the profound wake of Patrick O'Brien, whose sixteen-volume epic taught me all I needed to know, as well as providing months of joy.

For the indispensable stimulation, enthusiasm, editing, and critique during the writing process, I am indebted to Nicholas Meyer, Susan Cheever, Jesse Cohen, and Susan York.

For helping me find my way to this book's perfect publisher I am beholden to my agents, the incomparable Marion Rosenberg and the wizard Charlotte Sheedy.

Luckily for me, Michael Korda, who is that publisher, knows and revels in this period of history as I do. In his exhilarating editing, he revealed the secrets of time and the limitations of space, thus providing the reader with a better book.

Copyediting is too often the forgotten craft of book publishing. Fortunately I was assigned a woman of infinite patience, with a rapier pencil, who straightened out numerous errors and gaffes. To Carol Catt I offer my most respectful thanks.

Even with this amount of help, the book would not have survived the fraught process of writing it without my wife, Susan's, devotion to it. Her determination that it must be written overcame all distractions, objections, and practical considerations, mostly mine. To repay her support will take easily the rest of my life.

28 ~~28~~ DAYS

DATE DUE		
AUG 1 9 1998		
SEP 2 8 1998		
OCT 7 1998		
OCT 1 5 1998		
NOV 1 6 1998		
FEB 8 1999		

FICTION
Kinsolving, William.
Mister Christian

JMT

GAYLORD FR2